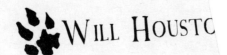
WILL HOUSTO

CW00820831

THE
SHOULDERS
OF GIANTS

HENRY BROOKS

*Bernard of Chartres used to say that **we are
like dwarfs on the shoulders of Giants,***

*so that we can see more than they, and things of
greater distance,*

*not by virtue of any sharpness of sight on our
part, or any physical distinction,*

*but because we are carried high and raised up
by their giant size.*

....

John of Salisbury
from 'The Metalogicon', 1159

Will Houston Mysteries by Henry Brooks
www.giant-shoulders.com

Published by PiquantFiction
www.piqfic.com

The Shoulders of Giants (2010)
Old School Secrets
The Cradle Snatchers
Student Jihad

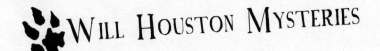

WILL HOUSTON MYSTERIES

THE SHOULDERS OF GIANTS

HENRY BROOKS

Copyright © Henry Brooks 2010

The moral rights of Henry Brooks to be identified as the Author of this Work has been asserted in accordance with the Copyright, Designs and Patents Act 1988.

First published in English by PiquantFiction in 2010—**www.piqfic.com**
PiquantFiction is an imprint of Piquant Editions.
Piquant Editions
PO Box 83, Carlisle, CA3 9GR, UK

ISBN 978-1903689-68-4

British Library Cataloguing in Publication Data
Brooks, Henry.
 The shoulders of giants. -- (Will Houston mysteries ; 1)
 1. Houston, Will (Fictitious character)--Fiction.
 2. Children of separated parents--England--Liverpool--
 Fiction. 3. Teenage boys--England--Cumbria--Fiction.
 4. Grandparent and child--Fiction. 5. Family secrets--
 Fiction. 6. Cumbria (England)--Social conditions--
 Fiction. 7. Suspense fiction. 8. Young adult fiction.
 I. Title II. Series
 823.9'2-dc22

This is a work of fiction. All characters, organizations, and events portrayed in this novel are either products of the author's imagination or are used fictitiously.

Cover design by ProjectLuz
Typesetting by To a Tee: **www.2aT.com**
Printed in the UK by J F Print Ltd., Sparkford, Somerset.

CONTENTS

Part One: LOVE   1
1   North for the Summer   3
2   The Baguette, the Barber and the Beast   14
3   War Stories   27
4   Three Unnatural Deaths   42
5   Fishing for Trouble   60
6   The Bin Monster and the Mysterious Stranger   76
7   The Mark of the Beast   90

Part Two: JOY   105
8   Spying at the Grave   107
9   The Beast Hunt and the Haunted House   117
10   Wild Aunty Joyce   130
11   The Merry Night   142

Part Three: PEACE   157
12   Facing the Lion   159
13   How Are the Mighty Fallen   168
14   Danger at the Mines   180
15   Uncle Sid's Secret   197
16   Fight to the Death   210

Part Four: PATIENCE   **227**

17   Famous for Fifteen Minutes   229

18   The Patience of a Saint   248

Part Five: GENTLENESS   **263**

19   The Fighter, the Footprint and the Frenchman   265

Part Six: GENEROSITY   **283**

20   Horses, Hiking and Hannah   285

21   The First Pitch   299

Part Seven: FAITH   **309**

22   Damsels in Distress   311

23   The Brave Men of Buttermere   326

24   Ancient Kings in the Hills of Gold   339

Part Eight: HUMILITY   **353**

25   The Value of Hard Work   355

26   Stan's Secret   365

27   Murder Mystery and the Mafia Showdown   376

Part Nine: SELF-CONTROL   **397**

28   The Loweswater Show   399

29   In the Ring   411

30   One Riot, One Ranger   423

31   The Reunion   444

Author's Note   459

PART ONE

LOVE

NORTH FOR THE SUMMER

W hat on earth am I doing here?' I wondered.
Eight enormous bikers had parked themselves
on the traffic island in front of the bus stop.
They were shouting and making obscene gestures at the
shoppers who were hastening over the zebra crossing. When
everyone else had scattered to a safe distance I was left alone,
surrounded by my luggage, on the wrong side of the crossing.

I watched them out of the corner of my eye, hoping they
wouldn't notice me. These guys were the real deal—straight
out of an American movie. The biggest one of all, obviously
the leader, I dubbed Mohican Man. He was a giant tattooed
creature with wild eyes and a face like a lion ready to strike
his prey.

I stood there waiting. My stomach was in knots and
my palms were sweaty. 'Come on Granny, where are you?'
I wondered. The men, only metres away, were restless—
spitting and jostling, itching for a fight.

An ugly bald biker with a thick Geordie accent shouted
at a passer-by. 'What you looking at, eh?' He smashed
his Newky Brown bottle on a stone planter full of pink
flowers. This left him with a lethal-looking weapon, which

he set down next to him as he muttered to Mohican Man and pointed up the street. I shifted my eyes to look. Three police vans had pulled around the corner and the officers were getting out slowly, as if waiting for the final order to move in. The shoppers huddled in clumps on the other side of the street, watching and waiting for the action.

Mohican Man looked at the others. 'You remember what I said?'

'Aye, no prisoners, Boss,' the Geordie said. 'We don't go quiet, you hear!' He drew himself up to full height as he turned around to face the police, who were now less than a hundred metres away. I could see the vein throbbing on his forehead and his nostrils flare as he walked over to his bike. There was a large Nazi swastika tattooed on his left temple. He reached into one of the side bags and drew out a knuckle duster, the kind with a retractable knife at one end, and placed it in his pocket. Then he set another object I couldn't quite see, with a rounded, wooden handle, within easy reach.

'Come on,' I thought, 'one of those shoppers should warn the police about the weapons.' 'Why don't you tell them yourself?' a voice inside my head asked. 'I'm just a kid,' I protested. 'I'm too young to die.'

As though he could hear me talking to myself, Mohican Man turned to look at me. His eyes cut into me and a rush of liquid fear coursed through my veins.

Then it happened.

An old Land Rover rounded the corner, pulled up and came to an abrupt stop on the traffic island just above where the bikers were parked. An old man hopped out, followed closely by a one-eyed Border Terrier. The man's hair was white and I could see that his face was lined and weathered, but his long-legged stride was swift and sure and his keen eyes darted from left to right. He was dressed in black wellies, brown cords and a navy lambswool jumper with leather elbow patches. He was chuckling, obviously enjoying a private joke with his dog, as he headed straight towards the gang. As this unlikely pair trampled into the midst of the scene, for a moment everyone—shoppers, police and bikers—froze.

Then Mohican Man narrowed his eyes and spat. The old man, apparently oblivious, came to a halt alongside Mohican Man's bike. He glanced at the bikers. 'Good day,' he said, as if they were a group of old friends. Then he turned his back on them and shaded his eyes with his hand as he searched across the road in my direction.

'Well Nelson,' he said to the dog, 'it's three-thirty by my watch. The boy should be here by now.'

There was something about his voice, his eyes—something familiar.

'Hey, you laddy, over there. Are you William Houston?'

And in that instant I recognized him. 'Yes Grandpa,' I said. 'It's me, Will.'

'Good lad.' He grinned. 'You've grown a bit. Bring your bags over and I'll help you get them in the Landy.'

Bring my bags over there? Was he crazy?

But he stood there, smiling. I didn't have a choice. Maybe if I made a dash for it, I thought as I picked up my bags, we could get away before the trouble erupted. I started across. I was just beginning to think we might get out of this alive when I noticed the dog, Nelson, looking disdainfully at Mohican Man's bike. He raised his hind leg. *'No!'* I thought. But it was too late. Nelson relieved himself in a short burst all over the back wheel.

Helpless, I watched the liquid trickle in the direction of Mohican Man's huge black boots. He advanced toward my grandfather.

'Oi! Old man! Your dog just pissed on my Harley!' His voice was low, seething with barely-contained rage.

Grandpa turned and eyeballed the giant. I was surprised to see that they were pretty much the same height. Grandpa's gaze fixed Mohican Man, and in that split second I saw him weigh and measure the giant and come to a decision.

'Young man, you'll have to speak up. I'm a little deaf,' Grandpa said. I was close enough to see, from the twinkle in his eye, that he was enjoying himself. I could hear the crowd whispering across the road and I wished the pavement would swallow me up.

'I said, *your dog pissed on my Harley!*' Mohican Man reached into his pocket.

Grandpa looked down at the unrepentant, tail-wagging, one-eyed Nelson and then over at the grubby bike. He exhaled in a half-chuckle, half-snort and looked back down at the dog. 'Nelson, it'll take more than that to get this machine cleaned up.' I saw Grandpa's eyes alight on the mysterious wooden-handled object in the bike's side pocket.

'What did you say? Are you trying to be funny with me 'cos if you are I'm going to–'

Before he could finish, Grandpa had reached down into the pannier and whipped back around to face him. Mohican Man found himself staring down the barrels of his own sawn-off shotgun.

'Careful, sonny,' Grandpa said. 'I killed the last Nazi who threatened me with my bare hands.' I heard a gasp from the crowd and noticed a commotion among the police. The other bikers were shifting nervously.

The only one who seemed calm was Grandpa. 'And what the devil have you done to this gun?' he asked. 'It's a 1928 Perdy. This would have been valuable.' He shook his head, full of regret, as he looked down at the disfigured weapon.

Mohican Man, who didn't seem to know whether he should keep his eyes on the gun or on the advancing police, raised his hands slightly. 'Okay, okay,' he said, 'you give me that gun and I won't hurt you.'

Grandpa bristled. 'Sonny, I've led men into battle on five continents and I'm still alive. Whatever gives you the idea that you can succeed where so many others have failed?'

'Well the gun—the gun's not loaded anyway,' Mohican Man stuttered. 'It's just–'

'Not loaded and the pins cocked?' Grandpa asked. 'Well then you'd better let me pull these triggers. It's not good for the springs on these old guns to keep them cocked.' Without releasing the enemy from his steely gaze, the old man removed the safety catch and let his fingers fall onto the triggers. The bikers all scrambled to the ground and Mohican Man fell to his knees, crying 'No!'

All of a sudden, the police appeared behind us. 'Please relinquish the firearm, sir, so no one gets hurt.'

Grandpa grinned down at the reduced and quivering giant and handed the gun to the officer behind him, flicking the safety catch on as he did so.

'Damn shame, would have been a nice gun, that.'

A look of relief swept over the officer's face. 'We're taking these men in for questioning about an armed robbery at a post office in Barrow this morning. I expect you won't mind coming to the station to answer some questions as well, sir?'

Grandpa looked at his watch and frowned. 'Cheeky fellow, I certainly would object. The lad and I have an appointment with my barber at sixteen hundred. Will! Nelson! Look lively or we'll be late!'

Grandpa grabbed one of my bags and marched off to the Land Rover, leaving the bewildered policeman holding the gun.

I trotted behind him, not quite fully grasping the mortal danger we'd just escaped. And at that moment I could hardly have imagined that this was only the first of many exciting encounters in store for me that summer.

But I'm jumping way ahead of myself. Who am I, and what was I doing standing alone in a small Lake District market town with my luggage? Let me rewind the tape.

Four hours earlier my parents had sent me, Will Houston, age fifteen, away for the summer.

My dad took me to the bus station in Liverpool. It was grey and raining and I'd never felt so rejected, so completely alone. I hardly spoke a word as he drove, but he had plenty to say—you know, the usual stuff. 'Don't be any trouble, remember to say please and thank you, make sure you offer to help ...' but I wasn't really listening.

I helped unload the car without a word. I handed my ticket to the podgy driver, who put my bags into the luggage bay.

Then I walked past Dad, towards the coach door.

He followed me. 'Well, I uh, here we are, we made it anyway, you will remember all the things I said?'

I nodded and glanced up at the coach.

Dad looked for a moment as if he might say something deep. But then he said, 'Well, this is it. You will remember to call your mother and ... oh, for goodness' sake tuck your shirt in and try to look a little smart. You know what your grandfather's like.' He checked his watch. 'Look, I'm late for a meeting ...'

'Nothing new there,' I thought as he broke off and ushered me toward the door.

'I, er, I hope it all goes okay for you and Mum,' I said.

'Yeah, it will be,' he said. He didn't look too sure. 'Look, I've got to go.'

'Yeah, I know, me too,' I said. I climbed on board.

'And offer to help your Granny!' he shouted after me. I blushed and glanced around at the other passengers.

I'd had this picture of myself travelling as an older teenager, going to visit friends or something. No one was going to be under that impression now. It got worse. Dad started talking to the bus driver in a loud voice. 'He's not travelled much, and he's only fifteen. Could you make sure he gets off at Cockermouth and isn't asleep?'

'Great, thanks a lot Dad,' I thought. I felt my cheeks burning. Why did he have to treat me like a child in front of other people? I slid down into my seat.

The coach doors shut and we started to move. Dad waved and, in spite of myself, I waved back. I was on my way into the wilds of the Lake District.

The coach passed a group of cliquey girls loaded down with shopping bags outside Matalan. They looked the same age as my sister. Louise was a real pain. We're talking about a girl who went into mourning (she seriously wore black for a week!) when Geri Halliwell left the Spice Girls. But then she cheered up when she started worshiping Britney Spears instead. Only last week, at the beginning of June, I heard her bugging Dad for the complete set of Britney dolls due out at Christmas. Like I said, a real pain.

And this was Mum and Dad's favourite child. I clenched my fists and stared at the seat in front of me. My nineteen-year-old half-brother Robert didn't get as much attention as Louise did either. But he'd already left home to become a trainee mechanic.

The coach trundled on and I adjusted the fans to get some cool air. 'Why are these coaches always so hot?' I wondered. When I stood up to take my coat off I saw there was an older couple sitting a few rows behind me. I hadn't been to see my grandparents for nearly a decade, and I tried hard not to remember that last trip. But it all came flooding back to me as I sat and picked some chewing gum off the headrest in front of me. Dad's property business had gone pear-shaped in the late eighties' property crash— just about the time Louise was born. Mum had been so stressed with Dad, the baby and me as a five-year-old, that she'd almost left him for good. She took us to stay with her parents in the Lake District for four weeks. I don't know all the details, but the doctor told Mum she had post-natal depression and he gave her some tablets that made her cry a lot less.

Dad came to visit us while we were there, but he argued with Grandpa. They must have made friends again, though, because Grandpa lent him some money to stop the bank from taking our house.

I used to call Grandpa 'Poppa Galloon' after he let me pop a balloon with a pin. I was so excited that I ran around the house shouting, 'Poppa Galloon! Poppa Galloon!' and the name stuck. At the end of those four weeks Mum made up with Dad, we all went back to Liverpool, and we never went back to visit Granny and Grandpa again. Granny drove down to see us at our house every now and again in her old white Metro.

From the city centre we moved away along King Edward Street and past Liverpool Hope University, where my parents met in the 1970s. Dad, according to all the stories, was a bit of a nerd, and Mum was a beautiful free-spirited art student. I never would have believed my mother was the lead singer in a band called 'Purple Haze' if I hadn't seen pictures to prove it. My dad admired her from a distance but never had a chance with her until she'd dropped out of school and was a struggling single mom to my half-brother

Robert. I have to admire my dad for raising Robert as his own. Dad always said that he'd got the woman of his dreams.

Just then the coach hit a bump and jolted me back to the present. I was getting hungry. How come you can stuff your face with Cheerios and be starving an hour later? I found some prawn cocktail crisps in my bag—Mum always knew my favourites. As we pulled along toward Aintree, I watched the courthouse go by—set back off the road with those familiar cold granite columns and obscured windows. 'And next on our tour,' I thought, 'the place where my family got all screwed up!' Men in black robes and stupid wigs stood around in front of the building, chatting in groups. I wondered if the pompous prosecutor who had got Robert sent to jail six months ago was among them. 'Arrogant, callous, pen-pushing ...' I thought. I kicked the footrest. 'If you only knew how much misery you cause with your so-called justice.'

It all started with the CD. Robert's new friends from the garage where he was an apprentice mechanic were all big into gangster rap, especially Dr Dre and his new protégé Slim Shady, a.k.a. Eminem. Robert had played his first single so often and so loudly that Dad finally smashed the CD to protect Louise's innocence. There was such a row over this that Robert went to doss at his friends' flat for the night, which became a permanent arrangement. Mum was against it at the time, and with good reason. They were a dodgy bunch, and a year later Robert and his friends were in trouble with the police for stealing and re-spraying cars. Robert was sent to Walton jail for two years and Mum got really run down about it all.

But the biggest problems were between Mum and Dad. I think Mum secretly blamed him for being so focused on work that he hadn't brought Robert into line before it got serious with the police.

Unfortunately, Dad had every reason to be preoccupied. Almost a decade after his first business crisis, he had another one. The bank wanted money for a loan and he didn't have it. Dad was so stressed about work and Mum was so worried about Robert, they ended up having a massive argument. I wish I'd never heard it, but it was hard to avoid. Loads of old hurts came to the surface, and before long they both said some major stuff and Dad moved out the next day.

I saw Dad four days later, when he came back to get some shirts. As he was leaving, Mum arrived back from work and they almost crashed cars as he pulled out of the drive. I don't know whether it was the shock of this that did it, but they managed to carry on a civil conversation in the street for about twenty minutes. That was when they decided what to do. They'd pack me and Louise off to stay with different sets of grandparents for the summer holidays while they tried to sort out themselves and their finances.

From that moment on, my fate was sealed. For the entire nine weeks of my summer holidays I'd be cut off from my friends, my home, my city, my computer—and sent to live with two old people I hardly knew and who probably didn't want me there any more than I wanted to be there. They didn't even have Sky! I could tell Mum needed space, though, so I tried to pull my weight as the older sibling and not give Mum too hard a time. At least my parents were talking again. Louise, of course, screamed for at least a week before she was sent to Nanna's flat in Cheshire. But what else would you expect from her?

I settled back in my seat as the coach moved slowly from one set of lights to the next. People milled about the city streets. They were all busy, getting on with life. But not me. I was on my way to Cumbria. 'What on earth will I do there for nine whole weeks? And will I even have a home to come back to in Liverpool at the end of it?' These were my thoughts, but I couldn't fully indulge my self-pity on an empty stomach so I opened another packet of crisps.

2

THE BAGUETTE, THE BARBER AND THE BEAST

Ladies and gentlemen, now that we're out of the city the steward will be coming round with snacks and refreshments. Expected arrival in Preston at 12:20 pm.'

I watched a boy on his dad's shoulders coming out of a McDonalds. They were laughing. Dad and I had exchanged a lot of cross words in the last months. I bit my lip. I bet that boy's dad didn't find fault with everything he did. Of course, he was probably too young to disappoint his dad—at school or anywhere else.

I couldn't even remember when it all started with my dad—maybe it had been going on my whole life. He didn't seem to care as much about what Robert did, so he went easy on him. Louise always did better at school—and she was a girl, so that's different. But I'd always been just average, and I knew that drove my dad crazy. Mum said I was artistic and creative, like her. But Dad didn't care about that. I knew I was a crap reader, but I loved stories. At least I enjoyed English and History, even if I wasn't that good

14

at them, because in those classes I could dream of being someone else in another world. I could do that when I played computer games, too. Wouldn't my History teacher love to know his class reminded me of gaming. I stared out the window at the houses and trees flying by. I was on my way to another world—just not one I particularly wanted to get to.

The bus bumped over a level crossing. I gazed down the tracks. That's what we were, my dad and I—a train that split off at the points and now we were heading in separate directions.

'When are you going to grow up?' he'd asked me countless times. I didn't know any grown men who seemed particularly happy. My friends' dads were pretty much the same as mine. Johnny Sutton and Pete Hackney were my best mates, and we decided we wouldn't grow up just to be miserable. Becoming a man, whatever that was, hadn't done anyone we knew any good. When we talked about these things, and looked at our parents, we only saw things to criticize. I got out my new text-phone and sent a few texts to the lads.

They didn't text back right away. Probably because they were having too much fun without me. Maybe they were at the mall checking out the girls. We were all obsessed with girls, of course. I spent a lot of time dreaming about finding the perfect woman, but every time I actually tried to talk to a girl at school I couldn't think of a thing to say. Even though one or two had told Johnny or Pete that I was cute, I got tongue-tied trying to talk to them, too.

I watched more houses go by and went through my usual list of worries. I'd choose the wrong wife. Or I'd never find anyone. Or I'd find the perfect girl and lose her to my best friend. I'd never get a proper job like my Dad and I'd never have any money. I'd die poor and alone. I couldn't help worrying about this stuff sometimes. I hoped adulthood would be like the secret access to level eight on my 007 'Golden Eye' game—you turn a corner and there it is, you're in. And then I could have a special fridge just for beer and a massive wall-mounted projector for my Playstation games in my own place where no stressed-out olds would hassle me about bedtimes and tidying up. One thing I was sure about was that I was in no hurry to be like any of the grown-ups I knew.

The coach headed north toward the M6 and we left the city behind as the bus carried me North to my fate. Ricky Martin's number-one hit 'Livin' la Vida Loca' on the radio only added to my sense of misery and injustice. Nine weeks. Sixty-three days! What on earth was I going to do for over two months in the most boring place in the world? I'd brought my PlayStation, my Game Boy, and my mobile phone. Mum and Dad must have been feeling mega-guilty because they both gave me money. The total came in just under £250. I decided to get my mind off things by playing with my Game Boy. I dug around in my backpack but couldn't find it. I dumped the contents of my bag onto the seat beside me. I started to panic. It wasn't there! 'Louise!' I thought. I remembered seeing her in my room this morning. 'The sneaky little ... of all the ...wait until I get my hands on her—' I threw everything back into my bag, cursing under my breath.

I tried to calm myself with vengeful thoughts. She would pay for this. An entire summer with old people and nothing to do and no Game Boy. At least I had my PlayStation. I hoped I'd remembered to pack all my games. But at that moment a terrible, dark foreboding came over me. A distant memory. Sitting on the rug in front of Granny's TV watching cartoons. Sitting in front of Granny's tiny fuzzy black and white TV! My PlayStation wouldn't work on her TV. I grabbed my third and last packet of crisps from my bag and opened them with such force that half of them spilled all over the seat. I stuffed them into my mouth. This is not happening, I thought. This is not happening.

As we pulled out of Preston Station I noticed we'd picked up a scruffy-looking boy, even younger than me. His thin brown hair needed to be introduced to a comb, as my mother would say, and there were muddy marks all over his tracksuit. I felt a bit sorry for him, but mostly I was just glad he didn't choose a seat too near me. I brushed more prawn cocktail crumbs from my new Kappa tracksuit and tried to get back to planning my revenge on Louise, but I couldn't concentrate. The boy, a few seats in front of me, was trying to get the attention of a bald man sitting across the aisle from him. The man, dressed in a blazer and cravat, kept one hand on the tatty Harrods' carrier bag on the floor in the aisle. The boy kept leaning across the aisle and peering into the bag. The man looked blankly forward, trying to ignore him.

'What's in the bag, mister?' the boy asked. He had a thick Lancashire accent. The man carried on staring at the seat back in front of him, pretending not to hear. 'C'mon, tell us ... I'll give you a Midget Gem.' The boy reached out a grubby hand and a crumpled bag of sweets. 'They're good for yu, got vitamin E111 it says on the packet.'

The man glanced at him quickly, then looked away again, 'It's my lunch,' he said.

'Ooh,' the boy said. He leaned so far over the aisle I thought he might fall into the bag. 'What yu'got then?'

The man sighed. 'It's a prawn sandwich, if you must know,' he said.

The boy slumped back in his seat. 'Eeh, I love prawns, me. Can I have some?'

'No you can't,' the man said. 'It's my lunch!'

People around the coach were beginning to listen in, and I saw a few quiet smiles. Once we were on the motorway, the man tucked a serviette into his shirt and started to unwrap his baguette.

The boy, not in the least put out, was still looking over and trying to engage the man in conversation. 'Is it a good one?'

No reply.

'I love 'em wid salt and vinegar crisps, me. Oooh, right nice they are.'

He went on and on like this until the man finally said, 'Look, do you mind? I'm trying to have my lunch.' And then under his breath but so that even I could hear, 'Find someone else to annoy.'

The boy was silent for a few moments. I was beginning to feel sorry for him when he started again. 'I were only saying, like cos a lot of people haven't had 'em wid crisps that's all, and ...' There was no stopping the boy. I never imagined there could be so much to say about prawn sandwiches and salt and vinegar crisps.

Twenty minutes later, as we approached Lancaster, Prawn Sandwich Man made a dash for the facilities at the back of the bus.

The rest of the passengers were then treated to a prolonged and thunderous demonstration of what out-of-date seafood can do to a man's guts. Diarrhoea is not really a laughing matter, but this was something else. The duration of the performance was nothing short of heroic. But this, combined with the sheer volume and range of sounds that this man achieved, made me feel that I was witnessing something quite outstanding. The other passengers sat in shocked silence. Children who had migrated to empty seats to play rushed back to their parents. One bold toddler, having approached the steps near the toilet during a brief pause, ran screaming back to his mother when the second movement began without warning. I noticed the driver looking back at the passengers every few moments as he loosened his tie. He was clearly wondering why his training hadn't covered emergencies like this. I'd never seen a bus approach a station with such speed and hard braking as we experienced pulling into Lancaster that day.

But our arrival at the station only intensified our awareness of what was going on in the rear of the bus. For when the low, rumbling, diesel engine was turned off we realized that we had only been hearing the performance at half volume and with, as a musician would say, 'the bottom end' missing. Mothers tried to pacify their terrified children. One family, after a hurried consultation with the driver, decided to pay the extra to take the train to Kendal. They bustled off the coach as soon as the doors opened, glancing back just once at the rest of us—as if we'd never be seen again. I watched our coach driver, soaked to the skin, bending down at one side of the coach. He may have been getting bags out of the hold, but I reckoned he was inspecting the underside of the coach for damage.

The driver seemed as unwilling to leave the bus station as Prawn Sandwich Man was to leave the toilet. He strutted around outside making calls on his mobile, no doubt to Head Office. Just when I was beginning to think that maybe someone should call an ambulance, or a plumber, the noise stopped, there was a flush, and the man appeared. His face was drained of colour. He made his way back to his seat and the coach was silent. Everyone was very interested in looking out the windows.

Everyone, that is, except the scruffy boy. He overflowed with sympathy. 'Of course, that's the thing with prawns,' he said. 'You got to watch 'em! It's what my Gran says anyway.' He paused, but only briefly. 'And eating too much fruit, will give you the ipsy-pipsies an all–'

'Shut up,' the man snapped. 'I don't care what your Gran says, just shut up and leave me alone.'

The old lady sitting opposite me had been keeping a straight face for a while, but I saw her shoulders begin to shake.

The coach started off again. The suspense mounted as the boy looked out of the window, for I knew he couldn't be silent. 'Anyhow,' he finally blurted out, 'better out than in.'

The coach erupted in fits of laughter. We all looked round at each other and it was a relief not to have to hold it in any longer. When the old lady to my left managed to stop laughing she wiped her eyes and said, 'Well, that's got him told!'

We left the motorway at Junction 36 and headed north through the lakes and mountains. Windermere, Ambleside and then Keswick passed as we continued deeper into the unfamiliar rocky landscape. The further we travelled, the bigger the expanses of mountains and rocks, the smaller and more alone I felt. I turned away from the window and blinked back tears. I rescued a little spider who was about to be squashed by the head of the man sitting in front of me. I watched him crawl over my sleeve. Did he climb aboard in Liverpool too, I wondered? I checked my phone. No texts back from the lads. Would I be able to get top-up cards in Cockermouth? Would I even find reception in Cumbria?

When we arrived at Cockermouth the scruffy boy got off first and wandered away down the street. The coach driver humped my luggage onto the pavement, and then I was alone. There was no sign of Granny, or her old white Metro, anywhere. It was a sunny July afternoon, a bit colder than Liverpool but fresher and cleaner. A man selling *The Big Issue* was standing nearby.

'I'm sure they'll be along any minute,' he said.

I smiled back and we struck up a conversation. I bought a copy of the magazine—my mum had always told me to do that—even though it's a bit dull. The man thanked me and I let him keep the 20p change. He found another customer and, since there was still no sign of Granny, I decided to pop into the newsagents to get my top-up cards. As it turned out, I didn't need any top-up cards. My network had no coverage in the Lorton Valley. It was official. I was stranded.

As I rejoined my luggage, I noticed those eight bikers on the traffic island. And you know what happened after that.

Once we were in the Land Rover, Nelson, bouncing proudly between us, kept looking to his master. Grandpa jerked the Land Rover into gear and, as he slowed at the next junction, he looked down and then let out one of his jovial snorts, 'That'll do, Nelson, that'll do. Stupid dog,' he said affectionately.

The dog looked satisfied and farted loudly. Grandpa and I both burst out laughing.

'I'm afraid Master Nelson is speaking German again!' Grandpa said. I could have sworn Nelson was grinning too. Old Land Rovers have a half sliding window at the front and, although I had never seen one before, I quickly learned how to open it.

Grandpa was asking me about Mum, Louise and Robert, but all I could think about was what just happened. I looked over at him. He was definitely old, but he was also the bravest person I'd ever seen. And he was even cooler than the only other cool oldies I knew of—Clint Eastwood and Sean Connery.

We bounced along the road to the small fishing town called Maryport. Grandpa pulled up outside a glass-fronted building on John Street with a sign that read 'Gareth Baldwin—Barber'. I'd only been in unisex salons but I'd seen barbershops in old movies.

'Now Will,' Grandpa said, 'come and meet some grand old fellas. Anyway you could use a trim'.

I'd been thinking about getting a quick trim and maybe my highlights done again, so I followed him.

The shop smelled musky and damp and a line of three old men sat in a row opposite the door. Their faces were weathered, as though they'd spent all their lives at sea. They didn't have a full head of hair between them and I wondered what on earth they were doing in a barbershop. I soon learned that they met there once a month for a trim and a chat.

'Afternoon Major,' croaked a tubby, red-faced man on the end as Grandpa marched in. 'New recruit?' he asked as he nodded stiffly at me. The others chuckled.

Grandpa snorted. 'As you were, Gunner. It's my Susanna's boy, William. He's digging in with Elsie and me for the summer.'

As the 'crack' (as they called their conversation) wheeled into motion, I was lost. At first I thought I couldn't understand them because they had more hair than teeth, but then I realized my problem was the thick West Cumbrian dialect. All four men, as it turns out, were decorated war heroes of one sort or another. They reeled off story after story and discussed which of their 'marras' (friends) had 'deed' (died) lately. I sat quietly, trying not to look too bored.

'Awey, lads,' Mr Baldwin greeted them as he appeared from the back of the shop through a stained, purple nylon curtain. 'What's the crack?'

'Now then George, where's thou been, lad? With the horses again, eh? We've bin waitin' ten minutes now and Major is not yan to hang around yu' know!' They all laughed heartily, including Grandpa. Although he was more refined than these rugged working-class men, I could see he was also bound to them by an invisible bond of brotherhood.

'Now then, Major,' the old man in the middle said, 'what's all this I've been readin' in the *Times'n'Star* about the famous beast which prowls that fell out'back of your house. They says more sheep's gone missin' and farmers are up in't arms that council's done nowt about it. I hope you've been keeping an eye on that dog of yours after dark. I've always said he has the look of a wild'un!'

Everyone laughed except Nelson, who turned his deaf ear to the comment. A beast? What was this all about?

'Joking apart, Jim,' Mr Baldwin said, 'I saw t'half eaten carcass of the fell pony near Cold Keld and there's no dog, fox nor anything else that I've ever seen could'a cut up another creature so badly. The look in that horse's eyes told a tale that chilled me through, whatever it had seen had near scared it to death before ever a claw reached its throat.'

The men all shook their heads. 'Now,' Mr Baldwin continued, 'I know the Major can handle his self but I still say that ye' shouldn't go near that moor after dark, gun or no gun, and I'd not have the lad out a my sight if he were my grandson.' He looked across at Grandpa as if maybe he'd said too much. There was fear in his eyes, and Grandpa gave him a serious stare.

'Aye, I hear you, George, don't worry I'll not let it get Will … unless he proves too much trouble for Elsie,' Grandpa said. The laughter was on again, and so went the rest of the afternoon as Mr Baldwin did his best for each of them with his clippers. By the time it was my turn, I was a little scared and knew that highlights were completely out of the question. So I sat in the hard leather chair, inhaled the pungent odour of gents' hairspray, and asked for 'a slight trim, but keep it looking like David Beckham, please'. I knew that if anything would get me the right girl it would be my sandy hair, which I spent a lot of time waxing.

'Aye, right you are marra, I know what thou's on about,' Mr Baldwin said.

But Grandpa's snort should have served as a warning. Mr Baldwin, who probably was a good husband and father and in all other respects an honourable and sincere man, was not to be trusted with hair clippers. He took a number four to my head with such determination and speed that by the time I was able to shout out it was too late.

'That's—that's not how Beckham cuts his hair,' I gasped.

'Aye, but he would if he came here lad,' Mr Baldwin said. The old men roared with laughter.

I must have looked near to tears, for Grandpa said, 'Now, lad, don't worry. It'll grow back.' For the first time that day I was glad I wouldn't be seeing my friends for nine weeks.

Football, as it turned out, was not Mr Baldwin's thing. He followed the horses, and I thought it was a shame that he hadn't found a career to do with horses rather than ruining my life. Back in the Land Rover Grandpa told me that his nickname was Gary Baldy—on account of his ability to make even the hairiest men appear bald in just a matter of minutes. At only £2.20 for this special treatment it wasn't surprising he was a favourite with the local mums, whose children abbreviated a 'Gareth Baldwin Haircut' as a 'G.B.H.'—not an unfair description.

As we bounced over the mountain roads to Granny's I hit a new level of misery. I had no mobile, no games, no friends, no hair. What did I have left? My name, my grandparents, Nelson. Oh, and nine weeks of utter boredom. I fiddled with my mobile.

Grandpa glanced over and said, 'You'll not get much in the way of reception with that thing at our place, lad.'

'I know, a woman in the shop told me.' I put it back in my pocket.

The old man chuckled. 'They say that when a man is stripped of everything he's free again.'

I wondered if that bit of wisdom had come from one of Mr Baldwin's customers. I felt a lot of things at that moment, but I did not feel free.

'We'll be at your Gran's place soon,' Grandpa said after a few more miles of silence. 'I expect you'll barely remember it?'

'I remember the donkey,' I said. 'Is he still alive?'

Grandpa laughed. 'They live a long time!'

We'd always called it 'Granny's place' because the little Lakeland farmhouse had been in her family for hundreds of years. Even when I was a child I remember thinking that the huge craggy mountains across the Lorton Valley were incredibly beautiful. I felt dizzy just looking up at them, like somehow they were there solely to find me out, to make me feel small. The cliffs were so steep they reminded me of tower blocks in the city, and I wondered whether people in the farms below were ever crushed by falling boulders. And there were more and more ranges of mountains that peeled off into the distance as far as I could see. Granny and Grandpa owned a lot of land, and they let most of it out to other farms. But they kept one large field at the front of the house for Alfie the donkey. This field covered about nine acres, all the way down to the crystal, mountain waters of the River Cocker, the fastest flowing river in England.

As we pulled into the yard Granny rushed out, wiping her hands on her apron. She was younger than Grandpa, with bright eyes, rosy cheeks and a warm smile. I liked her a lot, for she always made a fuss over me. She gave me a big hug.

'How's my William? Oh you've shot up!' she said. 'I see you've met Grandpa's barber!' She glanced over at Grandpa and shook her head. I brushed a hand over my remaining hair. 'Never mind, lad, it'll grow.' She smiled. 'Come in, William. Let's get you settled in your mum's old room. I've got some jacket tatties in the oven and a nice home-baked cake for pudding ... I expect you're hungry after that long journey?'

'Yes, I am a bit. Thank you, Granny.'

She put her hand on my arm. 'Oh it is good to see you again.'

As we walked toward the house I glanced up beyond the garden and fields to the dense woods on the lower slopes of Low Moor. What was out there, I wondered, that had made those men so afraid? Was something out there right now, watching us with hungry eyes? I banished the thoughts from my mind.

Granny's legendary cooking was on offer, and I was starving.

3

WAR STORIES

Granny's house seemed smaller than I remembered. She chatted away as she led me upstairs, not noticing my awkward passage around old pieces of furniture and through doorways. Mum's old room was a little musty but it still smelled like lavender and old books. The last time I'd been in this room, ten years ago, Mum had been sitting on the bed crying, holding baby Louise. But the room, with one small window that opened out east over the valley, seemed familiar. Almost like home.

I sat down on the bed and the metal springs under the horsehair mattress creaked under my weight, and then Granny's.

'Things worked out last time and they will this time,' she said. She patted my hand, and I nodded and blinked back the tears.

'Yeah, I know,' I said.

'Oh Will, you were always such a serious little boy. Your mum and dad are going to be okay. Don't fret, dear.' Granny always knew what I was thinking and just what to say. 'Dinner's at six,' she said. 'I'll let you get settled in.'

I unpacked quickly and went downstairs. The smell of dinner cooking drew me straight to the kitchen, where I found Granny talking in low tones to another woman about her age.

'Ah, there you are, Will,' Granny said. 'Do you remember your Grandpa's little sister?'

'Aunty Dora,' I said. 'Of course I remember. Thank you for the money you sent at Christmas.' Aunty Dora always sent us each a fiver at Christmas and on our birthdays.

'Hello dear,' Aunty Dora said. When she gave me a hug I felt how thin and fragile she was compared to Granny. 'Your Gran told me about your folks,' she said softly. Her eyes were filled with love and understanding. 'You'll be all right, William Houston, and we're going to pray for Susie and Dave.' She turned back to Granny and added, 'Another evacuee from Liverpool.' Granny nodded, but I had no idea what she meant.

'Supper's ready, William,' Granny said. 'We're just waiting for your Grandpa.'

Granny banged the pan at the door and Grandpa arrived moments later. Nelson was at his heels, eager to inspect his rations. Nelson got his name after he lost his eye fighting a huge, bear-like dog called Ripper from the Kern Howe Farm across the river. That fight also left him deaf in one ear. He used this partial deafness to full advantage when he didn't want to be called. I remembered how mad Granny used to get when she'd call him away from digging a hole in her garden and Nelson would pause, turn his deaf and blind side to her, then carry on digging as if she hadn't interrupted.

Granny's cooking tasted just as good as it smelled. I don't know who was the happier—I, every time she refilled my plate, or she, to see me eat.

After dinner Grandpa went down to the river with his fly rod to see if the sea trout were rising and Aunty Dora, who he always called his 'little Dora', went with him. She was completely devoted to her big brother. I couldn't imagine Louise ever wanting to spend time with me.

I helped Granny with the washing up and called my mum. I didn't want to hear anything negative about Dad so I didn't ask, but I told her about Grandpa and the bikers.

She didn't even seem surprised. 'Oh, that's nothing compared to what he and his brothers got up to in the war,' she said. 'He wouldn't tell you himself, but Granny and Aunty Dora probably would. You should ask them.'

'Granny,' I said when I joined her in the kitchen, 'what did Grandpa do in the war?' I sat down at the table. 'Oh, and what's an evacuee?' I asked.

Granny looked at me for a good few seconds. I knew she loved me, but it felt like she was weighing me up. Then she sighed and went back to washing the cake tin. I decided she didn't think I was old or mature enough to hear those stories but then, as she continued to wipe the tin, she started to tell me about our family.

'Your great-grandparents, Albert Wallace and Betty Finch, were born in Wallasey, Liverpool way back at the beginning of the century. Betty's family was Irish and she was a little wisp of a woman, so I've heard ... small but mighty. Your great-grandpa was an easy-going character. He was into his pigeons and preferred to be in the allotment rather than at the pub.'

Granny straightened her back and then bent back to the dishes. 'By the time Albert was your age he was an apprentice fitter at the Birkenhead docks. Betty was in service at Croxteth Park to the famous Sefton family. They were childhood sweethearts and were married in the summer of 1920—after Albert recovered from wounds he suffered in the Great War. I'd say Betty was fair pleased to have him back, as most young men from their neighbourhood never made it home. He was the goalkeeper at the Somme on Christmas Day when they played football with the Germans. After the game they all showed pictures around of their sweethearts and the Germans agreed that Betty took the best picture—she won him some chocolate! But then they went back to killing each other on Boxing Day.'

Granny paused, and I tried to take this in. I couldn't imagine playing football and chatting one day and looking at the same lads from the other end of a rifle the next.

'Albert never said much about the rest of the war,' Granny went on. 'Maybe he thought he could forget if he didn't talk about it. But I'm sure the responsibility was hard to bear. He was one of the few who survived the trenches, so he was the only link many bereaved families had with their young lads who never made it home. Later on he became a Methodist lay preacher.'

She nodded toward the dresser and I walked over to look at the picture sitting on top. Four handsome young boys—two soldiers, one sailor and one airman—smiled back at me, full of life and mischief even in black and white. They leaned toward the camera, laughing, arms hanging round each other's shoulders—as if it took all they had to stand still, for one moment, for this photograph. I wished I knew what the joke was. Two of them were probably about my age, but their uniforms made them seem older. They looked ready to take on the world.

'Your grandpa, Reggie, had three brothers,' Granny explained. 'Little Dora was born later. The Wallace boys were the pride of their parents—and of the whole neighbourhood. Neighbours used to say that they felt sorry for the Germans if the "Wallace Boys" were crossing the channel.'

'They look so young,' I said, lifting the photo for a moment.

Granny pointed with her soapy hand. 'Your grandpa and Will were the younger two. They weren't even old enough to enlist, but they lied about their ages.' She shook her head. 'Your great-grandfather was furious when he heard what they'd done. He'd seen war first-hand. He tried to stop them, but they escaped over the back wall one morning and never looked back. Will was the youngest; he died in your grandpa's arms at Dunkirk a few months after that picture was taken. It broke Reggie's heart.' Granny looked down at the sink and wiped her hands on her apron. 'I never met Will,' she said.

I looked at the picture again. Will. I'd all but forgotten I was named after my mother's uncle. But of course she'd never met him either.

As if she could read my thoughts, Granny said, 'I think you do look like him.'

'How old d'you reckon he is here?'

'Well, your grandpa was seventeen, so Will would have been sixteen when that picture was taken,' she said. 'Cyril's the oldest. He joined the merchant navy, but he and Grandpa had a disagreement years ago and they haven't spoken since. Paul, the one in the middle there, was a Spitfire pilot. He was shot down in the Battle of Britain, somewhere in the Channel.' Granny shook her head again. 'Did you know that Will was awarded the Victoria Cross for heroism at Dunkirk?'

I remembered hearing about the Victoria Cross in history class. It was the highest award for bravery you could get. 'Really? Have you got it here? Can I see it?'

Granny looked round at me as if she'd let a horse bolt from the stable door. 'No, love, you can't see it,' she said. 'And promise me you won't mention it to your grandfather.'

I nodded. I recognized that sad and serious tone. My mum sounded the same way sometimes.

Granny studied the picture again. 'That was the last time they were all together,' she said. 'It must have been a poor thing to be a mother in those days. In some ways I'm glad that Albert and Betty didn't live to see what the war did to their sons.'

What happened, I wondered. Suddenly, a hundred questions filled my mind and I wanted to know everything—everything about this family, these people who were a part of me, this great-uncle who had my name and who died a hero when he was only a year older than I was. I'd never even thought about this before, but now I needed to know. Where should I begin? 'But why did they not live to see ...' I began.

But Granny had finished her dishes and was on her way out of the kitchen. 'I've got to pop out now, dear,' she said. 'Ask me later.'

I decided I might get some answers from Aunty Dora so I hurried out into the cool evening air and down towards the river. The mountains were a dark red and deeper in the valley everything was bluish and quiet. As I crossed the field Alfie came to nibble me, looking for a treat. As I approached the wooded knoll at the bottom of the field I could see the last of the evening sun warming the larch trees and making the mountains a bright red. I spotted Aunty Dora making her way up from the woods. She came to a halt on the highest point of the knoll, and as I approached she waved and smiled.

'Ah, William,' she said. She motioned for me to sit beside her on the grass. 'How are you feeling? How's your mother? Did you get through on the telephone?'

'She's okay,' I said. 'Sends her love.' I sat down and we watched the setting sun as it started to dip behind Low Moor. She must have sensed I was about to ask a question, because when she turned towards me there was a question in her smile. I took a deep breath. 'Aunty Dora, Granny was telling me about your family, I mean our family, you know—Grandpa and Uncle William and everybody—but she had to go out before I could ask her—I was wondering ...' I paused, but her smile encouraged me to go on. 'What happened to Great-grandpa Albert and ...'

She tucked her knees up to her chin like a little girl and looked out over the mountains for such a long time I thought maybe she'd forgotten I was there. 'Well, Will,' she finally began, 'my dad was the kindest, gentlest man on the Mersey. He was soft on me—he'd always wanted a little girl to fuss over and finally, nearly ten years after the others, I came along. He called me his 'little Robin'. Mum was tiny but full of energy. She was a whirl of laundry and dishes. She made me a swing in the laundry shed for wash days when old Mrs McNally from next door came to help. They'd put me in that swing to stop me 'helping', and we'd laugh all day. Mum was always laughing and singing.'

She laughed at the thought of it but then stopped and looked more serious. 'But one wash day she fell carrying a pan of boiling water across the yard and scalded her face and arms. I couldn't get out of my little swing and screamed and screamed as Mrs McNally tried to help. Mum's pretty face was scarred from then on, but Dad was so kind. "You'll always be my pretty little sparrow," he'd say as he kissed her scars.' She wiped her eye and went on. 'Dad was an air-raid warden in Wallasey during the second war. His leg injury from the Great War meant he couldn't enlist, and I think he was thankful of it. He never spoke a word about the trenches or what he'd seen, but when the boys all enlisted it broke his heart.

'My parents both died during the bombings,' Aunty Dora continued. 'Dad was so frantic one night getting everyone

33

to the neighbourhood bunker that he hadn't noticed Mum and Mrs McNally weren't there. He only realized as the sirens were lost to the sound of the falling bombs.' Aunty Dora paused. I wondered if she only saw the setting sun, or maybe the long-ago fires. 'It was the worst night Liverpool ever saw,' she went on. 'The other wardens tried to restrain Dad from going out but they couldn't. He had to make sure Mum was safe. He hobbled the entire length of Cherry Tree Lane back to Monk Road—where we lived—as the fire and explosions raged all around him.

'People talked about it for years afterward. No one could believe he'd been so brave. Afterwards people decided Mum must have stayed behind to nurse old Mrs McNally during one of her angina attacks. Dad made it back to her, his 'sparrow', and they were found all together two days later under a mountain of rubble. They say love is stronger than death, and I think their love was. In some ways I suppose I'm glad that they went together like that. I can't imagine how one would have lived without the other. When they were married, they promised that nothing but death would part them ... and that's how it was.'

'But—but what about you?' I asked. 'Were you in the bunker?'

'No, bless you Will, no—I was an evacuee. I was sent— evacuated—from Liverpool to the Lake District before the bombing started. That's how I came to know your Gran. There I was, standing on the platform of Keswick train station—before it was knocked down—and all the town and dales folk had been told to come and take in an evacuee child to help the war effort. I was only eight years old and very frightened. All the other children were picked, and I was left alone. Then a girl about my age walked up to me and said her family had a farm on the other side of those hills and I could come to stay with them so long as I didn't take a liking to her sweetheart, Johnny Robinson, as she had been going steady with him for two weeks.'

Aunty Dora broke off and laughed. 'Your Gran was such a funny girl, always falling in and out of love. I expect your Louise is a bit the same, living for that one man who will sweep her off her feet. Anyhow, that was Elsie, and we had a good time making the most of it as the months of the war wore on. Her family was very kind and, even though there was rationing, being farmers they had more than most. I was settling in nicely until that summer's evening—one just like this in fact. Elsie and I were coming up from the river after a swim before bed. As I got to this very spot on the knoll, I spied a soldier walking down the field toward us. I didn't even recognize him until he took off his hat. It was my big brother Reggie ... I'd not seen him for two years, and oh how old and worn he looked—as if he might crumple under the weight of it all.

'He was wearing his khaki dress uniform, and I ran to him and buried my face in his chest. "Is it over, Reggie? Can we go home now?" I asked him. Reggie introduced himself to Elsie and asked her if she would give us some time alone. When he told me that Dad, Mum, Paul and little William were all gone to heaven, and that our home had been bombed out, I just stared and stared at the weave on his jacket. It was all so unreal, I'm not sure how I didn't go mad. Reggie was in tears. He told me that Cyril had gone to pieces, that they'd had a big fight the week before and he'd gone off to sea. All we had now was each other, he told me, and through his sobs he kept reassuring me that I didn't need to worry. He'd take care of me, he promised, when the war was over, and we'd live together. And he did, bless him, even though it would be a few years before his war was over.'

She paused and I gazed over this meadow with new eyes. This place held sacred memories. I closed my eyes and tried to imagine my grandfather, on this very spot, breaking the news to Aunty Dora that her parents and two brothers had died. She'd called me 'another evacuee from Liverpool', but my story was nothing compared to hers. At least everyone in my family was alive, and safe.

Aunty Dora patted me on the knee. 'So, dear, that's why the three of us are so close. At that time they were all I had in the world.'

'When did Granny and Grandpa fall in love?' I asked.

'Well, after your grandpa had to go back, we prayed for his safety every night. I used to write him a long letter every week and Elsie would add her little bits at the end. Later she confided that he was the handsomest, bravest, kindest man she'd ever met and that she'd never look at another boy until she married him. Can you imagine that? She was nine years old—what a caution she was, your Gran! Well, she did hold on, though she never told another soul, and she prayed every night that God would spare "her" Reggie in battle and that one day she could make him a good wife. She never walked out with any other boy all through her teen years. Reggie moved up here when he returned from Burma in 1945 and rented a little cottage in Lorton for the two of us, with me keeping house. He did labouring jobs to pay the rent until an old army friend got him a position in their family corn business in Cockermouth.

When your Gran and I were both in our late teens, Elsie had grown into the most beautiful girl you'd ever seen. That's where your mum gets her good looks. It took a while for Reggie to get over their ten-year age difference, but eventually he did, and it was all I could have wished for— to see the two people I loved best in the world so happy together. Their love story was the talk of the valleys for years.'

She paused and smiled over at me. 'Well, dear, I need to be going home. I've not told you about Uncle William, as I think it's best for your Grandpa to tell you that story if he wants to—but don't press him if he doesn't want to talk.'

I nodded. Ask Grandpa! I felt too in awe of him to ask him, even though I really did want to know about him and William. I didn't have anything in common with him—apart from the fact that he was my grandfather.

'Good night, William.' Aunty Dora bent to kiss my forehead and made her way up the field.

I continued on, descending yet further into the dusky woods. I found him by the river, rod in hand.

'There you are, lad. Come to try your hand against these sea trout have you? Well, take hold of this and I'll show you. I've not had a bite this evening, and yet I know they're there.'

I took the rod and he showed me how to cast. He was a patient teacher and I was, to my amazement, what he called 'a natural'. Just when I'd given up hope of finding an opportunity to ask him about Uncle William, I felt three strong tugs on the line. The fish splashed and Grandpa whooped in delight. He patted me on the shoulder and reminded me not to jerk the line. Eventually, after much laughter and lots of instruction, we landed a nice sea trout. Grandpa insisted that I whack it on the head and showed me how to gut it. He and Nelson were both so excited I didn't dare show my disgust.

'Well, I think you're going to make a better angler than me, lad,' Grandpa said as we made our way through the woods.

'I'm sure it's just that you're such a good teacher,' I said. I was glad of the evening shadows so he couldn't see me blush.

'Hah!' Grandpa snorted. 'That's not what my little brother Will said when I took him to Birkenhead docks for the first time. I'd been before, and I was trying to show him what to do, but he thought he knew everything. We had my brother Cyril's rod between us, and we fought over it so much that I pushed him off the pier and made him swim to the mud bank! My mother was furious ... she beat us both with Cyril's rod until we were sorry. She was a mighty little woman, your great-grandma.' He shook his head at the memory.

As soon as he paused, I blurted out my question. 'Grandpa, what happened to Will?'

He turned to look at me. He seemed taken aback, but not displeased. He sighed. 'Well, I suppose I should tell you the story, lad. You're old enough to know, and I'm certainly not getting any younger. But it's not to blather about to all and sundry. This isn't some fairytale. It's your family history, your heritage. Maybe someday you'll be called upon to show courage you didn't know you had.'

I nodded, though I had no idea what he was talking about.

'Well,' he continued, 'when that day comes, remember you're not the first in this family. Y'see, sixty years ago Poland was overrun by the Germans, and our regiment, along with two hundred thousand other British infantry, stood with the remaining Polish units. We were just boys, a little older than you are now. We'd never seen such bloodshed, such destruction.' He shook his head again and bent over to give Nelson, who was dancing at his heels, a pat on the head. He straightened. 'We'd never seen such courage, either. The Poles fought tooth and nail for their country and their families. We were all pushed back over and over again by the German artillery and panzer divisions. They were relentless.

'Before we knew it, our backs were to the sea near Dunkirk and Churchill had decided to get us all home to regroup to fight another day. We all knew that Hitler would be invading Britain soon enough.' He paused, and I thought I detected a slightly wild look in his eye. 'It was a week that the Polish nation would want to forget, but their soldiers will always remember it in a folk song about a young English soldier who single-handedly stopped a column of panzer tanks in their tracks and saved thousands of retreating troops.' He paused again, and I heard the catch in his voice. 'They still sing that song today in their villages. Many people think it's just a myth, but it's not. That soldier was our Billy, my kid brother.'

I heard a hint of the Liverpool scouse when he said 'our Billy', and it hit me hard. These weren't old black and white movie heroes but real people. From my neighbourhood. From my own family. 'What happened?' I asked. 'Did you–'

Grandpa halted and looked back down towards the river. 'Billy was a smart kid,' he said, 'and when he heard those tanks coming that day he knew there was no time for our troops to get away. He decided if he could stop the first tank as it advanced down the narrow, medieval street then all the others would retreat. He ran off while I was looking the other way, and he took a mortar launcher and a bag of munitions with him. But instead of setting the launcher up on the ground he fired it from the hip, running like David ran toward Goliath. That first tank stopped, probably in amazement at the sight, but after about four shots he hit it, disabling its front wheels. It all happened so quickly, I didn't even notice he was gone until the tank had been hit. I'd sworn to Mother that I wouldn't let him out of my sight. But I knew my little brother, and I knew where I'd find him.' He paused again.

'Was he hurt? What happened?'

'I ran down the side of the street,' Grandpa continued. 'My C.O. was screaming for me to return to my position, but I couldn't obey his orders and Mother's at the same time. All I could hear was her voice and my pounding heart. I spotted him lying in the middle of the street, his ears bleeding from the noise. He turned to me and grinned. "Look, Reggie! I stopped the Krauts!" he shouted over towards me. Just as the words were leaving his lips, the disabled tank gave a burst of machine-gun fire and eight rounds hit his body. I ran out to him, but he was near gone as I lifted his head. His thin body was riddled with bullet wounds. He struggled for breath in my arms ...' Grandpa's voice was shaking now. I edged closer to him. 'My little Billy's life was leaking away in a pool of blood. "We showed 'em, didn't we, Reggie? The Wallace boys," he said. I told him not to talk but he lifted his hand to point and struggled on. "Just—just need to drop the buildings either side to stop the other tanks pushing through ..." He was choking as he spoke. "I'm dying, I think ... you'll tell Mum and Dad that we weren't running from them, won't you?" Those were his last words.'

Grandpa took a deep breath and went on. 'I wanted to stay there holding him forever, but the second tank was pushing through and there were only moments left. I grabbed the launcher to finish what Will had started out to do. I aimed at the buildings nearby and brought them down on the tanks. I had to leave him where he fell, but I made it to the beaches. Churchill had thought he'd be lucky to get 60,000 of us home. But the whole country prayed and every boat on the south coast was sent over to get us and 160,000 made it. No one could believe it, but it was all because of heroes like your great uncle. That's 100,000 families that were spared grief, but it was a bitter victory for our family.'

'Billy and I were both awarded the Victoria Cross. I wasn't facing down tanks for my country like he did, I was just trying to get him home safe to our mother like I'd promised.'

I was silent. I couldn't think of a thing to say that wouldn't sound stupid. Suddenly the highest medal for bravery didn't sound all that glorious anymore.

Grandpa cleared his throat. 'Still, that was a long time ago and here's the house. Off to bed with you now, you look tired out. I'll wrap the fish and you can show your grandmother in the morning.'

Tired as I was, I felt like a different person. More grown up, somehow, than the boy who had followed Granny up those stairs earlier that afternoon. So much had happened in just a few hours and I was afraid I'd forget some of it. So I found my notebook and started to write a sort of diary with the events of the day and the family stories I'd heard. And my fish—I was surprised how exciting it was to catch a fish. When I'd finished, I stared out the window and wondered if I could ever be half as brave as my Great-uncle Will.

When Granny came up to say goodnight she told me she knew a boy and girl my age who wanted to meet me. 'You'll see them tomorrow, dear,' she said. 'Sleep well.'

4

THREE UNNATURAL DEATHS

The smell of scrambled eggs and bacon woke me the next morning, and I knew exactly where I was. At home we were always running too late for anything more than cereal or toast. But the heavenly aroma of Granny's cooked breakfasts took me back to my last visit here, when I was five, as I lay for a few minutes under the eiderdown. One breakfast I'd accidentally put salt on my cornflakes. I hadn't dared to tell Grandpa but ate it all up. I hadn't thought about that in years.

Granny was at the stove singing old hymns to herself. She gave me a hug and an enormous plate of eggs, bacon, tomato and mushrooms. Grandpa came in with Nelson at his heels, sat down, and criticized the strength of the tea. I decided he probably wasn't a morning person but didn't let it interfere with my feasting. As breakfast continued, though, I noticed that Grandpa's grouchiness was aimed at Granny. He didn't like her singing or the smart clothes she was wearing. I was embarrassed but Granny bore his little digs with an easy, gracious air. She was chirpy about something and she wasn't going to be drawn into an argument.

When the second pot of tea was on the table Aunty Dora came in. 'Now William dear,' she began quietly in her pleasant, old-fashioned way. 'I hope you will be joining us at church this morning'

Now that was one of the only statements that could have come between me and the fork-load of bacon en route to my open mouth. I'd been to church a few times, and it had always been boring. Dad had gone to church at different times, and dragged us along, but he'd always grown tired of fighting the tide of Mum's cynicism. That morning I felt so alive and full of virtue after hearing my family's history that the thought of old hymns and dull sermons left me cold. I was burning to get out into the real world to do something heroic—save a life, fall in love, kill some baddies, perhaps even the famous 'Beast of Low Moor'. I could feel my family's bravery coursing through my veins and surely that, I thought, was enough for any man.

'Do you go every week?' I asked.

'If I can, yes', Aunty Dora replied. 'You know what they say, "Sow an act, and you reap a habit. Sow a habit and you reap a character, sow a character and you reap a destiny."'

Grandpa gave a snort as he shook his *Sunday Telegraph* and peered deeper into its pages.

'It will be lovely to have your company, William,' Aunty Dora said as she stood. I wasn't aware that I had given consent, but it seemed my fate was sealed. 'Let's walk, Elsie, it's such a lovely morning. Reggie are you?' Aunty Dora paused expectantly.

'No, I am not. I'm going to sit right here and read this paper and then take the dog out.'

When the breakfast dishes were done, we headed out into the sunshine. The mountains looked friendlier against the blue sky and everything smelled fresh. As we walked

43

down the path I saw a boy on a BMX bike doing little circuits further up the lane. There was something familiar about him, but I didn't know anyone in the Lake District except my grandparents and Aunty Dora. He looked a little rough, like a stray. I thought maybe he was a gypsy waiting to rob people's homes while they were at church. He looked in our direction and, when our eyes met, he smiled, waved and carried on. I could just hear my mother the social worker: 'Will, you must always treat people well, even if they're less fortunate than yourself. Never look down at anybody.' I'd always tried to do that—though when I brought home a stray kitten one day my dad decided I'd taken it too far.

It was about a twenty-minute walk to Loweswater Parish Church. Every time I looked up at the mountains from another perspective they looked different. At one point we were looking down a long valley as Crummock Water stretched back into the mountains. I felt like I was on location shooting a film or something.

Granny stopped to greet a scruffy-looking old guy in tatty jeans and a checked shirt. He had a paper in his hand and was arguing with himself in some foreign language. Even I could tell his scraggly grey beard needed a trim, and when he looked at me with his dark brown eyes I got the sense he wasn't seeing me but someone from another time or placc.

'I have another letter from them ... those animals,' he said in a thick accent that might have been German. Or Russian. 'They say I will pay them one thousand of your English pounds if I do not join in their system of global indoctrination. This is worse than what we had to endure in Mother Russia.' He shook the paper and I figured he was mad, but Granny smiled.

'But Professor,' she said, 'if you have a television then you will have to buy a license!' She chuckled. Clearly this was not the first conversation they'd had on the subject.

'Madam, you mock me,' the professor said with a little bow. 'I have books and in them I find beauty and truth. While I devour the work of great men it is my custom to plug the little television in and leave it to run fuzzy without the aerial and in this way I fulfill the words in the Bible, "thou preparest a feast before me in the presence of my enemies". I have explained this to them but they still hunt me down like a revolutionary.'

Granny shook her head and introduced me as 'young William on my way to church'. Professor Conrad Inchikov, she said, had taught Philosophy at Durham University. He'd lived in the old green timber shack on Grandpa's land for the last sixteen summers and spent the winters traveling in eastern countries.

The professor's eyes pierced through me. 'Youth!' he snorted. 'What did Sir William Neil Connor say about being young?' He looked up to the sky. 'Ah, yes, here it is: "I remember my youth and the feeling that it will never come back any more—the feeling that I could last for ever, outlast the sea, the earth and all men; the deceitful feeling that lures us on to joys, to perils, to love, to vain effort—to death; the triumphant conviction of strength, *the heat of life in a handful of dust ...*"' His voice had grown louder with each word and now he paused, levelled his eyes from heaven to me, and went on speaking softly. '"The glow in the heart that with every year grows dim, grows cold, grows small, and expires—and expires, too soon, too soon—before life itself."' He breathed in through his thick beard. 'What words, what immortal words,' he said. 'Now mark this, young William, that you do not waste your youth or your time in this valley!'

I nodded uncertainly. He looked exhausted. I decided not to ask him who Sir William Neil Connor was.

The professor turned to Granny and gently enquired whether Major Wallace was accompanying us to church.

'My husband was, like his father, a popular Methodist lay preacher after the war,' Granny said. 'But he's fallen out with God some time since.'

'Ah ... yes ... indeed, my dear,' the professor said sympathetically. 'What your Coleridge would call "Truths lying bedridden in the dormitory of the soul" I believe.'

Granny smiled. 'Yes, something like that,' she said.

And with a funny little bow he went on his way to do whatever loony professors do on Sunday mornings.

Granny stopped to gaze out over the valley and down toward the river as Aunty Dora and I went on.

'What a nutter!' I said.

'Oh, the professor's all right.' Aunty Dora smiled. 'He's a little eccentric, I suppose, but he speaks sense through his madness on occasions. He fled Russia in the sixties and was a friend of Solzhenitsyn, but he lives here now. They say he's very well respected in academic circles and all that fluff about the TV licence is just his bit of fun, what he calls "his only recreation".'

'Why did Grandpa fall out with God?' I asked as soon as Granny was out of earshot.

'Don't judge your Grandpa too hard, William dear. He's suffered a lot in his life, and so has your Granny. The war turned many people hard, but not Reggie. He came back stronger and softer, as if all he'd seen had given him new eyes for what was precious and important. He became quite a notable preacher in Cockermouth and these valleys, and he had the respect of almost every family on account of his bravery in the war. He never charged God with any wrong over the deaths of his parents or his brothers, but when his first daughter, Elizabeth, died he didn't cope very well. He was caught off guard. During the war you expected the worst, but not during peacetime. Reggie thought he'd seen his last tragedy for a while and couldn't take another. It's not that he stopped believing as much as that he couldn't face God again because he was so angry with him.'

'How did it happen?' I asked as I glanced back down the lane toward Granny. How could she be so loving, I wondered, after living through so much pain and tragedy?

Aunty Dora was slow to start, as if the memory was too fresh. 'This was in the fifties,' she said, 'before your mum was born. Your grandparents had been married only a couple of years. Your grandpa wanted a string of boys to name after his dad and brothers, but that was not to be. Instead your granny had miscarriage after miscarriage. I remember thinking that one more miscarriage would break her for good. And then came Elizabeth. She was a healthy eight-pound baby and grew up to be the apple of her parents' eye—and no wonder, after all they'd been through, bless them.

'When Elizabeth was five, we had a family picnic down by the river bend—near where you were fishing last night. It was a perfect day. She was a feisty little girl, so sure she could swim on her own, she must have snuck off to have a dip. All of a sudden we realized she was gone and heard the faintest splutter. Reggie was off like lightning, but he didn't make it in time. My poor brother carried her limp little body to the bank and tried to resuscitate her but it was no use. She was gone forever. From that moment on it was like there was a black cloud hanging over the family. Your mother's birth was like a ray of sunshine that broke through that cloud, but the cloud never went away.' Aunty Dora lowered her voice to a whisper. 'I've never really talked to him about it, but I think Reggie blamed himself for not being more vigilant, for not been quicker. It was like Uncle Billy at Dunkirk all over again and he couldn't take any more–'

'Come on, you two. It's nearly ten o'clock! We're going to be late!' Granny came up behind us and we doubled our pace. I looked over at her as we hurried along. She looked different somehow—stronger, more beautiful.

Loweswater Parish Church was an ordinary enough building—it didn't even have a spire—but when I stepped inside I was amazed by the view of Grasmoor fell which filled the huge window behind the altar. It was better than any painting they could have hung there. I could just hear Granny telling me it was a piece of artwork by God himself. I didn't mention it.

I was surprised to see the place was nearly full—mostly old people, but there were a lot of young families as well. A kind looking, ruddy-faced man greeted us as we walked in. He was probably about sixty and he was wearing a tweed jacket, grey slacks, a burgundy tie—and a huge grin.

'Awey lasses, who's this strapping fella with ya? Is it really our la'al William?' He smiled and held out a huge calloused hand.

'You'll not remember my baby brother, George, Will, but I dare say you won't have forgotten helping the "Smelly Man" with the lambing when you were a toddler?'

'The Smelly Man! Of course I remember,' I said.

'Aye, well.' He started back, pretending to be offended. 'I dare say that us shepherds don't smell like folks from the town, but we've more fresh air up here to cart away the smell!' He chuckled and banged me on the shoulder. 'Well, seeing you're up in the valley for the summer, lad, you can make yourself useful and help an old man with his sheep the odd day. I'll even let you drive the quad-bike if you're good.'

'Okay—sure, thanks,' I said. Sheep didn't interest me at all, but I didn't know how to refuse without being rude. And since I had to spend an entire summer without computer games, quad biking on the high fells might be fun. Great-uncle George gave us each a hymnbook and a prayer book and showed us to our seats.

I was sure everyone was staring at me, so I tried to look around casually without catching anyone's eye. I could tell there were some real characters in the crowd. One thick-set bearded man was talking to George in short, low grunts that sounded Irish to me. His white bristly hair and bulging eyes reminded me of a badger, and he was wearing a heavy overcoat tied with baling twine—like Greengrass from 'Heartbeat'. I decided he must be some sort of tramp and I wondered what he was doing in church.

Another man strode down the aisle to sit in the front row by himself. If the tramp was like a badger then this guy was definitely a fox. He was tall, about Grandpa's age, and wore a nice country tweed suit. It fit him perfectly, but for some reason it looked like it wasn't made for him at all. His cheeks were red and he wore his grey hair slicked back. An even older woman, dressed in black with a velvet hat and walking stick, sat down next to him. The man looked round every few minutes as if he owned the place. He caught Granny's eye and raised his head slightly to acknowledge her, and Aunty Dora, and then he fixed his penetrating gaze on me.

For some reason I couldn't take my eyes off him, but I felt a sort of fear spread through me, as if I were being lowered slowly into an icy pool. I couldn't tell whether his eyes were full of hatred, pain, or guilt ... or all three. I finally looked down, pretending to be looking for something on the floor. I knew he was still staring at me, and my cold fear turned hot as I felt my cheeks going red. Finally, out of the corner of my eye, I saw him turn back around with a faint satisfied smile creeping around the edges of his mouth.

I looked straight ahead to the altar and the view of the fells. There was a huge empty black pot and a plastic bag at the front where, in all the churches I'd ever been to, there would have been flowers or candles or a cross or something. Behind that was a boy with a guitar, probably about fifteen, and a girl at the keyboard. She was older, maybe nineteen, although with her deep red hair held back by a hair band and her long flowing skirt it was hard to place her. The boy's clothes weren't very trendy either, and they both wore glasses. But the music they were playing, kind of 'soft-rock-ballad', was quite calming. I hadn't heard anything like it in church before.

'Those are the new vicar's children, Richard and Hannah,' Aunty Dora whispered. 'Such nice children. I know your Gran wants you to meet them.'

I nodded. They came to the end of the song they were playing and smiled at each other.

The clock said it was five minutes past ten, and in the silence after the song ended the congregation began to fidget and murmur. I looked around for the vicar—someone in a robe, back to front collar, a bit limp, but I couldn't see anyone to match my description.

Aunty Dora leaned towards me again. 'You'll like our vicar,' she whispered. 'He used to be a bouncer and into organized crime in Glasgow before he met Jesus and–'

There was an almighty crash behind us. Everyone turned to see the huge south doors swinging open and crashing against the wall as a tall, broad-chested man with a ginger beard like a lion's mane strode in. He was wearing a leather jacket and holding a weapon. I was sure we were about to be held hostage.

But as he came closer I saw it was not a gun that he held in his hand, but an uprooted pear tree. As he dragged it past us I saw the tiny, newly-formed fruits on its branches. Most people looked shocked, but some were smiling with anticipation. Mr Fox raised his eyebrow and the old woman, who must have been deaf, did not move.

'Dearly beloved,' the giant began as he made his way to the front. He had a Scottish accent. I looked over at Granny. Could this man actually be the vicar?

'Do ye know what's missing in Great Britain this morning?' the tree-wielding giant continued. 'Do ye know what's missing in British men this morning? Aye, and in the women too?' He glanced at me for a moment. 'Can ye tell uz what's missing in oor country's young people?' He raised the pear tree, which must have been at least fifteen-feet high, and placed it into the empty pot, which he started bedding in with compost from the bag as he continued talking to himself.

'Well, what is it? "Oh Roger," you say, "it's television! Folks have got no time for family 'cos they're always glued to the box!" Aye, maybe.' He nodded and went on. '"Oh, Roger, there's no discipline in schools and young'uns are running wild!" Aye, maybe.' He nodded again and put another huge handful of soil in the pot. '"Oh, Roger, there's no morality anymore, folks just do whatever they want!" Aye, I see that.' He shrugged as if he weren't really convinced. '"Oh, but Vicar, if only there were men and women in public life who set a good, moral example. But there's no-one to look up to anymore ..." Aye, I hear what yer saying. "Oh, but if we could only get folk back into church!" Aye, perhaps.' He nodded again, brushed the dirt from his hands, and drew himself up to face his audience. 'I tell ye all right now that churchgoing, morality, discipline and having a good example to follow will not make ye any more like Jesus, and ye'll nae get to heaven on that stuff either.'

He fixed his gaze on a row of starchy, do-goody looking ladies who were fiddling with their cardigans with stern expressions. 'What's missing, ladies, is the fruit of God's Holy Spirit. And that's got nocht to do with self-improvement but everything to do with "Christ-replacement". What I want to know this morning, ladies, is this: how fruity are ye?'

The ladies weren't the only ones who looked flustered now. There was shuffling all around.

I was surprised to find myself actually listening to this sermon, if that's what this was. He was so loud, though, it would have been hard not to listen. I felt like I do in the dentist's chair when he tells me what he's about to do and then asks me, 'Is that all right?' Even though I had no reason to be in church except that my granny dragged me there, I didn't really have a choice but to listen. I certainly didn't need God in my life or anything. But as I sat there it did occur to me that a new millennium was coming, and I had to start thinking about the 'adulthood' thing. I guess it came to me then that I basically had too many unanswered questions not to give this guy a chance. I would never have come to a church for answers but, since I was there, it was only fair to let God have his say—if there was a God.

The tree-planting Scotsman continued. 'Andrew is coming up to read a paraphrase of Paul's letter to the Galatians.' A tall, stocky man in his mid-twenties approached the front.

'That's Andrew the vet,' Aunty Dora whispered. 'He's also the champion wrestler of the dale. You'll like him.'

I nodded and wondered why all the men here were so massive.

Although he looked a bit intimidating because he was so big, Andrew had a friendly, gentle face with a slightly squashed nose. He took his stand and I wondered how friendly he would look if you were wrestling with him. He cleared his throat.

'Now it's pretty obvious to anyone with eyes in
their heads how mankind's natural, fallen nature is
demonstrated; adultery inside marriage, cheap sex
outside it and everything else dirty in between. Mix
with all that the usual cocktail of man-made-DIY
religion, occult superstition and that insatiable appetite
for a drunken party life and what do you get? I'll tell
you what, one long hangover lifestyle; silly irritations
morphing into habitual anger management issues,
petty arguments blowing up into major feuds, which
in turn soon have all and sundry splitting off into hate-
fuelled cliques, envious and murderous. Like I told
you before anyone who opts for this lifestyle will never
inherit his intended position in God's kingdom.'

Just as I was thinking, 'Wow, that writer must have visited *my* school,' the vicar got up.

'Aye, Andrew,' he said, 'we'll pause there 'cos this is what the man's talking about ...' And with that he ripped two branches off the pear tree and held them high. Uncle George came down the aisle with two buckets. The first looked to be full of household rubbish, but the other was full of cow slurry. People winced at the smell as he passed their pews.

'Thank you, George. Now, can anyone tell uz whether ye can have the fruit without the roots? We'll leave this branch in the rubbish bin for the next nine weeks to see an example of a man who rejects God. Eventually his virtue shrivels. We'll stick this second branch in the slurry bucket, although we'll have to leave it in the porch because of the stew. Ye see, a branch with its roots in slurry is to show us a man who cuts himself off from the grace of God by planting himself in a "good-deeds-alone" form of Christian religion, God help us! That's the slurry, folks! That man may keep some fruit, but he'll never mature or increase. He'll always remain small and hard. Now, Andrew, tell them the rest. They look like they need to hear some good news.'

Andrew returned the vicar's grin and carried on with his Bible reading. 'Er, Where was I, oh yes, "Like I told you before, anyone who opts for this lifestyle will never inherit his intended position in God's kingdom. Why? Because that kingdom is run on love, the out-flowing of which is clearly seen in a life of tender affection, irrepressible joy, un-argumentative peaceableness, endurance in trials and stickability in relationships. Also an easy-going gentleness, fidelity and a compassionate outlook poised always for the benefit of others, and all this bound with a humility and self control that means no one could take offence."'

Andrew sat down next to a pretty brunette and I saw her squeeze his hand.

The vicar jumped up. 'Now,' he said, 'ye'll all recognize that last passage from the old King James Version: "But the fruit of the Spirit is love, joy, peace, longsuffering, gentleness, goodness, faith, meekness and self-control." Now friends, I want us all to return to what the prophet Jeremiah calls "the ancient paths" over the next nine weeks. We're going to study the character traits that make a real man and woman as they were meant to be. Today I want to talk about the most important of these, which is also the first: love.'

'Here we go,' I thought. 'The excitement's over and it's time for a doze.' But, to my surprise, what he said made sense. He was talking about the love of Jesus Christ, and it was interesting. I didn't really believe him, though, when he claimed that the very same love could flow through me if I let Jesus do it.

'Now that takes a lot of believing, Vicar,' I thought.

At that very moment he looked at me and said, 'Do ye doubt God can do this? Tell me, is it not the same sap running in the trunk as in the branch? And the same sap that makes the fruit? Think about it!'

I nodded. I couldn't help myself.

As the vicar told stories about Jesus' love and this love being the source of his miracle working power, his words brought images to my mind of real love in my own family. I thought first of Dad marrying Mum when she had another man's child, then of Great Grandpa Albert kissing his wife's scarred face and of the two of them giving their lives for others in the bombing. I thought of Uncle Will giving his life for the escaping soldiers at Dunkirk, and of Grandpa risking his life to get his brother back and then giving up his future to protect his little sister.

But then the vicar talked about how good examples weren't good enough. 'Yer branch needs to be connected to the fruit tree if ye want to have big fruit, too, my friends.'

I found myself wondering if it would work or if it was just religious talk. Part of me wanted to be a hero like some other members of my family. But that part was only a very little, deeply buried, part of me. The bigger part of me decided this was going nowhere and it was time to be going home for lunch.

'Christ is willing to make the best of us, but we must be willing to give him the worst of us,' the vicar was saying. 'You can'nae have this fruit if yer life's not plugged into the fruit tree. The *branch* does'nae produce fruit, the branch only exists for the tree to hang fruit on. So if yer not plugged into Jesus Christ this morning I want to encourage ye to ask him to help ye. Then he'll do this for ye.'

Uncle George came down the aisle again, this time with another branch. 'D'ye see this branch George is bringing down to us?' the vicar asked. 'It's a wild pear from his orchard and it's got nothing to do with this one I've got here ... except this.' He produced a large Bowie knife from under his jacket—much to the horror of the twitchy, tweedy women. He made a cut in the tree trunk then took the wild branch from Uncle George, slid it into the cut and bound it tightly with string. 'Now, if we've done that right we're going to see this wild branch become grafted into the main tree. Do ye get my point? Ye may be a wild'un—and I was, believe uz—but ye can get grafted in today if that is what ye want.'

I was in a daze for the rest of the service. It felt like a set up, and too easy to be true, but I couldn't get the idea out of my head. Was he talking to me? Was I a wild branch who could be a hero if I just joined the tree? I decided I needed to think about it more.

As we made our way out into the sunlight after the service everyone was in a flurry of excitement—except the old woman in black, who was being helped into an old Range Rover and whisked off for lunch, no doubt. But I didn't see Mr Fox. Where did he go so quickly? And why had he stared at me like that? I felt braver outside the church and walked toward the sloping graveyard to get a better view. I caught a glimpse of him, almost out of view of the milling crowd, standing alone near a grave. I could have sworn he was talking, although I couldn't hear what he was saying. He knelt quickly, as if to place something next to the grave, and then slipped out a side gate. He drove away in BMW 7 Series that looked out of place among the fells and country lanes.

As I watched the car disappear out of sight I also saw Hannah helping an old lady toward the gate. They were laughing like old friends. I walked back toward Granny, who was talking to a couple of older ladies. Aunty Dora touched my arm and nodded her head in the direction of the BMW. 'Careful who you stare at, William. That's your granny's older brother, Sidney Armstrong. He's not a man to trifle with.'

'That was Granny's brother? Whose grave was that?'

'His wife's. He goes there every Sunday. They say he paid a huge price to get that particular plot when she died. I can't think why, since it's right at the back. Still, he's got the money and, as to the reasons, well ... he keeps most things close.'

I saw the vicar heading in our direction and turned away toward the graveyard again. 'Is little Elizabeth's grave here, the one who was drowned?'

'Why yes, dear, it's that little white one over there.' Aunty Dora pointed and I wandered off.

Elizabeth Anne Wallace, 1952–1957

*sweet and courageous daughter of Reginald
Oswald and Elsie Jane Wallace*

*laid here to rest with greatest sorrow but also
in fervent hope that they shall all be together in
His Kingdom on the day when He shall wipe
all tears from their eyes*

I found tears coming to my eyes—quite unusual for me—as I thought of them all standing here forty-three years ago. I wiped my eyes with the back of my hand and started back, past the grave at which Mr Fox, a.k.a. my Great-uncle Sid, apparently, had been standing. The large headstone read,

'*Harriet Evelyn Armstrong 1932–1971*'. I did the sum out loud. 'Thirty-nine? Wonder why you died so young?'

I jumped when a voice from behind answered me. 'She won't tell you and no one else will either, lad. They all talk but they don't open their eyes. Don't want the truth, they want a nice peaceful valley ... but it's there, just below the surface if you dig ... aye, just below the surface and it's not pretty.'

I spun round. It was the old tramp, passing along the lane behind a low wall with his lurcher.

'Uh, sorry?' He was off before I could ask him to explain.

I looked back down at Harriet's grave. The tramp was right. She would never tell me what happened. I wondered what Uncle Sid had placed there. I couldn't see anything, but I did notice that the grass in front of the grave to the right was freshly trampled. I looked down again. The only footprints at Harriet's grave seemed to be my own. A small sandstone cross marked the grave to the right. The lettering was partly worn away. I could only make out the first few lines:

Here lies our beloved Ellen, daughter of John
and Josephine Patterson,

dear sister of John Stanley Patterson, who
give her up to God in the hope of a better
resurrection on the day when Christ shall return
for His own.

The dates weren't clear, but it looked like she had died in 1949. And there was a tiny blue cornflower, still fresh, lying in front of the cross. I had seen Uncle Sid kneel down, but this was very mysterious. Who was Ellen? Why did he make a pretense of visiting his wife's grave? And what did the old tramp mean about my great aunt's untimely death? I wondered if Granny knew more about it. And, if she did, would she tell me?

I waited until after lunch, while I was helping her dry the dishes, to ask Granny about Ellen Patterson.

She looked at me sharply. 'Ellen Patterson? What did you hear—'?

'Oh, I just noticed her grave today,' I said, trying to sound casual. 'It seemed—sad, next to Great Aunt Harriet's large headstone.'

Granny looked away out the window and nodded. 'Ellen was my best friend, and Dora's too, when we were growing up. Let me see ... I know I have her picture here.' She pulled a picture from the sideboard drawer. There were three pretty girls standing in a field. 'That's Dora, Ellen and me. We were baling hay. We would have been in our late teens when this was taken. Ellen's parents had the farm at Loweswater and we were all thick as thieves until she ... well, she ... died suddenly a year later.'

'How did she die?' I blurted out.

Granny looked down, wiped the frame with her apron and put it away. 'Well, Will, that's a difficult story. I mean, it's a private matter, dear.' She took off her glasses and rubbed her eyes. 'It was a horrid shame, that's all. Enough said for now, I think.'

She smiled weakly and patted my hand.

I nodded and reached up to put a bowl away. Every time I opened my mouth round here I seemed to stumble onto sad stories. But suddenly the summer seemed to hold a lot more promise. I'd have to solve the mystery of Uncle Sid and Harriet another day.

5

FISHING FOR TROUBLE

A fter lunch on Monday I decided to take Nelson for a walk. Actually, Nelson took me for a walk. We wandered through the field, past Alfie the donkey, and down to the river. I carried Nelson across at the shallowest point and we crossed the field on the farther side toward Kern Howe Farm.

The farm was not as I remembered it at all. There was black plastic strewn around the main building and dogs were barking at regular intervals from within its labyrinth of yards. Nelson was on high alert, no doubt wondering whether his archenemy, Ripper, was in residence. I had no intention of finding out and turned down along the hedge. I could hear tractors in the next field.

As we neared a small barn that faced the other field, I heard hushed voices. I stopped to turn back but Nelson kept trotting on to investigate further. When we reached the back of the barn, I peered through a hole in the corrugated metal sides. There were three boys sitting on hay bales drinking beer. They were all about my age, though one was maybe a bit older. In the distance I could see a tractor ticking over near a ditch where there were some abandoned tools. My heart was pounding, but my curiosity was stronger than my fear. I stayed where I was and tried to piece together their conversation.

It appeared that the older one, who had arrived on the tractor, had called the others together to plan a fishing trip in September that would make them all rich. He was tanned, handsome and quick-witted. He kept glancing around with his piercing blue eyes, as if their meeting was secret.

'So, you're all on for it then? It's gonna be a big'un,' he said.

It seemed the other two were being paid to do something in the ditch but had taken most of the morning off—to sleep off a night of heavy drinking at the Kirkstile Inn.

'Have you got the buyer sorted?' one of them asked.

'Are you sure they're gonna pay us right?' the other asked.

They weren't just going to catch fish, I realized. They were going to steal them. And they were all scared about being caught by someone called 'Stan the man'. They mentioned a hotel manager in Carlisle and cash, lots of cash.

I decided to get away before I gave myself away. Just then, another tractor arrived. The cab door swung open, and out stepped a stunning blonde in t-shirt, jeans and wellies. A large dog stayed behind in the cab. She sauntered into the barn swinging a plastic bag, jumped onto a huge round bale, and started separating the beer cans to toss them to the others. She was the best looking girl I'd ever seen. I decided to stay and listen some more.

The oldest was called Chris, and the girl, Carrie, was his sister. The big burly one was called Carl, and the other lad was a cousin but I couldn't catch his name. They were so cool and confident. They were sorted, and they were free. Chris, who reminded me of Brad Pitt, was completely at home with himself and the world. I could see the others idolized him, and he gave them their collective coolness. The more I watched them and listened to their jokes, the more I wanted to be like them, to be one of them. This was the kind of life I was searching for.

My thoughts were interrupted by a commotion near the second tractor. The large dog had jumped down out of the cab and gone mental.

Only then did I remember Nelson. But it was too late. He was already engaged in battle.

Carl charged out to the tractor. 'Ripper! What'ya doin' lad?'

Ripper? This was the infamous Ripper? What would I do now?

The brute beast was trying frantically to shake Nelson off his neck, but Carl lost no time in separating them. He held Nelson up by the scruff of his neck and laughed. 'Look, everyone, it's old Nelson come back for a bit more. Thought you'd learnt your lesson last time!'

Chris had called Ripper to heel with amazing effect. I was impressed, because he didn't look like the sort of creature that could be tamed easily—particularly when there was a fight at hand. Nelson looked longingly from Carl to Ripper and back to Carl. He obviously thought he'd had the upper hand in the fight and was keen not to lose his footing.

'Stupid mutt wants to bring it on, let's let them have it out together. He's alone, no one will know.' Carl's tone was vicious and Ripper, growling by Chris's legs, clearly agreed.

'Shush, Ripper,' Chris said. 'Carl, don't be a divot. Remember what that crazy Major did to Dad when he let them fight last time? How do you know he's not round the back of that hedge?'

I froze. I knew I had to do something to help Nelson, but what? At that moment Nelson, who couldn't bear to be held hostage any longer, released his own secret weapon. It worked.

Carl dropped him. 'Oh, what's that smell? You disgusting creature! He's farted on me!'

Nelson raced towards his foe, and I knew I could wait no longer. I ran around to the front of the barn but, before I could intercept Nelson, Carrie jumped off her bale and grabbed him. I stopped short and watched the worried and angry glances passing between the group.

'Who are you?' Carl asked. 'And what are you doing on our land?' He was blazing and squaring up to me for a fight. He was my height but twice as broad in every direction.

'I was just walking my Grandpa's dog and I didn't mean to—' I broke off. Carl came nearer, and I could smell the beer on his breath and see the bloodshot hatred in his eyes. 'And what did you hear, listening behind our barn, eh?'

Chris moved forward, leaving Ripper with the other boy. 'Yeah, all right Carl, I'm sure he means no harm.' Chris was cool and guarded as he asked me where I was from, when I'd arrived, who I'd met in these parts. If I hadn't heard their conversation I would have thought he was being polite, and not just making sure I wasn't one of Stan's spies.

As he relaxed, they all relaxed.

'You wanna beer?' Carrie asked, reaching into the bag.

'Yeah, thanks, that'll be great, cheers,' I said. I hated lager, but this was not the time to appear soft. They all watched with satisfaction as I took my first manly swigs. I was careful not to wince at the bitter tang. We talked for a few minutes about my family and the valley. When I told them the only place I'd been since I arrived was church with my Granny, they all rolled their eyes. I took another swig of beer.

Apparently the new vicar's children had been round with invites for their dad's Sunday services.

'That girl told me she'd never been to a nightclub!' Carrie said. She was watching me, and I was trying not to appear to be watching her. She was even better looking close up.

'Narrow-minded, religious, square-eyed dorks!' Carl said and he spat on the ground, 'Better not try and bash me with their Bibles, or I'll bash them.'

We all laughed as he shadowboxed round the barn. I took another swig. I felt my heart race every time Carrie smiled over at me.

It turned out that their family were tenant farmers for Uncle Sid. The other boy, whose name I still didn't catch, was their cousin. They were all keen to know what I thought of Uncle Sid and I said I didn't know him, which was true— we hadn't been introduced.

'Keep it that way then,' Chris said. 'He's not a man to mess with. He owns most the land in this valley and has fingers in every pie besides. Dad says the only one who's ever stood up to him and remained in the valley is your grandfather, and that's only 'cos he's kin and it were over fifty year ago. No, Will, the further you keep away from that old wolf the better.' His hushed tone and the dark look in his eyes told me he was deadly serious.

'Do you know why he fell out with my grandfather?'

'Can't remember—Dad told me once. It was something about a lost war medal or something.' Chris was studying me.

It did occur to me how strange it was that I was asking someone I'd just met about my own family. But I really wanted to know, so I forged ahead, trying to appear casual. 'What "pies" is he into then?' I asked.

'The sort of pies that the tax man doesn't know about,' Carrie answered. She warmed to her subject. 'The amount of flash cars coming'n'going from his grand spot, I don't wonder if he hasn't got half the Carlisle Mafia calling for tea each day. Dad says that since his wife died–'

'Dad says—never mind what he says,' Chris butted in. 'My marra in Cockermouth says that Harriet Armstrong's car going over that crag's edge into Crummock Water was no accident and all the dales folk at the time said the same thing. He married her for her money and he did her in for it in'all.'

'Come on, Chris, you know what folks are like, they're always yakkin' about summet. There's no proof.' I could tell Carrie wasn't really defending Uncle Sid as much as teasing her brother.

'I know what folks said at the time, inquest or no inquest. That man's a wrong'un, look at it. Even his own sister hardly speaks with him. Nay, keep away, Will, that's my advice.'

I nodded, but I was watching the two other boys as they ran out to the lane. Someone was walking a bicycle along the Lorton road towards us. In a few minutes I could see it was a middle-aged woman. She was dressed, strangely for a summer's day, in an overcoat. The bike was laden with bin bags and cases. It was an odd spectacle, and it greatly amused Carl and his cousin.

'It's Mad Annie taking another load of clothes from the charity shops to store in her cottage,' Chris told me. 'Hey Annie! Been shopping again? Got anything for me?' he shouted across the road.

At first it seemed she didn't hear him, or chose to ignore him, but then she turned and shot him such a look. I saw him jump. Even from fifty yards away I could see the wild madness in her eyes. She stared at us for what seemed forever—though it was probably only two seconds—and then she continued up the Buttermere road.

When she was far enough away Carl and his cousin threw stones in her direction, but I knew they were afraid of her too and would have run the other way if she had turned around. They laughed and swore at her. And because Carrie was laughing, I laughed too. I tried not to think what my mum would have said if she had seen me laughing at someone who was mentally handicapped. But Mum wasn't here, I was stuck here for the summer, and it was up to me to make friends and get on with my life.

I looked over at Chris, wondering why he was so quiet.

He took a swig and wiped his mouth. 'Aye, she's a crazy old witch is that yan. My dad said that them eyes could put a curse on you powerful enough to kill, but I don't believe in all that superstition—anymore than I believe that church can make any man better than another.'

I wasn't quite sure what he was getting at, but he looked so cool as he said it—almost like James Dean as he lit up a fag, took a long drag and looked across the field to the river.

I asked him what films he'd seen, what kind of cars he liked, where he went to school. We were very different, but we also had lots in common—mainly cars and films. I could tell Chris liked me. He kept asking me my opinion every time a new topic came up. I was chuffed but tried not to show it.

After awhile Chris nodded his head toward the ditch, and the other two boys went back to work. Chris, Carrie and I sat around laughing and talking over another beer.

Gradually Chris grew quiet and serious. He looked behind him to make sure the others were still at work and then nodded his head, as if he had reached a big decision. 'Do you like fishing, Will?' he asked.

'Yeah, I mean I've only done it once, the other evening, but I got a sea trout.' I brought the beer can to my lips again and was vaguely aware of that hazy feeling, where my words weren't quite my own.

'Good lad. But there's better ways of catching trout than fannying around with a fly rod. How would you like to join us tonight on a little fishing trip? We'll share what we catch and I'll get a good price for them with a marra of mine in Cockermouth.'

Although I felt uneasy about it, I heard myself say 'yes'. The look of pleasure in Carrie's eyes made the decision the right one.

Chris explained the plan. He couldn't keep the excitement out of his voice. I was to stand in for their cousin, who would be away in town tonight. We were to meet at the Salmon's Leap, the pool where I'd caught the sea trout, at ten o'clock. They'd be waiting for me on the other side and Carrie would wade over with our end of the net. I suspected he was using her as bait for me, but I didn't care in the least—and I didn't think she cared either.

'So,' I said, trying to sound naïve but watching him closely, 'do you own the fishing on the other bank?' I wanted Carrie to see that I could stand up to him, but I wasn't prepared for his flash of temper.

'Too much talk of who owns what in Lorton. The river's been there for thousands of years and them fish are there for whoever's bold enough to have 'em.' He narrowed his eyes. 'So don't you dare mention it to your grandfather—or your Uncle Sid—or he'll put an end to it. And us.'

'Cool it,' I said. 'I won't tell anyone.' I rolled my beer can between my palms. 'Anyway, who's this "Stan the man" you were talking about? What's he to us?'

'The man's a flippin' ex-SAS psycho—that's what he is to us. He's the "Becky."' When I shook my head he went on. 'You know, the "Beck watcher", the man who patrols the river for the Environment Agency. But most folk agree he's in your Uncle Sid's pocket—a sort of unofficial henchman. You'll never hear him coming until he's on top of you and givin' you, what he calls his "horizontal interview"'. He's a sad git with no life to speak of since his wife ran off with another man. So he takes it out on the poachers.'

That was the scary image running through my mind after I left my new friends and headed home with Nelson. As we turned on to the lane, the Professor appeared out of nowhere. Apparently even Nelson hadn't heard him coming. He fixed his beady eyes on me, and I blushed and stammered as I said hello. I wondered whether he knew something.

'William,' he said, 'have you read my countryman's great book *Crime and Punishment*?'

'Oh, well, I've heard of it,' I mumbled.

'You should read it, William, you should.'

'I will, Professor, thank you,' I said as I edged towards Nelson.

But the Professor went on, looking across the valley to the Clegg's farm. 'Dostoevsky says that "Extraordinary people have the right to commit any crime they like and transgress the law in any way just because they happen to be extraordinary." Do you agree, William?'

'Well, I don't know,' I said. 'I haven't thought about it, really.'

He sniffed, gave me a wry smile and walked away, saying at the top of his voice like some mad Old Testament prophet: 'That is youth, you see, not to think of the consequence!'

I was glad to get back to the house, though I was extra careful to act naturally so Granny wouldn't suspect I'd been drinking beer. I watched TV for awhile and Granny cooked my sea trout for supper. I couldn't quite enjoy it, though, as the guilt of what I was about to do gnawed away at me.

At 9:45 I stood up, stretched and said I was going out for some fresh air. Grandpa was watching Sherlock Holmes on the telly and I could hear Holmes's words following me down the hall all as I slunk off. 'It is my belief, Watson, founded upon my experience, that the lowest and vilest alleys in London do not present a more dreadful record of sin than does the smiling and beautiful countryside.' Was it just me, or was everyone talking about sin lately?

Nelson, lying on the floor in the kitchen, raised one eyebrow to look disdainfully at me as I left. I stepped over him.

I hated lying to Granny, but I wasn't going to miss the only fun I might have all summer.

Ten minutes later I'd descended into the valley in the darkness, and the weight of what I was about to do seemed heavier with every step that brought me closer to the river. Both the bravado and beer had, by this time, worn off completely. But the excitement of seeing Carrie kept me going. Before supper I'd shaved, put on some aftershave and changed into my best tracksuit. This could be my big chance with Carrie, and my future happiness might depend on it. Everything had to be just right.

I stood waiting at the Salmon's Leap. No one came, and as the darkness settled around me I began to panic. Every shadow took on the shape of the terrible beast of Low Moor.

'Oi, Will!' A shrill whisper made me jump. It was Carrie, making her way across the shallow section of river. She was dragging our end of an enormous net, and I helped her up the bank. The whites of her eyes and teeth shone in the moonlight and I got a faint whiff of perfume as I took the net from her.

I could just make out Chris and Carl getting the net into position on the other bank. Carrie was whispering, showing me how we were to position our end of the net and how we'd work the pool.

When the path narrowed, she motioned for me to hold the net by putting my arms around her. She smiled and whispered into my ear. 'Come on, Will, I won't bite. The bank is too steep here. You'll have to stand behind me.'

I didn't need a second invitation, and I put my arms around her waist to steady her. Between the fish tugging and Carl pulling tight on the other end of the net, it was quite a wrestling match for me and Carrie to stay on the bank. I was having fun. When we reached the end of the pool and the tension was slackened, she spun round in my arms. We were both breathing heavily from the exertion.

'Well, Will, I think you're getting the hang of this.' She lingered near my lips and I pulled her closer. When she didn't resist I realized that this was my moment, that this girl was the one, and it had all been so easy. But as I leaned forward to kiss her I heard a crackle of twigs somewhere behind us in the near darkness. She pulled back to listen and we both stood still, hearts thumping and hot-blooded romance draining away.

How in the world could I protect Carrie from the beast?

But she was the first to respond. 'We're being hunted! Quick!' She pushed her way out of my arms and toward the river with such force that I fell backwards into a pile of brambles. As I struggled to get up I saw Carrie desperately yanking our end of the net across the pool. The boys hauled the rest and, seconds later, she was on the other bank and they disappeared from sight.

My nylon tracksuit was caught in the brambles and, though I managed to tear free, my hands were badly cut. I was about to head across the river to join the others when, suddenly, something knocked me sideways onto the bank. The wind was knocked out of me. I could hear the beast breathing over me. I kicked my legs wildly and tasted blood in my mouth. As I struggled to get up my knees gave way in fear.

What was it? Where was it? The next thing I knew, its huge dark form came out of the shadows and landed on top of me, pinning me to the ground. I was frozen with fear. I had no voice. I had just shut my eyes and begun to pray to God, in whom I suddenly had no trouble believing, when I heard a voice—a thick, Geordie accent.

'All right, young man, I think it's time you's and me had ourselves a horizontal interview, don't you?'

'Who—who's that?' I sputtered.

'I'm your conscience, boy!'

'My conscience?' I repeated pathetically.

'Aye lad, your conscience, you know ... that little voice inside you that tells you someone might be watching? Well that's me!'

I struggled onto my side. 'Are you Stan?'

'Never you mind who I am, sonny, my question is this: who are you and what'ya'doon here? Another naughty bairn from the toon come to make a little pocket money?' His breath stank of whisky.

'I'm Major Wallace's grandson. I'm here for the summer. This—this is his land,' I stammered. I was starting to regain my wits, although Chris had said this man was not so much interested in the truth or the law as in dishing out what he called 'justice'. I supposed he could just as well tie me up and beat me as let me go.

'Are you now?' he said. 'Well, you tell me what you've bin up to 'ere, and who you've been with, and I'll think about letting you go, lad.'

I thought about betraying Chris, Carl and Carrie. After all, they'd left me behind. But maybe that was my fault for being slow. I was so scared I probably would have told him everything if I hadn't remembered that, in almost every kidnapping film I'd ever seen, it was never wise to give away any of your cards and leave yourself nothing to bargain with. Suppose this man was even more of a psycho than Chris knew? I decided to play this as cool as I could. 'I'll tell you what you want to know when you take me to the farm,' I said.

'You're a plucky one,' he said. 'Okay then, but don't try and run. I don't do "soft", you understand?'

I did understand. And I had no intention of experiencing another 'horizontal interview'.

Stan followed me up through the field and, as we approached the yard, I could see Grandpa's silhouette. He was waiting for Nelson to complete what he called his 'doggy business'.

'Evening, Major.' Stan was remarkably cordial under the circumstances. 'I found this bairn at Salmon's Leap just now with three others who seemed in a hurry to dump him and make off on the other side. He said he'd tell me which ones he's running with if I fetched him back to you. So here he is.'

The look on Grandpa's face as he put his hands on his hips was enough to make me shrivel up. I knew I could never make this right. The full weight of my crime against him crushed me. Even Nelson was scratching around with his 'I told you so' look on his face. It seemed easier at that point to keep my side with the guilty than rip myself open to forgiveness in the eyes of this old man.

I thought of the feel of Carrie's body close to me by the river. But then doubt split through my passion as I tried to rationalize her running away without me. In the pregnant pause that should have been filled with my confession I remained silent. And knowing looks shot between the judge and jury.

Grandpa drew near and broke the silence. 'Well, Stan, they say men are a lot like fish. Neither would get in trouble if they kept their mouths shut. I feel in this instance our young poacher is keeping his shut for fear of physical reprisals from the Cleggs.'

I raised my eyes to look up at him and he looked right back.

'Oh yes, lad, Stan and I know who you've been with. Chris Clegg and his family have been raping these pools since his grandfather was a boy. Except his grandfather John—God rest his soul—only took what he needed to keep food on the table for his family. But these reprobates destroy whole generations of salmon and trout for a few extra pounds to pamper their lusts for fast cars, cigarettes and partying. One more year like last year and the agency reckons the gene pool for salmon from our river will be completely depleted and we'll have no more coming up. None! Imagine it—thousands of years of life obliterated for Chris Clegg to have a nice sports car.'

Grandpa may have been wrong about me being afraid of the Cleggs, but now I understood why I appeared so odious to him. I had become part of the destruction of his beloved river two days after he had let me see her secrets.

Stan stepped in as he saw Grandpa's temperature rising. 'Aye Major, easy now. We've nee proof yet that it is them. They're quick vermin and careful too. Even if I'd caught them tonight it wouldn't have done the salmon much good.

I could have them sent down for a few months for the sea trout but they'd be out for the big salmon run in September or the spawning in October and the fish wouldn't stand a chance. It's like Northern Ireland all over again—fighting a losing battle to an enemy we can'nae touch.'

Grandpa looked meaningfully at Stan. I could see there was real respect between the men, as if they'd spent long hours discussing soldiering. Grandpa put his hand to his cheek and a wry smile crept onto his face. 'Right here is what we shall do. It's pretty clear that Will has been caught in the act and as the landowner I suggest, Sergeant, with your permission, that my young felon receive a two-month suspended sentence provided that he serves Her Majesty's Water Bailiff—at his leisure—to protect the river he has so heinously violated.'

Stan looked surprised. 'You mean I'm saddled with the bairn?'

'What I mean, Stan, is this: my grandson—*and everything he knows*—will be at your service when, and only when, you require his services!' Grandpa seemed to have some hidden purpose, and his knowing wink at Stan was to seal the deal.

Grandpa turned to me. 'And you can dig over and stone pick my two new vegetable plots out the back tomorrow morning.'

'Okay then,' Stan said. 'I'll be round at fourteen hundred tomorrow, young man. Wear strong boots and dark clothing that doesn't rustle.'

I turned to reply but he was gone, melted back into the darkness.

'Right, you young snap,' Grandpa said. He looked pleased but sharp. 'Straight to bed, and if you keep your end of the deal with Stan I won't tell your Gran or Mum. Now off you go.'

'Yes, Grandpa, and I am really sorry. I didn't think–'

He cut me off. 'Look here, boy, you did think—but not enough, like most people your age. Like Chris Clegg. Thinks his mind is broadening when it's just his conscience stretching. But some things can never be undone, never be replaced. Do you understand, lad? Some things are bigger than we are. The way the river is—well, it's one of those things. Now go on, get to bed.'

'Yes, okay.' I slunk away into the house, so tired that I couldn't decide whether I should be relieved or frightened of what being at Stan's service might mean.

6

THE BIN
MONSTER AND
THE MYSTERIOUS
STRANGER

I awoke early on Tuesday morning after a terrible night's
sleep. I tossed and turned all night—every hour I'd wake
up and feel guilty, then I'd drift off into either a strange,
frightening nightmare about the monster or a wonderful,
intoxicating dream about Carrie.

Grandpa greeted me when I came down to breakfast.
'So, it's true then—a good conscience does make the most
comfortable pillow.' He smiled. 'Come on, lad, learn from
my mistakes—you haven't got time to make them all
yourself! Sit down, have some tea.'

We sat in silence until Granny came in. 'Oh Will, just
look at those bags under your eyes! Do you want to try to
get some more sleep after breakfast? You look shattered.'

Grandpa didn't give me a chance to answer. 'No,' he said,
'the lad is raring to go at digging over the paddock. He can
get to bed early tonight if he needs to.'

'Yeah,' I said, 'I'm fine, really.'

Granny shrugged and was soon singing away at the ironing board. I watched her carefully for a few minutes, but it was obvious that Grandpa hadn't told her anything of last night's drama. I was relieved. To appear a lying traitor in the eyes of Granny and Aunty Dora would be devastating.

For two hours after breakfast I worked at stone picking in the vegetable plots at the back of the house—hoeing, bending, lifting, digging. The soil was thick clay, what the dalesmen call 'right clarty stuff'. The clay clods stuck to my boots. There were no shortcuts, and the work seemed endless. I limped over when Grandpa brought me a mug of tea.

'Enjoying the work?' he asked with a grin.

'Well, it's er ...' I didn't want to complain but I was too tired to think of something pleasant to say.

Grandpa handed me the mug and turned back toward his shed. 'Don't worry,' he said, 'no one likes work, but in it you have a chance to find yourself. Enjoy your tea. And make sure you get the roots of those dock leaves, they go down deep.'

When I went in to clean up before lunch Granny asked me to take the rubbish out. I was surprised to see a BMX bike leaned up against the wall near the bins. No one was around, but it looked like the one I'd seen the kid riding on Sunday morning. When I opened the green wheelie bin, it spoke to me.

'I am the Bin Monster! State your name and business here or I'll eat you!'

I jumped back, dropping the lid, and heard a faint snigger among the rustling of paper and crinkling of cans.

'What are you doing in my grandparents' bin?'

'I'm the Bin Monster! I live here,' came the reply with a muffled chuckle.

'Stop being stupid and get out. It's disgusting in there.'
What kind of a kid would actually climb into people's bins?

The lid swung open, and up popped the urchin with a grubby face and soiled tracksuit. 'I've been in worse,' he said. A huge grin spread across his freckly cheeks.

'You mean you spend a lot of time in bins?' I crinkled my nose in disgust.

'No, not really. I wanted to meet you, so I thought I'd surprise you! My name's Lewis. What's yours? I thought we could be friends and have adventures and stuff.'

Adventures? I'd seen this kid before, and not just on his bike on the way to church. Finally it hit me. 'You're the boy from the coach! Last Saturday, you got on at Preston and sat next to–'

'Oh aye, next to Mr Stinky Prawn Sandwich!' He laughed. 'Yeah, that was me. Hey, do you want to play or not?'

Play? What would we play? How old did he think I was? 'Don't you have any friends your own age to play with around here?' I asked.

'Not really, my friends are in Burnley,' he said. As if that explained it.

'What are they all doing there?'

'That's where we live—Burnley. It's in Lancashire.'

'Yes, I know where Burnley is but what are you doing here?' I was beginning to wonder if he'd run away.

'I don't rightly know,' he said. 'It's a holiday I suppose.' He looked confused, as if he didn't quite know what the word 'holiday' meant.

I couldn't believe it. As if I didn't have enough problems already, I'd found a runaway in Granny's bin. At least I knew what to do, since I'd grown up with a social worker for a mum. The rule is to tilt your head to one side slightly and speak slowly, nodding your head as you speak to show care and understanding.

'Lewis,' I began, 'do your parents know where you are?'

'No, not really.' His expression was blank.

'I bet you're hungry, aren't you?' I was really warming up now.

'Yes I am!' He grinned. 'How did you know?'

I nodded. 'Look, I have some Mars bars inside. Would you like one?' I knew it was important to gain his trust rather than to say something like 'I think we'd better get the police to call off the search and take you home.'

'Oh, yes please,' Lewis said. 'I love Mars bars!'

He followed me into the kitchen. Granny was upstairs, but I made him sit down. I knew I had to keep an eye on him so he didn't make a getaway with Granny's ornaments. Lewis ate four Mars bars and drank a can of Coke, grinning between mouthfuls. I wondered how long it had been since he'd eaten. Giving up my chocolate was a small price to pay—I couldn't imagine being in his shoes.

'Lewis, when was the last time you had something to eat?'

He shook his head. 'Can't rightly remember.'

'When was the last time you called your parents?'

'Ages and ages,' he said. He fumbled in his pocket and brought out an ancient, scratched up mobile phone. 'Out of credit and the reception here is terrible anyway.'

'Yeah, tell me about it,' I said. 'But isn't your mother worried about you? Hasn't she tried to call you?' I knew I needed to resolve the situation before I lost his attention. His eyes were scanning the larder shelves.

'What, Mum? No, she's too busy looking after the twins. She says that while they're potty training she won't have any time for me so I have to look after myself. Have you got any crisps?'

'Yes,' I said. I took a packet from the shelf. 'Here, take these. Is that why you left home, because she couldn't cope with all of you?'

'It's not really a home, more a caravan.'

So he was a gypsy. I leaned forward. 'What about your father—does he have time for you?'

'Who, Dad? No, he's away most of the time working. Mum says he sells stuff. We do see him the odd weekend, but even then he's mostly out walking on't hills.' He shrugged as he finished the crisps and glanced again at the larder.

I pictured his father, a Romany tinker selling pegs and dusters. Imagine growing up like that, I thought. I watched his eyes scanning the larder shelves and decided I'd give the kid anything he wanted.

'Can I have some fruit cake as well?' he asked.

'I'm not sure where my Gran keeps it,' I said. I could see from the boy's eyes, and around his mouth, that his father must look a bit like Fagin from David Copperfield. He was probably just as harsh. I shuddered.

'It's in that green tin on the middle shelf,' he said.

I looked at him sharply and went to the larder. I knew that Gypsy fortune tellers had some dark, ancestral, sixth sense. I opened the tin slowly. It was full of fruit cake. Now I shivered. This was spooky. I came back into the kitchen with the tin just as Granny came downstairs. I gave her my most serious look as I spelled out the situation in adult code.

'Hello, Granny, this is my new friend. He's left his "caravan" home and hasn't called his mother for ages. He's just having a little bite to eat before we help him get home to his family. I think that would be best for everyone, wouldn't it?'

Lewis took the cake and grinned at Granny and then at me. 'Yes, I suppose I ought to get back soon, it's nearly lunchtime. Nice cake, Mrs Wallace. Thanks!'

'You're welcome, Lewis.' Granny smiled. 'I'm glad you two have met. You should be good friends. I hope you've not been giving him too much to eat before his lunch, William, or his mother won't be thanking you.'

Lewis wiped the crumbs from his mouth and peered up at me before looking down to examine his shoes.

'How are the twins, dear?' Granny asked. 'I'm going to call down later this week with two pretty dresses I found in Oxfam.'

'But—but ...' I spluttered. 'You mean, they're not Gypsies?'

'Who? Lewis's family? Of course not, dear,' Granny said. 'Whatever gave you that impression? They own a static caravan at the park in Lorton and they stay up here in the summer. Lewis's dad sells insurance and comes up at weekends to be with them and enjoy the fells.'

Lewis chuckled and dashed for the door. 'Nice to meet you, Will! I'm glad I have a friend here now. See you later!'

Granny closed the door after him. 'Poor mite, none of the village kids will play with him. It's so nice that you've taken him under your wing. Your mother always had that same soft spot for waifs and strays.'

She was definitely overstating my virtues, but I didn't say anything. I was hoping Lewis wouldn't come back for any adventures before Stan arrived at two o'clock.

Grandpa and I waited for Stan in the lane, and he was bang on time.

'Do you see the slightly odd way he walks?' Grandpa asked as Stan came into view. 'He was captured by the Provisionals in Belfast in 1978 when he was a regular. He was found five days later in an abandoned warehouse. They'd drilled both his knee caps and left the drill bits in his knees. The doctors said he'd never walk again, but he did—

and he went on to join the Special Air Service. They don't make many like him, lad, so make the most of your time with him.'

Now, in the daylight, I could finally see what this mysterious man looked like. People say that you can tell a lot by someone's face. His was scarred with unread stories. He looked like he was in his fifties, with sandy grey hair and a grey complexion. He looked sinister, like a baddy hit man on the big screen. He wore a patched-up old Grenfell jacket, dark green, with dark green trousers tucked into his black combat boots. I tried not to look at his knees as he and Grandpa talked.

I heard the sound of the bike skidding before I heard the breathless voice. 'Sorry I'm late, found some snails on the road and was playing with them and lost track of time. Anyway, where are we headed?'

We? I was about to protest, and I was glad to see Stan had an even darker scowl on his face too, when Grandpa cut in.

'Well,' he said to Lewis, 'You're all off to learn from Stan how to protect the river from pollution, vermin and poachers. Stan knows the benefit of having many eyes and he won't mind you going along, Lewis, if you do exactly what he says. Will you Stan?' Grandpa gave Stan one of those knowing looks that made me wonder what I was missing.

To my horror, Stan nodded. 'Oh, wy'eye man,' he said.

Grandpa gave a jovial snort and went back to the house.

We followed Stan into the woods and down to the river, heading up the bank toward Lorton. Stan didn't say a word but he kept looking around and particularly at the ground.

I wanted to find out why Chris had made Stan out to be such a phantom. 'Can you tell us how you walk through the woods so silently at night?' I asked.

To my surprise, he seemed almost eager to share his knowledge. 'It'll take over half an hour for your eyes to fully adjust to the dark,' he said. 'You move at night with your ears. If you're up close, like, then you move only when the target moves. That way the localized noise your target creates will always drown your approach. Otherwise you have to stay downwind and keep still. If you have to move, then the rule is to keep your weight on the heel of the foot in back and feel forward with the other. There's nee magic to it. Some terrain will be faster than others, but if you have enough time anyone can learn to get from A to B quietly. Mind you, that'll only work on humans. Animals have better smell, hearing and night vision than you do.'

This was cool stuff. I saw Lewis trying to put his weight on his back heel as we went along but, after almost falling into the river, he gave it up and ran to rejoin us.

'That's Red Howe,' Stan said, pointing to a small wooded hill that rose sharply from the river. Then he walked along a bit further, studying the ground as he went.

'What are you looking for?' Lewis asked.

The way he asked the question, I had this image of Lewis wandering through the woods looking for a trail of sweets or Mars bars.

'Game, vermin and poachers,' Stan answered. 'If you know what ya'doin you can read these trails like a book. The regiment taught us to read game trails as part of our survival training.'

'Why?' asked Lewis.

'Well, 'cos if we got into trouble, we could bait the right sort o'trap for the right game. You can also read trails to help you find water.'

'Have you been in trouble a lot?' Lewis asked. 'I'm always in trouble,' he added.

'Aye, man, I have, more than you can imagine, and this stuff has kept me alive more times than I can remember.'

'But how d'you do it? I mean, how can you even find a trail to start with?' I asked.

'You're best going at first light, that way you can see where the dew and spider's webs are disturbed,' Stan explained. 'Good tracks depend on moist ground, and the definition and moisture content of a print will tell you of its age. See here,' he said, pointing to a tiny print in the mud. 'This is a mink, not an otter. Its tracks are well defined but dry inside, which probably means he was here yesterday. Mink is vermin and a threat to river life. We'll need to trap and kill this one.'

'Have you brought any traps with you?' I asked as I peered down at the tiny prints.

'No need,' Stan said. He was cutting something with his large 'Crocodile Dundee' knife. 'We'll make a baited spring snare ourselves. Here, hold this while I make the spring.' He handed me a length of abandoned fishing line he'd been untangling from some bushes by the river and began trimming a nearby sapling. 'We'll be lucky to get the mink unless we can find some good bait. We need fish for these fellas.' He carried on notching a stake near the trail and then went again to the water's edge. 'They love fish. I'll see what I can do.'

He knelt down and reached slowly into the water, under the tree roots and rock ledges along the bank. 'I don't want—to have to get in and get wet—so if I can just check these ledges—then I can get us ... Ah hah! Some bait!' And, like a magician, he brought a small brown trout up out of the water and came back to the snare.

'Wow, that was amazing! How'd did you do that?' I asked.

He just winked and fixed the fish to the snare. The supporting stake and noose on the bent sapling would act like a catapult if the mink were to even nibble the trout.

Stan looked up, then, and saw Lewis standing still, wide-eyed, mouth hanging open in amazement. 'Stop gaping, lad. Trout often hide under banks and stone ledges when they're not feeding. The only miracle is that I didn't get bitten by a rat or a mink! Now we need to cover our tracks and our scent. Grab me some dry grass and some leaves.'

When we had gathered a few handfuls of dry grass he lit it so that the smoke drifted over the snare. Then he covered our footprints with leaves and smeared mud over the spots of broken, bare wood left by his knife.

As we headed off downstream Stan taught us to identify different animals from their tracks and droppings. 'Grazing animals and grain-eating birds will never be far from water. They'll drink in the morning and evening. When those birds are flying low and straight, they're heading towards water. When they fly high and rest frequently from tree to tree, then they're coming from the water source. Bees are good indicators, too, and ants marching up a tree in a column will be heading for a trapped water source. You'll never find a fly more than a hundred yards from water either. Meat-eating mammals and birds usually get their liquid from their prey.' He paused and glanced around.

'What about the beast on the moor?' I asked. 'It's a meat eater. Could you track it, too?'

'Aye, I could, but that creature's no fox and anyone going after it would risk becoming the hunted as well as the hunter. In our training we were warned against even walking on the trails of big game like that. They can smell you—and your fear. Most of those predators have far better senses and abilities than an unarmed man and, once they've established a territory, you best keep away.'

'So you don't think it's a monster?'

'No, lad, I'm not superstitious—though I haven't seen any tracks either. But I've never seen claw marks like the ones that fell pony died of last week. And I've seen most things!'

'How big do you think it is?' I asked.

'Big. Aye, it's a big cat or something.' He looked at me sternly. 'And listen, small predators hunt at night but big, powerful ones hunt when they want. You want to stay away from the fell and those woods behind your Grandpa's night and day. If that creature decides that it's the top of the food chain, then it'll come out whenever it wants and when it does you'd best not be in its territory, do yu'hear me?'

'Yes, I wasn't thinking of–'

But Stan's raised hand cut me off. We were on a track leading around Red Howe, just above the river. Through the trees Stan had spotted a figure on the opposite bank. He was approaching our position with swift, deliberate steps. The stranger was tall and lean, wearing a beige mac, black scarf and a large floppy hat that hid his face. He had a shepherd's crook in hand and looked rather like a cross between Doctor Who and the Grim Reaper.

'Wait here. Do not speak. Do not move.' Stan whispered harshly and pointed his finger at us. He made his way down to the bank. The river was shallow at this point, and Stan waded across to meet the man who stood waiting for him, motionless except for an occasional shifty glance either side.

'I wonder who it is,' I whispered.

'I don't know,' Lewis said. He was picking his nose. 'But he comes up the river every Tuesday afternoon and goes back a few hours later.'

'How do you know that?' I asked.

'I watch him from me den on the bank near the village,' he said. Lewis was more concerned with the findings in his left nostril than he was with the mysterious stranger. 'Never seen his face, mind, he never looks up from't ground and that hat and scarf hides the rest.'

'But that's miles away,' I said. 'Why would anyone come all the way up here?'

Even though the two men were about a hundred metres from where we stood, I felt I had seen the stranger somewhere before. Something about his height and build and posture seemed familiar. The two talked for a few minutes, but we could make out only the occasional murmur above the sound of the river. Then Stan motioned over to where we were standing. When the man looked at us for a split second I saw those penetrating blue eyes and I knew in an instant. It was my Uncle Sid.

I shivered. Why was he trying to disguise his identity? Where did he go every Tuesday afternoon? And how was Stan involved with this man of whom such treachery was rumoured? The way Stan gestured with his head and hands made me think they were discussing me. I was frightened and paranoid. Stan nodded a lot. After another few minutes Sid walked on and Stan returned.

'Who was that?' I asked.

'Never you mind. There are some things you don't need to know,' Stan said.

Stan made us walk all the way to Lorton village in silence. This was very difficult for Lewis, who seemed to speak whenever something came into his head. Apparently he'd been pondering the mating rituals of snails. It made Stan cross, but Lewis didn't seem to notice. We checked a few people's permits and, when we arrived at the village, we were discharged. Lewis went home while I walked back to the farm along the lane.

At dinner my food was cold before I finished telling them all about my afternoon. I didn't mention Uncle Sid's strange wanderings, though I'd already decided to follow him next week to see where he was going.

Granny asked me to go out and lock the chickens in at dusk. The chickens were all inside the hutch but they were squawking in nervous spasms. It was when I began to bolt the hutch doors that I sensed I was being watched. It wasn't any particular sound—like the night before when Stan stalked us—but the feeling of sheer panic was the same.

My eyes weren't accustomed to the dusky darkness, and when I turned I couldn't see a thing. It felt like being blind. I was trying to stay calm, remembering what Stan had said about predators being able to smell fear. Out beyond the vegetable plot where I had been digging was the edge of the woods that ran up to the base of Low Moor. As I stood there I could have sworn I heard a creature exhaling and a shadow moving deeper back into the darkness. Had the beast come for me, to punish me for talking about it earlier? I ran back down the path, through the back porch and into the kitchen.

'It's there, the beast—it's there, I'm almost sure it is,' I gasped.

Granny looked at Grandpa. 'The chickens, are they okay? Did you lock them up okay, dear?' she asked.

I looked over to the gun cupboard and then to Grandpa. Nelson also looked up, as if duty called, but Grandpa sucked on his pipe. 'First lesson of engagement is choose your battles and your battlegrounds, lad, and don't be drawn by your enemy when he has the advantage.' He spoke through the corner of his mouth and glanced at the clock. 'And especially when the BBC are doing a good wildlife documentary in five minutes,' he said. He got up from his chair and gave me a knowing wink before making his way to the sitting room.

'Disturbing your Gran's chickens, eh? We'll take a look at its tracks at first light while the dew is fresh. It'll be early, mind, so I'd get yourself to bed now if you want to be a good tracker.'

It took me forever to get off to sleep, though. I wrote in my diary and eventually got up the courage to turn the light off.

My last thoughts, as I finally drifted off to sleep, were of Frodo from *Lord of the Rings*. He said that he wished the ring had never come to him and that none of the bad things had ever happened. I couldn't lose the feeling that likewise a strange, dark destiny connected me and this mysterious creature.

7

THE MARK OF THE BEAST

Wake up, lad, or we'll miss the trail!' The voice came into the mists of my dreams like a whirlwind of cold. It was my covers coming off.

I opened one eye, saw Grandpa standing over me, and remembered. Our hunting trip.

'Okay, I'm getting up,' I mumbled as I reached to pull my covers back over me. Any desire to be a burly hunter or to conquer the beast of Low Moor was gone. I just wanted my bed.

But Grandpa was persistent, and his enthusiasm eventually rubbed off on me. By the time Granny's poached eggs were sloshing around inside with two mugs of hot tea, I felt as feisty as Nelson looked. He wagged his tail and inched towards the door as Grandpa loaded the twelve-bore shotgun. The game was afoot and he would not be denied a little sport. He was not a little miffed to be put on a lead, but Grandpa wanted to make sure that he didn't disturb the trail before we could get to it.

'Mind how you go, dear,' Granny said. 'Don't let Will out of your sight and don't bring a lot of mud or blood back in my kitchen if you're back before lunch. Hilda and

90

Frieda Millstone called yesterday to organize an emergency meeting of the W.I. here at nine, and I don't want the place to be a mess.'

Grandpa looked cross. 'Oh, no, why did you say they could come here? What's wrong with the church hall?'

'Don't be uncharitable, Reggie. They mean well, and you know as well as I do that they won't be refused. She said she doesn't want to use the church hall because "it's best the vicar doesn't know", so I imagine it's a surprise party or something.'

'Who are they?' I asked.

'They're two friends of mine, dear, and they do their best to serve the Lord,' Granny said as she narrowed her eyes at Grandpa.

'Aye, but only in an advisory capacity!' Grandpa added.

'They are very nice, and they live their lives for others,' Granny said. 'Unlike some people ...' She looked at Grandpa, but he was unmoved by the accusation.

'Yes,' Grandpa said, 'and you can always tell who the *others* are by their hunted expressions.'

'Reginald Wallace, that is not the example that Will needs and I hope when they come you will show a little more tact.'

Grandpa winked at me. 'Will, the art of hospitality is making your guests feel at home—when you wish they were!' He chuckled and bent down to give Nelson a scratch. 'I think we can stretch to it, eh Nelson, eh?'

Nelson appeared to love Grandpa's humorous moments as much as I did and egged him on with a few barks.

'Go on then, get out of my kitchen until lunchtime and let me get on,' Granny said. 'And for goodness' sake don't do anything daft!'

'Don't worry, Elsie. Even if I run out of ammunition I'll chase the beast right around Low Moor with my walking stick rather than face the Millstone sisters so early in the morning! Have no fear, we won't be back too soon.'

We headed up the back garden, through the gate and into the field. As we approached the edge of the wood Grandpa took a long, thin old dagger from his boot and gave it to me.

'Take that just in case and don't tell your grandmother,' he said. 'I've led men into battle on four continents with that knife in my boot and it's always stood by me, so don't lose it.'

Nelson began to whimper, as if sensing the presence of some evil.

Grandpa looked around. 'You're sure it was here, Will?'

I nodded. The early morning mists were clearing in the thickets and I felt some of the panic of the night before tightening in my chest. But I swallowed hard and clenched the knife in my right hand. I was glad it was heavy and it looked reassuringly sharp.

'Okay, Will, let's see what you've learnt from Stan.'

'You mean to track it? But I've never—I don't know ...'

'Will, stop faffing, man, and tell me what you see.' Grandpa pointed. 'Start by that tree.'

I walked cautiously toward the tree. At first I didn't see anything unusual. But as I crouched to the ground, keeping my balance by jabbing the knife into a fallen log, I noticed a pathway of broken cobwebs and trampled grass. It was not a single trail. 'I see an area of trampled grass, but it's not a line as much as a patch about three metres by two metres.' I stood up, pleased and relieved that I was able to find something. A faint breeze brought another clue. 'Oh,' I added, 'and there's also a musky smell, sweet, like urine.'

'Good, good,' Grandpa said. 'What about prints or hoof markings? Can you see any of those? Move slowly over the site and use your imagination. Who has been here?'

I was too scared to let my imagination have free reign, but I scoured the site for a print. The grass was thick and there was no mud to preserve a print, so I spoke without turning. 'There's nothing. No print. The trail leads toward those rocks but I can't pick it up again. There's nothing'

'Good, good. Very interesting, Will. I hadn't thought this creature worthy of merit, but this has got my attention. And so close to the house. Very interesting. You keep looking for a print. I'm going to look beyond the rocks'

'But I don't see what you mean. We've learnt nothing except that something has been here.'

'On the contrary, my dear Watson.' He snorted with delight as he wandered off. 'We've learnt a great deal. A bullock, a sheep or a deer would have left hoof marks on that ground, so we know it's not any of the usual inhabitants. No, what we've got is a big creature with large, maybe even soft, feet to spread its weight. And I would guess that it's been pacing the edge of this wood, marking its territory and agitating over whether to break cover and take the chickens or something else ... or someone else even.'

He disappeared around the rocks and I went back to my search, but this time I felt like I was trespassing. If the beast had marked his territory, then we were in its domain. I was staring at the ground with such concentration that I didn't see a long shadow to my right until it was right beside me and a twig broke behind me. I spun around with my knife raised.

'Lower your weapon, young William. I doubt I am the one which you seek to destroy at such a young hour of the day.'

'I'm sorry, Professor. I was afraid you were the creature that's been stalking these woods.' I took a deep breath. 'What brings you up here so early in the morning?'

'I am here to clear my head and observe nature, my boy.'

'Ah, morning Conrad.' Grandpa arrived back looking pleased with himself. Nelson walked close to his heels, sneezing with exuberance.

'Good morning, Major. Your young scout tells me you are seeking leviathan.'

Grandpa smiled. 'Yes, that's right. I picked up the broken grass trail beyond these rocks. It continues into the spruce plantation under the fell, but it's too dense in there for me to get in.' He shook his head. 'But I didn't see any prints either.'

The Professor did not answer, but gazed at me in silent horror, his mouth gaping open.

'You may not need zem,' he said. 'Look.' He pointed to me. Or was he pointing behind me? I felt that chest-tightening fear spread over me as I saw Grandpa's face. My knife was next to my stomach and I turned quickly, raising it to my chest with my shoulders hunching upwards. But it was not a monster that I saw. I gasped. The bark of the large tree behind us—about ten or twelve feet from the base—was completely torn away. The three of us moved together, in shock, to inspect the damage. A creature with very large claws had been at work. It was not easy to say how large since the markings, some of them up to an inch deep, had been furiously inflicted in different directions and were all interlinked. But the height of the claw marks alone, and therefore the size of the creature, left my knees weak.

Grandpa spoke first. 'I think we'd better call the gamekeepers. They might not want to work up in the woods today. I've never seen the like of this before. I think I'll get the vet up here as well to see what he makes of this.'

Grandpa seemed to be lacking his usual bravado. I glanced over to the spruce trees in the distance and tried not to think about what might be watching us from there.

Grandpa was already heading back to the house, but the Professor had followed my gaze to the thicket. 'He who fights with monsters might take care lest he thereby become a monster. If you gaze long enough into the abyss, the abyss gazes back at you.'

I looked blankly at him.

'Nietzsche,' he said. 'Who else? He might have done well to heed his own advice.'

I nodded, as if I knew what he was talking about, and followed him back to the house.

As we neared the gate we heard raised voices coming from the kitchen.

'Oh, no,' I said. 'Some group called the W.I. is coming at nine and Grandpa didn't want to be there. Professor, do you know what a W.I. is?'

The Professor looked interested. 'No doubt as a student of science you will be acquainted with the work of the great English engineer Sir Alec Issigonis?' I shook my head. 'No? Well, he once said "a camel is a horse designed by a committee", and this saying is also true of the formidable group of local women known as the Women's Institute.' He chuckled at his own joke and then stopped abruptly. 'Tell me, William, do you know if the Millstone sisters will be coming this morning?'

'Yes, I think they're the ones in charge, aren't they?'

'Oh yes, yes, very much so,' he said. He looked wistfully toward the house and a flush came over his cheeks. 'In fact, in all my travels I have never seen anything more magnificent than the older Millstone sister. Frieda is like ... the bough of a great ship. She cuts through everything.' He paused and sighed deeply. 'I'm glad I did not marry young, William, for then I would have missed this great prize.'

The Professor in love? I tried to imagine him, slight as he was, cuddling the bow of a great ship. 'Does she love you back? I mean, I've heard she's a bit ... well, strong.'

The Professor gazed into the distance. 'Ah, my boy, let weak men have weak women. I have set my cap at one who embodies the very essence and strength of womanhood, the backbone of your empire. I wish to embrace her as she is in all her wild, untamed beauty.' He sighed again and shook his head. Then he turned back to me. 'And yes, I believe she does welcome my attentions, such as they are, and marriage cannot be far from her mind.'

'Well I think you're very brave,' I said. And I did.

He shrugged and wiped his brow with a trembling handkerchief. 'Russell says "to fear love is to fear life, and those who fear life are already three parts dead".' Come, William, though she makes my bones tremble, I must win her or die trying.'

He led me towards the house and I wondered if Granny would be glad to see him as her guests were about to arrive. The W.I. contingent had not arrived, but the BMX lying on the grass told me that Lewis was in residence. Grandpa—gun still in hand—was involved in a heated discussion with Granny in one corner of the kitchen. Lewis was at the table eating cake, unperturbed by the noise. He moved his head back and forth as he watched the argument, as if he were at a tennis match.

'Ah, William,' Granny said when she saw me. 'Could you take Lewis outside to finish his cake?'

'I'll wait outside too,' the Professor said. 'It's Miss Millstone I wish most particularly to see.'

The Professor waited in the lane, scanning the road anxiously. Lewis and I sat on the step and I filled him in on what we'd found at the edge of the wood.

'And now I'm being driven from my house by the Harpies of Netherside!' I heard Grandpa saying as he came through the door. But I could tell he was teasing.

He stood beside us and shook his head. 'Those two spinster sisters are of Prussian descent—which explains a lot. This valley hasn't seen a peaceful moment since they retired here.'

'Where are they from?' I asked.

'Harrogate,' he said. 'They were a matron and teacher at a famous girls' boarding school. And I imagine, Will, that these are more dangerous than the creature we were tracking today.' He winked. 'Adaptability is the English sportsman's greatest asset.'

My curiosity was even further roused. Who were these women who sparked such strong and opposite feelings? Grandpa escaped to the shed and the Professor paced the lane, wringing his hands and saying various unintelligible things as if in preparation.

At 8:55 on the dot, he was put out of his misery. With surprising speed, sitting erect like generals on white chargers, two ladies on old-fashioned bikes, complete with baskets and bells, came into view. They wore corduroy skirts, checked shirts and maroon cardigans. They rang their bells almost constantly to warn oncoming traffic. Two black Labradors trotted along obediently behind them.

Judging by the Professor's polite gesturing to the rider of the first bike, I decided she must be Frieda. And if she was like 'the bow of a great ship' it might not be unfair to describe her sister, Hilda, as the rest of it—or at least the ballast. She was substantial. They both came to an abrupt halt and swung off their bikes with surprising agility.

'Churchill, Monty, s-s-i-i-i-i-t-t-t!' The dogs sat. I was glad I was already seated.

Frieda turned to march to the house. She stopped short. The Professor stood between her and her destination.

'Ah, good morning Miss Frieda, Miss Hilda, and what a lovely morning it is, isn't it?' he rubbed his hands nervously.

'Oh, it's you,' said Frieda. 'What do you want?'

'Why, I came to talk with you, my dear.'

'Well you'll have to be quick. We're busy.'

'Yes, yes, indeed. Well, I was wondering whether you had considered the bees and the buttercups this morning?'

I coughed to cover a laugh. Was this the Professor's idea of a chat-up line?

'What did he say?' asked Hilda.

'He's on about bees again,' Frieda muttered. She fixed the poor Professor with a withering stare. 'Professor Inchikov,' she said, 'I sincerely hope you haven't been eating those mushrooms again.'

'No, no my dear Miss Millstone, you misunderstand my intentions. I meant the bees as metaphors ... as Dr Freud would say ...'

'Now look here, I do not want to know what that man said.' Frieda crossed her arms over her chest and shook her head.

'Who? What man? I didn't hear him,' Hilda said.

'Freud!' said Frieda. 'Freud!'

'Yes, yes, I'm not deaf, no need to shout. Freud, is it? Huh, dirty little man, S. E. X. on the brain!' Hilda curled her lip in disgust.

'Ladies, please ... we must be a little more open minded to what these great men have said–' the Professor began to defend nineteenth-century psychiatry.

'Open minded, you say? Some continental sorts are so open minded their brains fall out—not so with the British!' Frieda informed the poor man.

'Great men, indeed!' said Hilda. 'Damn lot of nonsense!'

The sisters left the Professor shaking his head and at a loss for words.

I braced myself as the sisters approached the door.

'Ah, you must be William,' Frieda said as I stood up to let them pass. 'Yes, I saw you in church on Sunday. You make sure you're helpful to your grandmother while you're here.' I nodded. 'And who's this behind you?'

Lewis was standing a little behind me, stuffing the rest of the cake into his mouth. 'I'm Lewis,' he said, spraying cake crumbs over my shoulder. 'I'm on holiday ... from Burnley.'

'Yes, I should say you are,' said Hilda.

'Yes, indeed,' Frieda said with a short sniff. 'And I suppose there's no soap in Lancashire?' She didn't wait for a reply. 'Let's go in and get started, sister.'

But Lewis, with his mouth still full of cake, muddy face and all, blocked their way. 'You can't go in there,' he said.

'Oh, indeed? And why not, may I ask?' Hilda looked like she might knock him to the side, though Lewis stood firm.

'Because there are fierce creatures trying to get in there. I heard the Major say so!'

'Dangerous animals? In the drawing room?' Frieda asked. 'Are you sure, boy?'

'Oh, yes, Major Wallace said that there's two of them. He called them "real tough birds" and–'

'Lewis!' I said, as it dawned on me what he had misheard and what danger he was actually leading us into. 'I wouldn't worry Miss Millstone. Grandpa will know what to do, so let's just let the ladies–'

'Tough old birds? What tough old birds?' Hilda said.

I felt myself starting to turn red. 'Well, I think–' I said.

Lewis interrupted me. 'I don't know their names, but the Major does and he told Mrs Wallace he knew what he'd like to do with them–' It was getting worse. He had to be stopped.

I watched helplessly as the Millstone sisters exchanged looks.

'Do with them!' Hilda's eyes were bulging in their sockets as she edged her way toward the doorway.

'Oh yes,' Lewis continued. He'd finally swallowed his enormous mouthful of cake and was ready to explain everything he knew—or thought he knew. 'The Major knows what to do with them, all right. He's got his gun out and he's waiting for them in the kitchen.'

In unison the sisters stepped back from the door in horror. 'He has a gun?' Frieda whispered.

And at that moment the door opened and Grandpa stepped out, gun in hand. I don't think those sisters were afraid of much, but at the sight of the gun and the look in Grandpa's eyes, they took another step back.

'Miss and Miss Millstone,' Grandpa said. 'How nice to see you.'

Nelson growled.

'Why Major Wallace, whatever are you doing with a–' Hilda asked.

'A gun?' he asked. 'Just off to the shed to clean it. Good day.'

Granny appeared at the door then and greeted the women with a warm smile. 'Come in, come in,' she said. They did, and we could hear their stream of indignant questions.

'What was that boy talking about?'

'More to the point, *who* was he talking about?'

Granny laughed. 'Oh that's just Lewis, dears,' she said. 'He's from Burnley.'

The other women arrived, including Aunty Dora, who had brought us some sweets.

Lewis insisted that the visitors were all Sioux warriors arriving for a war conference and that we ought to hide outside the drawing room window and listen in on the meeting. After seeing the severe expressions on the faces of most of the new arrivals I could see what he meant.

'We'll listen in,' I said, 'but only for five minutes.'

As it turned out, five minutes was enough. There was a large potted plant in the bay window, and we crouched down and peered past it.

'Now then, ladies, please take your seats so we can begin,' Frieda said.

But she paused as the back door opened and Grandpa entered the room. 'Morning, everyone. Don't mind me, just looking for the *Telegraph*.'

Hilda looked at Granny. Granny looked at Grandpa. Grandpa and Nelson, pretending not to notice, headed for his battered old leather chair. Grandpa sat down with the paper and Nelson, at his feet, glared around the room. Hilda glared at Granny. Granny cleared her throat.

Grandpa looked up from the sports supplement. 'Don't worry about me, dear. You carry on. I feel a bit like a lion in a den of Daniels, but it's no disturbance, really.'

I saw Aunty Dora cover a smile with her hand.

'Very well,' Hilda said with a final glare in Grandpa's direction. 'Let's begin. First I would like to thank you all for coming at such short notice to this emergency session. Thank you also to Major and Mrs Wallace for allowing us to meet in their home and making us all so welcome. Because this is a special meeting, all other business, including the harvest festival and displays for the Loweswater Show, will have to wait for our next meeting which will be two weeks from Tuesday.'

'Will that be at the hall?' asked a slight lady with large teeth and even larger glasses.

'Yes, Joyce. Same time, same place, so please don't be late. Now, as you know, I am not one to beat about the bush–'

There was a snort from behind the sports supplement.

'Uh, the bush,' she repeated. 'Simply put, I have been in long discussion about Sunday's fiasco with many of you and other prominent members of the Parish Council, and we all agree that something must be done.'

There were nods of approval from some of the more severe-looking women, but Granny and Aunty Dora looked blank.

'What fiasco, Frieda dear?' Aunty Dora asked.

'Well, the service of course. The tree, the theatricals–' Frieda waved her hand in disgust. 'I'm sure our dear departed Reverend Wooly was turning in his grave, poor man. That sort of thing might be suitable for Americans, but I, for one, will not stand for it.'

'Nor I ... damn silly nonsense,' Hilda said.

'Frieda, can we just clarify whether it's the Reverend Wooly's final position that you're worried about, or the tree by the altar?' Dora asked.

Frieda was not impressed. 'Please, Dorothy, do not be flippant about our dear reverend—God rest his soul. The people of this valley are used to things being done a certain way, with reverence and decorum. And the abrupt, vulgar nature of our new vicar is simply not to be tolerated.'

'Now Frieda,' Granny began in a firm tone I hadn't heard from her before. 'My family has been in this valley for centuries, and I've been going to that church since I was a baby, so when you talk about the people of this valley you have to let everyone have their say.'

'Yes, yes,' Hilda said, 'that's why we're here, so everyone can have their say.'

There was another snort from behind the paper.

Hilda glared at the back of the sports section and continued. 'All Frieda was trying to point out–'

'Now,' Granny interrupted, 'I've only heard the vicar preach three times and, yes, it is different from what we've been used to. But he speaks plain truth with gusto and I like it, and so do Dora and George and others. We need to at least give the man a chance before we hold secret meetings about him. And this is hardly business for a W.I. meeting.' Granny was fiery, and I was proud of her.

The Millstones looked like they weren't used to being stood up against, but they certainly were not finished.

'Elsie,' Frieda said, 'I'll have you know that I've found out that the man used to be a thug and a hit man for the Scottish Mafia. I do not want this man influencing the weaker members of the parish—and I don't believe such a man can be brought into line. We need a gentleman. Someone like the late Reverend Wooly.'

Aunty Dora could take no more. She was so soft-spoken that I was surprised to hear her voice in the midst of this heated argument. But she spoke with smooth confidence. 'Ladies, whatever our new vicar may have been in the past, he's been turned around by Jesus Christ and sent to us. Can't you see he's just what we all need around here? A little wake-up call. I mean no disrespect to the Reverend Wooly, but I've spent too many Sundays wondering what he was talking about—and not getting any younger.'

Grandpa chose this moment to lower his paper. 'Actually,' he said, 'from what I heard from George, Wooly's sermons were like the peace of God—they surpassed all understanding!'

It was difficult to judge, from behind the potted plant, how his joke was received. I wasn't surprised to see Aunty Dora hiding another smile behind her hand.

Grandpa rose from his chair. 'Ladies, they say that moral indignation is jealousy with a halo, and I believe we have a case of it here. You're welcome to stay for another coffee, but in respect to my wife and sister's feelings, I forbid any further discussion of this divisive matter in my house.'

Frieda and Hilda, maybe for the first time since the War, were outgunned and speechless. They both bent over behind their chairs to retrieve their bags. With their country seats facing the stunned members of the committee, Nelson saw his opportunity to make a small contribution to the meeting. He trotted over between the sisters' chairs and sounded off. With everyone assuming it had been one of the sisters, there followed an awkward silence and a bit of shuffling.

Lewis and I had to crawl away, in stitches, to a safe distance where we laughed for a full ten minutes. Every time I managed to recover myself and wipe the tears away, Lewis would pull the shocked expression of the sisters, sound off and set me off again.

After Lewis had gone home, though, and the house was quiet again, I found myself quite annoyed about the meeting. I hadn't realized quite how strongly I felt about this guy I hardly knew who seemed to be telling the truth straight in a way I'd never heard it before. How could people who were supposedly on the same side act like that?

And then there was Grandpa, who didn't even go to church. He was on the vicar's side, and that was good enough for me.

PART TWO

JOY

8

SPYING AT THE GRAVE

I followed Granny and Aunty Dora to church on Sunday morning, lost in my thoughts. Mum had told me on the phone the night before that she thought the country must be good for me. 'I've never heard you so animated about anything,' she'd said when I'd finally finished all my stories. I'd had plenty to tell her without ever mentioning the poaching incident.

I tried not to think about how I hadn't heard a word from Chris or Carrie since. For all they knew I could be in jail. But then, maybe they thought it was better for me if they didn't get in contact.

The closer we got to church, the more dread I felt. I had this gnawing feeling in the pit of my stomach.

At the church gate a couple were helping the lady in black out of a car. The couple, probably in their fifties themselves, were fussing around her. Their eagerness reminded me of how the boys in primary school used to treat my friend Daniel Potts. His parents owned a newsagent's, and everyone tried to be his friend so they could get some of the sweets he always had with him.

But the old lady shook her way clear of them and made her way to the gate on her own, stick in hand. When Granny moved aside to let her past I saw her face. It was pinched and lean, her skin grey with a yellow tinge from many years of smoking, the wrinkles around her eyes and mouth settled in a permanent scowl.

'Good morning, Mrs Pardshaw,' Aunty Dora said. 'How are you?'

That was all the invitation Mrs Pardshaw needed. We were treated to a list of complaints about her aches and pains, her incompetent doctor, even the weather.

'I'm so sorry,' Aunty Dora said when the old lady finally took a breath. 'That must be very difficult for you. Mrs Pardshaw, I'd like you to meet my great-nephew William Henry. He's come to stay for the summer holidays. We're enjoying having someone young around to liven things up–'

'Oh how ghastly,' Mrs Pardshaw exclaimed. 'Why did you let yourself be put upon like that? How inconvenient for you. People who have children ought to at least own the responsibility and look after them themselves.' And, with her grinning escort in pursuit, she continued up the walk into the church.

Aunty Dora patted me on the shoulder. 'Don't worry dear,' she said. 'Mrs Pardshaw is like that with everyone. I don't think she can even help it now.'

As we neared the porch I got a whiff of the slurry bucket with the branch that had been severed from the living fruit tree sticking out. Aunty Dora smiled over at me and wrinkled her nose. 'Do you remember which lesson that is, Will?'

'The man who planted his life in "good religious deeds" without giving himself first to God?'

'That's right,' she said, and she nodded at Granny as if to say, 'See? Even a teenager remembers the sermon a week later with these unconventional methods our new vicar employs.'

But even though I remembered the lesson, I wasn't convinced. There was still fruit on the branch and the leaves appeared healthy enough. My mother had brought me up to think that good deeds were the most important goal. And certainly my experience of most church people did little to improve my opinion of their superior virtue.

George greeted us and gave us our service books. 'And you remember, Elsie, about the party on Wednesday?'

Granny touched his arm and nodded.

There were the Millstone sisters, flanked by various other loyal combatants from the W.I., scowling and whispering. Mr Badger was grunting away near the back. Uncle Sid, who arrived a bit late, took up his seat next to Mrs Pardshaw near the front.

The fruit tree was still at the front of the church. What was it the vicar had said? That Jesus Christ would be our King and rescuer? I'd been moved by the passion of his message last week, but as I thought about it now I realized it really did sound too much like something from the film *Alien*. How could Jesus have possibly helped me with Carrie, for instance? Or rescued me from getting caught poaching? Or given me the power to kill the beast? Those were real life problems I had to deal with on my own. The grafted branch had survived the week, and the branch planted in the bucket of rubbish had withered—a warning, I supposed, to people like me who preferred to do things their own way. But I'd survived the week.

Richard and Hannah finished setting up their music and Hannah was talking to Andrew and Jane, the champion wrestler vet and his fiancée. Andrew and Jane were in the second pew and Hannah sat in the first pew, facing them. I watched her absent-mindedly until I realized that there was something about her. What was it? She wasn't my type at all. She wasn't like any of the girls at school, and she definitely wasn't in the same league as Carrie. But I couldn't take my eyes off her laughing and chatting with her friends.

When she glanced round and caught my eye for moment I felt my heart skip a beat and a sickeningly flighty feeling in my stomach.

I looked away and decided it was the mushrooms Granny had fried for breakfast. But when I glanced over at Hannah again I saw she wasn't nearly as animated as before. She glanced at me quickly before returning to the keyboard.

The Reverend Scott's entrance was anything but dramatic this week. He greeted the congregation and, if he knew anything of the plots against him, he certainly didn't show it.

Uncle George got up to read from his battered old Bible. His face was weathered brown. He smiled and spoke warmly, like the way a shepherd would speak to his sheep I imagined, as he paused over the old book to introduce the passage. I'd always known him to be cheerful even though, according to Aunty Dora, he hadn't had things easy.

Mrs Pardshaw moved along the bench slightly as George stood at the front to read, her arms folded and head down.

'The reading today is from the gospel of John chapter fifteen, verses nine to fourteen. "As the Father has loved me so I have loved you, continue in my love. If you keep my commandments, you shall abide in my love ... that my joy might remain in you and that your joy may be full. This is my commandment that you love one another, as I have loved you. Greater love hath no man than this, that he lay down his life for his friends. You are my friends if you do whatsoever I command you."'

The vicar, wearing a black polo neck and black trousers, looked more like the bouncer he used to be than the godly leader of this congregation. I never would have picked him out of a crowd as a vicar.

'Good morning, everyone! I hope ye did'nae forget oor special topic of study for the next few weeks. The nine fruits of the Spirit from Paul's letter to the Galatians. This is, for ye men, the true foundation upon which manhood is built. To build yer life with any other materials is a waste of time.'

How to be a man? I was listening.

'Today we'll be looking at the second fruit, which is joy. The playwright George Bernard Shaw said that true joy in life is "being used for a purpose recognized by yourself as a mighty one; being thoroughly worn out before you are thrown on the scrap heap; being a force of nature instead of a feverish selfish little clod of ailments and grievances". Aye, and this is not mere happiness that I'm talking about but something much deeper.'

Happiness, according to the vicar, is connected with worldly things. 'It's the religion of the masses,' he said, 'and people have appointed these *industries* to be oor guide to experiencing joy.'

I'd heard that sermon before from my teachers. Blaming all the really good things in life, the cool technology they never had, for all the world's problems. The vicar had definitely never had a Playstation. He might have had an exciting past, but he was still old and irrelevant. But, much as I fancied a nap, there was something about him that prevented me from tuning out completely.

'Another man once wondered "whether all pleasures are not substitutes for joy". Aye, and ye can no more separate joy from its roots in God than ye can separate suffering from

God. The latter would result in bitterness, and the former in boredom.'

Boredom, I thought. I could preach about boredom.

'Aye, that's right, folks. Boredom! The cry of each new generation who looks for joy in the new toys or new sensations that money can buy. But what's the result? Disappointment and boredom with the world that cannot satisfy them. But I can tell ye this morning that enjoyment is'nae a goal of itself. Enjoyment only ever accompanies important ongoing activity.'

Well, I thought, that's not true. I've certainly enjoyed myself even though I don't know that I've ever been involved in 'important ongoing activity.' I reminded myself that this was a typical religious spiel. These types always have a quick answer for everything. At the same time a little voice inside me reminded me that I *was* generally pretty disappointed with the world. And bored.

'Can the God who made ye not offer more than a half-fulfilled life, ma friend? Ye bet he can! An eagle can walk, and that's fine. Walking has its place. Happiness has its place. But have ye seen an eagle take to the sky? Aye, that's where the eagle belongs, flying. And flying on the wings of God-given joy is where ye belong, too.

'As an old man, the apostle John wrote a letter to the disciples who would follow after him. He said, "I write this that your joy might be full"—that is to say complete, mature. But how does he say that this will happen? He says it will happen when they *know* that they have eternal life through a living relationship with Jesus Christ. Now I ask you today: are ye sure that ye know Christ? For joy is the flag that is flying when the true king is sitting on his throne, when God is working within us.'

The Millstones were fidgeting and, for once, I understood how they felt. It was uncomfortable being asked these questions, invasive even. The vicar went on to give examples of people on both sides of the fence, and I thought of two examples of my own—George and Mrs Pardshaw. Two people couldn't be more different, but both were sitting here in church. Did they just have different personalities? Or was, in fact, the 'special something' that George had joy? I wanted to have some of this joy he was describing, but I wondered if there was an easy way to get some.

After the service I slipped out and positioned myself around the far side of the church to get a better look at Uncle Sid. Sure enough he approached the two graves, but he definitely stopped at Ellen's. He spoke softly and I couldn't hear much of what he said. I edged a bit closer and heard his parting words. 'She's had a better week and I'm looking after the other things,' he said. As he turned to leave I was keen to get out of sight, but in moving back I banged my foot on a gravestone.

I froze against the church wall, certain that Uncle Sid had heard it. He did. My heart pounded as I heard footsteps coming my way. 'Who's there?' he called out.

My only chance was to break cover and get back around to the front of the church before he reached my hiding place. I ran, and I didn't look back. When I arrived at Aunty Dora's side I looked behind me but realized the flaw in my plan. I didn't know whether Uncle Sid had seen me turn the final corner or not. I did my best to control my breathing and join in the conversation with Aunty Dora, Andrew and Jane. But I kept my eye on the corner of the church building. Presently Uncle Sid appeared, but he did not look hassled. He surveyed the crowd of parishioners gathered at the gate and I kept a low profile. I shivered as he looked us over, and when I snuck a glance at him I saw that same slow smile creeping over his lean face. He walked with leisure through the gate to his car and I let out a long breath.

Andrew seemed very pleased to meet me. He shook my hand with vigour and enthusiasm and, as my hand recovered, I asked him about the mysterious beast and what he thought about the markings on the tree.

'Well, I didn't get long to take measurements and I must confess to being a little baffled by it. If I had to make a wild guess I'd say it's a cross between a huge bear, because of the height of the marks, and the largest cat ever seen. The configuration of the claw was more cat-like than bear-like. I wish I could tell you more, but I'm not paid to investigate these things unless there's a paying animal owner or farmer reimbursing the practice for my time.'

'But surely someone should be doing something?' I said.

'Oh, the protocol traps have been put out, but there's no budget for this sort of thing. They called in some safari bods from the south who used up the allocated budget in two weeks and went home cheery with the cash, saying that it must be a fox.'

'A fox! How could anyone believe that? A fox attacking a pony?'

'Well, they'd come and gone before the pony incident but, believe me, it's still easy enough when the government's involved. For one thing, no one gives a monkey's because no one's responsible for it. And second, it's easier to believe the report of the "professionals" when it lets you off the hook from having to fork out any more of your precious budget.'

'But that's crazy!' I said.

'Welcome to the adult world, lad!' He smiled and turned to Jane. 'We need to be going.' She nodded and he turned back to me and offered his hand again. Mine had only just recovered feeling, but I took it. 'It's nice to meet you, Will. I know your Grandpa's looking into it, so you tell him to call me after hours if he needs any help.'

I said that I would, but his comments only further fuelled my growing fascination and dread. This creature lurked only feet from the security of Granny's place, but any heroic thoughts I had of tracking and capturing the creature were hideously tinged with the dread of being eaten alive by it.

I remembered the stories last summer of an amateur naturalist and his girlfriend who were studying the feeding patterns of grizzlies in Alaska. They'd both been eaten alive, and the terrifying screams had been recorded by a video camera with the lens cap on. The woman had apparently watched helplessly as her boyfriend was torn limb from limb before she herself was also devoured by the beast. When rangers later found and shot the bear, it was eating the man's arm—complete with wristwatch. I'd had a few nightmares about it last summer.

I was relieved that, when Granny and Aunty Dora were finally ready to leave, the vicar was busy tossing a baby in the air.

'Ah, the wee one who was heckling my preaching!' he said. Hannah giggled beside him and the mother came running.

I slipped past, figuring that I had enough problems without having to talk to the vicar about his Jesus.

I looked back one last time and saw Hannah leaning on the gate, chewing her thumbnail, and her brother sneaking up behind her. When he poked her in the ribs, she jumped a mile and her hairband fell down over her eyes.

'Richard Scott!' she exclaimed. She pushed him away and appealed to her father, who just laughed. When she took off her hairband and shook out her hair she caught my eye and saw me laughing too. She smiled back and I did a doubletake. She had the most beautiful smile I'd ever seen.

I couldn't get Hannah out of my head all the way home. I was glad when Lewis came over after lunch. For all his annoying habits and grubby ways, he was becoming like the little brother I never had. It was nice to have someone looking up to me and an excuse to play in the woods, fish, make traps and light fires without matches. No girls and confusing teenage feelings, no scary beasts or great uncles. I even did my bit and convinced him he should come to church next Sunday.

9

THE BEAST HUNT AND THE HAUNTED HOUSE

Thought you'd never show yourself lad!'

Grandpa was waiting in the kitchen with his gun when I stumbled in after a good night's sleep. 'Hurry and get some breakfast and let's go and see what's cooking in the woods.'

I yawned. 'Looks like you've already been out.'

He drummed his fingers on the table. 'Well yes, Nelson's been for his morning constitutional and we found some tracks we thought you'd be interested in and–'

'Reggie!' Granny appeared with a bucket of ashes from the fire. 'There you are—what have you got that gun for? I hope you're not thinking of hunting that creature, because you should leave that–'

'Rabbits, dear. We're going to get some er ... rabbits.' He couldn't resist one of his jovial snorts as he patted Nelson on the head. The very mention of rabbits sent Nelson into a frenzy of tail-wagging excitement.

'Rabbits with a wild fowling gun? I'm no fool, Reginald Wallace. But if you've not got more oil in your lamp than to go getting yourself mixed up in this business, then more fool you!'

Grandpa rose and put an arm around her shoulder. 'We're already involved, love. It's here on our doorstep and no one else is going to deal with it. I promise to be careful. The creature will be asleep now anyway—I just wanted to follow some trails this morning and see if we can't draw nearer to its den. Stan's coming too, so you'll not need to worry.'

Granny shook her head but said no more. Grandpa didn't mention me accompanying them but motioned with his head for me to meet him outside.

Fully awake now, I bolted down my breakfast.

'Will, I have an errand I'd like you to run for me this afternoon,' Granny said as I was heading for the door.

'Right, Granny,' I agreed. 'I'll see you at lunchtime.'

I found Grandpa near the shed holding the long-barrelled shotgun.

'Is that what Granny called a fowling gun?' I asked him.

'Aye, lad,' he said. 'I doubt a regular twelve bore will give us the power we need to bring this thing down. The fowling gun is designed to hit objects at a greater distance, but that's not all ...' He searched inside his gun cabinet. 'If I'm not mistaken, somewhere down here is a little something to make our job even easier ... Yes, that's it.' He held up a tattered box of cartridges.

'What are they?'

'I brought these back from Italy when I was wild boar hunting some years back. They're just the ticket for this trip. Now, what about you lad, we'd better get you a knife.'

'Betta get the bairn a gun, Major.' Stan, true to form, had come across the field without us noticing his approach. 'If he's not a man he's no business on this trip, and if he is a man then he'll need a man's gear to defend himself.'

Grandpa looked at me as he put on his battered Grenfell jacket. 'Well, Stan, you've spent more time with the lad than I have. Think he can handle his own weapon?'

Stan took a good hard look at me and sniffed. 'Well, he's shown himself to have a level head when he's been about with me last week. I'd say he'd be all right with a little training. But, mind, he's your kin, Major.'

Grandpa pursed his lips and winked at me. 'Okay then, but we'd better not tell your grandmother!'

He handed me a single-barrelled, twelve-bore shotgun and took me through the motions of safety in a few gruff sentences and demonstrations.

Then they started off, leaving me too stunned to do anything but stare shell-shocked at the weapon gripped in my sweaty palms. Nelson trotted eagerly round my ankles as I struggled to adjust to the unfamiliar weight of the gun and the undeserved responsibility. I nearly tripped over him as I turned to follow the men.

None of my computer target shooting software had prepared me for this moment. I thought I knew all about guns and shooting from cyber reality. But this was nothing like it. This was real and very heavy. The gun gave me an odd feeling and I carried it very carefully. I knew I was being treated like an adult before I had really earned it. Their confidence and expectation had two contradictory effects. I felt small and unworthy. But I also had an overwhelming urge to meet their expectations, to become more like them in some way. I was surprised when I realized that it wasn't the gun that made me feel this way, but the level of trust that Grandpa had in me. The camaraderie of being treated as an equal among men had a power all its own.

But the shoot-out between the forces of good and evil that I imagined as we trekked through the field did not come to pass. For in this, the first of a number of such expeditions, we mapped trails on an OS sheet and charted patterns of movement and known kill sites. I tried to swallow my disappointment as the unused gun wore a groove in my shoulder and banged against my ribs.

No trail we followed yielded a decent print because, as Stan explained, it had been too dry the week before and the ground wasn't soft enough.

In one place we followed tracks only to find that they suddenly disappeared without trace.

'Some fox!' Stan said as he scratched his head, puzzled.

Grandpa agreed. 'I've never seen anything like it, I must confess. As if it vanished into thin air!'

Although I didn't get to use the gun, I was learning tracking skills and hand signals we could use to move through the woods together without a sound. Stan even let me take the lead. Once I felt the hairs rising on the back of my neck in terror, as I imagined myself being watched, but there was no evidence—I didn't see or hear anything.

When Grandpa decided we should try another day, I trudged back to Granny's. My gun felt much heavier than it had when we left. At least in my virtual gaming world I was guaranteed some action. This real world seemed to delight in keeping boys waiting for the things they were wanting.

After lunch Granny asked me to deliver Christian Aid envelopes to people on her list. She paused when she came to the envelope for Mrs Pardshaw. 'Hardly worth going, never puts anything in it,' she muttered. 'No,' she said suddenly and shook her head. 'I mustn't judge the poor woman. No, Will, you must bring an envelope to her at the big house on the far end of Loweswater. Then that will be your lot.' She handed me the thick stack of red and white envelopes. 'Oh, don't look so down, you can take the bike and you'll be back in two hours.'

I took a deep breath. 'Granny, do I have to go to Mrs Pardshaw? She gives me the creeps and I don't think she likes kids.' Then, suddenly, I had an inspiration. 'Don't you think she might give you more if you went?' I asked. Then I had another brilliant idea. I could send Lewis. He wouldn't mind in the least. And it might even be amusing to see the old lady's reaction to my grubby little friend.

'Everyone has a story,' Granny was saying. 'You can tell she was a city girl. She doesn't have much to say to local women—even now, after being here all these many years.'

'From the city?'

She married Angus Pardshaw in the days when higher-class folks had fancy balls to meet up with other such folk. She was a pretty young girl looking for a landed gent, like most of her set.'

Pretty? I thought I had a fairly good imagination, but I couldn't imagine Mrs Pardshaw as a pretty young girl at all. 'So she married for land, not love?' I asked.

'Oh, I wouldn't say that, though that was part of it. Angus worshipped her. He was a nice lad, not snobbish like some. But Cumbria never suited her, and she made that very clear. They moved to his house in London after one winter. She had a job writing for those fancy society columns in the magazines. In London she could mix with the rich and mighty.'

'But what about him? Did he miss his home?'

'Yes, I dare say Angus wasn't all that happy there, really, although I always thought he put a brave face on it. I think what he wanted was to go home, raise a family and manage his estate. But she had some funny ideas. As you noticed, she doesn't like children and never wanted any of her own. She thought they would tie her down.'

'She doesn't look that free now!' I said.

Granny shook her head. 'No, dear, you're right.'

'What happened to her husband?'

'Poor Angus. They separated after two years and he came back up here. But he was only in his forties when he had a heart attack and died while she was still in London with her career, her fashion shows and her foreign holidays. She stayed there until she was too old to do her job.'

'What happened then? How did she end up back here?'

'Well, when she was no longer editor of the magazine no one was all that interested in her anymore. She had no money of her own, and the house and estate in Cumbria was the only real asset that she'd inherited as Angus' widow. She wanted to sell it, of course, but Angus wrote it into his will that she couldn't. So she's stuck there. He must have known she'd have no choice but to live there, and it's quite ironic that the one place she didn't want to end up is the one place she can't afford to get away from.'

'She doesn't have anyone? Family? Or friends?'

'Oh, there's plenty of us who've tried to befriend her, including Dora and myself, but we're not really her sort of society. She's so sarcastic and critical, she pushes folk away who try to get close. Dora's had a little more contact with her than I have. I'm too far below her, being from farming stock you see.'

'But what about Uncle Sid and those people who bring her to church?' I asked.

'Oh Sid's just hobnobbing. He's so desperate to be accepted in high society, he'd always do anything. If he only knew how she speaks about him to others he wouldn't bother. And the other two are some of Angus's relatives hoping to get in with her so she leaves them the house— since she doesn't have anyone else to leave it to. It's all so tragic, really, to be left with so little company after a lifetime. Anyway, come on or you'll never get away with me yakking.'

I was dying of shame at the thought of being seen riding Granny's folding bike. It would be so unfair if someone saw me on this bike when no one had seen me carrying a gun this morning. But I saw the sense in getting the job done quickly, so I decided to take it. Thinking about how Mum would praise me for having a mature attitude made me feel more mature.

Lewis met me in the lane and told me all he'd heard about Mrs Pardshaw and her haunted house. He gave me some refresher chews and began singing the song from *Ghostbusters* as we headed into Loweswater. As we rode along I realized it was the first time I'd felt relaxed all day.

Lewis insisted on playing 'knock and run' on the doors as we went around putting the envelopes in people's letterboxes. I told him to just stick them through, but Lewis would have none of it. Sticky, and with his mouth full of sweets, he banged loudly on each door, then sprinted back to his bike, squealing like a pig, and made off at top speed before the door opened.

'Lewis, you idiot! Stop it!' I protested.

'C'mon,' he spluttered and almost choked, 'you know you really love it!'

At every house I made him promise not to do it again. He'd promise, even as he'd run up to the next door, turn and eye me, and indulge again in his new form of torment. It was so embarrassing, but maybe just as embarrassing as his behaviour was the realization that I found it quite funny and would have been disappointed if he'd taken my pleas to stop seriously. Maybe I wasn't growing up as quickly as I thought.

We did the bulk of Loweswater in half an hour and, just as I was congratulating myself that we had nearly finished, we saw a horse and rider coming along the road towards us. The woman on the mount was slender and graceful. Her auburn hair flowed down her back from under her helmet and her tight-fitting jodhpurs and polo shirt were splattered with mud. It was Hannah, returning from a ride on the fells. I felt my stomach knotting once again. She looked very different, out of her Sunday best, and her face was radiant.

Though I tried to maintain my composure on Granny's shopper bike below her towering horse, it was obvious she'd seen us playing knocky over the hedges. I wasn't sure whether her tight smile was one of disdain or pity, but I could have died.

'Cor, you're pretty,' Lewis said with his usual tact. 'How old are you?'

Two dimples appeared in her cheeks. 'Seventeen,' she said. 'Perhaps a little too old for you?'

'Nah, I like you. D'you wanna sweet?'

'That's very kind, thank you, er–?'

'Lewis. Name's Lewis. This is my best friend, Will Houston. He's in my gang.'

'Ah yes, we've met. Sort of.' She leaned down to take the sweet. 'You're up for the whole summer?' she asked me.

'Uh, yeah, six and a half weeks left,' I said.

'Well, you must come and meet my brother. I'm sure he'd be in Lewis's gang, too—there aren't many boys his age round here.' The horse was pawing the ground impatiently and she leaned forward to pat his chest.

'We've always got loads of sweets,' Lewis said.

'I'll be sure to tell him.' Hannah tightened the reins. 'Thanks for the sweet, Lewis. It was nice to meet you, Will.' She trotted off, the horse swishing its tail proudly.

'Nice to meet you too,' I said.

'Cor, she's hot!' Lewis said far too loudly. 'Think she might fancy me!'

I pushed him into the hedge and told him to shut up.

'Now, Will, don't be jealous,' he said. He got back on his bike and overtook me as he hollered, 'Oooh, the green-eyed monster!'

I pedalled hard, praying that Hannah was out of earshot.

On the other side of the lake we met the Professor. 'Where are you going in such a hurry?' he asked.

'Mrs Pardshaw's haunted house,' Lewis told him. 'We're ghostbusters!'

The Professor peered down at him for a moment. He motioned further down the lake with his stick. 'You will find her house in darkness, behind the big gates and high wall.' Then he began mumbling something in Russian.

'What's he on about?' Lewis asked me, making a sign to indicate he thought he was crazy. Lewis was never subtle.

I widened my eyes at Lewis but he carried on. 'Er ... thank you, Professor,' I said.

'Those high walls we build around us to keep out sadness also keep out the joy, my young friend,' the Professor said.

'Oh right, thanks,' I said, trying to be polite as I flapped my hand at Lewis to stop. 'I'll remember that.'

'Good,' the Professor replied. 'Also remember Euripides, "Short is the joy that guilty pleasure brings".'

I had no idea what he was saying. 'Well,' I said, 'I met her on Sunday and I'd say she was fresh out of joy—but she didn't seem too bothered.'

He shrugged and, as we started off on our bikes, called after us, 'Unhappy people are strangely like those who sleep badly, they are always proud of it!'

There was no mistaking Mrs Pardshaw's house at the far end of the lake with its large gates and high limestone wall. Lewis finally stopped chattering as we approached the large Victorian mansion.

He skidded to a halt. 'There's no way you'll get me up there, Will. It's haunted! Everyone says it is!'

'Stop being stupid,' I said. 'We're just delivering an envelope.' I could sound brave and matter-of-fact because I had no intentions of going inside. So I laughed Lewis off and made my approach up the driveway, past the overgrown rhododendrons, alone. But as I got closer I saw a shadowy figure behind a raised lace curtain. I doubled my pace, hoping I could leave the envelope and be gone before she made it to the door.

The house, like its occupant, had an air of death about it. There were no flowers, only untended shrubs. The paint was peeling off the bargeboards and window frames, and there were weeds pushing up through the raised porch, which I now mounted with a pounding heart. As my trembling hand stuffed the envelope through the letterbox, I saw a distorted silhouette behind the etched glass of the front door. The handle twisted and the door opened.

Mrs Pardshaw's wizened face greeted me. 'Well, what do you want?' she demanded.

'Hello, hello Mrs Pardshaw, I've—I've come to bring you your Christian—um, your Christian Aid envelope, that's all,' I stammered.

I had the feeling that she knew exactly who I was and why I was there. I was right.

'Ah, yes, the Wallace's grandson,' she said, 'come to absorb yourself in the joys of this delightful corner of England and tire your grandmother out in the process.

Well come in, you could run a message for me too and save me an unnecessary trip.'

I couldn't see any other option but to follow her into the musty hallway. She was wearing black patent leather shoes with gold buckles, a tight-fitting black woollen skirt that fell above the knee, and a dark cardigan. Her gnarled fingers were studded with a collection of diamond rings and she wore a pearl necklace at her wrinkled throat. She was elegant, somehow, though half-fossilized.

When I spotted a glass of sherry on the hall sideboard I realized what the smell was—like my parent's drinks cabinet. We passed from the grand hallway into a large drawing room where, everywhere I looked, there were pictures of her in her 'society days'. She'd been quite a babe, in an old-fashioned kind of way, and in all the pictures she was posing with other beautiful people.

'Yes, even I was young once,' she snapped. 'Don't look so surprised.' Her words were sharp but a bit slurred and she gestured theatrically. I assumed the glass of sherry was not her first that day.

'I wasn't always here in this valley, you know. I did have a life ... once.' She gazed out the window and then back to her photographs. 'I was right up there with the celebs, when we—when I lived in the city. I used to dine all the time with royalty, film stars and the like. Oh, they all knew me ... they all needed me to write nice things about them for the glossies. See that picture there? That's me with Jackie Onassis. Many people said I was her double, do you ... don't you think so?'

'Oh, yes. Yes,' I said, shifting from one foot to the other and not daring to look at the door. Why was she trying to impress me? 'Did you work for a magazine?' I asked.

'Dear boy, I was not a journalist or anything common like that, if that's what you're thinking. I was a society correspondent. We had the power to make or break personalities, and they knew it. They wouldn't dare cross us. We were the king makers in those days, and I—I was the Queen Bee. But all that's gone now.' She waved her hand around the room. 'And here I am. I expect your grandmother has told you all about me?'

'She said that you don't have much company,' I said. It seemed the least offensive thing to say.

'Did she now? Well, let me tell you. It is nearly impossible to find people up here who have any decent conversation left in them. Nobody likes having salt rubbed into their wounds, even if it is the salt of the earth. The realms of the women's league and the W.I. are a bit alien to me.' Her upper lip curled in disgust. 'And I'm not sure that I would take to *knitting* competitions as well as some of your relations might.'

I couldn't believe I was actually feeling sorry for the W.I. after my encounter with them a few days before. I stood there, speechless, as she searched through a pile of papers. At last she dragged out a book.

'Ah, here it is. Tell your Aunt Dorothy that I tried to read this but found it woefully banal for my taste in literature. "Overly indulgent, American religious hysteria" is what I would have written if I had been asked to review it.'

She handed it to me. It was a book called *He Chose the Nails*, by Max Lucado.

'It's a book about Jesus?' I said.

'Emotional hogwash is what it is. But I should imagine she'll want it back all the same. I don't mind religion at the proper time, we all need an insurance policy, but these people who are forever pushing their religious preferences on the weak-minded are singularly distasteful. I do love to read good literature, but this sort of thing is just—drivel.'

She spat out that last word and sank back into her chair. She began leafing through a copy of *Hello*. The Beckhams were on the front page, looking supercool as usual, and she glanced at them before waving me away.

'I'll take the book back to Aunty Dora, then. Goodbye, Mrs Pardshaw,' I said and headed out towards the hallway, but as I did she called me back.

'And you, what will you do with your life, eh?' she asked.

'Uh, I'm not sure yet,' I said.

She looked past me. Finally she said, 'Well, see you don't waste your time.' She lit a cigarette and went back to her magazine.

Her scathing intellect might have had a glory of its own, but it was an empty majesty, and so sad.

I was glad to see Lewis waiting for me, hopping from one foot to the other. 'Am I glad to see you, Will! I thought I might never see you again. Did you see any ghosts or werewolves or anything? What'd she say?'

I didn't really have to answer as Lewis chattered on and on, most of the way home, about his own theories.

As we rounded a bend, though, he shrieked, 'Will, hide! It's Mad Annie! C'mon, I don't want to be cursed!' He ducked out of sight behind a hedge, as did I.

'Don't be so stupid,' I whispered. 'She's just an old woman who's lost it a bit.'

Though we were well hidden I could feel her eyes on me as she cycled past, with all her bags and panniers stuffed to overflowing with old clothes.

This valley was like those panniers, I thought. Stuffed to overflowing with characters and their stories.

10

WILD AUNTY JOYCE

I tell you, we're never going to be ready at this rate. Reggie, please can you get that gun off the table.' It was breakfast time, and George's party wasn't until that evening, but Granny was already in a whirlwind. It looked to me like she was making enough food for an army.

'Good morning, Will. What do you need me to do, Elsie?' Aunty Dora arrived at the door.

'Oh, Dora, thank goodness. You can tell your brother to get that gun off the table,' Granny said. She spoke from behind the biggest sack of flour I'd ever seen, which she was lugging from the larder.

Aunty Dora took care of the gun and sat beside me at the table. We both knew there was little we could do except get in Granny's way.

'Mrs Pardshaw asked me to give this back to you,' I said, handing her the book.

'Thank you, Will. Did she say anything about it?'

'Well, she said she thought it was overly emotional American drivel ... or something.'

When I saw Aunty Dora's face fall I wished I'd thought of a nicer way to put Mrs Pardshaw's harsh words. I could see she was upset that the little book hadn't broken through to Mrs Pardshaw.

'She probably didn't really give it a chance,' I said. 'It looks like a good book.'

'Oh, it doesn't matter Will, dear.' Aunty Dora smiled and patted my hand. 'I was just hoping she would read it. I think it would really help her—if only she wouldn't be so spiky.'

'She did say she liked good literature,' I said. 'Maybe it just wasn't the right book?'

'Give her *Mere Christianity* by C.S. Lewis and tell her to put that in her pipe and smoke it.' Grandpa had spoken from behind the paper, and suddenly there was silence in the kitchen. Granny stopped her clattering and Dora stared in bewilderment. Grandpa continued reading his paper, pretending not to notice.

'Well,' Aunty Dora said after a long pause, 'that may be just the ticket. C.S. Lewis is certainly more the sort of writer she would be used to and it is a good book ... yes, I'll find my copy and drop it in.'

'No need,' Grandpa replied without looking up. 'You can take my copy. It's next to my bed.'

Aunty Dora and Granny exchanged amazed and barely suppressed smiles. Could it be that, after all these years, Grandpa was starting to seek God again?

'Thank you, Reggie,' Aunty Dora said. I could tell she wanted to say so much more.

'So what's this party celebrating?' I asked Granny as I helped clear up the breakfast dishes.

'It's not "what" but "who"!' she said. She brought two more trays of freshly baked scones out of the oven before she continued. 'You're too young to remember, but she held you in her arms on at least two occasions before she passed on. I remember when we were planning a party for your first birthday she said she would hold out for one more party before she went home ... and she did. We had your first birthday celebration in her garden, and she went about two weeks later.'

'Who did?' I asked. This all sounded a bit creepy.

'Your Great Aunty Joyce, George's wife.'

Suddenly, it hit me. 'The pink bonnet!' I exclaimed.

'Ah, so you do remember then.' Granny smiled.

'I remember the story about that awful bonnet! She misheard Dad on the telephone and knitted a pink bonnet for me. They put it on me and took a picture for a laugh.' I'd never forget how Louise had scanned the photo, enlarged it, and passed it around to my friends on my thirteenth birthday. I could have died with embarrassment. 'But why are we having a party for someone who's dead?'

'Dead! Weren't you listening to the vicar yesterday? Dear Joyce is more alive now than she ever was when she was here ... if that's possible. Oh, she was a caution—game for anything, the life and soul of the party.' Granny paused to wipe her floury hands and passed me another photo from the kitchen dresser.

I recognized George straight away. Even in fading black and white and after all those years I could see his pride and joy over the woman standing next to him on the steps of what I assumed was Loweswater Church.

Aunty Joyce was a sharp, perky woman—not sharp in a nasty way, but sharp in wit. I saw it in her eyes, the corners of her mouth, a cheeky and eager expression that was unmistakeable and irrepressible. As I looked at them I tried to imagine them as Carrie and me. How would you know, I wondered, that the person you were marrying was the right one? I'd been trying to put thoughts of Carrie from my head. Should I take the fact that I hadn't seen her as a sign she wasn't really interested in me? I looked down at the picture again. 'Was she from the valley?' I asked.

'Heavens, no!' Granny said with a chuckle. 'She was from away, Whitehaven, and what a shock we all had when George brought her home to meet mother and father!'

'Why, what happened?' It was hard to imagine Uncle George doing something outrageous.

'Well, dear, I don't know where to begin ... I mean, she was just so different from anyone we had ever known in our family. She was a screen lass from the Haig Pit.'

'What's that?'

'She worked in a shed on the sea brows next to iron conveyor belts that brought the coal up from the seams. They had to screen the coal from the slate, hack it up and shovel in through grates in the floor for the wagons waiting underneath.' Granny shook her head as she ran a basin of hot water to finish the dishes.

'But that sounds more like man's work!'

'Aye, that it was, Will dear. It was very hard work and most women wouldn't do it. Apparently it was easy to tell a screen lass in town, for their hands would be covered with cuts and scars and their fingertips would be calloused from the work. She told me the air was so thick with coal dust you could chew it. And it was that coal dust that eventually killed her. She was only in her sixties, but her poor lungs were so full of tar that the emphysema drained the life from her.' Granny gazed out the window for a moment before she continued. 'Now we have only our memories and this little anniversary party to celebrate her life.'

'Every year?' I asked.

'Aye, Will, every year. It was her idea, you know. She said it would do all us stuffy valley folk good to have at least one decent knees-up a year! Oh, what a girl she was ... a real diamond in the rough. Those lasses put up with a lot of stick for the work they did.'

'Why was that?'

'Well, everyone else in the town looked down on them. They had a reputation for being coarse, and the factory girls would give them a wide berth at the dancing halls on a Saturday night. And some of them were game characters, if our Joyce was anything to go by. Screen lasses were always the butt of the men's jokes, but Joyce never cared about that. She had hungry mouths to feed and rent to pay. She said it was a happy enough life, and the other lasses were like family.'

'Why did she have hungry mouths to feed? Was she married before?' I asked. I was getting confused.

'She'd been married, but she didn't ever have any children of her own. No, she took care of her brothers and sisters. She was from a large Irish family and her father had had an accident down the pit and couldn't work again. In those days it was work or go to the poor house, so at the age of sixteen Joyce went to work as a screen lass with her sister. She met her first husband, John, at the pit, and they were married just after her eighteenth birthday.'

'What happened to him? Did the marriage fail or something?'

'Marriages don't fail, Will, it's people who fail. But no, that wasn't what happened. In those days folk stuck together more than they do now.' Granny wiped her hands on her apron again and turned to look at me. 'No, Will, there was a dreadful accident at William Pitt in 1947. Over a hundred men died. They brought up the bodies as the lasses looked on for signs of their fathers, husbands, brothers, sweethearts and friends, but there was no sign of John. John and eleven others were never recovered—their bodies were sealed up in the shaft. Oh, coal came at great price! Only three men made it out alive. A young lay preacher by the name of Birkett–' She paused. 'Yes, I have that right—John Birkett. He led two other young men out of that terrible place on their hands and knees, but the others wouldn't risk it ... and so they died down there in the darkness.'

Just thinking about such a horrible death made me feel short of breath. 'Why—why didn't the others go with him?'

'Well, they had a choice, to wait for rescue where they were or risk finding a way out. Poor John ... and Joyce, too, a widow at nineteen. But, do you know, she went back to work when the pit opened again the next day, right over the ground where her John was buried, and stuck it out for another few years without complaining. She supported herself and her family all those years. Aye, she was an amazing woman and no mistake, God love her.' Granny shook her head and looked up at the clock. 'Oh, goodness, Will. Is that the time already? We'll have to get going or we'll be late. I've got to get to Cockermouth to pick up some bits and you're supposed to be over at Thrang End to help with George's sheep. I'll drop you off on my way and George can bring you along to the party.'

'Oh, I'd forgotten about that. Should I bring clothes to change into before the party?'

'I wouldn't worry, lad.' Granny laughed. 'You'll only smell as bad as the rest of them—they'll not be getting home if there's George's home brew and dancing to be had.'

I found myself wondering about Aunty Joyce as we packed the car with trays of food. She must have been so brave and strong. She sounded like the complete opposite of George, the quiet, affable dalesman. How could two people who were so different, and from such different worlds, make a good couple? I vowed to find out more.

George and I whizzed all over Low Moor on his quad bike as the dogs darted back and forth to bring the Herdwicks down for dipping. It was a great afternoon—the air was warm and the freedom of the fell and the speed made me feel—well, alive. I smiled when I thought of how I'd been missing my Sega. There's no comparison between playing video games and flying over rough terrain with the wind in your hair. Obstacles and jumps rush upon you, out of nowhere, before you know it. George was a master at handling the quad. The way the suspension is rigged on bikes like that meant that a less experienced rider would be risking death, riding such rough terrain at the speeds we were doing.

George was a very different man out of his Sunday suit and in his natural environment. He was powerfully built and seemed a lot less old and much more confident. He was totally extreme in his negotiation of the many becks we had to cross. I shut my eyes and gripped his waist as we went airborne on several of them.

On flatter runs I could look down into the valley. I spotted Granny's place and the interconnected areas of woodland that made up the beast's lair. From up here I could see how clever this creature was to choose this place. There was loads of cover but also easy access to fields full of livestock. And it had a network of dense woodlands to retreat to if it were hunted, as well. I saw how difficult it would be to pin it down to one location.

As we made our way down to the lower slopes we saw a man furiously waving his stick to attract our attention. George rode over to him and introduced me.

'Will, this is Dicky Patterson, a shepherd from Ramthwaite.'

'Nice to meet you, Will,' Dicky said. He didn't look that much older than I was. 'You'll never believe what I just found, George.'

Dicky brought us to a clearing in the bracken where we saw the hideous remains of a mother and two lambs that had strayed from the intake fields and fallen fowl of the beast. Although the dismembered carcasses were a gruesome sight, it was the heads, still intact with wide eyes staring, that sent a chill through me. I deduced from this that they were fairly freshly killed, so I scanned the slopes for the nearest woodland cover. It was nearly a kilometre away.

I remembered how Stan had explained that, after a period of hunting, a dominant predator will establish larger and larger territories. In effect, they work to own the ground and everything (and everyone) on it. This open kill so far from woodland cover could only mean one thing: this creature was gaining confidence by the day. How long would it be before it began to see human intruders as a food source, I wondered as George and Dicky continued their conversation.

'And council reckon it's a fox and won't do anything about it,' Dicky was saying. 'I wonder at folks having no sense, George, I really do, like.' He poked the festering remains. 'I'm not leaving my stock on't this side of valley 'till this is sorted out, aye, and I'm not spending any more time up here neither.'

George stood lost in thought for a moment and then patted the fearful Dicky on the shoulder. 'Aye, you're a good lad, Dick. You get 'em away from 'ere before you lose any more and don't fret over much, lad, it'll be right soon enough.' George took one last look down at the remains of the sheep. 'I'll be seeing you later perhaps at the village hall for a crack?'

Dicky smiled. 'Heh, you know I'd not miss it for ought, George, aye, I'll see you later.'

We watched Dicky make his way through the bracken to his Land Rover, which was a short distance below in the intake fields that he rented from Grandpa.

I asked George a few more questions about the beast on the way back, but he seemed distracted. It hadn't occurred to me earlier that it was the anniversary of his wife's death, and here he was going to work and then face a party full of people afterwards.

'Uncle George, how did you meet Aunty Joyce?' I asked.

There was a pause and then a chuckle from Uncle George. He stopped the bike and we got off near a piece of broken fence. 'Come on, lad, I've been meaning to fettle yonder fence for a while. Give a hand and I'll tell you how I met that gay, bonny lass.'

George worked on the fence, and I mostly watched, as he told me the story. 'Well,' he began, 'you may not think it now to look at me, but I was a shy lad when I was growing up. Aye, wouldn't say boo to a goose and weren't much of a one for talking with the lasses neither. Mind you, I were quite good at cricket in my day, and it was when the Young Farmers of the dale were due to play the Haig Miners of Whitehaven that it all began.'

'I was driving the bus for the lads, not bin a great one for drinking and carrying on and such like, and I was waiting back of the Miner's Welfare club for the others when she appeared out the back door to empty bottles into the bin.'

'Was she working there? I thought she was a screen lass.'

'Aye, poor mitten, she did both. Up at four in the morning to the pit and evenings on the bar. It's a wonder she lasted as long as she did, but there was her dad's family to feed and things were different in them days.' Uncle George paused for a moment to consider the fence, though I could see he wasn't thinking about it at all. 'Mind you, Will lad, you should have seen her, she was a cracker of a lass. Long black hair, like a raven, and oh, how she laughed. She said her grandma was an Irish gypsy, and I well believed it.

Alt'lads loved her for it, in a nice way I mean. She had a way of making folk feel happier just for bin with her. Anyhow, where was I at? Oh yes, by the bins at the back of the club. She clapped eyes on me and we started cracking about this and that. I'd given up thinking about getting a wife. There weren't much to choose from in the valley and most of the ones I'd fancied were taken by the other lads. Oh how she talked, on and on like a bird. She laughed at me, being so clumsy around lasses an' all, but we hit it off right enough and we were good for each other.' George paused to wipe his forehead with the back of his hand.

'When I proposed to her it was on the same spot,' he went on. 'I made a right goose of myself but she said "yes" anyhow. I told her that I hadn't much to offer in the way of luxuries but I would do my best to make her happy and see to it that her family didn't want for ought. Didn't think she'd take me, me being a bit older and from away. There were plenty of other men from her sort of people, you know, townsfolk, young miners and that, but she said yes to old George! Said I was her Boaz and she was my Ruth, you know the Bible story?'

I didn't, but I was more interested in hearing more of his story, so I nodded. 'What did they make of her here?' I asked.

'Ooh, it was a rough time for the lass and no mistaking. My folks weren't best chuffed a bit at her, and the valley people can be just as snobbish as them in London when they want to. Our Joyce was a screen lass from't pit and they all thought they were a cut above her.' He paused to cut the wire with his pliers. 'Aye, but she was a princess inside, Will lad, that she was, and no mistake. A bit of a rough diamond in some of her ways—I mean, she liked a pint of beer and cracked with the lads at the Kirkstile, where she worked for a while. That was a bit unheard of for a lass, but that was just Joyce. There was no harm in her, just loved to crack with folks.' Uncle George handed me the pliers.

'In fact,' he went on, 'I would say that the church in those days was half full of folk she had got to come along from't pub. They say joy is a net of love by which you catch souls. Well her joy was such a net, lad, and no mistake. Fair packed the church, she did. And she won them all round in the end—well, most of 'em. She never complained about the way folks were to her, just accepted them and loved 'em all the same. Most of the young lads and lasses in this dale went though her Sunday school classes, including young Dicky back there, and they all loved her, bairns and parents. What she'd suffered in life had made her real with folks, and the way she talked about the Lord wasn't just talk. It was real, and folks wanted a bit of it for themselves. They'd all know where to go if they needed someone to talk to. She'd never judge, like some folk do, and she'd never gossip in a bad way about folk. That was our Joyce. What a girl.'

'Didn't you have kids of your own?' The question was out of my mouth before I'd considered whether it might be a hard one for him.

'Oh we did, Will, but the Lord took 'em to be with him before they were born. It were a hard time for her, and it fair grieved me to see her go through such a sadness. I was devastated myself at the time, but it was nothing to her being the mother and all.' He straightened up to stretch his back. 'Anyhow, after six times we decided to stop before it finished us off. Joyce got asked to do Sunday school. She was an Irish Catholic by birth but never put a lot of stock in labels and buildings. "Folks is folks and God is God, out else is folks being daft!" she'd say. Anyhow, the kids took to her right away and she did all she could for them. After thirty years, we felt like she had kids and grandkids enough for three lifetimes.' Uncle George burst out laughing. 'Aye, they spent more time round at our laal spot than their own homes, some of 'em.'

'I would say that by t'end we had a hundred times more joy than sorrow. The Lord has a way of seeing to that, Will. Like it says in the book, "if you wanna find life, you've got to giv't away". We gave up our evenings and weekends for them little 'uns and it was like the Lord give us a family. There's that saying, ain't there, that those who bring sunshine in the lives of others, cannot keep it from themselves?' He grinned and roughed my hair with his big, square hand. 'Right, lad, that's the fence done. Let's get back to the hall before we miss all the fun.'

George's kind eyes were full of tears as we walked back to the quad. 'Aye, I don't half miss her, Will lad, but I wouldn't have changed it for the world, except to keep her.'

We got the sheep into George's intake fields near what he called his 'laal cottage'. I had a look round the yard and outbuildings while George finished up. I could just imagine Aunty Joyce busying herself with farm work and her adopted generations of valley kids.

One of the barns had obviously been used for the youth club. Tattered and bleached posters hung on the walls and manky sofas sat, empty now. 'Not a bad thing to leave behind you, these memories, these people,' I said out loud as I thumbed through a photo album. Kids from the seventies and eighties at all sorts of activities always with Joyce, laughing, in the midst of them.

Uncle George called me back to the yard. It was time to walk down to the village hall. I'll go for Uncle George and make the best of it, I thought as I closed the album in the big silent barn.

THE MERRY NIGHT

George laid a hand on my shoulder at the doorway of the village hall. 'Turn around, lad, and look at that,' he said.

I turned and scanned the road and the pub and church below us. It took me a moment to realize what he was talking about. When I stopped looking for something to look at and noticed the sweep of mountains and lakes before us, the sight actually made me catch my breath. It was the most beautiful view I'd ever seen.

'Aye,' Uncle George said, 'you could travel far and wide and never see a prettier piece of God's creation.'

The village hall, on the other hand, was not quite so spectacular. The dusty floorboards, the musty smell, and the pale green crockery were all as ancient as they were familiar from every other village hall I'd ever seen. I was sure not much had changed since Granny and Grandpa's wedding reception there almost fifty years earlier.

The place was half full of people already, following Granny's orders to set out the chairs and tables. Uncle George set up some brown plastic kegs on a window ledge.

'George's famous home-brewed beer,' Granny told me as she handed me a pile of plates. 'Now don't get the wrong idea, Will—he's not a drunkard, but Joyce always encouraged him to have enough beer in case of a party and his home brew became a legend ... round here anyway.'

'What's this, little sister? Not bringing shame on us for the home brew, are you? Remember it says in Matthew's Gospel that when God came in the flesh, he came eating and drinking alcohol and it was them religious hypocrites who said, "Look at him! He's a greedy drunkard, mixing with social and religious outcasts".' He put an arm round Granny. 'Hope you're not getting religious, Elsie!'

She pushed him away. 'I'm just telling him about Joyce. Now off with you and get those slides ready.'

I looked round the room, wondering who had been in Joyce's Sunday school class when they were children. A number of farmers were fresh in from the fields too and stood in little groups, talking and laughing. Though most of the women were bustling around getting everything ready, they too were chattering and laughing and teasing.

'Awey, George, lad!' came a shout from one of the farmers. 'Is thou going to put sum a that ale in the pots for us, or just fiddle with it all night? Dick here is fair parched from't fells and might pass out at any minute, like!'

George laughed. 'He'll have to get it himself,' he said, 'as I'm to get this picture show working before the party starts.'

The farmers lost no time in gathering round and pulling a few pints for themselves.

I felt a bit of a spare part so went over to help Uncle George. He asked me to operate the projector.

Dicky brought a pint over for George just as the first slide came onto the screen. It was a black and white picture of a young woman in her teens standing with three other miners. As it came into focus, George said, 'Aye, that's our lass with her dad and uncles.'

Dicky put his hand on George's shoulder as he handed him the pint. 'Aye George,' he said, 'it were a good day for us like when you brought her here, Father says. And she were right good to us when mother passed on, don't think we would have coped without her comin' over.' George put his arm round Dicky's shoulder and blinked back the tears.

Dicky turned to me. 'And what about Will? Will he be sipping a little ale with the lads this evening?'

'Well,' George said, looking nervously toward his older sister who was organizing some large metal urns for tea, 'I suppose the lad's done a man's work, but make it a half in a mug in case Elsie sees or else I'll get it.'

I was chuffed to be included with the men. The others grinned and raised their glasses to me as I winced at the bitter taste. 'Go on Will, lad, it's not that bad!'

Grandpa and Nelson arrived, as did many others, and there was more joking and backslapping, before George called us all together for the start of what they called 'the Merry Night'.

'Aye, well, thanks for coming everyone, don't seem like a year since we were all here. Anyhows, you know I'm not one for yakking but I do want to say that this was our lass's wish, that the people she loved best would get together to have good crack once a year. If she were here now, Joyce would be telling you that some of 't best gifts God gives us is each other and she wanted you all to take a good look around each year and not forget it. If she were here now, she'd be telling you that valley folks don't know how to party like folks from Whitehaven. Well, tonight we'll give them a run for their money!'

This met with applause, and everyone raised their glasses to her memory and all the joy she had brought to the valley.

Grandpa turned down the lights and the slide show began. The first was a picture of a plaque that read:

There is a wonderful mythical law of nature
that the three things

we crave most in life
—happiness, freedom, and peace of mind—

are always attained by giving them to
someone else.

'Hear, hear!' someone said, and others echoed.

There was a roar of laughter, though, at the next slide. It was me in the bonnet! There were great shouts and more hilarity as Grandpa singled me out as the victim. I was grateful that it was dark and that I had control of the projector.

The slides filled in the details of the stories I'd heard about this lively woman. Now I could see her with George, teaching the children, bringing life and laughter to family occasions.

I don't think anyone was seeing in focus through the tears as the final slide came onto the screen.

But Aunty Joyce wanted this to be a party, a celebration, so when the band struck up everyone made their way to the floor.

I watched George slip out to the back porch to greet a dark figure standing in the doorway. I edged closer to see who it was and was surprised to recognize the man I called Mr Badger. I sidled past the Professor, who seemed to have a taste for the home brew and was merrily eyeing the Millstone sisters. But before I was safely past him he touched my arm and pointed to Mr Badger.

'Beware, William, for there is a man who lives far away from other men.'

'Oh, right,' I said.

'I believe it was Aristotle who said that anyone who is not able to live in society, or has no need to because he is sufficient of himself, must be either a beast or a god. Mark it well, young William, and keep your distance.'

I nodded, but this man intrigued me—not least because he claimed to know something more about the death of Harriet Armstrong. 'But he's talking to Uncle George,' I said.

The professor stared at the two. 'Each has his past shut in him like the leaves of a book known to him by heart and his friends can read only the title.'

'Pardon?' I said.

'That's Virginia Woolf, my boy. It's like that man, Mr Demas. As I say, beware. Do not dig out his past but be happy to only read the title, for I fear that Demas has been digging all his life. And what he has uncovered deep under those mountains was a thing best left buried.'

The Professor nodded at me, as if he had made his meaning perfectly clear, and made his way across the room to his beloved Frieda.

Titles, books, mountains and digging? I shook my head as I made my way over to where I could hear the two men talking.

'Are you sure you'll not be staying?' George was saying as he put his hand on the dishevelled man's broad shoulder.

'No, George, I don't belong at places such as this. I just wanted to pay my respects to you and Joyce, that's all. I've not forgotten all she did, and you know if there's ought I can ever do to repay you, you just have to ask.'

'Aye, Jack, I know and I will. Thanks for coming. See you at church on Sunday then,' George said as Jack turned to leave. Demas gave no answer but disappeared into the night.

As George turned to come back in he bumped into me. 'Now then, Will, what are you doing there?'

He must have realized I'd been listening, so I got straight to the point. 'Who's that man and why won't he come in?' I asked.

'What? Old Jack Demas? Well, that's a long story, lad. Why d'you want to know?'

'Just interested—he seems strange, that's all. How did he get like that? I mean, where's he from and that?'

'He came from somewhere near Glasgow, originally, to work in the mines that used to be all over here in Lorton, Borrowdale and such like. He took quite a shine to Harriet Willis, the daughter of a wealthy corn merchant from Cockermouth, but there was no real chance of him ever having her. That was where your grandfather worked after the war you know. He was thick with John, the Willis's older son. Anyhow, Jack made some daft vow that he would get rich in the mine and then win the lass, even though she was barely seventeen. I wasn't very old myself at the time, but I remember folk talking about it all right. It was the sort of nonsense that's in romance books and such, but that's what he did. He set himself up for a right fall, he did, and that's what happened, poor lad.'

'Why? What happened to him?'

'Well, Sid had also fallen for Harriet, and he persuaded the daft lass to elope with him to Gretna. They got married there without her folks knowing.'

'Ah, Harriet Armstrong,' I said. I could picture the large gravestone. 'So Willis was her maiden name, then?'

'Aye, lad, but our Sidney was only after her brass—and he got that, as well as a whole pile of misery with it. Like old Spike said on the telly, "money can't buy you friends but it can get you a better class of enemy!"' He chuckled.

'Why was he miserable?'

'Oh, Harriet was a nasty, spoilt child and she made a right fool of him. She'd been swept off her feet by this handsome, older fella, and she probably married him to spite her old man as much as anything else, but she soon tired of our Sidney. She drank all the time and had a string of posh fellas who were always round when Sid was out. As hard as our Sidney tried to fit in with the posh lot, it weren't no good. He was from a different stable to them lot and they weren't about to let him forget it. I felt a laal bit sorry for him, really. Our family was miffed with him for his carrying on, and then there was her parents, too. Well, I'd say Sid dug himself a lonely laal pit to live in.'

'Why? What did her parents do?'

'Well, Sid's a lot of things but he ain't daft, and Harriet's father saw that. He couldn't undo the marriage so he made the best out of the job and got Sid a job in his estate office. The old man hated him, mind, but what would you expect? Anyhows, poor laal Jack Demas took ill with the notion of losing the lass. I guess they'd say today that he had a nervous breakdown. He had this big thing about not being grand enough for't lass, and in his madness to be good enough for the posh folks he became a proper recluse. He kept working the lead mines to get silver long after the mining companies had stopped work there. He were right obsessed with getting rich enough to deserve her.'

'Is that the end of the story?' I asked.

'Well, Jack still lives in a mine near Force Crag, under Grisedale Pike. I'd say he would've been dead long since but for the kindness our Joyce showed him. Being from mining stock herself, and a game one for a crack, she took him food and such from time to time and eventually got him to come to church. But I'd say she was the only person he spoke to for years and years. Folk say that he's amassed quite a bit of silver and stashed it away, but I don't know aboot that. Folks who didn't go to church never saw him to look at until the day of Joyce's funeral as he'd taken to getting about by night mostly.'

'And that's why he hates Uncle Sid? Because he stole his sweetheart?'

'Well, there's that and other stuff,' George said. 'But I'm not the one who you should ask about that. Come on, let's get back to the dancing.'

The place was hopping, and as I scanned the room I realized no one was exempt. I watched Grandpa make a beeline for the Millstone sisters, who had taken up positions near the fire door. I imagined he wanted to bury the hatchet with them, and before long he had Frieda on her feet and swinging with great agility—for their age, or for any age for that matter. I shifted further back against the wall, the better to be invisible and observe.

The poor Professor, bereft of his beloved Frieda, found an easier conquest in Aunty Dora. She also moved with great grace and agility to the various tunes the quartet of musicians was banging out.

Uncle George came up beside me. 'Come lad, help out an old fella and take this young lady off my hands.' He moved aside and there was Hannah, slim in a blue silk dress, her hair in ringlets. Her cheeks were flushed and she, like George, was quite out of breath from dancing.

'Well, yeah, I'm not sure what I'm doing, really,' I stammered.

She laughed and wiped her brow. 'You and me both, but it's good fun,' she said. She gave her glasses to George. 'Could you put those somewhere safe? They keep falling off my nose every time I jump!'

She held out her hand to me. It was warm and moist, and she dragged me into the middle of the circle of dancers. They all clapped and we had to dance this sort of highland jig.

The more mistakes I made, the more she and the others laughed and, the more they laughed, the more I laughed too. Some dances just degenerated into fits of giggles on all sides. At one point, though, I had to take her by the waist and waltz her down the line and, though we were in a noisy, crowded room, it was as if we were the only two in the whole universe. She looked at me once or twice, and I wondered what she was thinking. Her eyes were dark brown with a hint of green around the edges. If she wasn't smiling or laughing, her cheeks were dimpling in a way that meant she was about to. After two dances I had to let her go as she'd already pledged one to the Professor and one to my grandfather. Aunty Dora was my next partner, and then Jane, and I thought that if my friends and even family from Liverpool could see me they wouldn't have recognized me, such was my exuberance. And I knew I owed part of that to a woman who had once knitted me a pink bonnet.

Early morning tracking with Grandpa became a part of my routine that week. Grandpa felt we were making progress, learning the beast's habits, but I often felt impatient and discouraged. In the afternoons I joined Stan on a series of excursions. My penance seemed less like punishment every day and Stan was daily becoming more sociable. He even promised to take me into Cockermouth to choose a suitable outdoor knife for my new-found hobbies. This almost compensated for the fact that he made me go out with him on Wednesday afternoon when Lewis and I had planned to follow Uncle Sid on his mysterious weekly journey.

'There's always next week,' Lewis consoled me.

On Friday evening Lewis came by after supper to ask me to go for a bike ride with him. He'd already eaten, but he had enough room for two pieces of Granny's pie.

'C'mon,' he said. 'No one's about. It'll be fun. Stop worrying about your image.'

He knew that I didn't want anyone to see me on Granny's old bike, but I could hardly say that in front of Granny.

'What are you worried about, Will dear?' Granny asked as she cleared Lewis's plate.

'Oh nothing,' I said, glaring at Lewis.

He grinned. 'Great!' he said. 'Let's go.'

No sooner were we on the road, however, than we ran into Carrie and Carl Clegg. They were coming out of a field on a tractor. They stopped and waved.

I wanted the hedge to swallow me up. I knew I'd run into them sooner or later, but I hadn't decided how I'd handle it, and I definitely wanted to be looking cool when I saw them. Not riding along on Granny's bike with a grubby little kid in tow.

Most nights I played back the conversations I'd had with Carrie in the barn and by the river that night. I couldn't get her out of my head, and I'd decided that she must like me too, but that was only half the picture. Being involved with her meant being involved with her family, and being involved with them meant having a part in their poaching plans for later that summer.

Every day I spent with Stan had helped me to better understand how hazardous their scheme would be for the fish stocks in the river. They'd also hinted to me that they had people involved who would take Stan out if he were to turn up to arrest them. I had come to respect Stan and even to like him a bit, and the thought of having any part of a criminal operation that might injure him seemed doubly damning. But I really wanted to be one of them, to be cool and accepted. That urge never seemed that strong unless I was actually with them, and I was unprepared for how I'd react to seeing them again.

'Oh hi,' I said lamely, although they couldn't hear me over the noise of the tractor. Carl turned off the engine and they both climbed down quickly, as if they'd been waiting for a moment like this since last Wednesday.

'All right, Will? We thought you'd died! Where've you been hiding for ten days?' asked Carrie.

'Yeah, we thought you'd split on us for good after the other night,' Carl said. 'Did you get away from Stan?'

'No, he caught me and took me home,' I answered him, though I was looking at Carrie for a reaction—or maybe even an admission of regret that she'd abandoned me. Neither was forthcoming.

'Did he make you talk? About us and stuff?' Carl asked. This was what had really been troubling him: had I dobbed them in?

'No, I didn't say anything but he knew it was you anyhow. But he doesn't know anything about the other stuff,' I said.

'What stuff?' asked Lewis, who wasn't really interested in the conversation but didn't like being left out.

'Mind your own business and go back to the caravan park, you scruffy git!' said Carl. He pointed his finger at Lewis.

Lewis, however, was not in the least intimidated by this oversized oaf who stood glaring down at him. 'Get lost, fatso. I was talking to my mate, not you,' said Lewis. He'd found the chink in Carl's armour almost immediately. Though Carl was strong from bodybuilding and farmwork, he also had an excess of puppy fat.

'That's it, you little rodent!' Carl said as he grabbed Lewis by his t-shirt, nearly lifting him off the ground. 'Suppose

I give you a good thrashing now while your mummy isn't around to help you.'

Lewis was helpless, and yet he seemed unafraid of the bully. 'You can't!' Lewis shouted, although I heard a slight waver in his voice that told me he was scared. He knew as well as I did that Carl was capable of doing some serious damage—and it wouldn't even trouble his conscience that he was fighting someone five years younger and half his weight.

'Oh? And why not?' Carl laughed. I could tell he sensed the growing fear in Lewis's eyes and relished the power he had over him to terrify.

'Cos Will won't let you!' he said. And he turned to look at me, full of trust and confidence.

Carl stared at me with a smirk on his face that said he knew I wouldn't interfere with Lewis's punishment. I looked at Carrie, who didn't seem to care, then back at Lewis, and finally back to Carl's amused glare.

My brain processed the strangest series of thoughts and conclusions in those few seconds. First was my natural inclination to laugh along with Carl and Carrie but then, for some reason, an image of Grandpa at Dunkirk cradling his kid brother, my Great-uncle William, flashed through my mind.

'And why won't he?' Carl's voice rose with excitement. 'I'm gonna smash my fist into your dirty little nose!'

'Because, because ... he's my fr—' Lewis spluttered as Carl raised his fist.

'Because I won't!' The authority in my voice surprised even me. I placed my hand on the arm Carl was using to grip Lewis's t-shirt. 'That's enough, he's learnt his lesson.'

Carl glared at me and I thought I might be about to get Lewis's lesson when I heard Carrie saying, 'Yeah, come on Carl, that's enough. Let's get back.'

I pried Lewis out of Carl's grip. It was like taking a bone away from a dog. Carl was fuming that his prey had been stolen in such a humiliating way and when Carrie had gone back to the tractor he whispered, 'Don't you ever cross me again like that towny or it will be you next time.' Then he turned to Lewis. 'And you—you better keep out of my way or I'll run you over.'

Lewis recovered quickly enough to grin at him as he walked back to the tractor.

As Carl walked away, Lewis let out a phoney cough with the words 'fat boy' clearly audible underneath. Carl, his back still to us, paused, but then pretended not to hear. He climbed into the cab, shut the door and kept an eye fixed on Lewis and then on me.

'Ooh, that were a bit scary, thanks for rescuing us, Will,' said Lewis with a grin. 'Look at 'im, big fat bully on his big old tractor and his big fat shaved head–'

'That's enough, Lewis! You keep your big gob shut next time and stay out of trouble,' I said. Carrie waved at me as they drove away. I think she'd been impressed, although that hadn't really been my intention.

That night I lay awake thinking about her. I tried to put out of my mind the memory of her abandoning me at the river, but it was hard. I tried to imagine her as my wife, like Uncle George and Joyce, but that was difficult too. I couldn't imagine her settling down because she seemed so untameable and independent—even though that was part of why she was so appealing.

When I talked to my mum on Saturday night I decided I'd ask her the question that I'd been afraid to ask the week before. 'How's it all going with dad and the business and stuff?'

There was a pause. 'It will be a while, Will, if this can be put right,' she said. 'I mean, you do know that don't you?'

'Sure,' I said. I did not know that. Not at all.

'You should call your dad, Will. He's having a really hard time.'

'Okay,' I said. That was the last thing I wanted to do.

After we hung up, my stomach was churning and my palms began to sweat. I'd done pretty well not thinking about all this over the last two weeks because they'd been so busy, but now here it was. My parents were on the brink of divorce and there was nothing I could do about it.

I picked up the phone again right away and then put it down. Dad's disapproval was all I needed right now. But I'd promised Mum.

I called Dad at his rented flat. He put on a brave, casual voice, but there were so many silences I knew his mind was in a hundred other places.

'Are you all right, Dad?' I finally asked.

'Well, I'm under a lot of pressure, Will. The doctor gave me some tablets to help with the stress, though.'

'That's good,' I said. 'That should help. You know, with Mum—and everything.'

I heard a long exhaling on the other end of the line, then there was another pause. 'Look, son, you might as well know that I can't see any way out right now but to sell the house. Things still aren't good with your mother and—I don't know ... I mean, I really don't know.'

'Yeah, but Dad, we'll be all right?'

'Yes, I'm sure we'll sort something out.' His voice was hollow and a thousand miles away.

We talked about footy for a bit and then said goodbye. I was in shock. By the time I got back to Liverpool, I might not even have a home to go back to, much less a mother and father in that home.

The dread of all this stalked me through the dark hours that night.

'Where are you, God?' I almost said out loud as I turned over again. I wondered what it would take, what kind of prayers I'd have to say or good deeds I could do to make everything right again. The worst part was, I really didn't think there was anything I could do. The grandfather clock in the hall struck three.

In that dark night, of course, I could have had no idea that those chimes were actually heralding one of the most important days of my life.

PART THREE

PEACE

12

FACING THE LION

Will ... Will ... oh look at you, dead to the world. Wake up, lad, the eggs are on.' Granny opened the curtains

'Ah, Granny,' I groaned, 'I've hardly slept.'

'Poor lad,' she said. 'Well, you can have a lie down after lunch. Get a dressing gown on and go down to the kitchen while it's all hot, eh?'

I groaned again and shielded my eyes with my arm. The fact that it was Sunday morning did not help. Not even Granny's breakfast or Nelson's antics at the breakfast table could lift my anxious spirits or unknot my stomach.

'I don't feel all that well, Granny,' I said. 'I really think I need to sleep.'

'Nonsense, dear. You'll feel much better once you're out in the fresh air. Church is just what you need right now. Go and get ready, for we don't want to be late.'

There was no way out. I sulked and Grandpa snorted with amusement. But I noticed that he did nothing to stick up for me.

In the end we drove down, as the clouds were dark and ominous.

'Aye, the forecast is for a wet week,' Grandpa told us.

The church was buzzing that morning. People were congratulating George on a great party Wednesday night. Everywhere I looked, people were talking and laughing and exchanging stories. I tried to catch Hannah's gaze, but she only had eyes for her music that morning. She barely resembled the girl I'd seen on the horse and at the dance. She seemed to have a special collection of really dated clothing that she saved for Sundays.

As we sang I noticed Uncle Sid stiffly twisting round to inspect the congregation. Once again he made a point of staring at me for some moments before turning away. He gave me the creeps and I wondered if Lewis and I should go through with our plan to follow him on Wednesday afternoon. Mrs Pardshaw was there in black, stiff and unsmiling as the rest of the congregation belted out the words to the hymn. A draught of cold air behind me signalled the late arrival of my Mr Badger, Jack Demas. For the first time I noticed that the place where he sat was as far as he could physically get from Uncle Sid.

I tried to imagine both men as young but couldn't. It seemed to me they must have been born old and disappointed. I decided I'd ask Granny to let me see some pictures of Sid and the others when they were young. Since I had a dull, wet week ahead I could pass the time doing some detective work and be ready for the big day on Wednesday.

During the third song I tried to focus on the service, and that was when a strange thing happened to me. The more I sang and thought about the words and what they meant, the calmer my stomach felt. For the first time since my phone call with Dad the night before, I felt a bit of peace, a little hope. I was trying to rationalize this when the music stopped and the vicar addressed the congregation.

'Well everyone,' he said, 'I'll tell ye this: if the people in the Western world would hear what I'm about to offer free to ye this morning, then there would not be enough church buildings in the world to service the crowds. I'm serious now—what I'm about to offer free is so much in demand that it's become a multi-billion pound industry. Sadly, even in churches, even this one, mibbe only a quarter of the people will take what I'm about to offer ye.'

I saw Mrs Pardshaw look up. She's probably as curious as I am, I thought.

'So what's the great need? It's all about peace of mind.'

Okay, I thought. Now here's something useful.

'I read recently in a survey,' the vicar continued, 'that eighty-five percent of doctors' patients come with stress-related complaints. I'm not knocking medication as such, mind you, but young King David on the run and Peter, fast asleep the night before his execution, had something better.'

There was a murmur of recognition through the crowd.

'Tell me,' he said, 'if ye put the ten-year-old lad of an airline pilot in charge of a Boeing 747 in mid-flight over London and left him alone, how would he feel?' He paused while everyone drew their own conclusions. 'Aye, pretty anxious I would say! And do ye think he'd feel any better if ye put Classic FM, playing some soothing music, on the radio?' The vicar paused as a few chuckles rippled through the congregation. 'Nae?' the vicar said. 'Well, what about a relaxing massage to his neck and shoulders to help the wee lad with his jitters?'

'Course not!' Like a pantomime audience the congregation began to call out, gradually gaining confidence.

'Nae, of course he'd consider ye bonkers. What about some aromatherapy oils to ease his state of mind?'

'Of course not!'

"Mibbe a doctor could prescribe some medication to take away the sweaty palms and butterflies? Ye may think him a little young, but some doctors might even want the wee lad to chill out with some marijuana.'

'No!'

"Well then, how about a special lucky charm guaranteed to bring safety to any traveller who wears it?'

'Of course not!'

'Better still, a self-help guru might empower him to view his current position in a more positive light?'

'Aye,' the vicar said. 'You may laugh, but that's the kind of stuff ye're offered every day to help ye cope with stress. And oor situation is far more acute than that of the lad in the aeroplane. I'll tell ye what *will* reassure him: to get his dad back in the cockpit and behind those controls. *He'll not be happy until he's got his dadie back there!* And the same is true for us. We're hurtling through our stress-filled lives toward death at an unstoppable rate with no one to drive for us. We need oor Father back. Let's turn to the Bible, shall we?'

He read from Philippians 4:7 and 9. 'Aye, Paul's been in more scrapes than I have, and if he found something to give him peace of mind then I want a bit of what he's got. Listen to this: "And the peace of God, which passeth all understanding, shall keep your hearts and minds through Christ Jesus ... Those things, which you have both learned, and received, and heard, and seen in me, do: and the God of peace shall be with you."'

He let it all sink in while he took a swig of water, keeping his eyes fixed on us the whole time. 'Aye, so what did Paul do? I'll tell ye. He entrusted the driver's seat of his life to Jesus Christ, that's what. I guarantee that if ye do that too, ye'll have peace. Jesus says, "my peace I give unto you: not as the world giveth, give I unto you. Let not your heart be troubled, neither let it be afraid." Ye'll not be getting this type of peace of mind anywhere else.'

Sure, I thought, there's a logic of sorts here, but to give control to an invisible God or Jesus seems so weird, so out there. But he was right about the alternative stress busters. Most of them didn't really work.

The vicar continued. 'Jesus says, "Not as the world gives." This means that there is a peace on offer from the world, but his is different. Jesus says that yer hearts will no longer be afraid when ye've got him, and that's really what I'm coming to. "He is our peace", as it says in another verse. I think it was Jimi Hendrix who said, "When the power of love overcomes the love of power the world will know peace" ... exactly what happened when Jesus died on the cross!'

The vicar paused for a moment before he finished. 'Take Jesus at his word,' he said. 'Ask for his help. I'll be available after the service to talk and pray with people who've never done this before if ye like.'

The rest of the service went by in a blur. All of the problems in my family—from my brother in jail to me fighting with my sister to my dad's business and my parent's divorce—went through my mind. I couldn't solve any of them on my own, not even fighting with Louise. No essential oil would help with any of it. And a lucky charm would never help track and find the beast or solve my dilemma about Carrie or the Cleggs—or anything else. What the vicar had been saying made sense to me. And if Jesus was alive and was the solution to all my problems, known and unknown, what was I to do? I'd never made any decision about what I believed or didn't believe. But I saw now that not making a decision was itself a decision. Finally my need for help outweighed my other shallow arguments, and I decided I needed to meet and talk to this fiery man of God when the service was over.

And, before I knew it, the time had come. Instead of going to the church door the vicar took up a seat near the altar, in plain view of the milling congregation who watched him nervously. I'd expected to wait at the end of a long line of people whose hearts and consciences had been similarly pricked, but there was no one else. It could have been my own nervousness, but it seemed to me that people were watching this enormous man out of the corners of their eyes as he scanned them beating a hasty retreat to the back of the church. The rain was coming down hard and most people lingered there at the back, making conversation and hoping it would pass. Granny was talking to Andrew and Jane, and Dora had gone over with a copy of *Mere Christianity* to talk to Mrs Pardshaw.

I was on my own in the pew, well churned up inside.

When I stood up, I didn't feel all eyes upon me or hear the twittering and hushed voices from the back grow more excited. For that moment, they weren't there. Carrie's face came to my mind. It was disapproving, but I kept going and she disappeared. It was just me—with all my history, my short bursts of brilliance, my problems and my rubbish. I carried them all with me up the aisle to the altar. Richard and Hannah were putting away their music and stopped abruptly when they saw me approaching. I didn't see their faces. I looked straight into their dad's eyes.

I became afraid. I felt naked, I felt dirty before a Holy God. I felt it wouldn't be safe to go on. A line from a book Dad read to me when I was nine, *The Lion, the Witch and the Wardrobe*, popped into my head. The girl Lucy had asked Mr Beaver if the lion Aslan was safe, and Mr Beaver had said that, of course, he isn't safe. He is *good*. He is the *King*.

And so I walked through my fear and, as I did, an unexpected thing happened. Those eyes that had held such terror for me began to fill with tears of joy. The giant got up and walked towards me, and then I was aware that everyone at the back had gone quiet. While the valley looked on, the very man whom I'd avoided meeting, came and placed his huge hands upon my shoulders. His eyes were streaming now. It all made perfect sense to me at that moment, though I couldn't have explained it in words.

'I'm Will Houston,' I said. 'I need God too—'

'Aye lad, I know ye do. Welcome home.' He smiled. 'He's been waiting for a fair wee time.'

He led me over to the side where we sat down and he talked more about what it meant to be a Christian. 'Ye bring yer sin, laddie. His Father will adopt ye as his own, and ye'll become a subject of another kingdom.'

By the time he had finished, I was ready. I knelt down and he led me through what he called the sinner's prayer. It was a simple prayer but an unbelievable experience to speak these powerful words of confession and trust.

The vicar gave me a bear hug and then stood to face the rest of the congregation who were still watching but pretending not to. 'Aye,' he said, 'and there's more joy in heaven over one sinner who repents than over ninety-nine who don't need to.'

I felt weird—lighter somehow, like I'd been scrubbed raw, and vulnerable. I had tears in my eyes, which I wiped away.

'I think ye've met ma Hannah,' the vicar said. 'And this is ma lad, Richard.'

Hannah, who seemed quite emotional, gave me a hug. 'Oh, I'm so pleased for you,' she said.

'Yeah, well I wonder whether Jesus could help me with my dancing,' I said with a grin.

'Oh,' Richard said, 'you're a follower of Jesus for thirty seconds and you already believe in miracles!'

We all laughed and Richard shook my hand. He chatted for a bit and I was surprised to find that he was okay, and not at all like I had imagined him to be. He was confident and quite grown up, but not in a bad or boring way.

'We should meet up this week and do something,' he said.

'That'd be great,' I said. 'I'll give you a call when this rain stops.'

The heavy rain had turned into a light drizzle, and people were filing out into the churchyard. I saw Uncle Sid skulking away but didn't trouble myself to follow him. Wednesday would come soon enough.

I'm not sure it would have been possible to follow him anyway, with all the well wishers who thronged about me. Granny and Aunty Dora both had eyes shining with tears, glowing smiles and warm hugs.

Uncle George gave me such a handshake that I thought there would be nothing left of my hand when he let go. 'Well done, Will lad, I'm glad to see you've got a good head on those shoulders.'

After Andrew, Jane and several others had also spoken to me, the vicar's wife came over.

Jan was a warm, elegant woman with blue eyes the colour of the Mediterranean that rested on me as if I were the only person of importance in the world. Her calm manner and kindness reminded me of Aunty Dora. 'Well, William Houston, you've made quite a stir and I am glad to meet you at last. I hope your Granny will let you come to visit Richard and Hannah this summer. There aren't many young people their age and I think you'll get along famously—especially after this morning. What a great morning!'

'Thank you,' I said. 'I'd like that. Richard and I talked about going fishing this week.'

'Oh, I'm pleased,' she said. 'We'll see you soon, Will.'

I noticed as we left through the gate that many people were still staring at me—almost as if I had done something out of the ordinary.

I didn't know much at that point, but I did know that in a sense they were correct. I had come face to face with God that morning—and that was far from ordinary. I didn't know exactly how everything else would work out, but I knew that somehow it would. I knew I'd made the most important decision of my life, and everything else was detail.

But as the saying goes, 'the devil is in the detail'. And so it was, as that week would show. I had come face to face with God that Sunday but would face down the devils of hell before the week was out.

13

HOW ARE THE MIGHTY FALLEN

Come on, Will, there's no such thing as bad weather—only inappropriate clothing! My, when I was your age a bit of rain was nothing!' Grandpa was not at all interested in my feeble excuses.

Granny came to my aid. 'Reggie, leave the lad alone. It's bucketing down. Take Nelson out later.'

Grandpa shook his head and sighed and he and Nelson headed outside without me.

Granny and I sat by the fire for a morning coffee while Grandpa was out. She was easy to talk to—not like most adults. After what had happened at church the day before there was so much I wanted to say, and even more I wanted to find out.

'I guess I do know I've done the right thing. But, I mean, there are so many things that I can't change in my life. But yesterday I saw I could do that, I mean, stand up and that. I think it was the first time I made any link between me going my own way, doing my own thing, and Jesus Christ nailed to that cross. You know, I hadn't really seen that I was part of the problem. I don't know—it's so weird, and it sort of feels like someone else is speaking.'

Granny smiled and put her mug down. 'The Bible says you're a new creation in Christ, Will. You're still you, of course, but transformed on the inside. How do you feel generally? Did you sleep better last night?'

'Well, yeah, I guess a bit better. But my head's been buzzing with all this stuff. It's like there's something new in me, something alive, like you say. I don't know exactly how to describe it, but I do know I'm not so churned up about the future. I mean, I still think about it but the butterflies aren't there anymore.'

Granny nodded. 'Dad's flying the plane?'

I smiled. 'Yeah, that's it, I guess.'

'Here, Will, I found this Bible last night. It was given to your mum when she was about your age, in Sunday school. I'm sure the vicar will talk with you more about it, but Christians need to know and read God's Word. It gives us strength and peace, brings us closer to God.'

'Thanks, Granny,' I said. I flipped through the Bible and read mum's name in the front. It was a bit yellowed with age but obviously hadn't been read much. I wondered how I'd describe what happened yesterday to my parents. 'Do I just start here at page one of Genesis?' I asked Granny.

She smiled. 'Well, you could. But I think when you're just starting to learn what it means to follow Jesus it's good to start with a Gospel. There are four Gospels in the New Testament. All of them tell the story of Jesus from a slightly different perspective. I think I might start with Luke's Gospel if I were you. It's easy to follow, and though you'll recognize some of the stories about Jesus it's quite another experience to read through a whole Gospel as a new follower.'

'Well that's a wild day!' Grandpa came in through the door, drenched to the skin. Nelson, after shaking himself off in Granny's kitchen, looked very chirpy.

'There's only inappropriate clothing, dear,' Granny said with a wink as Grandpa slunk upstairs to change.

Soaked through as Grandpa was, he seemed barely moistened compared to our next visitor. Just after lunch there was a knock at the back door and a very wet and hungry Lewis plonked himself down by the Aga. Granny fussed around him with a towel as he eyed the remains of our lunch with that orphan look I recognized from the day I first met him.

'It's no use,' Granny said. 'The poor lad's soaked to the skin. Go upstairs with Will, Lewis. And Will, you get him something of yours to wear for now.' He grinned and scampered upstairs, where he chose what had been my best tracksuit. I didn't mind. Over the last few weeks I'd changed my mind about nylon. My encounter with the bramble bush by the river that night with the Cleggs hadn't helped, but I also realized I didn't want to be thought of as a city boy.

'Hey, you haven't forgotten about Wednesday, have you?' Lewis asked as he went through my stuff.

I looked out of the window at the fierce clouds over the crags opposite. 'No way,' I said, 'we'll find out what that fox is up to but we'll have to be ready and you can't be late!'

'Okay you two,' Granny called up the stairs. 'I've got a treat by the fire when you're ready.'

Lewis was even more pleased with himself than usual, stretched out in front of the sitting room fire, cocoa and cakes in hand.

Granny started her pile of ironing. 'Now I wonder how I can keep you out of trouble this afternoon?' she asked.

I knew exactly what we could do. 'I'm sure Lewis would be very interested in the family pictures you said you had— and so would I,' I said.

Granny raised an eyebrow at me before putting down the iron and going over to her dresser. She brought out a scrapbook and an old chocolate box stuffed with letters and photos.

'This,' she announced, 'is my family. It may look a bit of a jumble but you'll have to be very careful with these photos. They're precious. The ones in the box are mainly Grandpa's things. He was never one for putting stuff in albums, but there's lots in there to see.' She put them down on the coffee table and I wiped the crumbs from my hands and picked up the album.

'Thanks, Granny,' I said.

There were pages and pages of family picnics.

'Aye, no one in the valley ever went on foreign holidays in those days,' Granny explained, 'but we did know how to have a good time. Mother would pack us up a picnic and we'd go off for the day. Mind you, days off were rare. Sundays were always a great day for gallivanting, though. After church, my father would hitch up a team of horses and put us on the back of the hay wagon and take us off all over the place. We'd go swimming at Crummock, fishing in Loweswater and rambling on the fells above Borrowdale. They were grand days.'

'What about this one?' I held up a picture of a tall, handsome young man standing in a quarry.

'Oh that's our Sidney, at Strathbrow Quarry where he worked during the war,' Granny said as she started on one of my shirts.

'But didn't Uncle Sid go off to the war to fight?' I thought of the picture of Grandpa and his brother William, looking so young in their uniforms I'd assumed all young men their age had gone to war.

'Oh no, not Sidney,' Granny said. 'He could have done, but he got a job there in the quarry so he didn't have to go, it being a reserved occupation and all.'

'What's a reserved occupation?' I asked.

'Well certain jobs which couldn't be done by't lasses still had to be done during the war, and quarrying was one of them.'

I knew Granny well enough by now to detect the defensiveness in her tone and I wanted to find out what was behind it. 'Did he work there so he wouldn't have to go and fight?'

Granny put the iron down and looked out the window at the rain. 'Aye, maybe, but sometimes I wish he had gone for all the trouble he caused over those years. I mean, I'd never wish him dead, but he let himself down badly in those years—and us, too—the family, I mean. The war might have knocked a bit of sense into him before he made such a mess.'

Lewis nipped out to the toilet and I thought maybe she'd tell me more while he wasn't there. I knew about Sid and Harriet, but there had to be a lot more to his fall from grace than eloping with a posh girl. 'Why? What'd he do? Uncle George told me a bit about Harriet and that ...'

'Oh, that was the least of it,' Granny said. She pressed the iron firmly onto a shirt collar. 'Did he tell you how Sid used Harriet's father's money to swindle all the poor folks' farms off them in the valley? Our family name was mud in those days. People have long memories in these parts, and all the while Sidney grew fat off other folks' hard work.' She looked out of the window again, across the valley, before she continued quietly. 'But that weren't it, not the worst of it anyway, though it were bad enough for one lifetime. No, that were not the worst of it, lad.'

She came over and shuffled through the pictures until she found the one she'd shown me before of herself, Dora and Ellen, in their late teens, baling hay. Ellen was, as we'd say at school, 'a real babe'. It hadn't registered before, though, that there was also a toddler in the photo with them.

'Who's the toddler?' I asked.

Granny looked up and smiled. 'It's her baby brother, poor mite.'

I looked at Ellen's face again. Her hair was short and curly and her smile brimming with a mixture of innocence and independence. It was hard not to like her—even in black and white.

'Poor Ellie Patterson,' Granny continued. She shook her head. 'I think I told you she was my best friend, and a sweeter, more fun-loving girl was not found in this whole valley—until my brother came along.' She went back to her iron and attacked a pair of trousers with short, stabbing movements.

'Why?' I asked. 'What did Uncle Sid do to her?'

'He took a fancy to her and, like everything he's ever touched, he ruined her. Dora and I were the only ones who knew. She fell pregnant to him, which was bad enough in those days, but by the time we found out about the pregnancy he'd lost interest in her and was going after Harriet. Poor Ellen. She died in childbirth on the same day Sid took Harriet to Gretna.' Granny's voice caught, and I looked up from the photo to see her take off her glasses and rub her eyes. 'So you see, Will, why we barely speak after all these years. It was a terrible thing.'

'I saw him by her grave,' I said. 'I think he wants everyone to think he's visiting his wife, but I saw him put a flower on Ellen's grave. He didn't see me, though,' I said. I was proud of my discovery and thought somehow this information might be useful to Granny, but she was sombre about the revelation.

'Well, I should hope he's feeling a bit guilty about it, but there's nothing he can do to change what he did. Ellen's gone, and no amount of pining will bring her back. He brought misery to both women. He's had a fair bit of misery himself, but that would be no less than he deserves for what he did.'

I'd never heard Granny speak so harshly. I heard Lewis's footsteps. 'Did the baby survive?' I asked.

'No, dear,' Granny answered. 'She didn't, and Ellen's parents moved away that summer after the funeral.'

The rain had stopped, at least for the moment, and Lewis was anxious to go out. We started down the lane and saw Aunty Dora on the far side of Ramthwaite Village, on her way up from Lorton to see us. An almighty shower started as we greeted her. Lewis said he could get back dry if he pedalled quickly enough. So he sped off, although he must have been soaked through for the second time that day before he got a few hundred metres. Dora and I took shelter under the bough of a large oak tree, which protected us from the worst of it.

I told her what Granny had said about Ellen and about how cross Granny had been. She nodded. 'Ah, well you see, William, it was doubly hard for her because Ellen made your Gran promise not to tell Sidney that she was pregnant.'

'So Sid never even knew?' I was flabbergasted. 'But why not tell him? I don't understand.'

'Well, of course she didn't know that she would die in childbirth, although it wasn't an easy pregnancy. Ellen didn't want a man who would only want her out of duty for her child. I'm sure she would have told him once he'd made up his mind about which woman he wanted, but that day never came. Ellen was proud that way, and I can't say I blamed her for it. We all want to be loved for who we are. She wouldn't beg him to come to her and quite frankly, after the way Sid behaved eloping with Harriet, I think she would have been better off without him.'

'Oh that's rough—I mean, that's really sad.'

'Yes it was, and your poor Gran took it especially hard. She had to tell Sid after the funeral, and I don't think she's ever really forgiven him or herself—though why she blames herself I don't know. Maybe she felt she could have done more to stop Ellen from falling for him. I mean, she of all people knew what Sid was like. Sidney may look respectable enough now, but I quite feared what he could have done as a young man. He was their father's favourite child you know, and spoiled. He was so much brighter than George and Elsie and they hoped he would make something of himself. But he was bent on his own pleasures, and what a time he had—down the pubs and dance halls of Workington and Cockermouth. That was when the do with our Will's medal happened but-' She stopped suddenly, as if she'd said something she should not have.

I'd heard fragments about the disappearing medal and wanted to hear the whole story. 'Please, Aunty Dora,' I said, 'tell me the rest. I really want to know what happened that night.'

Aunty Dora looked at me for a long moment before answering. 'Now look, Will, you must never mention this in front of your grandfather. It all happened a long time ago, but it's still a bit hush hush, understand?'

'I won't mention it,' I promised.

'Well,' she began, 'when our Will died in your grandpa's arms all those years ago at Dunkirk, something died inside him, too. Having to leave his body there to be run over by tanks and not getting him home to our mother hurt him so deeply that he could barely speak about it for years. The Victoria Cross and his dress uniform were the only things he had left of his little brother, and he brought them north with him when he came to look after me. We both stayed with Elsie's family for a few weeks while we got a place of our own sorted out. And one night during that time Sid stole the uniform to go out on the town in Whitehaven.'

'Oh, no,' I said. 'How could he do such a thing? He didn't take the medal as well, did he?'

'Yes he did, though no one knew it. That night he got in a brawl outside the Empire dance hall with some sailors and the medal got lost, ripped off the ribbon. He came home the next morning in a drunken stupor wearing the torn and soiled uniform with the pin end but nothing else. He didn't even know he was missing it.'

'How did you all find out?'

'We were still in bed when the revellers came down the lane. There were five of them, singing at the top of their lungs. Reggie was already up milking the cows and went out to see what the noise was about. There was Sid, wearing our Will's uniform. Reggie was fuming about Sid's lack of shame over it, but it wasn't him that started the fighting. Sid and his mates started it. They were all pretty tough farm lads but Reggie sorted them out, all of them, and good riddance to them.'

'It was only when he stripped Sid's unconscious body of the uniform that he noticed the medal was missing. And, well ... that was it,' Aunty Dora said. She shook her head.

'Why? What happened?'

'Well, we didn't see him for a week,' she said.

'Where did he go?'

'I never knew. I was going out to shut up the chickens one wet night and there he was, soaking wet. He hadn't washed or shaved or eaten. He sank to his knees and opened his hand and let the pin and ribbon from the medal fall to the ground. He said he was sorry for taking off and that he would never leave me alone the way he'd left poor William in France. Oh, he was in a bad way.'

'But he did get better, right?'

'Oh, with a lot of love he came round after a time. Elsie's mum was a wonder and Elsie, who was about seventeen then, had her own way of perking him up.'

'I can't imagine what he went through,' I said. 'What happened to Sid?'

'Kept a low profile. He'd already moved away from the farm and his father forbade him to visit for a while until things settled down. We had the uniform washed and somehow Sid came into possession of what was left of the ribbon and pin. The sorry business with Ellen and Harriet happened a year later, so you see it's quite a story.'

'What really happened to Harriet, Aunty Dora? I mean, not what the gossips say ... what *really* happened?'

'Oh, none of us knows more than the gossip. We weren't talking a great deal to Sid by then and he's the only one who will ever really know. I know he suffered at Harriet's hands—she was a nasty girl, always was and made a right fool of him with her lovers, but whether she pushed Sid so far that he staged her suicide ... who can say? I can't.'

She folded her arms, shivered and squinted up at the clouds. There seemed to be no break in the rain. 'You'd think it would take an extraordinary type of person to take another's life, but then again maybe anyone can—given enough incentive. Harriet's death certainly made Sid a richer man, but that's proof of nothing. There was no witness, so no one can say. Mind you, no one crossed Sidney after that! And every time something dark or unexplainable happened in the valley, folk would lock their doors and tell naughty children that Sidney Armstrong was out and about and might come to get them if they weren't good. People are forever gossiping. Some say that he stalks the river in tramp's clothes, though I would say that's just folk being a bit daft. Look, Will, the rain's letting up finally. Let's head up to the farm and have a nice cup of tea.'

We walked up the lane, back through Ramthwaite. I held my peace about what I knew. He did stalk the valley in trampish clothes and I would, with the help of my faithful companion Lewis, solve the riddle of these weekly outings. I was sure it had something to do with his wife's mysterious death. There was no way, it seemed, to solve the murder mystery. Aunty Dora had hit the nail on the head—there was no witness, so there could be no further investigation. What did Morse or Sherlock Holmes do when their investigations ran into a dead end? Without Sherlock's pipe or Morse's penchant for ale I mulled it over with a cup of tea.

With photos of their younger selves in the book on my lap, I watched Granny and Aunty Dora talking and laughing together. I'd heard my mum say that to know someone is to love them, and I felt like I was beginning to love these women even more now I knew them better. Older people were definitely not dull, grey or irrelevant after all. When I'd arrived even a few weeks ago I would have been ready to reject their wisdom just because they didn't know anything about mobile phones or the internet. That *is* crazy!

I saw the story of the summer of 1947 through photos of Granny and Grandpa. He was a powerfully built man, and he was determined looking even then. Little Elsie was not so little anymore and had grown into a beautiful young woman while he was away fighting in Burma. How must it have felt to come back to this young woman who loved him after having seen and endured so much at war? And Granny—it was a remarkable love that she had had for her Reggie since girlhood. I thought their romance would make a good film.

That night I tossed and turned with nightmares. Uncle Sid was stalking me along the banks of the river and the farm had disappeared, leaving me nowhere to run to. I kept hearing Aunty Dora's words, 'But there were no witnesses, so we'll never really know' ... 'No witnesses', 'No witnesses', 'No witnesses' ... over and over again. Around three o'clock, though, I awoke with a startling thought: there was one man who claimed to be a witness—old Jack Demas, who lived at the mine. That first Sunday at church he'd said something about people in the valley not wanting to open their eyes but that it was all there under the surface and it was not pretty. Surely that meant he saw something or knew something.

I decided to get Lewis to visit the mine with me. Maybe we could get some information before Wednesday. I hardly slept after that, as my mind churned with a mixture of dread and excitement. At five o'clock the cockerel ushered in the day when I would learn that there was more than one kind of beast in the valley.

14

DANGER AT THE MINES

Come on, Lewis, pick up, pick up, I thought as the phone rang and rang. When he finally answered, I could barely hear him over the cartoon music in the background.

'Lewis? Lewis, it's me ... Yes, I know it's early ... What? No, I don't watch *Looney Tunes*. Look, get up here as quick as you can—there's something we've got to do before tomorrow ... What? Yes, now. Lewis, it's dangerous.'

The 'D' word worked like a charm. He turned off the TV and was at Granny's door within the hour.

'Forty-eight minutes from door to door,' he said, grinning and out of breath. 'Impressed?'

Mouth full of cereal, I nodded.

'Am I in time for breakfast?' Lewis sat down at his place at the table and Granny obliged.

I never knew how Nelson would choose to spend his day—sometimes with Grandpa, sometimes with me, and very occasionally Granny would be favoured with his presence. He usually looked earnestly at me as I approached the door. And he wasn't necessarily in it just for the food. He seemed to have a special sixth sense that detected the potential for adventure, trouble and even a fight if he was lucky. That morning, just as Lewis and I were about to close the door behind us, Nelson leapt from the couch and ambled towards the door. The look on his face said, 'All right, if I must ... but there'd better be some action.'

The sky was grey and ominous and a bruising wind fought us as we cycled off towards the mine, Nelson trotting by our wheels. Lewis was up for the adventure but it was like a TV cop show for him, while it was personal and up close for me.

'Ooh, dead creepy, like the "terrible two" adventure at smuggler's mine!' he said when I told him about our mission.

Although I never would have told him so, I was glad to have Lewis with me. He was funny without realizing it and our days together had been good fun.

Only as we cycled the lanes with Nelson gaily trotting by our wheels did the seriousness of our mission begin to sink in. Uncle George had pointed out where Demas lived—high above the valley in the shacks outside the lead mine. We could only take the bikes so far, for there was no track from the Buttermere Valley to the mine. I was showing Lewis the map when we heard a rustling in the bushes nearby. We froze. When the Professor appeared we both let out sighs of relief.

'Ah, young William and Master Lewis! Where are you bound on this dismal day?' he asked with a grin. He was clutching a bouquet of harebells.

'We're just going to ... to ... to see someone,' I said. The old man seemed nice and harmless enough, but after all I'd been learning recently about the web of mysteries in the valley I decided I didn't know enough about him to be certain he was trustworthy.

But my caution was unnecessary, because he'd overheard our conversation. Looking up towards our destination he said, 'Ah yes, I see ... Mr Demas.' He scratched his beard. 'What did Conrad say? "His soul was mad. Being alone in the wilderness, it had looked within itself and, by heavens I tell you, it had gone mad!" Poor fellow.'

'I don't know if he's mad, Professor,' I said with a sideways glance at Lewis. 'Uncle George thinks he's okayish, says he just finds it hard around people.'

The Professor looked past me and then he smiled. 'Ah yes, I knew it, of course! The Bible. "For Demas hath forsaken me, having loved this present world." Very apt indeed. But an enigma indeed for a man who once loved worldliness to be living with the gods on Mount Olympia herself.'

I nodded vacantly as he pottered off.

Lewis gave a muffled snigger. 'Weeeeeeeeeeeeeirdo!'

After we hid our bikes in the bushes and continued on foot I began to feel uneasy but said nothing to Lewis. Nelson was urging us on, running ahead and circling back. This, according to Nelson, was exactly what life was about. Perhaps he imagined a hundred fearsome bulldogs awaiting conquest over the next brow. For Lewis danger was the stuff of comics and cartoons and not something to be wary of. He soldiered on as he started on his lunch and began to leave me well behind. Pretty soon the valley became the mountain, trees gave way to gorse, gorse gave way to bracken and then bracken gave way to heather. Up and up we went as the mists swirled and disappeared and the valley below became a cosy patchwork of fields and woods.

At a lunch stop halfway I had to contend with two sets of forlorn eyes peering into my lunch box. Lewis, his own lunch long gone, was keen to help me out. Nelson seemed to assume that we were in equal partnership in all things—danger, adventure and provisions. The dog had inherited a militaristic view of things. He stood to, alert to danger as he gave the odd glance back towards me to see whether I had finished unwrapping my sandwiches. A fellow comrade in arms would not hesitate to give his lunch, or even his life, for him. When the food was ready, Nelson looked over at Lewis to let him know it was his turn to take watch. He then positioned himself next to the grub, having a good look over it to see what he would like to share with me first. In the fact of such strong expectations I had to give in. I'd never had a dog before, and in the vacuum of uncertainty about what I should give him and how much the little chap did rather better than Lewis and considerably better than I did—with my own lunch!

Though we walked through mists and strong winds we could see the mines clearly. Giant spoil heaps spilled down the hillside at various intervals. The scale of them made me feel very small indeed, though Lewis was in his element.

'Cool,' he said, 'the mines of Moria from *The Lord of the Rings!* D'ya reckon there'll be any goblins in there, Will?'

'Don't be a spoon, Lewis. This is serious business. Let's find where the mine buildings are and do what we came for.' As soon as the words were out I felt sorry for snapping at him. I hadn't realized just how tense I was—nor had I realized until that moment that one slip-up here could be the end of us. And it wasn't just the Professor's warning about Demas that was bothering me. The loose mounds of slate everywhere looked sufficiently dangerous.

After a twenty-minute scramble we found what we were looking for, though from this nest-like position far above the valley I could see why we hadn't seen the buildings earlier. From directly underneath, the sheer gradient of the spoil heaps hid the cluster of red brick buildings. But, once we were on top, we were gob-smacked by the commanding view of the valley. I imagined you'd be able to see for miles on a clear day.

'Cool,' Lewis said. 'I bet this is what it looks like to God, seeing all those tiny cars moving on the little roads next to the lakes with a teaspoon of water in them.'

If the view was grand, the buildings were just the opposite—derelict, with broken windows and shattered corrugated asbestos roofing. One or two shacks further up the slope looked to be still intact, so we continued on up the windy mountainside.

When we arrived on the crow's nest plateau we came to a small stone building half covered at the rear by slate spoil from workings further up the slope. A dirty rag of a curtain hung in a window and an old tin pan of water sat by the door. It was obviously occupied, but there was no sign of Mr Demas. Before I could object, Lewis and Nelson marched straight to the heavy wooden door and knocked. There was no answer. Lewis lifted the latch and, to our surprise, it opened. We went in. I noticed a large key in the lock on the inside of the door. I thought it was strange that he would go out without locking up.

'Do you think he really lives here?' I asked Lewis in a half-whisper. 'Look at this place. It's like going back in time—except for that.' I pointed to a small paraffin Primus stove on a slate ledge by the window.

'Yeah,' Lewis said. 'Creepy. D'you think he has any biscuits?'

I groaned. 'Lewis, stop it. You can eat when we get home.' I kneeled beside the fireplace. The ashes were still warm. 'What do you think he burns in this? There aren't any trees for miles.'

'There's the wood pile,' Lewis said. He pointed to some large chunks of timber off to the side.

'Lewis, those are pit props from the mine that he's chopped up for firewood. They used them to hold up the roofs of tunnels. Do you think he's been taking them out all these years? The tunnels would collapse without them—they'd be deadly!'

Lewis was more interested in trying to find the switch for an oil lamp. 'It's so dark in here!' he said. 'But this one doesn't work.'

'It's an old oil lamp, Lewis. You light it, you don't turn it on. How do you think he'd get electricity all the way up here?'

Lewis looked around. 'There's no telly, either!' He shook his head in amazement. 'Is that where he sleeps?' He pointed to a cast-iron frame in the corner with springs and a thin horsehair mattress covered with dark grey blankets.

'I suppose so.' I shrugged. The crockery was chipped tin enamel and there was a rocking chair by the fire. That was all, except for the great number of books lining the shelves. Quite a few of them were historical romances. The story of Jack's love for Harriet Armstrong and his nervous breakdown after Uncle Sid eloped with her would probably make a great novel. There was also poetry by Wordsworth, Coleridge, Shelly, Keats, Southey and volumes of Shakespeare. There were philosophy and history books as well. I imagined him up here on a cold winter night, reading to escape from his desolate existence.

The slate flag floor led through to a dark pantry at the back, where we discovered that this was no ordinary mine cottage. As our eyes became accustomed to the dark we saw lamps, shovels and picks as well as wooden mining props as big as railway sleepers. These props weren't chopped up and drying out for firewood—they were actually propping up a doorway that led into the mountain itself.

'Mines of Moria indeed,' I whispered as I peered through the rag-curtained doorway into the pitch-blackness of the shaft. I dropped the curtain and started back towards the main room but Nelson stayed by the dark entrance sniffing. He whined and looked up at me. He had smelt something and wanted me to investigate but I wasn't interested. I'd always been afraid of the dark, and that was just in my bedroom.

'No, Nelson,' I said. 'There's no way I'm going to lose myself inside a mountain on the whim of a dog.' 'Ooooooh, oooooooh!' Lewis made ghostly noises near the curtain as I retreated.

'Shut up Lewis. C'mon, he's obviously not here, let's look round outside.'

But as he went on moaning and whooping in ghostly fashion I thought I heard another sound. Lewis stopped, his eyes wide. 'Did you hear that? It's the ... that ... flippin' Balrog monster come to get us!' he whispered.

Nelson cocked his good ear to the black passageway and whined loudly. He looked up at me, an appeal to lead the troops forward. 'This is the way to the action you promised me,' I could almost hear him saying.

I turned to leave, but I hesitated. There was a niggling thought in my mind. Was the sound I had heard something like the word 'Help'? My palms were sweating and my legs were shaking.

'Lewis,' I said, 'Nelson's right. We have to investigate. Let's strike up some lamps and have a look.'

And, as I made the decision, a strange thing happened to me. I felt an incredible sense of purpose and peace. It wasn't that my fear was gone, but I knew I wouldn't face this dark chasm alone. I knew that I was destined for certain journeys in life, and this was one of them. A phrase echoed in my head, 'I will never leave you nor forsake you.' Not until some time later did I read these words in the Bible for myself.

Having said that I'd never felt so out of my depth as I did when I entered that mine. On and on we went, down narrow passageways that led us deeper and deeper into the heart of the mountain. I began to wonder if we were entering some mythical place after all. We lost all sense of time and direction. At each junction we cried out 'Hello!' in unison and then listened for a reply. A cry always answered us in return, making it clear which way to go. Lewis was a nervous wreck, and I tried to show that I was not, but Nelson led the way and steadied us both with his eager little face and twinkling good eye.

After what seemed like ages we came to a pile of rocks and timbers blocking the tunnel. I'd thought we were getting to our destination, and the noises had gradually become more discernible, but this was an unexpected and abrupt conclusion to our journey. Suddenly Nelson leapt onto the pile of rocks in front of us and started barking and scraping at the rubble until, to my horror, he exposed a hand protruding from the rubble. I nearly jumped out of my skin and Lewis screamed and ran back up the passage.

'The goblins are coming to get us! Run, Will, run! Run for your life!'

Then I heard the eerie voice again. 'H-e-l-p me.'

'Quick Lewis, get back here! Someone's trapped under this rubble,' I said as I started to pull away the larger rocks. What I'd assumed was the end of the tunnel was, in fact, a rock fall.

With Lewis's help it was only a matter of minutes before we were looking at the haggard face of Jack Demas. He was very weak, and his legs were trapped further back. He didn't talk but cried uncontrollably as we uncovered him.

'Mr Demas, we daren't move any more rubble in case we bring those larger rocks down on your head ... do you understand?' I couldn't tell what his mental state really was and he made no verbal response. I began to panic. How could we get his legs out? Help was too far away.

'Will, look at his hand,' Lewis said.

His bloodied fingers were pointing to the props behind me. I looked at the props, back to his hand, and understood what he was thinking. Lewis and I propped one over his head like a bench to protect it from falling rubble and slid the other alongside his trapped legs, using it as a lever to try to free him.

We worked for what seemed forever, and I thought our arms would give out from exhaustion but eventually we had one leg free and then the other. Only one rock fell while Jack crawled out, but the prop took the full weight of it.

Jack rolled onto his back and lay there a few minutes before pulling himself up against the shaft wall.

'Are you all right, Mr Demas?' I asked. I wondered if he would make it back through the tunnels.

After a long pause he looked up. 'What day is it, lad?' he asked. His voice was hoarse and dry.

'Um, Tuesday—Tuesday afternoon,' I said.

He shut his eyes. 'Oh God, two days ... seemed like a year.'

I crouched down. 'You've been trapped in here since Sunday?'

But he didn't open his eyes. 'Out of the depths I cried to you, oh Lord, and you heard my voice ... Thank you ... Thank you.' Then he opened his eyes. 'You're George's nephew aren't you?'

'Great nephew, we ... we just came to see you about something when–'

'No! You came in answer to my prayers. My prayers ... without any faith or hope ... but God still answered them. "If I descend to the depths you are there, even if I make my bed in Sheol, there your hand will find me"' Mr Demas shook his head, dazed. 'I never thought God would hear me, not me, but he did. Maybe he is as good as that vicar says he is.'

I tried to think how I could have been an answer to his prayers. But no, I was pretty sure we'd just decided to come up here to find out what we could about the situation with Uncle Sid. Still, what were the chances that anyone would come up here? And that we could arrive today, just in time?

I was amazed but relieved that he was able to walk and seemed to have no broken bones. His clothes were torn, and he was badly bruised and cut, but it was a miracle he was no worse. His powerful build and heavy overcoat must have protected him.

We made our way back to the cottage and watched Jack devour some rabbit stew straight from one of the pots near the fire. He drank large amounts of water from a coffee pot and, eventually, he spoke. 'I owe you a debt I can never repay, but if there is anything that I can ever do, anything that is in my power for either of you, then one day I will do it. I swear it.'

We both nodded, unsure what to say. I was glad Lewis didn't ask him for biscuits.

Jack wiped his brow. 'Now, what are you doing up here? This is no place for you. Does your Grandmother know that you've come?' Lewis and I exchanged glances. 'Hmm, I thought not,' he said. 'Well, what is it then?' As he waited for our reply he reached for a bottle off the shelf and, with shaky hands, loosened the cork. He took a long draught, screwed his eyes shut and twisted his face, and drank again. Some of the liquid flowed down over his stubbled chin and gave off the strong smell of homebrewed alcohol.

'Well we wanted to know,' I began, 'I mean, I wanted to know what you meant when you spoke to me that day at Harriet Armstrong's grave.'

Jack lowered the bottle. 'Oh, you do, do you?' I could see the pain in his bloodshot eyes and the bitter set of his mouth from the hurts and injustices of the past. He belched, wiped his mouth with the back of his hand and took another swig. 'I wasn't always like this, you know. There was a time when I was well thought of in these parts. My father was a Greek migrant who worked his way up as a ship's engineer in Glasgow, where he met my mother. I followed in his footsteps but became interested by the money that could be made mining for precious metals.' He eyed me carefully, as if he knew my thoughts. 'Yes, that's right,' he nodded. 'I was a greedy young man and my father was sad to see it, but I was determined not to always be poor as they had been. I would have it all, and I knew how to get it.'

'Is that why you came to Cumbria?'

'Aye, I came here when the mines were at their peak, but not just for this one. There are mines and disused workings all along these fells where they mined tin, lead and gold.'

'Gold?' Suddenly Lewis was interested.

'Gold in Cumbria?' I asked. 'Are you serious?'

I thought he was pulling my leg, but his face was deadly serious, stern and foreboding. 'Aye, there's gold. Under Maiden Moor and round Hindscarth, though no gold has come from there for years. But I see you're interested at the idea—the slim chance of maybe you finding some and getting rich, eh?'

He'd read my excitement correctly. I'd always wanted to be rich and important—it was probably my biggest goal in life.

'Well,' he continued, 'gold is a cruel mistress, and silver too. She pays you less than she extracts ... like these mines.' He sat for a minute gazing out the window, as if yearning for freedom from this place, this mistress. 'Weather's set in stormy for a while. You'd best stop here a while till it clears.' We took a place by the hearth and I made a fire while Jack washed his wounds in silence. I could tell by his unsteady movements that the alcohol was taking effect.

I pressed on with my questions, anxious to find out more. 'Did you want to marry Harriet, Mr Demas? That's what Uncle George said. Did you want to get married very much?'

His face hardened after my first question but softened after my second. I'd assumed his love of wealth and his obsession with this aristocratic young woman consumed him completely, but I was wrong. There was something else that drove him—something worse and more consuming, something the darkness in the mines had nurtured in him over the long years—his hatred of Sid. 'So you heard from George, did you? Well George is a good man and he will have told you true enough what happened. I will tell you seeing you're so set on it.'

We agreed. Lewis rose to let Nelson out and managed to send an old can flying. He slouched in the narrow doorway, avoiding the drips and glancing at the darkening sky.

'Well, now, some people seem to have plenty of chances with life ... success, women, that sort of thing, but it was never that way with me. In my haste I've always gambled my chips in for what I wanted and done okay ... until I came to Cumbria, that is.' He looked at the ceiling and sniffed. 'It started out as a good year. I was working at the Lorton lead mine, just down from your Gran's place. I was the celebrity of the summer, having just designed some pumping gear to clear the abandoned mine of water. I had put all my savings into the scheme and I was the toast of valley as I had brought some much-needed jobs after the depression they'd suffered since the war.'

He paused to apply a wet cloth to a wound on his leg.

'Was that when you met Harriet?' I asked.

'Aye, that's it. Her father was an investor in the mine and brought her along to the opening. He introduced us and we had a chance to talk. She was younger than me but not much, and her father liked me too. He was a shrewd man and could see that if the mine was fruitful once again, as it had been in its heyday, then investors like him would be very well off. I fancied that he intended me for his daughter if things worked out. Oh, and she was a beauty—a bit headstrong, but a rare beauty.'

He tightened the bandage and winced before taking another drink. 'I dreamed of it every day and night, having her ... but it was not to be. Those uncut seams didn't prove to be as lucrative as we'd all hoped and the operation failed ... I failed ... and with it went all my chances at wealth and winning Harriet. But that's mining, a bitch of a mistress.'

'Oh no,' I said. 'So what did you do?'

'I was under a lot of stress—working long hours, trying to keep the investors out of the picture until I could find a way out ... but there was none. Eventually Harriet's father forced us into insolvency, little realizing that in the same week his daughter would be running away with that scoundrel, Sidney Armstrong. How that man came from the same womb as George and Elsie I will never know. He crept into Harriet's affections somehow, and just to spite her father she ran off with him.'

'Is that when you came here?' I asked.

'Here? D'you like my little hut then? Huh! Well, after the creditors cleaned me out I had nothing and no one. I was suicidal with despair and grief over the mine and Harriet. I'd decided to leave the country and return to Glasgow when I met a lad at Keswick train station who worked at this mine here. He said there was labouring work if I wasn't too proud to do it, and that was when I made my biggest blunder.'

'Why? I don't understand.'

'Aye and I hope you never do.'

'Mr Demas?'

'Well, I needed to make peace with my father. We'd exchanged harsh words before I left and I knew I should have gone home. Most of the money I'd lost in the mine was his and mother's savings. But I chose what seemed like an easier path that led me here. I guess I was a prodigal who never went back to his father. It appeared easier, I say, but this mine has worked me through to the bone and that's the truth. There's not a day goes by when I don't wish I'd taken that train. But now it's no use. My parents both died, penniless, over twenty years ago and I'm left here, still working my passage.'

For a moment I thought he was going to cry, but though his grey bottom lip trembled slightly he dragged his sleeve across his nose and removed the remorse. 'It took me months to recover from the shock of losing the mine and Harriet, but when I did come round there was still something alive and strong in me. It was that love of silver! Oh, just to see it there in the pot when it's refined, so pure, so perfect ... to think what it was worth, that I'd cheated it out of the rocks ... and that it belonged to me, not to some bunch of stuffed gentry! I'd worked for the firm for eight years before the mine closed, and I'd mapped out every seam that had more to come.

Sometimes I hid the best faces from the boss, taking a note of where it was for a rainy day. I knew when their mineral licence would expire, and I was ready to return a week after the firm left. I set up a smelting plant in the lower sheds and extracted all the lead I could and did all my own silver extraction until one day I decided I would go and cash in some of what I had made. But then it happened ...'

'What happened, Mr Demas?'

'It was really the mine ... she wouldn't let me return to the valley. As I approached Keswick town for the first time in years it dawned on me how different I was from the townsfolk. The years I had worked in isolation had become the walls of a prison, but now that I was free to go and face people it was worse. I became agoraphobic in public places and had to return to her, to the mine. That was many years ago. Your Aunty Joyce and Uncle George were the only people I saw for decades. Eventually Joyce persuaded me to come to church, and that was the start of me getting out again, but I still can't stop around people long—even now.'

'So you live way up here.'

'Aye, lad, well, there's plenty of timber in the mines, game on the fells and books still to read. George pops in every now and again when he's up with the sheep and I keep myself to myself and I reckon there are worse off people in the world.'

'Yes, but don't you ever dream of really being, well, down there in the valley?' I was thinking about what the vicar had said on Sunday about peace of mind. What would old Jack have made of that challenge?

He smirked. 'I don't remember what it is to dream like that, lad. I just get by all right here. I took from my parents and from these hills what I had no right to, and now they can have what's left of me in return.'

I felt a heavy sadness for him, but there seemed nothing else to say. I decided I had nothing to lose by asking again about what he said that day in the graveyard. 'And so Harriet's death, when we talked three week ago ... what did you mean?'

'I thought you might get round to that. You're persistent, aren't you? Well, what I saw, I saw, and knowing that devil Sidney, I knew what it meant, too.'

'What do you mean?'

'Well, I was going over the fell to Buttermere to buy some more paraffin for my stove when I saw them. I knew the car well enough, and I could see something wasn't right as well. It was tearing along Crummock Water at great speed and swerving all over the place. I ran down to the edge of Rannerdale Knott as it neared the huge bend there on the rocky precipice. The passenger door opened and Sidney jumped free from the car just before it crashed through the wall and fell fifty feet into the lake below.'

'So you mean he was there all the time, but—'

I thought I had it now, but Jack interrupted. 'But why did the enquiry say that she'd been alone in the car and missed the corner when drunk at the wheel? I'll tell you why. Because he picked himself up and slunk off and lied through his teeth about his whereabouts.'

'But you saw it. Why didn't you do something?'

'Oh I did, but the police were in Sid's pocket and, as I later found out, never filed my statement. No, they told Sid what I'd seen and Sid sent me a message saying that if I didn't want to go to prison for my illegal mining activities up here then I should hold my tongue over things that didn't concern me. I'm sure he fobbed the policeman off with the story of my madness and gave him some cash for his trouble. His alibi stood up in court. I can't imagine how he bribed mad Annie to lie for him, but she did.'

He covered his eyes and pinched his brow with his left hand for a few moments. 'The bastard walked away and poor Harriet was left not avenged because I was too afraid to exchange this prison for a heated one elsewhere. So there you have it—all I know and all I'm going to tell you. Like I said before,' he said as he straightened up to look out of the window, 'it's not pretty under the surface, this valley ... none of it.' He grimaced. 'Good, looks like the rain's past. You'd best make your way back before it gets too late.'

He saw us to the edge of the spoil heap upon which his home was built and, after assuring us that he would be all right alone and swearing us again to secrecy, we descended the slopes to the valley where we found our bikes intact.

His parting words rang in my ears all the way home. 'Just remember, Jack Demas never forgets a favour or a friend.'

Jack Demas frightened me, and I was glad to scramble down to the security of the valley. I wondered if Aunty Joyce had been scared of him at all. The 'what if' haunted me all the way home. What if we hadn't gone up there? Would he have died alone in the mountain? How long would it have been before they found him? It was strange to think that God had used me to rescue him, even to answer his prayers, as he said. I knew Jack Demas needed more help than we were able to give him, though. I probably knew more about him now than anyone. I tried to pray for him, though I didn't really know what I was doing. I told God that I was available if needed. It seemed to be the right way to say it.

My nightmares that night were filled with images of Uncle Sid stalking me down dark caverns. I kept waking to wonder: should I really follow through with my plans to follow a cold-blooded killer?

15

UNCLE SID'S SECRET

Wow, that's a stinger verse!'

Granny looked up from putting my pile of clean laundry at the foot of my bed. 'Which verse, dear?'

'Er, this one ... "The heart of every man and woman is deceitful above anything else in the universe, and desperately wicked: who can untangle it?" It's in the book named after Jeremiah.'

Granny went to the door. 'You'll have to decide whether you believe the Bible, that we're all bad through and through or ...'

'Or what?'

'Well, or that we're basically good with a few bad bits. I know which description I think fits. Anyway, I thought you were going to read Luke's Gospel.'

'I finished it yesterday and thought I'd have a look around the rest of the book.'

'Good lad.' She smiled. 'Anyway, get up now—I want to clear away the breakfast.'

It was raining again and I wondered whether even Uncle Sid would be about his secret business on such a foul day.

But by mid morning it had cleared up considerably and I watched at the window for Lewis, who was downstream in Lorton at his den. There he had a good view of the fields where he said he'd seen Sid walk every Wednesday. The plan was for Lewis to wait until he saw him and then pedal as fast as he could upriver to Granny's place to get me. There was no sign of him all morning, and by lunchtime I was uneasy. Worse still, Granny extracted a promise from me over the lunch table.

Watching for Lewis all morning had given me too much time to think over what Jack had said the day before. By the time we ate lunch I just couldn't hold in my questions any longer. So I asked Granny about Uncle Sid's evidence at the inquest after Harriet's mysterious death.

Instead of an answer, she gave me a warning. 'Will, you have to promise me that you'll not get involved or in any way meddle with Uncle Sid's affairs. You've no idea what kind of man he is. Do you hear me?'

'Okay, I'll keep away.' I looked down at my empty plate as I said it, aware that I was sitting here just waiting to break the promise I was making.

But I was worried enough to take some precautions. I left a note pinned to the back of the chicken shed door that told Granny about my mission and what time I would be home. I knew she wouldn't go out there until it was time to lock the chickens up at dark. The plan, of course, was to be home in time to take it down well before dark. It gave me a strange feeling to think of where I'd be if Granny did find the note.

As I waited for Lewis I grew more and more anxious. Finally there was a clattering in the yard and Lewis sped in as fast as his grubby bike would go. He was panting and out of breath from the uphill ride from Lorton, but his smile told me all I needed to know.

'He is coming then?'

'Yeah, about half a mile downstream. But it's fair misty in the valley—I had a hard job making sure I didn't lose him.'

'A little mist never throws Morse off the trail, and it won't bother us–' I stopped suddenly. 'Hey, if I'm Morse, then you're—Lewis!' I'd never thought of that before, and we had a good laugh while I put on my jacket. We closed the door behind us as quietly as possible. Granny was upstairs and Grandpa had gone out with Stan to make one last reconnoitre of the woods. We'd worked hard tracking many of the creature's movements the previous week, and Stan thought that by Friday we'd be able to put together all the data we'd collected to come up with a fairly accurate picture of the creature—and a plan for putting an end to the killing.

Lewis and I headed off in high spirits but soon sobered up as we descended into the patchy fog in the river valley. I remembered Grandpa explaining that these mists frequently come in the summer after long periods of rain. The valley base was cold and eerie. As we entered the woods at the bottom I took one last look back up the field at Granny's place—my home these last three weeks. I could barely make it out. The mist was thick in some areas and thinner in others, so navigation was difficult and tracking even harder.

We waited about ten minutes by the bend in the river near Kern Howe Farm for the fog to lift. But then we decided we'd better go further, up to the open fields. We didn't want to miss Sid and waste another week so we moved on, slowly and silently.

I knew the river fairly well from my trips with Stan, and I chose a rocky knoll with a view across the river. We waited another five minutes that seemed like fifty. Sitting still was even harder for Lewis. He only finally settled down when I told him, in jest, to pick his nose or something and stop making noise. Obedient as ever, he found great consolation in the suggestion and set to work quietly enough, occasionally pointing out to me some particularly rich picking.

Suddenly we heard a series of sounds coming fast upon us from behind. I wheeled round, dreading that I would see Sid, but to my relief and delight it was Nelson. In my haste to leave the house I must have shut the door on him—and he must have made an escape at the first available opportunity and followed us along the river. He looked happy to see us, though I also detected his stern reproof. How could we possibly plan another adventure without his services?

He immediately took up an observation post on the knoll with one of his 'Okay, lads, I'll take it from here' expressions. Because we were near Kern Howe Farm he was probably planning a further assault on his bitter rival, Ripper, who we could hear barking from time to time.

There was a sudden break in the mist, and there before us was the figure we'd been waiting for. We both took cover and I held my breath until he was out of sight.

'Cor, like the grim reaper, him, long coat, stick an'all,' Lewis whispered.

My heart raced as we quietly made our way upstream, keeping to the dark cover the way that Stan had taught me. We followed about one to two hundred metres behind Sid and kept him in view as much as possible. His was an easy route, along the edges of the fields near the wooded riverbank, but ours was a more difficult one. Up and down the banks, along rocky ledges, through thickets of hawthorn and brier, with the mist every now and again obscuring our target. We were exhausted after a mile or so when we saw Sid ford the river.

We followed even more carefully now, and our patience soon paid off. He came up before another farm by the lane that ran toward Granny's place and then crossed it onto a small track that led up to a small outcrop of rocks and trees only barely visible some two hundred metres away through the mist. We followed the lonely figure as he strode on and on. He never stopped, never looked back. As we made our way over the road we caught a glimpse of him disappearing into the trees at this outcrop. We waited for a moment and followed his steps up the track, through two more gates that read 'Private: Keep Out', and then into the small wooded area. Lewis's face was pale and it was unnerving to be able to hear his heart thumping. We paused there in the trees and there was a sudden movement. I froze as footsteps swiftly approached us from behind.

'Young William!'

I jumped and whirled round. 'Professor! Thank God, I—'

'I see you look after your great uncle with unnatural interest,' he said. 'Have your grandparents told you nothing to keep you from him?'

'Well, not really ... why? What do you know?' I asked as my heartrate slowed a bit.

'I know very little about your uncle, but I have often felt him to be like Marlowe's Faustus, the man who traded his soul for power ... yes, yes, "all things that moved between the quiet poles were at his command" you see.' The professor must have detected from my face that I did not see, and so he went on. 'Marlowe was not the only great writer to write about your uncle.'

'A great writer wrote about my Uncle Sid?'

'Well not him exactly, dear boy, but one like him. Listen to this: "Everything belonged to him—but that was a trifle. The thing to know was what he belonged to, how many powers of darkness claimed him for their own. That was the reflection that made you creepy all over. It was impossible—not good for one either—trying to imagine. He had taken a high seat amongst the devils of the land—I mean literally. You can't understand—how could you?" Ah! But I see you have his look in your eye, and my persuasions will not keep you from it, so go if you must but do not say you were not warned.' He tapped his stick twice on the ground and made off up the lane.

'Gaga!' Lewis said as he shrugged and grinned.

We went on, and as we rounded a bend in the track we came upon a cottage with a slate roof. The ground around it was unkempt and overgrown, but there were piles of bin bags outside and a bike leaning up against the wall. It struck me all at once—it was mad Annie's bike, and this must be her home. Annie had been Sid's alibi, according to Jack, but why would he sneak up here alone?

'It's mad Annie's house,' I whispered. 'Chris Clegg told me she was a witch with magical powers. Maybe Sid comes here to put curses on all his enemies.' I didn't mention to Lewis the fear I'd seen in Chris Clegg's eyes when he saw her. 'C'mon,' I said, 'let's go!'

'You can't make me go any closer,' Lewis said. 'I wouldn't set foot in that old lady Pardshaw's house and I'm not going any further. I'll wait by the gate. You shout as loud as you can if there's trouble.'

Nelson seemed spooked, too, and chose the gate option.

So I went up to the cottage, in the dampness and mist, on my own. I couldn't see any sign of Sid but heard sounds from inside the house. I positioned myself just under one of the windows. After a few moments I peeped through the window and there they both were in the room.

It was lit by a candle sitting on the table. There were black bin bags stuffed with clothes stacked everywhere.

And there was Uncle Sid, gently combing Annie's hair and talking quietly to her. Every so often he'd step over to the stove to stir something in a pot.

I couldn't believe it. What was going on? Why was he here? It was all so strange, so completely different from the sinister plot I'd imagined.

Even from my small experience I could tell Annie was mentally handicapped. She showed no emotion, she didn't say a word, and all the while Sid kept on with his combing. What was she to him that he paid her weekly care visits? And why had she given an alibi for him twenty-two years before?

They couldn't be lovers—she was at least twenty years younger than he was, and I couldn't see Sid in that situation. No, there was something else. But what? I repositioned myself so I could see her face better. She was the key, but who was she? Where had she come from? I saw that in candlelight she was actually quite pretty. I was sure I'd seen her face before, somewhere else. Mentally I went up and down the church pews, the people I had met in the valley, but I couldn't find a near match. Who was she?

Uncle Sid put down the comb, told her he would be back in a minute, and left the room.

She turned her head, slightly, and it came to me. Her face was a mirror image of Ellen Patterson, the woman Uncle Sid had loved all those years ago but had abandoned for the wealthy Harriet. But Mad Annie was too young to be Ellen herself. She must be a relation. What was it Sid had said at the grave? That he would 'take care of her'? But who would he take care of for Ellen unless it was—Ellen's child? Could that be it? But the child had died at birth and Ellen's parents had moved away.

Lost in my thoughts I hadn't heard the silent step behind me and, by the time I felt a bony hand on my shoulder and a chill down my spine, I knew it was too late. I was caught, and I broke out in a cold sweat. The hand that gripped my shoulder slowly turned me round to face my fate.

His slate grey eyes bore into me. I couldn't speak. His expression was smooth, almost without emotion. I felt as though I'd been trapped in his web and was about to be eaten alive. My strength melted away.

A wry smile crept onto his lips. 'I was wondering when you would get here, young nephew.' He smiled at my surprise and nodded. 'Yes, I knew that you were following me. I knew you would from the day you recognized me with Stan by the river, and particularly after you spied on me at the graveyard. In fact I expected you last week, but I understand you were busy.' He paused again and nodded, registering my jaw dropped in amazement.

'How—' I squeaked.

'Yes, I do make it my business to be informed. But you don't look to be too troublesome. Please, come inside ... be my ... guest.' He stared into me, waiting.

I felt as though he were reading my thoughts, my fears, everything. I tried to reply, but I couldn't even remember why I was there, or my name. I didn't want to go inside with him, but how could I resist?

'I—I—I can't. I mean, Granny told me not to, I mean, I shouldn't be here, I–'

He appeared pleased by my admissions and carried on as if nothing I said mattered. And, in a way, he was right. 'My, you do look like your mother. She was a favourite niece of mine, you know?' He paused. 'Yes, your mother was about the only one of them that would speak to me for years.

Maybe you and I will be friends, too? We'll see. Come inside and meet Anne. Do you know who she is?'

I found I could form complete sentences again as he ushered me to the door. 'Yes, she's your daughter by Ellen Patterson—but I don't know how, as Granny says she died at birth.'

Sid seemed taken aback by my thorough answer, but not undone as I thought he might be. Was that respect I saw in his eyes? Or merely a recognition that I might be more use to him than he had supposed? 'My, you have been a busy little bee, haven't you? Yes, you are correct. And since you know already and have me at such a disadvantage ... I will tell you the rest. Your grandmother told you all she knew, and for years I barely knew more myself until Ellen's parents contacted me with the news.'

'The news that your daughter was alive? But why hide it from you for so long? I don't get it.'

He paused at the doorway into the sitting room where Anne was waiting. 'It's quite simple, really. Anne was all they had of their daughter, and they hated me and didn't want me to lay claim to the baby. Unfortunately, at that time they didn't know how the traumatic birth had also damaged the child. They moved at the end of the summer to Newcastle, where they could live near relatives and escape the gossip.'

'But when did you find out? I mean, how...?'

'They contacted me about twelve years ago. They weren't able to look after her any longer, and they knew I had risen in the world and could arrange things for her. They contacted me through my solicitor to make arrangements.'

He introduced me to Anne, who sat calmly entranced by the candle in the dim, musky room. 'William, this is Anne. Anne dear, this is William.'

'Nice to meet you, Anne,' I said.

I thought I saw a flicker of acknowledgement, but it might have been the candlelight.

'I evaded responsibility in my youth,' Sid said, 'for which I daily suffer regret. I see Ellen very much in Anne's eyes. I loved her mother very much, but I didn't know that she was with child when I started to court Harriet.'

'Aunty Dora said that Ellen didn't tell you about the child because she wouldn't force you to be with her for the child's sake.'

'Did she?' There was a catch in his voice. 'She was a proud girl, Ellen was ... I don't blame her, how could I?' He began to brush Anne's hair again as he looked out of the window toward Loweswater, where this drama had all begun fifty years previously. 'I like to think that I would have done my duty by her, but I was young and full of ambition for greater and greater things. Perhaps I would have, perhaps I would have abandoned her for Harriet. I don't know now. I'll never know. What's done is done.' Sid paused and rolled his tongue around his teeth and cheek.

'Her grandparents sent her back, and now I have a chance to make some small amends to the child and to Ellen by providing for her ... a very small penance, I would say, but no less than I deserve.'

'Why didn't you tell people when she came back? I mean, why keep it a secret for so long?'

'Listen, William, I know what they all think of me—the family—so self-righteous. Do you think they would welcome me back for my good deeds? I'm sure they wasted no time in telling you of all the terrible things I've ever done.' He looked out the window again. 'They're so sure they know God's mind on every subject that I needn't give them reason now to feel sorry for me, or give them cause to pardon me.

As if I needed to grovel to them for forgiveness. No, I've kept my council about Anne and I'll continue to do so. The Bible says a man's good deeds should be done in secret or else he will lose his reward. There are some things that I must make right in my own way without interference, and I shall need you to give me your word that you will never speak of what you've heard and seen today to another soul.'

He fixed me with stern eyes.

'I won't, I promise,' I said. And as I made the promise I remembered the promise I'd made to Granny just that morning. Some promises were hard to keep, but I would try. I couldn't help but think that if people knew his story it would be easier for him somehow. This route he'd chosen, to pay God in arrears for his sinful youth, didn't seem to give him the peace of mind that I'd experienced on Sunday.

'Good,' he said. 'We have an agreement and I, in turn, will not tell my sister that you've been following me after she told you not to.' He nodded—as if he knew more than I had actually told him.

'But I never said she said–'

He held up one hand to silence me as he scrolled through a text message on his phone with the other. He read, somewhat triumphantly, 'Sorry Granny, I've followed Uncle Sid somewhere up the river, can't explain now, if not back by 6:00 pm could be in trouble, Will.'

My note from the chicken coop door. Who could have found that? And texted it to him? Sid had eyes everywhere.

'But how did you—I mean, who texted you—'

'I'm surprised no one warned you against trifling with me,' Sid said. 'But never mind that now. All you need to know is that your secret is safe with me. The note will come to me later for safekeeping and your grandparents won't suffer any *more* disappointments with you ...' I blushed as I thought of the poaching episode and Grandpa's face that night. 'If,' Sid continued, 'you help me with something next week. Don't worry, it's a small matter, but you might feel you want to oblige me ... to preserve your reputation at home, perhaps. You will meet me at my house in High Lorton next Wednesday, at one o'clock, and I'll tell you what I wish you to do.'

I opened my mouth to object but didn't know what to say. I was cornered. He had me totally. Somehow he knew I couldn't bear disappointing my grandparents again—especially not now that I was doing so well at being a man and a proper Christian.

'Don't look so surprised, nephew. You may have thought that our confessions today made us somehow equal. Believe me, they do not. You have given me your oath regarding Anne, and I will hold you to it, and I will keep my word regarding this matter of your duplicity when you have run this small errand for me. Are we agreed?'

I nodded.

'Good, then you'd better be on your way. Your friend will be cold out there by the gate.'

He returned to combing Anne's hair and I made my own way out of the cottage. As I walked down the track Lewis ran to keep up with me. I said nothing but shook my head and shrugged my shoulders to fend off his questions. I couldn't tell him most of what had just happened. I felt defiled, dirty, owned. I didn't know what awaited me next week, but this power Uncle Sid exercised over me held me in its grip so tightly I knew it couldn't bring anything but trouble. I felt as though he had a leash around my neck.

As soon as I got home I checked the chicken house. The note had indeed been taken, and care had been taken not to leave footprints in the soft ground around the area. Sid had destroyed my confidence in my amateur-sleuth powers, but I was desperate to know who my betrayer was. I paced the path looking for where my secret adversary might have entered. Eventually I found the fresh print of a grippy walking boot, about size ten, near the trees where the beast had left such terrifying markings. I made a note of the size and pattern in my notebook. As I looked up and beyond to the woodland further up the fellside I wondered whether I was being watched even now. I went back to the house quickly and did not look back. I wasn't about to give my enemy the pleasure of seeing me afraid.

That night at the table I was quiet.

'Are you all right, Will lad?' Granny asked.

I nodded, and Grandpa reminded me that he'd need me over the next few days to deal with matters 'out back'. He moved his head to motion towards the woodlands.

'I'll do whatever you need, Grandpa,' I said. I didn't add that I'd be glad to be around Grandpa and Stan for some time. I felt safe with them, even though I'd be back in the beast's territory. It had grown bold enough to make open kills outside its wooded hunting ground, and now we were going deep into its home patch.

As I tossed and turned in bed that night I couldn't help but feeling something like sorrow for Uncle Sid. Angry and resentful as I was at the way he'd treated me, I couldn't get out of my mind how unhappy he must be. What must it be like to try to pay for all those past mistakes on his own, knowing that he'd never really make it better or get rid of his guilt? He had no peace, no one to share his burden. But I couldn't talk to anyone about it because he'd made sure that I, like him, would bear his secret alone.

16

FIGHT TO THE DEATH

Wakey, wakey lad! Today's the day, I know it! Get up and get your kit on.' Grandpa popped his head in my door and I heard his light steps running down the stairs as I rolled out of bed. Where did he get all his energy, I wondered.

Even Nelson had a wicked twinkle in his eye as we ate our fried mushrooms.

'Quick, lads,' Granny said as she poured the tea. 'Dora and I are off to the shops in Cockermouth and we want an early start.'

'Right, Nelson! Now down to business!' Grandpa said as soon as she was out of the door. He brought some maps from a chest in the drawing room and spread them out on the table. He examined his watch and motioned toward the door. It opened, and Stan entered the room.

'Morning Major, Will, Nelson. Is there a brew on?'

I fetched him a mug and, as we all stood in the kitchen, I could see from their glances that I'd missed something over the last few days. Stan was holding several rolls of tracing paper.

'What is it? What are you not telling me?' I asked.

Grandpa snorted. 'You'll find out soon enough, lad. Come on, Stan, let's get started.'

'Okay gentlemen,' Stan said. 'What are we up to?'

'Victory, that's what we're about!' Grandpa said. 'As Winston Churchill said, "Victory at all costs, victory in spite of all terror; victory however long and hard the road may be; for without victory there is no survival." You've got everything, Stan?'

'I think so,' Stan said. 'And I hope the bairn is ready for today's excursion—he looks a bit tired.'

'I'm all right,' I said. 'What's all this with the map and the tracing paper? What have you been up to?'

'What we have been up to, young William,' said Grandpa, 'is this: we've been conducting a sieve analysis of the Wild Wood and connecting woodlands on the Low Moor side. And what you're about to see is the correlation of all our mapping work over the last ten days.'

'Sieve analysis?'

'Well, it's really a fancy way of looking at lots of information layered over and over, and that's why we've got the tracing paper to put over the map,' said Stan. Neither of them could contain their excitement. Stan laid his first roll of tracing paper over the map. 'See here, this is the one which you started, and I completed it. It's all the known kill sites.'

'Okay, and what about the others?'

'Well, this one here has all the areas where we've found positive prints.' He laid this paper over the first. 'Then this next one shows where we've seen claw markings on the trees, and then the next where we've found droppings. And this—shows all recorded sightings of the creature,' said Stan proudly as he laid the final paper down over the others.

Grandpa and I leaned over eagerly, searching for the pattern.

I'd come to know the woods fairly well over the past weeks but didn't yet know them nearly as well as Grandpa or Stan did. So I didn't understand the look of alarm on their faces as the final piece of tracing paper was laid down.

'What is it?' I asked.

'I had a hunch about this two days ago,' Grandpa said. He frowned at Stan.

'Yes, I wondered why you didn't mention it. I was thinking the same thing myself on Tuesday afternoon when we found those prints near the Scout camp,' Stan said.

'What prints?' I asked. 'What camp site?'

'On Tuesday afternoon we followed the trail that runs close to the village,' Stan explained. 'We'd thought the creature had got very bold to come so close to the farms, but that wasn't the worst. It became clear that it had paid a great deal of attention to prowling the perimeter of the small clearing and campsite where the Scouts go on weekends during the summer months.'

'Now,' Grandpa continued, 'we haven't mentioned this to anyone yet as we weren't sure.' He paused, cleared his throat, and looked at Stan. I'd never heard my grandfather sound so deadly serious. 'But we very much fear that the creature is looking to make a human kill at the camp, where the Cub Scouts from Cockermouth will be this weekend. These other survey results and the amassed data that Stan put together here show beyond a shadow of a doubt that that is where the beast has spent most of its time in the last three days. Who knows? Maybe it saw that large group there last weekend and is just waiting for the next one to arrive.'

'But what are we going to do? I mean, someone has to warn them not to go there.'

'There'll be no need to do that,' Grandpa said. He folded his arms. 'It'll all end today, because we're going to end it. Right, Stan?'

'Right you are, Major. We'll put a stop to it all right.'

'But how can you be sure you'll find it?' I asked. I was half-terrified, half-exhilarated by their determination.

'Because of that!' Grandpa pointed triumphantly to one corner of the map.

'Where all those dots are? What are they?' I asked.

'Well, my dear William, if you examine the general direction of the tracks, they seem to converge around here.'

'Where is that, exactly?'

'It has to be its lair—it's the old quarry at the back of Thrang Wood, not far from the Scout camp. And that's where we can make a search this afternoon. But first we must make sure that we have everything we need. Stan, have you got your checklist to hand?'

'Aye, Major, it's all here.'

'Good, 'cos there's nothing more likely to get us peace as to meet the enemy well prepared—so says old George Washington, and he knew what he was talking about.'

And so we spent the rest of that morning making preparations for the final hunt of the beast of Low Moor. There were guns to clean, and I was pleased to have back my little single-barrelled twelve-bore shotgun. Stan checked the springs and the locking action to make sure it wouldn't let us down. Grandpa had his wildfowling gun as well as a range of knives.

Stan stood looking out the window as he cleaned a pump-action shotgun. 'I've often found this very useful over the years,' he said.

Stan and I would each carry a small medical kit and Grandpa would carry a larger one in his rucksack. Stan had walkie-talkies, and I checked that the batteries were all charged up and ready. We packed hot drinks, sandwiches, chocolate—and raw rabbit meat as bait for the beast.

By mid-morning, everything was ready. I had my cartridges loaded into a belt that I'd wear around my waist and Grandpa's 'Fairbairn Sykes' commando knife strapped to my leg.

Just before lunchtime there was a knock at the door. I assumed it would be Lewis and was preparing my explanation as to why he couldn't come with us when I opened the door to find Andrew standing there. I hadn't seen him apart from Sundays, and it caught me off guard to see him in a camouflage jacket over a rugby shirt.

He stooped to come through the door and looked around at the assembled party with a grin. 'Well then, it seems I've been missing all the fun. I'm afraid I didn't pack a lunch but I see we have plenty!' he said, looking at the food on the table ready to pack in our sacks.

'I suppose we do,' Stan said. He appeared less than happy to share his lunch with a man of Andrew's size.

'Good timing, Andrew,' Grandpa said. 'We're nearly ready. Have you got the gun?'

'It's all in the car,' Andrew said as he bent down to give Nelson a scratch behind the ears. Nelson, sniffing round his legs, seemed to have a special attachment to Andrew.

'What gun?' I asked.

'The gun we're going to use to bring down this beast!' Andrew said.

'I daresay the bairn thought he was going to shoot the beast with that old gun of his!' said Stan. He smiled as he pointed the knife he was sharpening at me.

I blushed. It had occurred to me.

'No, William,' said Andrew. 'We're going to see if we can dart the creature first, or at least we hope to do that, if we can get a clear shot.'

'Aye, but are you sure you've got enough of that drug of yours to put this animal to sleep?' asked Stan. 'From what we've seen it looks to be a fair sized creature.'

'No, you don't have to worry,' Andrew said. 'This Immobilon is the proper stuff.' He reached into his pocket and pulled out a very small bottle wrapped in several bags and bubble wrap. Andrew placed it on the table carefully and pointed at it triumphantly. 'This stuff is hardly ever used these days—it says so in all the vet's books I've read. They recommend that you don't touch it. That little bit there cost about £100, and the only reason I've got it is because it's out of date. And we've only got it at the practice because of the zebras at the animal park—it's about the only thing that'll bring them down!'

'But why don't the vets use it if it's so good?' I said.

'Partly the cost, I suppose, but more importantly, it's well dangerous!' He placed two pairs of thick blue rubber gloves from his other pocket on the table next to the bottle. 'You have to wear double gloves to use this stuff and you have to have two people, because of the reversal drug which must be on hand at any moment.'

'What's the reversal drug?' I asked.

He brought another bottle out of his pocket and handed it to me. It had 'Revivalon' written on the label.

'Immobilon's so lethal that if I get one drop of it on your skin it could kill you within seconds, and so I have this reversal serum on standby—first for our safety but also to bring the animal round after we've got it tied up. We can't muck around with this stuff. Stan has had training to administer Revivalon, so we're safe. If anything does go wrong, the exposed man must be given an equivalent shot of this stuff into a muscle, but preferably a blood vessel, to save him.'

I looked at that dangerous little bottle with awe. I hadn't considered that we might not be killing the beast.

'We can only syringe the dart after we see the size of the beast,' Andrew explained, 'as too much Immobilon will kill it. And only when we have the animal in range can the dart gun be pressurized.'

I doubt the beast will wait around for that, I thought. I didn't say anything but was glad to have my gun ready and loaded.

Grandpa and Stan went through our check-list, safety precautions, using the walkie-talkies and first-aid procedures.

It was almost one o'clock and I could see Grandpa glancing at the clock and getting edgy. 'I think it's time we should be going,' he said. 'Elsie will be back any minute now and I don't want her making a fuss.'

Stan and Andrew exchanged smiles.

'Sorry Major,' Stan said. 'We forgot that you're under the thumb—and probably too old to be going out so late in the afternoon!'

'Aye, do you need your nap first?' Andrew asked.

Grandpa laughed and followed Nelson to the door. 'What a lot of fuss and equipment over a trifling little matter like a stray animal in the woods,' Nelson seemed to be saying.

We set out at last, and it wasn't long before the weight began to get to me. The combination of cartridge belt, gun, knife, rucksack, provisions, walkie-talkie and medical kit dug into my waist and shoulders, but I made sure nobody knew it.

Stan and Andrew strode out in front, discussing the protocol of using the drug over and over again lest any mistake should be made. Grandpa and I paused to look at the tree near the house that had been so savagely scraped by the beast. One of the marks was twelve feet up. Although we'd been joking about Nelson's eagerness for the hunt and felt confident in our own abilities, seeing the tree was a stark reminder of what we were about to do. This was not a game. This was the real thing. We'd done all we could to protect ourselves, but we still didn't know what we were fighting against—and this was a great weakness.

'Come on lad, let's get at 'im!' Grandpa slapped me on the shoulder. 'Toward thee I roll ... To the last, I grapple with thee, from hell's heart I stab at thee; for hate's sake I spit my last breath at thee.' He looked back at me and smiled. 'Oh come on, surely you've read *Moby Dick?*'

I shook my head and looked back at the tree one last time.

As we entered the darkness of the woods I had that eerie, tingling sense that I was being watched. But I also felt like I was trespassing in someone else's domain—uninvited but observed. We made our way through the Wild Wood, up the back of Ramthwaite and along the narrow tracks through arching conifers where the Scout camp was. Stan and I found still more droppings and paw prints as we went along. When Andrew saw the prints he became more and more convinced that what we were chasing was a large cat of some sort. But he still couldn't reconcile the size of the markings on the tree near Granny's place with the size of these prints.

'Maybe,' he said, 'the beast climbed the tree and scratched and scratched as it went up and down?'

I wasn't convinced but I hoped he was right. 'Oh that's a relief then,' I said. 'It must be much smaller than twelve feet long.'

'I'm not so sure,' Stan said. 'A cat of any size like the one we're tracking can be just as dangerous to humans whether it's six-feet long or ten-feet long.' He went on to list several terrifying facts about the speed of Siberian tigers and the ferocity of other sorts of lynx and cougar.

My relief left as quickly as it had come.

'That reminds me of a story I heard last week from the Reverend Scott,' Andrew said with a grin.

'Cowboy stories?' Grandpa said. 'I've heard he's keen on that sort of thing.'

'Yes exactly, he's been reading the autobiography of Davy Crockett. On one occasion the young Davy Crockett was on a wilderness expedition, alone, and he decided to sleep in a tree. He was awakened in the night by the ferocious growling of a mountain lion, not fifteen feet away. He leveled his famous gun, 'Old Betsy', at the approaching cougar, took aim and fired. After a cloud of smoke had cleared, Crockett found himself staring at the cougar—with only the skin torn off the front of its face! The musket ball from his gun had removed the skin, but it hadn't penetrated the skull. As the animal gathered its wits it launched itself at Crockett, who batted it aside once with the gun before laying it down to take out his Bowie knife. During a fight to the death, in which Davy Crockett's leg was badly mauled by the creature, he eventually inflicted so many stab wounds that it died. This won him much acclaim with a scouting party of Comanche Indians the next day. They made him an honorary member of their tribe because he had done such a deed with a knife. What do think of that, young Will? Better than the movies, eh?'

'Yeah, cool,' I said. 'But that's just Hollywood and legend, isn't it?'

'No way, this book the vicar's reading is Davy's own life story in his own words. They made them tough in those days.'

I didn't really want to think about how the skulls of these beasts could withstand a musket ball. I looked down at my own shotgun and prayed silently that I would have more success if the need arose.

After half an hour trudging through the woods on high alert, we eventually came to the quarries.

'Ah now,' Grandpa said as he scanned the area, 'the beast's lair is here—somewhere.'

It was surprising to come upon such a broad clearing in the dense woods. I noticed a large cut into the hillside where, Grandpa explained, the slate had been hewn more than two hundred years ago to provide materials for dry stone walls, house building and slate roof tiles. Now all was dark, forlorn and damp. The dense thicket of conifers provided excellent cover from almost all sides, and you could look out from this secluded dell up onto the fells from only a few angles.

There was a faint southwesterly breeze that afternoon, so we kept downwind of the quarry area. As we skirted the outlying pine thickets the palms of my hands became sweaty. My thumb constantly flicked the safety catch on and off and on again so that I'd be ready in the event of an emergency. Stan pointed out the remains of several young sheep near a cave toward one side of the quarry. 'Well, Major, they weren't there the other day, were they?' he whispered.

Andrew had halted in a clearing and we all gathered round as he got his dart gun ready.

'So, young Andrew,' Grandpa said, 'you're pretty sure that we'll have a chance to get a shot in?'

'Well, I reckon whatever it is is having an afternoon nap inside that cave, but I'll have to get a little closer than I am now if I'm going to have a good shot. I'll need to just get down over behind that boulder, I'd say. Then Stan and I can lay everything out ready. From there I reckon we're in with a good chance of making a clean hit when the creature comes out for its feed.' He spoke slowly and steadily, in a low whisper. He didn't seem the least bit nervous. Stan didn't appear to be afraid either.

I, on the other hand, was getting jumpier by the minute. 'Please, God,' I prayed, 'let Andrew use enough of the drug and get a good shot.'

Andrew and Stan put on their two layers of rubber gloves each and, armed with their guns, the deadly sedative drug, and the reversal serum, they made their way down past the boulder until they were in the base of the quarry, directly in front of the opening to the small cave.

'Nervous, lad?' asked Grandpa as he loaded his gun.

'A bit,' I said.

'That's okay, Will,' he said. He stooped to pat Nelson, who was anxious for us to join Andrew and Stan. 'Nerves are a good thing—they keep you sharp. It's not nerves that stop a man acting as he should when he should. That's fear, and that's what you've got to watch. Don't ever be ruled by fear, Will. Have courage and hold fast to the job in hand. We're here to provide covering fire for the others if things go wrong. They're counting on you, and so am I. I know you'll do your duty.' He gripped me on the shoulder and sent me to cover the left flank of the quarry. He took the right, so we were equidistant from Andrew and Stan's lookout. Our plan was to make sure the beast didn't escape.

I was more nervous than I let on, but I followed Grandpa's instructions and tried not to let fear take over. I knew that duty means doing something because it's right—regardless of feelings. They were all counting on me, and the last thing I wanted was to disappoint them.

I made my way round the side of the quarry and hid under the low branches of a Sitka spruce. We waited for hours. In the early evening, the bulk of Low Moor and the dense plantation of Sitkas caused the light to fade fast. As it grew darker, I began to wish that I hadn't watched so many scary films. Images from those films, together with my active imagination and the very real danger we were in, nearly paralyzed me with fear until I wasn't sure that I could move if I needed to. With each passing minute my heart beat faster as I stared into that dark hole in the quarry. I was fifteen and about to die a savage death, I thought. I need to escape. Granny must be worried by now, I thought. What would Mum say when she heard the news of my death? That's fear taking over, I told myself sternly. Focus.

The tension mounted as the light ebbed away. The forest threw out its own dark shadows and I heard the unfamiliar night sounds of the woods. I could still see Stan and Andrew clearly, but I wondered what we'd do if it got much darker. Cats can see in the dark, humans cannot. I shuddered.

And then, suddenly, the waiting was over.

There was a disturbance somewhere far back in the conifers, directly behind Stan and Andrew. At first I thought maybe it was a large mammal—a deer or stray sheep. But a horrific wailing and snarling pierced the darkness. I almost dropped my gun. Back in the city, late at night, I used to wake sometimes to alley cats fighting. It always mystified me that such small creatures could make such a noise. This sound was similar, but greatly magnified. I took great gulps of air and fought the urge to run—to run anywhere, just to preserve myself. 'Have courage and hold fast,' Grandpa had said. 'I know you'll do your duty.' His words and his confidence gave me the strength to stay where I was.

Stan and Andrew wheeled around, caught totally off guard. The beast had not been in its cave, as we'd assumed, but was coming from behind. I shifted slightly to get a better view of Andrew, who quickly loaded a syringe with Immobilon and placed it into the dart that Stan was holding for him. I glanced over at Grandpa, who had raised his gun. I decided to do the same and raised my weapon, released the safety catch and trained it toward the undergrowth. And then it came again, this time louder and more terrifying—a deep-throated wailing, snarling, vicious sound. I gripped my gun to steady myself and glanced over to see whether Andrew and Stan were ready.

'Come on, you're going to be too late, hurry,' I whispered under my breath. But then I saw the accident happen.

Andrew withdrew the syringe from the dart, and the next thing I knew Stan was shouting, 'It's soaked through!' Some of the Immobilon must have touched Stan's skin! I saw Andrew quickly pull out another syringe to fill it.

'Andrew!' Stan cried.

But Andrew was steady in his task. I watched in horror as Stan clutched his heart and reached out to steady himself on a nearby rock with his other hand. Within seconds, Andrew had given him the injection and was crouching over him.

'Some of the drug made contact with his leg and the antiserum is causing palpitations. I'll have to get him to hospital quickly,' Andrew whispered to Grandpa, who had moved from his cover and was crouching on the edge of the quarry. 'I can carry him, but I'll have to leave you here.'

'Okay, come on, I've got you covered,' Grandpa said.

Andrew lifted Stan onto his giant shoulders as though he were a sack of potatoes, scrambled up the bank and disappeared into the forest. Grandpa scrambled down the bank with his gun still trained toward the noises that couldn't have been more than fifty feet away at that point. Where was it, why wouldn't it come out?

He beckoned me to join him in picking up Stan and Andrew's gear, and I scrambled down from my hiding place.

'Come on, lad,' he said, 'we'll have to finish this business another day when we've got more back-up. Don't look so worried. Stan'll be all right. He's a real tough character, that one. Let's just get this stuff and follow them down to the road before that creature gets here to give us any trouble.'

Nelson made several advances towards the trees, as if he would go to take care of the enemy himself, and Grandpa, with his gun trained towards the trees to cover our retreat, heeled him back.

'Okay Grandpa,' I said, 'I think I've got everything.' I was shaking and hoping not to show any hint of fear or relief.

'Okay laddie,' he said. There was the twinkle in his eye, as if this sort of adventure happened to him all the time. 'You make your way towards the bank and Nelson and I'll cover you, won't we Nelson?'

It was only when I was clear of the bank, having pulled Nelson up with me by the scruff of his neck, that I saw it coming.

Out of the darkness and through the trees, with a ferocious speed and purpose, came our long-awaited enemy. It was a grey-brown creature, catlike, but with colossal proportions. It sprang into the quarry and flew toward Grandpa, who wheeled round to defend himself, tripped on a rock, and was flung backwards.

'Good God!' he shouted. His gun lay on the ground, several feet away from him.

Then the beast was on him. Its eyes were a deathly pale yellow, its teeth too large for its hideous mouth, and its long body taut and muscular.

Grandpa raised his hands to fend off the creature, but its vicious claws were already tearing into his skin. Nelson leapt down to defend his master. For a split second I looked on, stunned, as if it were all a strange dream, or a computer game or a film. I could do nothing. Grandpa was going to die. The creature disposed of Nelson with one strike of its powerful claw.

'Shoot it, damn it! Shoot it now!' Grandpa gasped.

The sight of Nelson lying next to my grandfather, who was being shredded with hateful speed, suddenly filled me with a deep strength of resolve. It was a mixture of love for my grandfather, and Nelson, a hatred of all that would harm them, and a reckless abandonment to protect them at any cost. I dropped everything I was carrying except the gun and took aim. In one hideous second I realized that with the slightest waver I could hit Grandpa instead of the cat.

'For God's sake, kill it!' he screamed in a high-pitched gasp. I squeezed the trigger, and there was a thunderous bang. When I opened my eyes I saw that I'd hit the creature's back leg. It had wheeled round and, leaving the now silent and motionless form of my Grandpa, was heading towards me through the clearing grey smoke.

The image of David Crockett and his knife came to me in that moment. I had no time to reload but stooped to pull out my dagger as the animal flew toward me. I was on the bank, uphill, and that was my one and only advantage. I knew I had to use my height and leverage to full advantage immediately. I launched myself from the bank, and we met in midair. I slashed at the beast with my dagger as it caught hold of my shoulder and waist with its claws. But as we both reeled back I landed on top, crushing the creature under me. It snarled with rage and I got one good stab at its ribs. I felt that I might have done some damage, and maybe I did. But this animal was pure muscle and, for every stab I made, it tore back at my hands and arm.

Within seconds it had thrown me clear and was up, poised for the next attack. The dagger had flown from my hand and was lying just out of reach. The beast circled and snarled. My bloodied hands were shaking and I couldn't reach the knife. The beast limped slightly and was bleeding from the stab wounds in its side but showed no sign of tiring or turning. It did not fear me. I belonged to it now. It was built to fight to the death; there was no way to retreat.

Then there was a yelp and a bark and, bloodied and battered as he was, Nelson came to my rescue. He rushed all at once upon the beast and, for a vital split second, drew his attention. When I turned back, knife in hand, the gallant little fellow had plunged his teeth into the neck of the beast and was hanging on for all he was worth. This was my chance, and I knew it. With all the strength and speed I could muster I flung myself at the distracted beast, who reared to greet me with Nelson still hanging on.

We embraced in a deadly lock and I felt its claws ripping into my arm and side. It was excruciating, like cold steel cutting through to the bone, but I lashed out, plunging the dagger time and time again into its side. Its eyes were ignited with rage and I could smell its foul, humid breath as it bore down upon me and I turned my head to protect my face from its teeth. I got three more good stabs in before it overpowered me and we all fell back. My head banged against a stone on the ground. I began to feel faint as the beast lashed again and again at my arms with its paws. Then, all of a sudden, I saw its mouth opening toward my face with tremendous speed.

Instinctively I raised my left hand and its jaws closed about my left wrist. In that moment I managed to ram the dagger high up the animal's rib cage near its heart. The third time, just as my right arm was ready to give up, I felt the dagger sink in to the hilt. The beast gave an almighty wail and released my mangled forearm. And then, as quickly as it had started, it was over. The beast reeled back and slumped over on its side. It gasped for breath after breath as those pale, unyielding eyes bore into me. Beyond the beast Grandpa lay motionless in a pool of blood.

Nelson was lying next to me. I made my way over to Grandpa and began to sob. Blood was spurting from a huge rip in his arm. It's a major artery, I thought. Please, no. I took off my belt and strapped his arm up tight to stop the flow. That was the last thing I remembered.

PART FOUR

PATIENCE

17

FAMOUS FOR FIFTEEN MINUTES

I've got a bit of movement, I think he's coming round.' I heard a voice, far away, miles above me.

'Okay, give him another shot. I don't want him getting excited before we can get him to A and E,' said another voice in the distance.

I started to come round again in the back of an ambulance bouncing along the lanes. I heard the siren and fought to keep my eyes open as a paramedic attached something to the drip on my arm. There was an overwhelming, metallic smell of blood—like being at the dentist, but worse. A warm rush went through my body. I felt sick. I passed out.

Beep. Beep. Beep. I felt drowsy and thirsty. Very thirsty. It took me awhile, lying there half awake, to recollect what had happened. Beep. Beep. Beep. A hospital. I was in hospital. There was a rustling of curtains and I opened my eyes. Andrew's face gradually came into focus.

'All right, Will, take it easy.' There were bloodstains on his jacket.

'Grandpa,' I croaked. 'Grandpa's bleeding and he's going to die if we don't–'

Andrew put his giant hand firmly on my shoulder. 'It's okay, Will, your grandpa's here. He's going to make it, thanks to you stopping the bleeding. You've done all right, now just stay calm.'

'Nelson? What about Nelson? He saved my life but ...' my voice trailed off and my mouth felt numb and dry.

Andrew laughed. 'Don't worry, about Nelson. He was unconscious, but it would take more than a cougar to kill him! He's down at the practice and one of the partners is stitching him up. And, before you ask, Stan's okay too. He's on the same ward as your grandpa. Everything's going to be okay. You need to rest. You're going to need all the energy you've got.' He raised an eyebrow, and even in my groggy state I saw the twinkle in his eye.

'Why?'

'Why? Because you're quite the hero lad and there'll be reporters and TV crews here before long to visit the 'Beast Slayer', so you'd better get some shut-eye.'

The curtain rustled again and Andrew stepped aside so a Hispanic-looking doctor could approach the bed.

'But you don't have to worry about that, Mr William Houston. I will not let them disturb my patient until I am sure that he is in a fit state. I am Doctor Michael and you, my boy, are lucky to be alive.'

'Am I badly hurt?' I asked.

'No, but you could have been and you probably should have been. You have injuries to your left leg and arms and I operated on these last night. They were more punctures than lesions, that is to say tears in the skin, and so we have given you a range of inoculations to insure there is no further infection.'

'But will I be able to use them again? Will I be able to walk?'

They both looked at me for a moment and Andrew burst out laughing.

'Of course you will!' the doctor said.

'Haven't you been listening?' Andrew said. 'The cuts weren't too bad. I think you can thank the Grenfell jacket for that.'

'Oh,' I said, feeling embarrassed. 'There was so much blood everywhere.'

'You are coming round from a minor operation and will be returned to the ward when the anaesthetist is happy that you are suffering no adverse effects to the drugs,' the doctor said. 'Until then I cannot stress enough that you should remain calm.'

When I was wheeled down the corridor to the ward later that morning I saw nurses smiling at me. 'Well done,' a few said. The nurses on the ward lined up and clapped as I was jolted through the doorway. 'Good on ye, lad!' another patient called out. This felt good, very good in fact, my cheeks flushed. A doctor looked up from his clipboard and smiled as I passed by.

Grandpa and Stan were already there in Room B361. They were beaming at me. The nurse wheeled my bed into the space next to theirs, clanked on the brakes and hoisted me up to the same level. Directly opposite us were three thickset, bullish-looking men sitting up in their beds. They were pursing their lips over their copies of *The Sun* and *Autotrader* magazine. A television blared out the daytime shows from a fuzzy set overhanging someone's bed.

'Well, lad, I would say you've earned your stripes,' Grandpa said with a smile and a moist look in his eye which showed pride and gratitude beyond his words.

'Aye, you did a good job, laddie, well done,' Stan wheezed from the other bed. He tried to sit up, winced, and swore under his breath.

I smiled. It was strange to see them in pyjamas. They looked so much smaller, almost unrecognizable.

'Tell us what happened, Will,' Grandpa said. 'All we know is that you strapped my arm and somehow killed the beast.'

As I recounted the detail, they hung on every word. They drew their breath and shook their heads and exclaimed.

'What a beast that were!' Stan said.

'Aye, I can tell you now I feared the end,' Grandpa said.

We were comparing our battle wounds when we heard a disturbance in the corridor.

'No of course we're not the general public!'

'I should say we are not!' Those were two unmistakable voices. I saw Dr Michael hastening after the two intruders and heard his soft intonation but couldn't make out his words above the huffing and protestations of none other than the Millstone sisters.

'Ah, good, some sport,' said Grandpa as he rearranged his covers. 'This should be interesting, since they only let family and church ministers visit.'

'I'll bet they get in to see us,' said Stan, who was straining over from his bed to peer at the spectacle. 'Say twenty pounds, Major?' he wagered.

'Well, I would tend to put my money on your side,' Grandpa said with a chuckle. 'But in the interests of the sport I accept! Twenty pounds it is.'

Meanwhile, the commotion at the staff nurse's desk continued.

'No, we're not family. Church ministers? What a ridiculous question, do we look like church ministers?' Frieda demanded.

'Damn lot of nonsense,' Hilda said. 'I don't know what's wrong with people in hospitals.'

'No proper ventilation—it makes people odd!' Frieda said. She took off her raincoat and tucked it under her arm. She was not leaving anytime soon.

'Ladies, I am sorry, but unless you are family or church ministers you cannot visit these patients until tomorrow. Hospital rules,' Dr Michael said firmly.

'That's ridiculous! We haven't come all the way from Loweswater to be sent back by a cleaner!' Hilda said.

Grandpa and Stan were in hysterics, which was actually causing them some pain.

'Madam, I am a doctor!' Dr Michael said. His voice trembled, but I thought he hid his anger well.

'Oh, I see.' Frieda peered down at his badge. 'Can't read it without my glasses. What does it say, Hilda?'

Hilda bent forward and squinted. 'I can't read it either.'

'It says Dr Michael.' He raised his voice. 'That is my name, Michael!'

'All right, there's no need to shout. I'm not deaf, Dr Migwell. Well, not as deaf as her, anyway!' Hilda said as she glanced at her sister.

'Deaf? I'm not deaf, heard every word,' Frieda said. She turned to the doctor. 'Dr Manwell, we may not be clergy but we have come from the Loweswater W.I. and the Mother's Union which, in every sense, represents the parish. Besides, people have said that we both have a unique way with the sick. We are very close personal friends of the Major's and merely require a few minutes to drop these gifts off and check that they are being properly looked after before we go.' Her voice was both plaintive and indignant and I sensed she had won.

Dr Michael threw up his hands and left them in the hands of a nervous looking staff nurse. 'I give in, nurse, let them do as they please. But just five minutes.' As he passed by the door I heard him muttering, 'Not paid to be insulted by racists.'

'What on earth is the matter with him?' Hilda asked the nurse, who just smiled.

'Latin sorts! Temperamental, too much sun.' Frieda said as she watched him disappear down the corridor.

The nurse pointed the way, and the women made their advance. Stan and Grandpa recovered from their hysterics just in time for the arrival.

'Doesn't look like anything much is wrong with you if you can sit up grinning like a Cheshire cat,' Hilda said, trying to hide her relief.

'Good morning, ladies, how nice to see you.' Grandpa said.

Frieda had paused in the doorway and was glancing at the bed opposite Stan, where one of the tough looking men was slumped with his *Sun* newspaper open to page three as he gazed blankly toward the television set. As if it was her perfect right and as natural an action as cleaning up one of her dog's messes, she marched over to her unsuspecting victim and removed the offensive object.

'What do we do with rubbish?' she demanded.

The man looked blank.

'Rubbish goes in the bin!' she answered as she strode to the bin near the window while all three men looked on in bewilderment. 'Stuffy in here, Hilda, isn't it? Need some air,' she said as she wrenched open the window.

The cool morning air sent all three men further under their covers, but they chose to fix their eyes on Oprah Winfrey rather than tackle the women at the end of their bed.

'And what on earth is *this* rubbish?' she demanded as she followed their gazes to the screen. 'Americans!' she spluttered, and proceeded to pull the plug. The next thing I knew she was at my bedside, ready to sort me out too.

'We were nurses you know, Major,' Hilda said. 'You don't have to look so scared. Now let's just make you comfortable.'

Apparently this meant that we all had to be sitting up straight. It became painfully obvious that the design of hospital beds had changed quite a bit since their nursing days, but with a series of violent jerks they soon had us— and the beds—where they wanted. We all managed to smile for them despite the agony of our newly jolted injuries.

Then we received our gifts. First there was what appeared to be a funeral wreath, which was left over from a W.I. demonstration the preceding Tuesday. It was very large and looked as if it would be more at home at a grand naval funeral than in a hospital ward. Hilda tried in vain to cajole it onto the bedside table before she eventually hung it above Grandpa's bed, on the medical apparatus. Then there were cartons of prune juice, which we were instructed to take twice daily.

'To keep you regular,' Frieda said. 'As you know, constipation is a great scourge among hospital patients.'

'Naturally we brought you a copy of today's *Telegraph*,' said Frieda with a withering glance to her left at the man whose paper she had binned, 'and I dare say the Major will let you read it when he has finished.'

'But only if you behave!' Grandpa said as he wagged his finger, which sent Stan into another fit of coughing.

There were also some chocolates to keep our spirits up. Last of all, Hilda slid a small bottle of brandy out of her bag.

'Well, Hilda, that's very kind, but I'm not sure it will go with the medication,' Grandpa said, hesitating in jest.

'Nonsense. Brandy is just the thing to go with every medication. Everyone knows that. Here, take this,' she said as she sloshed a generous glug into Grandpa's hospital beaker and then into mine and made us drink.

'I think I need some medicine too,' Stan said as he looked over longingly.

'No, Stanley, we brought *you* some Kaolin and Morphine. Now open wide.' Stan, for once without strength to resist took his medicine and winced as it went down.

I managed to finish my double brandy before the staff nurse came in and commented on the strange smell. She was of course referring to the brandy but Frieda, who took the comment personally, pointed out that it was hardly surprising since they never opened the windows and that it was no wonder there were so many sick people in the hospital.

Grandpa was quite revived by the tipple and offered to keep the bottle for later, to which Hilda agreed. The sisters were about to leave, satisfied that their ministry to the sick had been adequately discharged on behalf of the W.I., when Hilda spotted my Sikh anaesthetist, complete with turban and beard, coming with the drug trolley to do the ward round.

'Oh, good!' she exclaimed. 'I nearly forgot ... your tea major!' She reached into her sturdy leather handbag and produced some packets of teabags. 'Quick, Frieda, stop that man with the tea trolley and I'll give him these.'

Frieda obliged. 'You there! Please wait here a moment my man! We have some tea for Major Wallace.'

Dr Hassan had treated me earlier that morning, after the operation, and he, Andrew and I had had a good laugh before I'd been transferred to the ward. He looked enquiringly toward me. I grinned and gave him a knowing nod to wait and receive his medicine as we all had to.

'Right, I've got them all now,' Hilda said as she stood up. 'What's the man's name, Frieda? Does he speak English?

What ... is ... your ... name?' She spoke this last question slowly and very loudly.

'I am Dr Hassan.'

Hilda barged over to him with handfuls of teabags. 'What's that? Speak up, man!'

'It's Hassan.'

'No, no, not Assam. The Major likes Darjeeling for breakfast with an Earl Grey, Lapsang mix in the afternoon. Look, I've written down the instructions, it's all in the bag. *Instructions ...in ... the ... bag!* You can read, can't you?'

'I will do my best,' he said.

'Very good of you, thank you,' Frieda said. Then she turned to us. 'You've got to be firm with these people if you are to get anything done properly.'

'Well, Stan, I believe that's what the Church of England calls "errands of mercy"!' Grandpa said once they had left. In another fit of laughter he bumped his head on the titanic wreath.

The next visitor was similarly impatient with the staff. 'Where is that man?' she demanded, and almost instantly she was in the doorway, glaring past me to Grandpa. She ran to his side. 'Reginald Wallace, you stubborn, infuriating, thoughtless man! What on earth did you think you were doing, taking Will on a dangerous trip like that? He could have been killed, and you could have been too if Will hadn't rescued you—you reckless, old—'

'Come now, Elsie, stop making a fuss. We're okay, give me a kiss,' Grandpa said. He was still floating on the effects of the brandy—as was I. I took a sip of water, hoping it might mask the smell.

'I will do no such thing,' she said. Granny turned to me and sat on the side of my bed. 'Poor William, how are you sweetheart? I called your mum and dad, and they're on their way up now.' She patted my arm and sniffed. 'What's that smell?' She grabbed my beaker and I grinned stupidly. 'It's brandy!' she declared. 'This boy is drunk, Reggie—what have you been giving him now?'

'Hold your horses, Elsie, the Millstones made us have a little tipple.'

'Oh did they? And I suppose they brought that funeral wreath as well? Well, that is just great—his parents coming up this afternoon and him smelling like a tramp!'

I could tell Granny wasn't really cross, but I knew she'd had a nasty shock when she got the call the night before. Apparently she and Aunty Dora had spent the night at our bedsides—and they hadn't slept much when they finally did go home to sleep.

We did get her to chuckle about the prunes and poor Doctors Michael and Hassan.

'And to think I waited nearly ten years to marry you!' she said as she bent over to kiss Grandpa goodbye.

Grandpa snorted. 'And wasn't I worth it?'

Granny didn't answer him as she walked out, though I could see she was smiling.

As the additional medication began to take effect, the television droned in the background while Grandpa and Stan retold the story of the beast. It almost sounded like a fairytale. A good story, I thought. This year I could write an amazing essay on 'What I did this Summer'. But my teachers wouldn't believe me. And since I had such a great story they probably wouldn't assign that topic, for the first year ever. Maybe I could write the story anyway. Where would I begin? I drifted off.

I woke to a soft, familiar voice. My mother. I opened my eyes to see her and Dad standing beside my bed. She smoothed my forehead, inspected my wounds, and gave me the third degree.

'But what were you doing with a knife and a gun?' she asked. She shook her head and looked over at her father, who was trying to make small talk with Dad.

'I think we'll have him transferred to a hospital in Liverpool,' she said when Dr Michael came in.

'I assure you that's not necessary,' Dr Michael told her. 'He'll be discharged in a few days as long as his wounds start to heal without infection.'

Mum didn't look convinced but decided she'd stay in Cumbria until I was discharged and take me back home then.

This thought scared me almost as much as the beast had. I was finally having my first real taste of adventure, and the last thing I wanted was to be carted back to the city to spend the rest of the summer in front of my computer. But I knew I couldn't act like I had when they packed me off up here only a few weeks ago.

'Please let me stay,' I said. 'I mean, it's up to you, because you're my parents, but I really like it here and I'm helping Grandpa with some gardening—and other things, and I'm making friends. I'm learning so much about who I am, too. You know, about my family history, and—and tons of other stuff.'

My parents both looked at me and then, for the first time in a long time, at each other.

'The lad's right,' Grandpa said. 'I won't hear of him going now. He's really settling in, and I need his help. I'll make sure he doesn't get into any more scrapes.'

At this Mum looked sceptical, but they both agreed I could stay if that's what I wanted and it wasn't too much trouble for Granny.

Dad was worried, though, about how to handle the media. Journalists had already contacted Dad and Granny for information and he didn't want it to get out of hand. I couldn't wait to talk to them. This could be my first step to something big.

'There's something else, Will,' Dad said. 'I'm also concerned about animal rights activists.'

'What do you mean?' I asked. 'Are they worried about Nelson? Because he's fine–'

'No, Will, the cougar. When your mum and I came in there were two women outside the hospital being interviewed by Border TV. They were carrying placards and whipping up a frenzied defence of the cougar.'

'But that's ridiculous! We had a dart ready and poor Stan–'

'I know, I know,' Dad said. 'They're just showing their ignorance, but we need to handle this carefully so people have the real story.'

'Will I get to be on TV?' I asked. 'I hope my friends in Liverpool see–'

'No, Will.' Dad shook his head. 'I think we need to make sure you have as little contact with the media as possible.'

'Aye, your father's right, Will,' Grandpa said. 'Those reporters can be more dangerous than wild beasts.'

And I handled the wild beast so I can handle the reporters, I thought. But I didn't say that. I didn't want them to think the notoriety was going to my head, which of course it was. As we continued to debate my future stardom, Reverend Scott's huge form filled the doorway.

'I'm sorry to intrude on yer family reunion,' he said, 'but I couldn't help overhearing and I think I might have a solution.' The vicar strode into the room and introduced himself to my parents as well as to Grandpa and Stan. He seemed to build an immediate rapport with the men in particular, and they were eager to hear his proposal—as was Dr Michael, who had just come in too. Suddenly the room seemed very small indeed.

'Well Roger, what is it that you're suggesting?' Mum asked.

'Well, I gather that the bairn wants to stay in Cumbria but ye're afraid that the intrusion of the press in the aftermath of yesterday's heroics will prove too much for his ego and Elsie's patience.'

Dad smiled in spite of himself. 'Yes, that's about it.'

'Well, I do have a suggestion, but I need to ask the doctor a question first.'

'I am all ears, Vicar—what is it?' asked Dr Michael.

'Would ye say that, given a steady recovery and nae further infection, Will might be able to ride a pony in five days' time? Not fast, mind ... just trotting along.'

To my surprise, Dr Michael didn't even hesitate. 'Of course he could. As I've said to his mother, he should be discharged in a few days. He'll be walking tomorrow, maybe even this evening—no, I see no problem with him riding a horse ... provided he doesn't fall off!'

There was a general chuckle.

'Aye,' the vicar said. 'Well then, let'uz tell ye ma idea. Next Thursday ma family and I will be taking oor annual holiday. This year ma lass persuaded us to hire ponies and do a trekking, camping and walking holiday in the valleys around Loweswater. Ma wife suggested last week that it would be nice for ma lad Richard to have someone his own age to lark about with and ma wife, who has a soft spot for yer lad, suggested that William join us for the trip. It will only be for a few nights, and we won't be far from home, but it would get Will away from the media storm until it blows over. What d'ye think?'

My parents exchanged glances. Mum looked apprehensive but Dad seemed to like the idea.

'What do you think, son?' he asked.

'But Will can't ride,' Mum said. 'He went once in Wales, but that was years ago and then there's the expense. We can't put upon your family like this–'

'Please,' the vicar said with a smile. 'You will'nae be putting upon us. My daughter will select Will a sturdy naig and lead rein him till he feels confident. And as for the money, well he can pay his own way if that makes ye feel more comfortable.'

Mum seemed fine with that, and they all looked for the final vote from me. The thought of being out of the limelight and giving up the chance to rub shoulders with David Beckham was painful. But, on the other hand, being with the Scotts—and particularly Hannah—seemed like such a good idea I didn't hesitate.

'Well, Grandpa,' I said, 'if you're sure you can manage without me ...'

'Of course I can manage,' he said. 'Besides, Doctor Michael says he needs me in here for about ten days, and Stan can spare you I dare say, so go on—have some fun.'

I grinned. 'Thank you,' I said to Reverend Scott. 'That would be great.'

At that moment Hannah arrived in the doorway, carrying a bag from the hospital shop. She hesitated when she saw the room full of people and walked gingerly to the end of my bed. Her father did the introductions. She came close to my bedside and gave me a little wave. 'Hey, how are you?'

'How do I look?'

'Pretty awful, actually, but better than I was expecting.'

'The lass has been worried sick, more like!' the vicar said. Mum raised an eyebrow.

Hannah didn't take him on. 'Well of course we've all been worried,' she said. 'Anyway, look, I got you this—it's my favourite.' She took a fruit and nut bar out of the bag and handed it to me.

I smiled at her. 'Thank you,' I said.

'He doesn't really like nuts in chocolate,' Mum said.

I glared at her.

'Oh, I'm sorry,' Hannah said. 'I should have thought.'

'No, don't worry,' I said. 'I really appreciate it.' I smiled again and she tried to smile back.

'Aye,' the vicar said, 'don't worry, pet, you and I can share it on the way home—if you dun'nae tell your mum! Will here has agreed to come with us next week.'

'Oh, that's wonderful!' Hannah smiled, for real this time, and then glanced over at my mum. 'I mean, that's good, Will, as long as it's okay with your parents? And the doctor?'

Everyone nodded, and Hannah assured me she'd choose a better horse for me than she did a chocolate bar.

After the vicar and Hannah left, the nurses helped me into a wheelchair and I spent the rest of the afternoon with Dad and Mum. They seemed to be getting along, but I didn't know if that was just for my benefit and I didn't ask whether or not Dad had moved back home yet.

'I do believe you've grown up a bit over the past few weeks,' Dad said as he patted me on the back. 'You seem more—mature.'

'Oh, it's the country air!' Mum said. But she was smiling and I could tell they were both pleased.

Mum had tears in her eyes when she left. She stood between my bed and Grandpa's. 'I could have lost both of you,' she said, shaking her head.

'Don't worry, lass, we've had our last big adventure for awhile, haven't we, Will?'

I nodded and squeezed Mum's hand.

'Aye,' Grandpa continued with a twinkle in his eye, 'the big game hunting around here isn't what it used to be.'

Mum gave me a hug, Dad gave me money for the holiday, and they left to have dinner with Granny before driving back.

'I'll see you at Granny and Grandpa's fiftieth wedding anniversary,' she said. 'It's only four weeks away.'

'Listen, I'm proud of you son,' Dad said. 'Don't forget to call us, let me know if you need anything.'

'Fifty years,' I said to Grandpa after they'd left. 'That's a long time!'

'Aye, that little sentence "I will" turned out to be two life sentences!' he joked.

He was, I could tell, looking forward to having a big do. He'd hired a marquee for the field and outside caterers. 'Aye,' he said, 'we didn't consult the ladies of the W.I. on that one, and you should have seen the consternation that caused—an unexpected bonus!' He chuckled again, though I could see all this laughter was still causing him some pain.

When our dinner arrived we all had another good laugh trying to identify what it was. Dr Hassan, who was by then off duty, appeared with a big grin and a tea tray.

'Ah now,' he said, 'I did promise to do my best. And I didn't quite dare to disobey the sisters! You make sure you tell them, won't you, that I followed orders?'

We promised that we would, and Dr Hassan joined us for a cup of Grandpa's favourite Earl Grey and Lapsang mix, which I thought was pretty awful.

Dr Hassan had probably never seen such an array of characters. 'There's been some excitement around our little hospital today,' he said.

'Were there many reporters out there?' I asked. 'I might do some TV interviews tomorrow,' I said with a glance at Grandpa.

Dr Hassan smiled and tweaked his moustache. 'He that can have patience can have what he will,' he said.

'That's cool,' I said, 'is that a proverb from your culture?'

He laughed. 'No, Will, that was Benjamin Franklin!'

Between the excitement of meeting the press, the anticipation of the riding holiday and my painful wounds, I didn't sleep much that night.

I finally drifted off just before breakfast was served and interrupted my dream, in which I was a Blue Peter presenter. I told Grandpa about my dream over our cups of hospital-issue tea. Dr Hassan had gone home.

'Hey laddie, they may love you now but that's 'cos you're feeding their machine. Just remember that no matter how rich you become, or how famous, when you die the number of people at your funeral will still pretty much depend on the weather!'

I smiled, but he couldn't snatch away my dream that easily.

'The press come from another world,' Grandpa said. 'Treat them with courtesy but don't change yourself for them, for they will forget you soon enough, or turn on you for another story.'

As it turned out, Grandpa was right. The reporters were only after thirty seconds of news footage to feed the public hunger for novelty sound bites. They had no interest in me or in my long-term career as a star.

I was fascinated by what went on behind the cameras with the TV crews, but by lunchtime I was exhausted by telling my story over and over. And I was bored.

One particularly pushy woman from a magazine completely ignored the nurse's hints that I was tired and needed a break.

'Just one more thing,' she'd say before she'd ask another loaded questions about animal rights, my feelings about and experience with guns, my knowledge of cougars, and so on. It quickly became clear that, regardless of my answer, she would still want to ask 'just one more thing' to show me in an unfavourable light. We'd made it clear to the other journalists that our adventure had been, in essence, a conservation exercise turned survival scenario, but she didn't seem to be interested in the truth and Grandpa saw what was coming.

In a stroke of genius he reached over and spilt his tea on her notebook and suit.

'Oh, I am most dreadfully sorry, how clumsy of me! Here, take this napkin to dry yourself.'

'No, no, just—honestly, it's ruined,' she said, dabbing away at the stain with her tissue.

'My dear, I think you have enough. And, as the nurse has told you, William needs to rest now.'

She glared at Grandpa. 'But Mr Wallace, I just have one more question.'

Grandpa's eyes sparkled. 'Yes, Madam, but I still have *one more* jug full of water. So if I were you I'd leave while I had the chance. Good day to you!'

As she stomped out of the room Stan wiped his eyes and let out his long-suppressed guffaw.

'As Hilda said yesterday, "You've got to be firm with these people!" Jolly good advice!' Grandpa said as he fished out his own handkerchief.

But what if she publishes nasty things about us?' I asked.

'Don't look so worried, lad. How did Kipling put it? "If you can meet with Triumph and Disaster, And treat those

two impostors just the same ... you'll be a Man, my son!"
Count yourself happy to be alive and free from the Millstone
sisters!'

I drifted off to sleep again, freed from my dreams of
fame and fortune. I imagined riding over the mountains
with Hannah, and that brought me round to Granny's
parting comment to Grandpa the day before. How did she
know that he would marry her after waiting those ten long
years? How could she have been so patient? I thought she
might tell me more, to while away my hours in the hospital.
I didn't know then that she would bring Lewis with her
and that he would bring his own form of entertainment to
lighten the dullness of the hospital routines.

18

THE PATIENCE OF A SAINT

D o you need more pain medication, lad? You look a bit miserable.'

'No, Grandpa, I'm okay. I just miss being at church this morning, that's all.'

He relaxed back into his pillow. 'Well, you've certainly changed your tune in the last few weeks.'

'Yeah, I hope so. I mean, I hope it's for the best.'

He smiled pensively and went back to the paper.

Stan was discharged after the morning ward round. Grandpa and I were sorry to see him go. I'd grown to appreciate his humour and, without whiskey, Stan was less bristly. He'd been invited to the vicarage for lunch and, when Grandpa had teased him, he'd replied, 'Eeeh, stop your noise, man. I'm just having a bite to eat with the fella, I'm not going religious!'

I was hopeful for Stan that he would actually have more than a bite to eat. He never spoke to me about his wife's betrayal, but I was sure the Scotts could help him if anyone could.

The afternoon passed slowly until Aunty Dora, Granny and Lewis turned up. Lewis was a bit sheepish and awkward at first, but he soon forgot his shyness as he made me recount the attack in graphic detail.

'Oooh, I bet it were right spooky!' he said, rolling his eyes. 'You should have taken us along, you know, for back-up.'

Eventually Granny wheeled a weary Grandpa out to the hospital garden in a wheelchair for some fresh air.

Lewis followed them. 'Mum gave us two quid to get us both some sweets from the shop. I'll get you a Dr Pepper and some Timeouts if I can—won't be a moment!' Granny commissioned him to get Grandpa some Alka Seltzer as well.

I was glad to have a few minutes with Aunty Dora. She'd come to be a solid reference point of love and calm in my life over the past few weeks.

'Well, dear, it appears you have more of your grandfather in you than you gave yourself credit for. We're very proud of your courage. Well done. I expect you're glad it's all over.'

'Yes, except I don't know what the papers will make of it. There was one nasty reporter in yesterday who was out to criticize us.' I told her how Grandpa had dealt with her and Aunty Dora laughed.

'There's a famous saying about critics, Will. That it's not them who count "but the man who is actually in the arena, whose face is marred by dust and sweat and blood, who strives valiantly, who errs and comes up short again and again" and then the end of the quote I remember best: "who, at the best, knows, in the end, the triumph of high achievement, and who, at the worst, if he fails, at least he fails while daring greatly, so that his place shall never be with those cold and timid souls who know neither victory nor defeat."'

'That's cool,' I said. I wondered if I'd ever be able to reel off profound quotes like everyone else up here seemed to do.

'Well you'll find it in your Uncle Jim's little book.'

'Did I ever meet Uncle Jim? I know I've seen his photograph on the piano at home and everything. He was a builder, right?'

'Yes, that's right,' she said. 'But he was gone long before you arrived.' She gazed out of the window. 'In fact, he died in this very hospital. Seems like an age ago now.'

'Here? What happened?'

'Well, we were married in the summer of 1956 and we were very happy. He ran a small building firm that his late father had started, and Jim's mother taught me how to keep the books. Those were good years, and I'm glad we had such good ones before the illnesses came.'

'Illnesses?'

'Yes, it all started when he did a small extension for your Uncle Sid. There had been some problem with the plastering, but Sidney refused payment on the whole job. It came at a bad time for the business and even when the work was put right Sid withheld payment with excuse after excuse.'

'But that's terrible!' I said. I could easily imagine it, though.

'Oh, it's just the way some people do business—you'll learn that as you get older. Anyway, it was during that stressful time that Jim took a bad turn. The doctor said it was hypertension—you know, high blood pressure, and he gave Jim something called Rauwolfia to help. It appeared to do the trick, though he had to take large doses because he was quite a big man. But no one told us about the side effects, and that was the worst of it.'

'Oh no,' I said. 'Why? What were they?'

'Terrible depression,' Aunty Dora said. 'He was so low most days that going to work was more than he could face.

Sometimes a week could go by without him getting out of bed, which was very difficult for us. The business went to the wall and we had to sell the house and move in with Jim's mother, who wasn't very understanding about Jim's condition. Well, most people weren't in those days. She kept telling him to pull himself together, which made him even worse. It made her angry to see all that they had worked for disappear, and she was worried too, I guess.'

'But what about the doctors? Didn't they stop the medication or something?'

'Oh eventually they did, but by then it was too late. Something chemical had changed inside his brain, I think, and no matter what they tried he didn't ever fully recover. They didn't have all the treatments and knowledge then that they have now. Anyway, we coped because we had to, but eventually Jim had a stroke and he died a week later, right here at this hospital.'

'Oh, that must have been so hard.'

'Yes it was, dear. You see, I had to live with him and some of the time he was only partly the man I fell in love with. But they do say true love is when the other person's happiness is more important than your own. Poor Jim, it wasn't his fault but he took a lot of his frustrations out on me, it wasn't easy … but I promised him for better or worse, and that was that. I'd never go back on that promise. Sometimes I used to lie awake praying that God would give me my old Jim back, and every once in a while I'd see a glimmer of sparkle return to his eyes and I'd remember, but those were just a few brief seconds over the years.'

'Did you blame Uncle Sid?' It was really his fault, I thought.

'Oh, to my shame I secretly blamed lots of people: Sidney, the doctor, Jim and his mother, and even God for that matter, but in the end blaming people doesn't do any good. As the vicar says, "Life isn't about getting a good hand but playing a bad hand well." I don't think I'm a fatalist, Will, but I do trust God to know what he's doing with my life. So I just waited it out, took one day at a time. It was never very glamorous, I know, but I trusted God for enough strength for the day in front of me and then got on with it.'

'Sounds rough to me,' I said. I didn't know what I'd do if horrible things like that happened to me.

She smiled sadly. 'Yes it was, dear, but we'd never learn to be brave and patient if there were only joy in the world.'

'Were you a bit relieved when it was over?' I blurted out. 'I mean, I know I might have felt a bit—trapped—or something ...'

'Well, yes. That's a very hard question, but yes, I think in a strange way I'd been mourning for Jim for years before he died. I felt a great relief that his trial was over ... though I couldn't have known that mine were just beginning.'

'Why? What happened next?'

'Well, I looked after Jim's mother for another eleven years after Jim died. She was getting on by then and needed someone to care for her. I couldn't move out then, when she needed someone—not when she had taken us into her home in our time of trouble. So I stayed on and looked after her too. But oh Will, what a woman she was—always complaining, nothing ever good enough or done right. She had never really liked me anyway, and was always mocking me. She was keen enough to go to see gypsies to get her fortune told and to read her horoscope, but would she stand any talk of the Bible or God? Oh, would she get worked up! She was hard work and she almost finished me. In fact, I'd made up my mind to get her into a home when the Lord showed me the verse about "doing unto others as you would have them do unto you". Well, I knew right then and there that God was calling me to go on caring for her. I said, "Lord, I haven't got any more to give" and do you know, almost immediately the verse came to me, "Come unto me all you who are heavy laden and I will give you rest, learn of me ..." You know the one, don't you? Well that was it, I had to keep going, and do you know it was the best thing I ever did.'

'Really?' I found this hard to believe. 'Why?'

'Well, the more I started to pray for God's patience and love to flow through me, the more she opened up. Her bitterness and restless agitation started to subside, and eventually she did pray with me and read the Bible. She died peacefully a few years later, and to this day I thank God that he caused me to keep going for her.' Aunty Dora smiled and patted my hand. 'So there you go, that's my story, and look, here comes your grandpa.'

I watched her as she and Granny helped Grandpa back into bed. The heroes aren't all on TV, I thought. To keep going all those years under those difficult circumstances, to give the best years of your life for no medals, no money, no kudos. She did everything out of commitment to those around her and to a God who could 'work out all things for good'. She'd never have a TV reporter ask her about her amazing deeds, and she wouldn't want that, but it made me blush when I thought of my dreams of fame and of my pride in my own accomplishment. I had to kill the beast to survive, but I didn't think I would have stuck around to fight the monsters of illness and bitterness for year after year.

Grandpa was in his element with two women fussing over him. 'Yes, just pull that pillow up a bit, please. There, that's better. Now where's that cup of tea?'

'I'd say you're nearly well enough to be getting your own tea,' Granny said.

Grandpa winked at me.

'I'm not really allowed to tell you.' The bossy staff nurse was practically shouting down the phone at the nurse's station. 'Well yes, we have got Will Houston up here ... And what do you want me to do about it? ... Well, a lost boy isn't really my concern. I have got a ward to run, you know! ... No I will not send someone down ... Well you send someone if he's so much trouble ... He's been what? Sick on you? What am I supposed to do about that?'

As she talked I realized that Lewis had been gone an awfully long time. What could he have been up to now? He was ushered back to the ward a few minutes later looking more sheepish than usual, and nearly frogmarched up to the nursing post by an angry auxiliary nurse.

'I do not see why I should have to leave my patients to play escort to Vomiting Vernon!' she said, hands on hips. Lewis slipped into the ward as the staff nurse rose from her desk.

'All right Lewis, what have you been up to this time?' I asked. 'You've been gone ages!'

'Weren't my fault,' he said, slumping into the chair next to me. 'I found the shop all right but I couldn't find me way back.' He'd been walking along counting his change and took a wrong turn. Then he got distracted as he heard the groans of a patient with a nasty open head wound being wheeled down the corridor past him. Lewis felt sorry for the man and followed the procession in the hopes of being able to help the poor fellow. By the time they reached a ward, Lewis was informed that his services would no longer be needed.

'Never heard a doctor swear before!' he said.

Then, having no idea where he was, he experimented with the lifts and ended up near the mortuary in the basement.

'Eeh, it were right spooky ... there were three of 'em laid out on't slab. Weren't no one there and I fancied a look so ...'

Aunty Dora was horrified. 'No, Lewis, not the dead bodies?'

He grinned ghoulishly. 'Well that's not exactly how the morgue bloke put it, right angry he were.'

'I'm not surprised!' I said.

'Eeh, Will, he looked just like Dr Frankenstein with a big apron an' all. Well, he tried to grab us but I weren't going to let him experiment on me so we had this chase round the big tables!'

Aunty Dora was incredulous. 'Lewis, you shouldn't let your imagination run away with you.'

But Lewis was in earnest. 'No, really, you should have heard him, he said he'd do this and that to me if he laid his hands on me. But I were too speedy for him ... and look, I got away with all me body parts! I took the back stairs and found myself in the maternity ward, which were nicer, though them lot are a bit touchy.'

He came upon a baby that was crying in a room on its own, picked it up and winded it.

'Not that anyone thanked me,' he said, 'she were quite cross really.'

He found a warmer reception on the geriatric ward.

'They seemed friendly enough. One thought I were a doctor and I didn't want them to be upset too, so I told 'em all to have an Alka Seltzer to eat and a swig of your Dr Pepper for them what were struggling, not having teeth an' all!'

'Oh Lewis, you didn't!'

'I did! Actually most wanted another and I didn't want to be mean. Eh Will, you should have seen 'em—they were bouncing!'

This whole row of patients, for obvious reasons, soon caught the eye, and nose, of the nurse. She penned Lewis up in a waiting room until hospital security could get there to interview him. Thinking it might well be his last meal, he ate all our chocolate bars, finished off the Dr Pepper.

'I even had a few Alka Seltzer to calm me nerves.'

Then he was bullied 'by the man with the keys' while a fat little nurse stood by with her hands on her hips, tutting about how she'd have to change all the patient's sheets and clothes. Lewis did a hilarious imitation of her.

'Then she told me me face was pale and did I fell all right, but by then it were too late,' he said. 'I didn't mean to get them, I just felt right queasy and I opened my mouth. But you should of seen it Will, it were like a volcano! All over both of 'em.' Lewis shook his head in wonder over his own abilities. 'It did the trick, mind—they weren't half keen to get rid of us after that, Will.'

'I expect they'll get over it,' I said. My stomach hurt from trying not to laugh.

'Oh, aye, and I feel much better now. Quite ready for me lunch, actually.'

When Lewis went to give Grandpa the last two Alka Seltzers, Granny took his place by my bed.

'Well I must say you're looking a lot better, and I can see your Grandpa's on the mend as well.'

She smiled at me and I remembered what I was going to ask her. 'Granny, Aunty Dora told me that when you were just a girl, during the war, you said you knew you were going to marry Grandpa one day?'

'Yes, that's right,' she said.

'But how did you know?'

She laughed. 'Oh, girls say lots of silly things about boys.'

'Yes but you waited, didn't you? I mean, you didn't go out with other lads when you were my age because you waited for Grandpa. How did you know?'

She smiled. 'Do you have someone in mind?' When she saw my blush she put me out of my misery. 'With me and your grandfather it was easy, Will.'

'Yes, but how can you say that? I mean, it was nearly ten *years* of waiting, and he was at war and you were so much younger. You had so much stacked against you, really.'

Granny smiled. 'It was easy because God told me beforehand—and when he says something will happen, waiting is easy because you trust he knows what he's doing with your life.'

'That's funny,' I said. 'I mean, that's almost exactly what Aunty Dora said to me.'

'Ah, well then,' Granny said. She stood up and looked over at Dora, who was saying goodbye to Grandpa. 'You've heard it from the horse's mouth. She knows more about patience than anyone else I know, so it must be true, William. Her favourite verse is that one in Romans chapter five, the one that talks about continuing to praise Jesus "even when we are hemmed in with troubles because we know how troubles can develop endurance in us, and how that endurance in turn forges the tempered steel of other virtues, keeping us alert for whatever God will do next". So whatever it is you're mulling over, remember to trust God with the timing.' I nodded and she kissed me goodbye.

'Oh, and William,' she said as she turned to go, 'the Reverend Scott told me after church this morning that he and Richard will be coming over to see you tomorrow— to go through some of the details of your next adventure.

I told him I disagreed with the doctor about your going, but there you go. I've spoken my mind but I'm sure you'll be in good hands if anything should happen.'

After they left, Grandpa and I settled in to watch some more TV. There really isn't much else to do in hospital and, though I was up and walking a bit I wasn't up for going very far—or for taking the risk of getting lost and landing up in the morgue.

A nurse came in with a handful of envelopes. She fanned them in front of her face and smiled. The perfume smell was overwhelming. 'Here's your fan mail,' she said with a smile.

Some of the letters were from girls my age and older and some asked me to text them with my number. Like the interviews, this novelty turned out to be one more thing that didn't quite live up to my expectation. If I'd known a few weeks ago I'd be getting mail from all these girls I would have been thrilled. We didn't get a mention in the *Sunday Telegraph,* which annoyed Grandpa, but most of the other papers included a feature about us. Most of them had a sickly looking shot of me in bed. There wasn't anything negative in them, to my relief, and most of the articles were very complimentary although they varied in accuracy. But by the time I'd scanned through the pile of papers the novelty of seeing my name in print had all but worn off as well.

I was surprised to see Carrie appear that evening. She only stayed for a few minutes and I was relieved that Grandpa was down in the day room. She asked me about the media and the interviews and thumbed through some of the fan mail. She seemed more attentive than usual, but she arrived so close to the end of the visiting slot that she had to leave before we could really talk. She was easier to talk to than Hannah was, though. Carrie was a full-on babe and I realized as she sat next to me that I still liked her—a lot.

After she left, though, I found myself thinking about Hannah. I still wasn't quite sure what Granny meant by 'endurance', and I was less sure how God would tell me something that I could wait for with confidence all those years. So I tried not to rush ahead in my imagination to romantic scenes with Hannah. 'Trust what will be to God,' I told myself. And as I tossed and turned I prayed for God's will to be done. That felt right, but then when I did fall asleep I dreamt about Carrie.

Grandpa was in the day room again and I was alone on the ward the next day when the vicar arrived with Richard.

Richard was fifteen, like me. He had gingery brown hair and a few freckles. It struck me again that he was confident but not cool in the conventional sense of the word. He didn't strut with his shoulders or put on any of the mannerisms that my friends back in Liverpool put on to appear big and tough. He was mature, interested and attentive.

The more we talked and planned, the more excited I became. Richard and his dad planned to climb the Pillar Rock and Napes Needle, two rock towers that sounded awesome. The Pillar was situated along the Ennerdale Valley, where we'd be camping.

'It's an almighty cathedral spire of rock, there's an uber-classic climb I've been wanting to do on the west face,' the vicar said. 'And the Needle's a sharp shaft of rock under a thunderous looking mountain called Great Gable. It is a decent bit of rock, lad, but I guess there's a chance you won't be allowed to do anything more than watch,' he said to me.

I nodded, although secretly I hoped I'd be able for much more than watching.

When Richard left to go down to the day room to introduce himself to Grandpa I thought I ought to say something religious.

'I was sorry to miss church yesterday,' I said. 'Was it good?' What kind of a stupid question is that, I thought, as soon as it was out of my mouth.

But the vicar nodded. 'Aye, it was. I spoke about endurance, or "stickability", and it went well enough. No one fell asleep anyway!'

'That's exactly what I was talking about with Granny and Aunty Dora yesterday,' I said. 'I mean, they heard your sermon, but I was asking them about it. Isn't that weird?'

He smiled. 'Nae, not really weird at all, Will. The Lord saw to that, and I know a bit about what God's brought those two women through in their lives, so I'd imagine it was a better sermon than I could preach. She's a remarkable woman, your aunt, from what I've heard.'

'And her faith is so uncomplicated ... you know, almost simple—in a way.'

'Clear waters, like clear foundations, do not seem so deep as they are. Usually it's the muddy ones that look the most profound.'

'Yeah, I guess. Well, it made sense to me anyway.'

'Aye, well it would do, tried and tested—a sermon written over fifty years with steadier hand than I've got and on priceless paper.' He eased back in the squeaky chair. 'Aye, good ... good. I'm glad to see the Holy Spirit at work in yer life, lad. I've bin thinkin' about you a lot since you came up to the front of church last week. It was rare thing. There was a mighty anointing upon the whole place as ye stood. Have ye mibbe felt or heard the Lord speaking to ye this week at all since?'

I hesitated, unsure of what to say. 'Um, I'm not sure ... I don't think so. Should I have?'

'My sheep hear my voice, that's what the book says. It's the shepherd's job to teach the sheep to hear. But ye'll see that soon enough, don't fret. Have ye got a Bible?'

'Not my own,' I said.

'Ach, well we'll get wee Hannah to dig ye one out,' he said. 'Ye must have one of yer own, lad. Like gold dust, living water ... ye'll see.'

'Thank you,' I said.

'Good lad. I can see something in ye which pleases God, and that gives me joy for ye, Will. Stick at it, lad, and ye'll be fruitful. Remember, the mighty oak tree was just a wee acorn that stood his ground.' He paused while I thought about that.

We talked about my family, and school, which felt like another world away now. I wanted to know more about him and his gangster past, but I was afraid to ask. I had only a glimpse into it when we were talking about next Sunday, when we'd all be camping in some remote valley with our horses.

'Aye, we're up to gentleness next week,' he said, 'and I've got Andrew to preach the sermon. It's his first time preaching but he'll be okay. There's nae gentler giant than that lad. I'm a work in progress and it may be providential that I'm not spouting off about one of ma weaker points.'

'Do you find it difficult to be gentle, then?' I asked. I thought vicars ought to have everything sorted out.

'Difficult? Aye, ye could say that. Not so much with Jan and the bairns, but more with other folk and tense situations. Ye see, Will, I was raised in a rough part of

Glasgow and a man had to be a certain way to get on. I'm big, and so I did get on, but not in the right way. I was a verra violent man and dished out a lot of beatings and had a fair few myself an'all. The world makes ye hard in yer heart, and ma heart was like stone for a lot of years. There was nae room for compassion or weakness ... that is, until something stopped me dead in ma tracks.'

'What was that?' I asked.

'Ach, lad, ye're always asking questions,' he said. 'I'll tell ye the whole story another time, mibbe when we're out on the naigs, eh?'

'Okay,' I said.

Richard returned then from his chat with Grandpa, and the vicar consulted the nurses about my medications and restrictions for the holiday.

And, though I was anxious as ever to be discharged the next day and begin the next leg of my adventure, I tried to be patient. Granny had brought my mum's old Bible for me and I stumbled upon the perfect verse in Philippians. 'Let patience have her perfect work, being confident of this very thing, that He which hath begun a good work in you will see it through until the day of Jesus Christ.'

PART FIVE

GENTLENESS

19

THE FIGHTER, THE FOOTPRINT AND THE FRENCHMAN

Please, Will, just one more picture so we can see that scar?' Wearily I showed the photographers my wounds again as we crossed the car park on Tuesday.

For some reason the media thought my discharge was worth reporting, even though I hadn't been in any danger over the weekend. I was relieved to escape from the prying cameras and microphones into Andrew's car and I was even more excited to be heading back to the mountains. I missed the space, the freedom, the beauty of it all.

Andrew was in high spirits. He was taking me home via the practice, where Nelson was nearly to be discharged as well.

'He's been restless without your grandfather,' he said. 'He'll be pleased to see you.'

It was a happy reunion, but I was shocked when I saw the extent of his injuries. He was trying to impress me with his usual bravado and eagerness, but I could see it was hurting him to walk, let alone stand on his hindquarters. The stitches looked raw and he had sustained injuries to his abdomen and neck. Seeing Nelson's wounds was another stark reminder of how close we'd all come to death the week before. I was sad to leave the little fellow, who looked mortified that he wasn't considered well enough for home and more adventure. I thought of that blind guy in *The Great Escape* when he said something like, 'Take me with you, I can see, I can see perfectly'.

'It'll be your turn to go home soon enough,' Andrew consoled him as we left.

Granny was out, so Andrew took me to the Kirkstile. Chris Clegg was driving past the entrance in a tractor as we got out of the car. When he saw me he reversed back and beckoned me over.

'I'll meet you inside, Will,' Andrew said.

Chris had a cigarette hanging from his mouth like James Dean. 'All right, Will lad? I've not seen you for a week or two, sounds like you've been having adventures.' His tone was sarcastic but I nodded. 'Carrie says she saw you and I've been meaning to catch up with you an' all, to give you something for helping out.' He stepped out of the cab and handed me a twenty-pound note.

'Thanks, but I can't take this,' I said.

But Chris folded my hand round the note and slapped me on the shoulder. 'Shut up, you earned it and there'll be plenty more when we get together in a couple of weeks for a night out. You won't have to worry about Stan then, I've seen to that.'

Three rough-looking young farmers pulled into the yard in a pick-up and saluted Chris. After a short exchange across the car park they went inside. The money in my hand felt dirty, or rather I felt dirty for taking it. But Chris was so cool that I felt unable to refuse him.

'Chris, this stuff about Stan,' I began. 'Well, he's not going to get hurt, is he? I mean, he's–'

'Will, relax. It'll be no more than he's done to people I know and it probably won't come to that if we're careful. Will, look at me.'

I looked at him. 'I'm inviting you to be part of the biggest salmon catch that ever happened in Cumbria,' he whispered, 'because I like you ... and so does Carrie. We're going to make poaching history and a few quid into the bargain. Look, do you not remember *Danny, the Champion of the World?*' He watched me nod and smile. 'Aye, well it's no different from that only with fish ... Come on Will, lad, we're going to be famous.'

'But what about the fish stocks?'

'Awey, them fish have been going up there forever.' A car sounded its horn behind us and Chris climbed up the steps to the cab. 'I'll crack with you about it more at the Loweswater Show in a week or two, eh?'

He kicked some Budweiser bottles across the floor of the cab and shifted the tractor into gear. He was cool, and he might be right about the salmon stocks not being at risk, but what about Stan? Stan had been like a mentor to me over the last weeks. I knew he wasn't well liked, but he'd been good to me. What would they do to him if he did catch them? Could I feed Stan false information about the location so he'd be miles away? That way at least he'd be safe, even if the fish weren't.

I didn't want to be involved at all, but I felt that I'd somehow committed myself by taking the money. My desire to be accepted by Chris and his gang was definitely at war with my sense of right and wrong. I tried to forget about it. After all, the Loweswater Show was about a month away and I wanted to enjoy being out of the hospital and being a bit of a celebrity after my ordeal.

The restaurant staff all greeted me with smiles and wanted to know how I was feeling. I wasn't particularly hungry so I made swirls in my bowl of soup with my spoon while Andrew chatted away about the Loweswater Show. It was the big annual event for our end of the valley and he was in training to defend his wrestling title. He thought I should enter, too.

'Me? I don't know anything about wrestling—except that they wear funny-looking embroidered pants on the outside of their leggings.'

Andrew laughed. 'You don't have to wear them if you don't want to, but it is traditional.'

'So how does it work then?' I tried not to sound too interested so he wouldn't just sign me up for it.

'Oh, Will,' he said, 'it's the sport of sports—man against man using only your wits, your balance and every muscle in your body to keep your opponent between you and the ground. It's hard to explain until you've done it for yourself, but it's like what lads do all the time mentally. I mean, they're always wondering whether they can outwit and out-wrestle that fella on the other side of the pub. There's nothing malicious about it, just a boy thing I guess—testosterone and all that. Anyhow, Cumbrian wrestling is the best and most civilized way men have invented to put that to the test without falling out about it. In fact, they always make you shake hands with the other bloke after each round. You've got to try it, Will. I mean, you're young and agile and you're not slow-witted like a lot of people your age. You'll probably wipe the floor with them in your weight class.'

'Listen to him, southern prat talking about the sport as if he were born in the valley!' This loud challenge came from one of the rough-looking farmers who'd greeted Chris. They were sitting at the bar a few feet away.

Andrew looked at me and spoke in a low tone. 'Archie Pritchard, last year's runner up, didn't take it too well.

Try not to make eye contact and we might be spared any trouble.'

'He's just stirring it up, Andrew,' I said.

Andrew smiled. 'Well you know what they say, "Malice is of a low stature but it hath very long arms."'

Mr Pritchard, however, was in the mood for confrontation at all costs. He carried on with his loud and insulting comments about off-comers and namby-pamby Bible bashers. His two companions were an appreciative audience.

'Aye,' Andrew continued. 'Archie's a gifted wrestler, but he doesn't bother to get in trim. He's always relied on his natural ability, and that worked for him until I moved up here four years ago.'

The bartender was looking worried but Andrew gave him a reassuring 'don't worry, there won't be any trouble' smile. Andrew didn't seem riled or fearful, but he did tell me to get ready to leave as he gathered up our used glasses. I could feel the tense danger in the room. I assumed Andrew was planning to walk away from the situation—which seemed okay to me, if maybe a bit limp considering the level of insult he had sustained. But I was wrong.

Andrew leant over once more. 'Remember Will,' he whispered, 'the Bible says, "let your gentleness be known and experienced by all men because the Lord is very near". It's my text for the sermon on Sunday, and it looks like I'll have a chance to live it first!'

He raised an eyebrow, stood up with the glasses and walked over to the group by the bar. The confidence in his saunter suggested that he was about to belt Archie.

'Good,' I said to myself. 'Smug git deserves it!'

The others swiftly moved aside and Archie braced himself, but as Andrew went past him to deposit the glasses on the bar he spoke to him in an unusually friendly manner. 'Now then, Archie, what's all this ranting about? You're a fine wrestler and you'll have a chance to beat me in a few weeks at the show.'

Andrew held out his hand but Archie stood motionless, staring with cold, bloodshot eyes.

The two were well matched. What Archie lost in height to Andrew he made up for in girth. He was six feet tall and broad shouldered, but I assumed from the bulge above his belt that he was a little too fond of the beer.

Archie quickly recovered from the shock of Andrew's friendly gesture and brandished his brutish fists. 'Strutting around the valley as if you own the place,' he spat. 'I'll beat you at the show, marra, and I'll beat you with these now if you step outside.'

'The wrestling ring,' Andrew said, 'is the perfect place for men like you and me to test ourselves against each other. The pub yard is not. You'll have to wait for the show.'

'Coward! You're chicken!' Archie said.

'It's called self-control, Archie,' Andrew said. And he stepped forward to show he wasn't afraid. 'I'm off to work now, and you may still choose to have a go in the car park, but you'd end up in jail and miss the show and I know you wouldn't want that!'

'You pussy!'

Andrew smiled as he turned to leave. 'No, Archie, it's the law of a civilized society. And in this instance it has protected you.'

Once we were safely in the car I asked, 'What would you have done if he'd followed you out here and started on you?'

'I was quite certain he wouldn't. But I don't know, Will— we might both have been hurt badly, I suppose, but that's why we have laws—and wrestling—to keep everyone safe.

Just like a river needs banks, big boys need something to contain their competitive side within the bounds of safety.'

I could see what he meant and I wondered if I could ever win a wrestling contest against Chris Clegg. I tried not to think about that either. 'Andrew,' I asked, 'what did you mean about the Bible verse back there?'

'Well,' he said, 'the way I see it, when the Bible says "the Lord is near so be gentle" it means you can afford to back off from fighting a lot of your own battles and leave room for him to fix stuff. I mean, if you came down to our surgery in Cockermouth and passed by all those sick animals, no one would expect you to do more than be gentle with them and pat the dogs and horses on the heads. If you started getting worked up by the numbers of sick animals and then barged in and started getting rough with my surgeon's scalpel, think what a mess we'd have on our hands! I just think that sometimes we need to give delicate things to the master physician. Does that make any sense?'

'Yeah, it does. But letting go of the game controls is scary.'

'I know, Will, but trusting yourself with the scalpel is a lot worse.'

'Yeah, I guess ... I don't want to end up like Archie anyway!'

Granny still wasn't back when we arrived at the farm, so I unpacked and put a few of my get well cards on the shelf. She'd put fresh flowers from her garden on my bedside cabinet and Mum had sent some cuttings about me from the *Liverpool Echo*. There were also letters from my two best friends at school, Johnny Sutton and Pete Hackney. They both said how much they were looking forward to next term and told me that our 'cool' ratings had gone through the roof. 'Loads of people who'd never talk to us before stop me in the street 'cos they know I'm your friend!' Pete wrote. I couldn't quite imagine being back in Liverpool—or going back to school.

I was sitting at the end of my bed reading the letters, and so for the first time I actually read the tapestry picture hanging above my pillow. The first word caught my eye. It said, 'Gentleness can only come from the strong, only the weak are cruel.' I copied it down in my journal and then I added, 'God, please make me strong and gentle—like Andrew.' It really was strange to see themes like this in my conversations and events in my life, and even in pictures hanging in my room, but every day I was more and more convinced about how real and amazing God is.

It was quiet that night without Grandpa and Nelson, but I knew Granny was glad to have me home. I could tell she was still a bit shaky about our close call. When I phoned my mum after supper she told me that the headmaster of my school had paid her a visit. They wanted to do an article for the school website and needed a photo of me in Cumbria.

Stan called round later that evening, too. He left his boots off in the hall under Granny's watchful gaze. She made us some cocoa before retiring to bed. Stan and I talked for a long time. The vicar had made quite an impression on him and I think he just wanted someone to listen as he thought through it all out loud. It was exciting to hear him talking about God and he didn't smell of booze, which was also a good sign. I was tired, though, and after awhile, in a half sleepy state, I caught myself staring past him at his boots lying in the hall. For some reason, one was on its side. The grip pattern was unusual but it looked somehow familiar. Where had I seen it before?

Then in a flash it came to me and I felt this cold horror creep over me. I had to be sure, so I excused myself to go upstairs to the toilet and found my notebook. And there they were—the footprints of Uncle Sid's secret accomplice who had texted Sid the week before with my note to Granny. But how could that be? Stan was one of us, a good guy. Was he really a Judas? I was confused. And then I remembered something else. Tomorrow was Wednesday, and at one o'clock Sid was expecting me to run some errand for him. In all the excitement I'd completely forgotten that I was still now in his power.

I wanted to march back downstairs and confront Stan, but my conversation with Andrew that afternoon kept coming to mind. Here was another one of those delicate situations that called for the master physician's knife and not mine. Stan was just starting to climb out of the hole he'd dug for himself after his wife had left him for another man. He'd been through more stuff in his life than I could possibly imagine. He could have any number of reasons for working for Uncle Sid. I had to give Stan the benefit of the doubt. I had to proceed with gentleness.

But a thought about how I could turn this to my advantage did occur to me as I wrestled with this question. I knew from watching spy films that feeding false information through known informers was a clever way of outwitting your enemy. If I gave information to Stan, chances were it would reach Sid's ears. The only thing Sid had on me was that I had deceived Granny and Grandpa. If I could make him believe that I'd come clean with them, I'd be free from his grip.

'What are you up to tomorrow, then?' Stan asked as he stood to leave.

'Oh, not much in the morning,' I said. 'Then I'm off doing some errand for Uncle Sid in the afternoon.

Granny's not too keen, though, says he'll have me doing all sorts.'

Stan looked up from lacing his boots. 'You told her, then?' he asked. He'd slipped up, but I carried on seamlessly.

'Oh yes. I didn't want to go, knowing how they don't really get on, but seeing as he's family too I'll see what he wants me to do. If I don't like the errand I'll just walk away. I mean, it's not like I have to do anything for him, is it?'

After Stan said goodnight and slipped off into the darkness I went to bed rather pleased with myself. But I was still dreading the next day. It only occurred to me as I lay in bed that I'd told whopping lies. I felt guilty about it and decided I'd come clean with Granny ... just not tomorrow.

Wednesday was dull and overcast. After an early lunch I went down to Sid's place in High Lorton. I leaned Granny's bike against the huge gates and walked up the drive to the colonnaded front door. The massive Georgian mansion seemed out of place among the cottages of the village.

'Good afternoon, William. I see that you've recovered from your heroics last week ... good ... good. Well come in, lad, and let me show you around.'

He was far friendlier than I'd expected. Had Stan relayed the message?

Uncle Sid showed me his library and the various documents he'd been working on to force the Environment Agency and the National Rivers Authority to take action to preserve the Derwent and Cocker rivers. Most of the stuff went over my head, but he was passionate about it.

'A lot of bureaucratic idiots!' he spat. 'They'd all quite happily sit by and pass toothless legislation but never lift a finger to save what we're about to lose. The river systems are being poisoned by farm waste, starved of life by river-straightening earthworks and poached to death by organized gangs. No one is responsible, no one cares.'

Apparently he'd funded various research projects designed to drag these 'halfwits', as he called them, and the general public, out of their inertia. This was a very different side of my Uncle Sid.

He showed me round his huge empty house.

'Harriet and I never had children, of course,' he said as he showed me through a series of spare bedrooms. He seemed quieter, wistful. I saw only a few family photos—a few of his parents and a nice one of him fishing with my mum. There were aerial photos in his library of developments he had been involved in—some in the area and some abroad.

He pointed to one of these pictures. 'That's Tignon, just south of Marseille. It was the biggest development I ever invested in. Things didn't work out as planned and I lost a lot of money. That was about five years ago now. But there's a delicate situation brewing and I need you to do a little favour for me this afternoon. It relates to the Tignon project.'

I tried to look him in the eye but couldn't quite do it. I felt like I was in a cage with a snake, like there was something else going on and I had to be constantly watching my back.

I tried not to sound too committed to the idea. 'What is it, Uncle Sid?'

'Oh, just a small thing. I need you to deliver a package to a hotel in Cockermouth where some of my French associates are staying. They're waiting for me to contact them and ... well, it's very complicated and I doubt you'd want to know.'

I looked at the photo again and thought how I would like to know. Was this a baited snare?

'Well,' I said, 'if I do agree to go I'd like to know what I'm getting myself into ... I mean, what's in the package, for a start?'

Sid hesitated for moment and then moved closer. He fixed me in his gaze. 'I'm sure I don't need to tell you that you are never to repeat what you hear in this room.'

'Of course.'

'Very well.' He glanced at the windows and began. 'You see, I borrowed a great deal of money to get this development through its final stages. The man staying at the Wordsworth Hotel tonight is a legal representative of the other investors. They are what we would call venture capitalists. They gambled on the success of the development, as did I, only it didn't go according to plan and now they're very keen to get back from me everything they lost.'

'But they gambled the same as you did. Didn't they know the risks? Why would they come back to you like that?' I knew a little more about this than most people my age since this was part of my dad's job.

'Well, William, I made certain unwritten pledges to these investors about the success of what they were investing in. And they're holding me to those even though they knew there was an element of risk in that type of coastal resort.'

'But if it was unwritten they won't have much chance getting it off you in the courts.' I did know that much.

'My dear William, it is not the courts where these men seek to get their redress ... how shall I put it? They are the sort of people who try to avoid the legal system. Do you understand?'

'You mean the Mafia? You're in business with the Mafia?'

'No, I believe the Mafia are Italian. These gentlemen are French. They're men who have grown rich in a number of ways, probably no less honourably than the established banks, and when they spot lucrative investments they can invest because they're free from the traditional entanglements of banks. They were happy to support the final stages of the Tignon development, taking an equity share in lieu of inflated interest. Unfortunately the equity didn't match their expectations, and now they want the remainder of their loan repaid with the interest they originally waived. At the last count it was just under three million euro.'

'And if you can't pay it?'

'If I can't pay then they will take certain measures against my family.'

What family, I wondered. 'Can you afford to pay them?' I thought I should check.

'No, not immediately. I will need time. The brown envelope is a first installment, a peace offering if you like.'

'But what if they won't take it in bits? I mean, suppose they want it all now?'

'Then there will be trouble for my family.' He hesitated, and the dreadful truth began to sink in.

'But Uncle Sid, you haven't got any family—close family, I mean.'

He looked up. 'Yes I have. I'm not talking about Anne, they can't know about that, but they will target the others. They would waste no time paying my sister Elsie and my brother George a call, and I don't know whether they would go further than that. Your own family are next in that line ...'

'No! No, they can't, you can't, I mean you can sell this house—'

'No, Will, this house is already mortgaged to the hilt. My only option is pay them slowly if they will have it.'

'But what if they won't? No, we have to go to the police.'

'*No!*' he shouted. I jumped and he went on more quietly. 'No, they mustn't be involved, trust me. They must not be involved. There's nothing they can do. They can't protect the family from these people. Our only hope right now is to play the hand we are playing. Mr Gerrand is waiting for me to contact him this afternoon, but I dare not be seen near him in case he is being followed. They don't know you and no one will suspect a teenage lad walking into the hotel. Ask at the reception for his room and take him the package with the note inside and then report back to me. That's all I ask. Since you made me tell you everything, you can see that you're doing this to protect your own family—and your own neck.'

I couldn't believe this was happening. 'Well, I'll need some time to think.'

'I wouldn't have asked you if there were any other way, believe me. It's been painful—and dangerous—for me to divulge this sorry affair to you. But I know you're a canny lad and I can trust you to keep your word. Forget what I said last week about telling your grandmother—I didn't mean that. But I do ask you now to do this ... for all our sakes. Will you?'

'Okay, I'll go,' I said. I took the package from his hand.

'Good lad. If you're quick you can make the next bus into Cockermouth. It leaves the village in eleven minutes.' He'd obviously not anticipated a refusal.

He showed me a back way through his garden and over the fields to the village bus stop. I scarcely had time to consider what I'd landed myself into before the bus had pulled out of the valley and I was minutes away from Cockermouth. The bus stopped on Main Street at about two o'clock. I looked over to the statue where the bikers had been and spotted the Wordsworth Hotel on the other side of the street.

I popped into the newsagent to get a plastic bag to put the brown parcel in. I thought a boy with a bag was far less conspicuous. Remembering the courage of my grandfather that day I first arrived, I coolly walked across the street to the hotel and made my enquiry at the reception. I didn't notice anything suspicious about the characters around or inside the entrance. 'I'm here to see Mr Gerrand, I have some stuff to give him.'

There was a spotty guy a little older than I was working at the reception desk. 'I'll just look and see if we got him ... oh yes, room six on the first floor. You can leave it here if you like and I'll take it up to him later.'

'No, no, thanks. I'll bring it up to him if that's okay. Room six, you say?'

He nodded and went back to playing cards on the computer. I climbed the uneven staircase and walked slowly down the narrow corridor. Room six was the last door on the left.

For some reason I'd pictured guards in black suits standing outside the door. Too many films, I told myself as I approached the door. I couldn't hear anything except my own heart pounding. I was terrified to knock but more terrified that someone would open the door and find me standing there spying. I knocked. Nothing. I hadn't knocked very hard, so I waited long enough to not appear rude or impatient and knocked again. There was a shuffling, and the door opened.

'Yes, what is it?' A small man in a bathrobe with a bath towel around his shoulders stood before me. His hair was wet and his face was flushed and dripping. He seemed so ordinary I was completely taken aback.

'Oh, I'm—I'm sorry to disturb you,' I stammered. 'I, um, I'm from Mr Armstrong. I have a package for you. Are—are you Mr Gerrand?'

He looked at me for a moment, nodded, and started to dry his hair. 'I see, please excuse me like this I have very bad hay fever and was trying to clear my lungs with steam from the bath. It is not a good time of the year for me.'

I nodded and smiled sympathetically. I knew all about hay fever, though I didn't think the pollen was too bad at the moment. 'Yeah, I get it too. Have you got some antihistamine? You can get it at the chemist over the road here,' I said, pointing. Was I really giving medical advice to a man with Mafia connections?

'Thank you, yes, I think this is what I shall do later. Now you say you are here for Mr Armstrong? I was told to expect him today sometime. I trust he is in good health and that you are a precautionary measure?'

I nodded and handed him the bag. He motioned for me to come in and took the parcel over to his dressing table. He opened it, frowned and opened his briefcase. He took out some documents and examined them through a pair of half-rimmed spectacles.

'This wasn't what I was expecting,' he said.

'I think there's a note for you inside the envelope as well,' I said. I took deep breaths, trying to stay calm.

He peered at me again over his spectacles. 'I see, I see. Then let us hope the note weighs more than the package.' He found the note and read it then re-examined the documents from his briefcase. His nose was streaming and he kept grabbing tissues to stem the flow. He was obviously agitated that things were not in order. He peered inside the package once more and then leaned back in his chair and looked out of the netted window. Then he turned to me. 'Well, that's that I suppose. You may tell your employer that I will put his offer to the syndicate and they will, no doubt be in touch … one way or another.'

'Do you think it will be all right?' I asked. I tried not to sound as scared as I was.

'I'm afraid you have the wrong man if you want answers. I'm a solicitor and merely discharging matters in the UK on behalf of my clients. My brief finishes here and I cannot divulge any further information without the authority of my clients. Thank you for the information about the chemist. You know the way out? I don't think I can really accompany you dressed like this.' He smiled and then sneezed.

I said goodbye and closed the door behind me. I hesitated outside the door, at first just to calm down, but then I heard Gerrand's voice.

'It's Gerrand ... Yes I'm sure he is busy but he will want to speak to me ... Yes, I'll wait.' I waited, too. 'Good afternoon ... Yes, I understand you're busy ... Yes, well that is why I'm calling ... No, I'm afraid he is offering five percent up front and quarterly installments thereafter for three years ... Yes, I know ... Please don't shout, I can hear ... Yes ... No, I would prefer if you didn't involve me ... Oh well if you insist I will attend, but only to be your eyes, nothing more ... No ... I don't care who you are going to send over to sort him out ... Please don't shout ... Yes, yes, that's better ... The hotel? Yes, it is serviceable I suppose. Book it for when? Let me write that down. The twentieth, two weeks, Wednesday. How many rooms? ... Sorry ... Sorry, can you say that again? The reception is not good ... Four rooms, yes ... Very good, I will do that ... Yes ... And you will contact Mr Armstrong this week to let him know what is expected of him? ... Yes, please don't swear ... Yes, I know, you have been very patient ... No, no, I don't think you are at all unreasonable ... Okay, okay ... I will count the deposit before leaving tomorrow. Yes. Goodbye.'

I crept away, sure that what I'd heard was very bad news for Uncle Sid—and for all of us. The twentieth was a little over two weeks away. Was a hit squad coming over from France or somewhere to persuade Uncle Sid to find the money?

The bus ride back to Lorton seemed to take for ever. I kept hoping that I'd wake up and discover this was all a bad dream brought on by my pain medication. I went straight to Uncle Sid's, but he wasn't in. It finally occurred to me that it was his day to visit Anne, so I scribbled a note explaining what had happened and popped it through the door. I had sworn that I wouldn't divulge what Uncle Sid had told me, but I'd made no pledge regarding the extra information I'd obtained from Gerrand that afternoon. What should I do next? The trekking holiday was to begin the next day. I decided not to tell anyone just yet until I'd spoken to Uncle Sid next week. He'd hear from these heavies in the meantime, I was sure.

We spent the evening packing for the camping trip. I didn't have much proper outdoor gear so it was a bit of a scrounge session between old stuff that Granny could dig out and what we could borrow from the Scotts. Richard was in high spirits on the other end of the phone and was more than willing to share anything he had with me—even if it meant him using his sister's cast-offs. I was beginning to look forward to spending time with him almost as much as with his sister.

'Dad's taking an air rifle in a holster on the horse so he can look like a proper cowboy!' Richard told me. I could hear Hannah in the background laughing and saying how embarrassed she'd be if he went through with it.

'Yehah!' Roger shouted.

This was going to be an adventure, I was sure.

PART SIX

GENEROSITY

20

HORSES, HIKING AND HANNAH

Will! You're up early.'
'Good morning, Granny. I've taken Nelson out and done the chickens. There's seven eggs on the side.'

'Thank you very much, dear. You can take a dozen with you for the camping trip. Oh, is that a pot of tea? I am impressed. How's the weather?'

'It's perfect,' I said. 'Everything's perfect.'

It was a fine summer's morning. Wispy clouds soon vanished as the sun rose and the lush ash trees around Granny's place swayed under in the fresh morning breeze. A cuckoo called across the valley and the Clegg's cattle lowed. Every time I heard those cattle I thought of the decision I had to make in a few weeks about the salmon poaching. Between that and Uncle Sid and the Mafia and my parent's separation, I had a lot on my mind. I was learning, though, not to worry so much about the future and to concentrate on what faced me each day. And what was in front of me that morning had all the makings of the best adventure yet. A week away from all these troubles—and time with the girl who might be part of my destiny. It seemed like a big thought—destiny. And, although sometimes it felt like I was trying on shoes a few sizes too big for me, thoughts about God, my future, Hannah, and even becoming a man were beginning to feel more comfortable.

I called Grandpa before I left.

'Aye, I'm better and stronger than ever, lad, don't you worry about me,' he said. 'Have a good time now and don't be any trouble for the Scotts.'

Granny waved me goodbye with numerous warnings, and soon I was biking down the road with my heavy rucksack and the wind through my hair. I felt as strong as I ever had. The only medication I'd packed were anti-inflammatory tablets.

Richard greeted me and led me out to the field where Hannah was waiting to give me some riding instruction. Her hair was tied back and she was wearing the same polo shirt and joggers I'd seen her wearing the other week. She was naturally flushed and pretty without make up. She smiled when she saw me and led a large brown pony over to me.

'Hello Will, you look loads better. This is Brigham. He's very experienced and not at all skittish. I, er, put a little something in the saddle bag for you, for the journey.'

I reached in and pulled out a dairy chocolate bar. 'No nuts! Thank you.'

'You're welcome. Dad says you've ridden before?'

I didn't want to sound deficient. 'Well, yes, I rode a few years ago in Wales—but we didn't gallop or anything like that.'

She smiled, and I could tell she'd already ascertained that I was completely ignorant of horses. She explained the various straps around the horse's neck. Words like snaffle bridle, clip rope and head collar went whizzing over my head. I watched and nodded, trying to look intelligent.

Richard stood near us, laughing, with his arms folded. 'Hannah, give the guy a break. We only want to ride the blessed creature, not enter for Crufts!'

'Shut up, Richard. And don't be so ignorant. Crufts is for dogs. Anyway, it's important to know what things are called. So stop showing off to Will and go help Dad with the bags.'

He walked away laughing, not at all put down by his sister.

'Sorry about my brother, he can be an awful big head when he's got friends around. Now then, where was I? Oh yes, the saddle.'

Hannah lengthened the stirrups and looked at me again to make sure I was watching. Brigham was enormous. Sixteen hands is big, but it's hard to get over the scale and power of an animal that size until you're standing next to it.

He winced slightly as Hannah tightened the belt under his belly. I stepped back nervously, but Hannah stood her ground and spoke to him in a calm but firm voice.

'Okay,' she said as she turned back to me. 'The stirrups should be about right, and if you feel the saddle slipping let me know and I'll do it up another notch.'

I hoisted my foot up into the stirrup (it was higher up than I'd thought) and then tried to find something suitable to grab onto.

'No, not that bit, use the cantle ... no, the *cantle,* the high bit at the back of the saddle ... here!'

I grabbed the thing she was pointing at and made a go of it and was soon in the saddle—not very elegantly, but it was a start.

As Hannah tried to talk me through the finer points of using the stirrup, the exact position of the leg, the posture of the back and the way to hold the reins, Roger and Richard came out. What a sight they were! Roger looked like something out of a Clint Eastwood movie, complete with cowboy hat, boots and leather jacket. He carried a western saddle under one arm and a rifle under the other. He took one look at me trying to get my fingers right for the reins and laughed, as did Richard.

'Ach, lassie, for heaven's sake leave the poor lad alone. We're off trekking, we're nae going to Crufts!'

Richard giggled and Hannah smiled as well

She had a sense of humour, but she also held her ground. 'There's a right way to do things, that's all. I understand that doesn't mean much to Butch Cassidy and the Sundance kid, but it needn't affect Will if he wants to learn properly. Really, Dad, please tell me you're joking about taking that hat and gun!'

'Aah, wheesht woman, ye sound like yer mother. Everyone knows there's Injuns in thae hills. Besides, if we dun'nae see them then we'll get some rabbits for the pot! I hear Will is a crack shot ... even if he does like bigger game!'

He went on with his teasing as Hannah and her mum fussed around my horse, making sure the 'injured' lad was going to be okay.

Jan had the same deep auburn hair as Hannah. She asked me about the cougar and my hospital stay and my grandfather, and listened, as she always did, as if I were the only person in the world.

Her dappled grey Welsh pony was called Galadriel and Roger had what he called an Appaloosa Pinto Stallion.

'He's ma proper little Injun pony,' he said. Jan and Hannah laughed, saying it was no such thing.

'It's just spotty, Dad,' Hannah said.

Hannah did have an American pony. Her father had bought him from someone in their last parish for her fourteenth birthday—just when he began his fascination with the Wild West. It was a feisty chestnut and white Pinto gelding called Tonto. She explained that gelding means 'snipped' and Pinto referred to his big splodges of colour, like the Indian horses in the films. Richard had a brown pony like mine called Twiggy.

'He stinks,' he said, waving his hand in front of his face.

I quite liked the smell of horses, but Richard was more interested in speed. 'The stable owners told me Twiggy could really go!' he said.

The ponies were from a stable in a village called Brigham, about a mile from Cockermouth. I assumed that my pony was named after the village, but as Roger was securing my rucksack to Brigham's back he told me about the remarkable horse that he was actually named after.

'When Buffalo Bill was just plain old Will Cody, in the 1850s, he was contracted by the Kansas Pacific Railroad to supply buffalo meat to the railroad workers. It took a naig with real nerve to race alongside thunderous herds, and a buffalo can outpace most ponies and turn far quicker too. Well, Will claimed to have the best buffalo hunter of all, and his name was Brigham.'

'Oh, Dad! Lay off the Wild West until we get going at least!' Hannah said.

'Ach, whisht lassie, Will is interested. I can tell a kindred spirit. Now apparently this naig, Brigham, would ride alongside a beast without being steered, allowing the rider's hands to be free. But he'd only give Cody two shots before moving on to pull alongside another buffalo. Once, when a surprise herd was approaching and Brigham had been pulling a cart, Will rode him bareback with a cart harness still attached. Some US cavalry, seeing this twenty-one-year-old on a cart horse approach them, assumed they were both amateurs. But no sooner had the chase begun than Brigham outpaced the steeds of the officers and, with Cody's keen knowledge of the animals, they overtook the buffaloes in a ravine and shot twelve before the officers got a shot fired! Fancy that, eh! And that's not all—nae, for that naig carried him heroic distances when being chased by Injuns.'

'I knew it!' Jan said. 'Impossible to resist resist telling the stories once you have that blessed hat on.'

They all laughed and I watched them a bit enviously. They seemed to have so much fun together. Roger didn't seem nearly so scary to me now that I saw him with his family and the kids teasing him.

'Aye,' Roger continued, 'and there's plenty more stories where that came from.'

'Dad, leave it out!' Hannah said.

'Aye, okay, another time, Will. We have to get started. Have we got all the gear ready, Mrs Scott?'

'We're just missing the surprise member of our party, but I think I can hear him coming now.'

We heard hooves behind the hedge and an exasperated voice. 'Come on, Alfie, we are really late and I haven't got any more sweets. Honest I haven't.'

Alfie? Granny's donkey Alfie? Lewis appeared at the gate, dragging Granny's podgy donkey behind. 'I'm dead sorry everyone, he wouldn't move or ought like that 'till I'd given him all my sweets. I wanted to save one for you, Mrs Scott, for letting me come—but Alfie sniffed it out. Hi Will, couldn't let you come without me this time. I got Mrs Scott to let me come and look out for you—you know, you being a bit poorly and all.'

'We're so glad you can come along with us, Lewis,' Jan said. 'Did you bring everything on the list I gave you?'

'Oh yes, no bother, even got the brush. Mum said I'd to have one too if I were going with a vicar. I didn't know whether you wanted a dustpan as well but I brought one. Is it for the horses?'

Everyone except Jan burst out laughing as Lewis pointed to a dustpan and brush strapped to poor Alfie's side. 'No dear,' she said, 'I meant for brushing your hair.'

'Eh, I'm not brushing my hair with that!'

'She meant a hairbrush, you wally!' I said.

'But I haven't got one, never needed it.'

'Aye, and you won't be needing it on this holiday either,' Roger said with a smile. 'We're heading to the high mountain plateaus away from civilization, laddie, so ye'll be okay. It's just my wife fussing as usual.' He winked at his wife. 'Now come on, you lot, let get this show on the road!'

Roger made a point of showing off the air rifle going into its holster. The boys gathered round while the girls shook their heads. Jan said she would lead rein Lewis for the 'first stint', as Roger called the advance. Richard charged off to the other side of the field on Twiggy and Alfie, possibly attracted by Twiggy's powerful odour, toddled up the field in pursuit. Lewis was a natural riding bareback and Jan declared that she might be out of a job. Twiggy and Alfie were inseparable, and it was also useful because it meant that Twiggy didn't carry Richard too far in front.

I thought I was doing rather well. Trotting along up the field seemed very natural, and I only had a little twinge of pain from my leg wound. Hannah kept an eye on me and restricted her comments to riding technique. I was trying to think of ways to sidetrack her, now we were alone at last, but I had to concentrate on how much tension I was putting on the reins and using my knee, heel and stirrup correctly. At least we were together and she was enjoying teaching me. It was a start.

Roger and Jan brought up the rear, and it was clear how delighted they were to see this extended family trip taking shape so well. I was struck by their generosity in sharing a very special and limited family time so willingly with people they hardly knew.

We rode past the Kirkstile Inn and then turned onto a track heading out into the upland fells around Kirkgate Farm. The track was enclosed by a wall on both sides and the imposing peak of Melbreak loomed over our heads. It was so steep and craggy it looked like a leftover volcano. We emerged onto the bracken-clad hillsides above Mosedale Beck as it snaked its way back down to the pub.

Brigham was as steady as the stable had said he was, and he was patient with me as Hannah tried to get me up to a canter. Unfortunately I couldn't concentrate on my leg position and keep my rhythm at the same time. Poor Brigham obeyed my kick. It was not pretty or dignified and definitely did not convey the cool image I wanted Hannah to see.

'No Will, ease back a little. Let the horse dictate the lift.'

'I ... can't ... make ... him ... stop ... bouncing me ... ooh, eeh, ouch!' I told her between bounces. She giggled and dropped back to be with her parents.

Surprised to be abandoned, I did what I'd seen the cowboys do. I jerked the reins a bit and, when nothing happened, I gave them a proper go. Brigham came to such an abrupt halt that I almost went flying over his head. The others went whizzing past.

'You're doing fine,' Richard called out, 'but don't be too rough on your poor pony!'

'It's not the pony that I'm worried about!' I shouted after him.

We stopped for lunch at the head of the Mosedale Valley at a place the shepherds call Floutern Cop. On our left were the moorlands of Whiteoak Moss with Hen Comb rising into our northern skyline, and to our left were the craggy summits of Great Borne and Herdus.

'This is where Harriet Martineau made that difficult crossing with her ponies during that terrible storm,' Jan told Hannah.

'I remember that from her journals,' Hannah said. 'I'm glad we're here in the summer sunshine.'

After lunch by the tarn we mounted up our rested steeds and plodded off down Gill Beck into the Valley of Ennerdale.

We had done about five kilometres, and after another two we were on the floor of the valley and heading up a minor road to Bowness Knott car park—where those without ponies had to leave their vehicles. As we rounded the bend, the jaws of this majestic valley were opened to us and we trotted down the track to the lake to continue our journey. The Forestry Commission had planted Ennerdale with conifers, and it felt like we were in the wilds of Alaska instead of England.

The mountains were impressive, too. As we ascended the forest tracks Roger explained that this was a climber's paradise. He pointed out Pillar Rock, Gable Crag, Proud Knott, Raven Crag and the Needle. The valley went on and on. Jan finally succeeded in getting Roger, who was keen to get to base camp, to agree to a rest by the river for half an hour. The horses drank while we paddled and threw stones.

Roger went upstream with his fly rod and I joined him after a few minutes.

'I'm afraid I haven't the patience to be a fisherman, lad,' he confessed.

'Try directing your cast near that shaded pool on the far bank,' I suggested. Grandpa had taught me a lot in a short space of time, I realized.

On the second cast he got a bite and, though it was only a very small brown trout, he was excited and thanked me profusely. He couldn't wait to show it to Jan.

'Ah, Roger,' she said. 'I've never seen you come back with a catch before! I'll cook it later—but you'll have to gut it.'

I went over to join Hannah, who was gazing into Tonto's eyes and talking softly to him.

'Do you think he can understand you?' I asked.

'Yes, they're very intelligent animals.' She looked up at me and smiled.

'I helped your dad catch a fish upstream.' I was eager to impress her, but her praise went straight to her dad.

'Oh, that's great. Good old Dad, he hasn't had a lot of joy with fishing. Is there enough for a meal?'

'Well, just for him really, it's not very big.'

'Oh,' Hannah said. She patted the horse. A cry and a splash broke the awkward silence.

We ran to the bank just as Richard was pulling Lewis out of the river.

'The river is so shallow you've done well to completely soak yourself,' Richard said, laughing.

'I was trying to be careful, honest I was, but I lost my balance. At least I won't have to wash later.'

Jan sorted him out with some shorts from his bag and he rode bare-chested the final four kilometres up the valley. Richard rode beside me and we talked about the plans for the next few days. I found out that beneath his half-nerdish façade Richard was a bit of an adrenaline junkie. I was determined to try to keep up. Every time he mentioned how he hoped his dad would do this and that scramble or climb with him, I made sure I let him know I was up to it if he was.

I wasn't intimidated by him because I knew Richard had lots more experience in mountain climbing and riding, but I was impressed by what a boy my age could do. And I wasn't about to let the city-boy side down if I could help it. Alfie wasn't going to be outdone by the larger ponies, either. The old donkey's stamina amazed me. Richard and I laughed about it.

'I dare you to mention that to my dad,' he said. 'He'll tell you the story of how General Custer teased Buffalo Bill for taking a government mule to guide a party sixty miles to Fort Laramie.'

So I told Roger about how impressed I was with Alfie and, sure enough, I received a detailed account of that very incident. It was hard to keep a straight face with Richard riding just behind his father and raising his eyebrows at me.

The account finished with the moral of the story: 'The general himself was only a young man in his twenties, but he had a magnificent white stallion. That stallion was quite outdone by Will's mule, however, on the journey to the fort. And Custer was amazed the next day when Will saddled the same mule to ride back again. So, you see, big is nae always best!'

Jan and Hannah meanwhile had been making a fuss of Lewis. Now that Lewis was a bit cleaner from his dip in the river, he made a more desirable object for Jan and Hannah to fuss over. He kept them entertained on the final leg of our journey.

It was after five o'clock when we arrived at base camp, having come almost the entire length of the valley. We emerged from the pine forests out into open mountain valleys with Great Gable and Kirk Fell looming above us.

The River Liza wound its way over glacial drumlins up to Gable Crag, and to the south were the less imposing summits of Brandreth and Haystack. They were awesome, but not picturesque. I felt as though we had entered a giant's amphitheatre of rock, scree, beck and grass. I felt a long way from home and, but for the experienced company I was keeping, would have felt very intimidated.

Roger sent Richard and me to select a good site and we chose a little patch of dry, level ground between the confluence of Sail Beck, as it came tumbling off the mountain, and the River Liza. We were near enough to the edge of the forest to benefit from its shelter from the winds that sped up the valley, but not so near as to put the camp in jeopardy of a midge invasion. We pitched the tents, one for the Scotts and one for me and Lewis. After we had fetched wood for the fire we realized that no one had brought matches. Roger delved into his tent and emerged with an axe.

'Come, lads,' he said to me and Richard. 'I'll teach'ye how to make fire with an Indian fiddle!'

I had no idea what he was talking about but followed him and Richard into the woods to collect what he needed.

Hannah and Lewis, meanwhile, were collecting kindling. Lewis followed Hannah everywhere. She seemed to have adopted him for all jobs relating to the horses and camp chores. When they returned to the camp with the kindling and heard about our match-less predicament, Lewis confided with the ladies that he always carried a cigarette lighter with him. Hannah told me later that they were so relieved and grateful that they quite forgave him when he told them he used it to light cigarette butts that he found lying around the beer garden at the pub in Lorton. 'It's cheaper than buying your own,' he'd explained. 'Not that anyone will sell them to me, and it's a lot better for you than having a whole one!'

Unaware of this startling revelation, Roger, Richard and I were deep in the forest having our bushcraft survival lesson. According to Roger, a man who knew what he was doing could survive in the wilderness with just an axe. Roger declared himself to be such a man—although from Richard's comments I got the distinct impression that the translation from theory to practice was a bigger leap than his dad ever had patience for.

'Right now, piece A, the base. With this we take oor knife and make a shallow pilot like so, then we cut a V in the side of the base where the pilot hole is ... like that.'

I was impressed. We'd used one of the guy ropes to make the Indian fiddle, something like the bow and arrows that we made as kids.

'Aye, but ye can use the roots of the spruce tree if ye din'nae have any cordage of yer own ... aye, it's all here if ye know where to look.'

All we needed was the tinder and kindling.

'Will, ye'll find plenty of that lichen on the north side of the spruce trees, it's excellent stuff and, incidentally, it will always tell ye which direction north is if ye're in a survival situation without a compass'.

While I was gathering an abundance of the stuff, far too much as it happened, Richard was shaping a smooth stick, one foot by one inch, with his Bowie knife. This was called the drill. When Roger was happy that we had all the fire lighting gear we needed, we swaggered triumphantly back to rescue the girls from cold tuna and pilchards.

I thought they looked pleased to see us as we set about our magic display of Indian fire-making technology and, at first, all went well. Roger assembled the rig by placing the base piece on the ground and inserting Richard's 'drill' into the pilot hole. Then we placed the fiddle, or bow, around the drill and another hollowed piece of wood on top to protect the hand of the person doing the fiddling. Richard made a good start of spinning the drill backwards and forwards with the bow. Then Roger took over and I kept the tinder handy, watching out for the smouldering shavings that would soon appear in the V-shaped notch. We held our breath for about thirty seconds—until we realized that the wooden drill was too soft and was breaking up in large splinters under the pressure.

At that point Lewis grabbed the tinder from me and casually lit it with his lighter. Even Roger, beaded with sweat and frustration, burst into laughter. Roger later learned from his Ray Mear's book that it was no wonder we had trouble, as we really needed a harder wood for the drill and base.

The women made no end of fuss of Lewis for being so clever. And, of course, he lapped it all up.

As the fire burnt down to produce enough embers for cooking we took a dip in the icy river. Roger insisted on entertaining us all after dinner with his harmonica.

'It's amazing,' he said. 'I niver thought I had a talent for music, but now I've discovered it!'

'Ah, and it's such a shame you can't accompany us in church, Dad,' Hannah teased him.

After a short recital, which wasn't actually too bad, we watched the stars. I'd never seen them appear so close, bright and clear.

When we turned in to our tents at about ten o'clock Roger declared he'd sleep out by the fire, western style, with the horses. I had a good night's sleep—even though I was woken in the middle of the night when I heard Roger abandoning his fireside post for the comfort of the tent!

21

THE FIRST PITCH

We woke to a glorious morning and a great breakfast cooked over the open fire. While Roger arranged the climbing gear and Hannah tended the ponies, I helped Jan with the washing up on the riverbank.

'I'm a bit nervous about climbing the crags today,' I admitted.

'When I was a girl,' she said, 'I once kept a cocooned caterpillar and waited for it to hatch on my bedroom windowsill. The poor thing struggled and struggled to break out, and so I decided to make it easier by cutting the cocoon with my nail scissors. It was able to come out, but its wings were shrivelled and unformed and useless for flying. I was so upset, and it was years before someone told me that God had designed the cocoon to be a struggle to develop muscles in the wings of the butterfly.'

'Trying to tell me something?' I said.

'Sort of, just don't let fear shape you, okay?'

I nodded.

When Roger discovered that he had left some gear behind he was quite flustered. 'Ach, we're missing a whole set'a crabs and a belt! We can'nae take poor Will without all the proper gear. Richard have ye seen–'

'Relax, Dad. I've got the carribeenas, and if that belt is missing Will can wear mine and I'll use a sling.'

'Don't worry,' I said, 'I'd rather not go than have you in danger, Richard.'

'It's okay, Will. The sling's nearly as good and ye do need to have all the proper equipment yer first time. But are ye sure ye'll be okay climbing? Ye were in hospital just a few days ago...'

'I'll be fine, barely feel a thing now—besides, I'm not going to let you have all the fun!'

Jan was looking forward to a day by the river with a good book and Hannah was planning to take Lewis for a canter on one of the other ponies.

'Are you sure you don't want to come with us?' Richard asked her.

'It's not like I haven't done the Pillar before. You boys go and enjoy yourselves. Lewis and I will be fine.'

'Aye,' Richard said, 'providing he's a more obedient pupil than Will!'

'Hey!' I said. 'I did everything she said. Didn't I, Hannah?'

'Will,' she said, 'you've come a long way in a short time, but there's still room for improvement if you want to impress me!' She smiled cheekily and I wondered if we were talking about horse riding or other matters.

By nine o'clock we were heading up onto the crags. We ascended Sail Beck onto the mountain called Looking Stead. From our sunny vantage point on the ridge we had a majestic view of all the great peaks in the area. There wasn't a soul to be seen in any direction, and that morning the wilderness belonged to three men on the Pillar ridge in the western Lake District. We wouldn't have swapped that feeling of freedom and adventure for anything.

'Aye, lad, there's nothing like rock climbing to get a man's blood pumping in his veins. As Hemingway said, "bull fighting and mountain climbing are the only real sports ... all others are games."'

As we dropped off the ridge at the coll after Looking Stead, we wound our way along a path traversing under the vertical crags of the ridge. We were in the shade now, and cool gusts of morning air chilled us so we stopped to add a layer of clothing.

'We dun'nae want to arrive with cold muscles and get them strained on the first pitch,' Roger said. 'Are'ye sure yer okay, lad?'

I nodded.

'Dun'nae worry, lad, this was the first real climb for a wee laddie from Keswick called George over a century ago. He cut his teeth here too and lived to tell the tale. They say he was so green that he nicked his mother's washing line to use as a rope but felt a bit of a daftie when he saw a load of alpinists already on the rock. Poor George was so taken aback by how nice these men were and how they did'nae laugh at his silly washing line that he thought he'd like to be a climber too. Good job, for he grew up to be the great pioneer George Abraham, whose black and white climbing photographs got many a man out of his armchair and onto the crags.'

With the image of this curious man arriving on the crag with his mother's washing line, we rounded from Hind cove into Pillar cove and there before us was the Goliath that we had challenged. The Pillar looked like the crumpled spire of a cathedral, separated from the vertical cliffs beside it and rising into the sky over a thousand feet above us.

I felt shaky. The elation I'd felt in the sunshine back on the ridge had completely evaporated. I felt so small and out of place in this half-lit giant's rockery. This feeling of fear reminded me of how I felt when I followed Uncle Sid to Anne's cottage. I'd imagined how it would all go and that I would be in control, but the reality was far different. Those kind of imaginings were from Sega world. But a world I could control, I realized, was a world without possibilities and adventure, without frontiers or challenge. Although I knew I didn't want to live in the shadow of the gaming world, right at that moment I wanted desperately to retreat into the comfort of a video game and not face the stone-cold reality of what lay before me.

As we got closer, Pillar Rock got bigger and bigger. The summit passed out of view as we arrived on the Western side to do what Roger called the 'classic approach'.

'Aye,' he said, 'the Pillar was first scaled one hundred and seventy years ago, and Herman Prior wrote in about 1870 that a man climbing the route we're about to do takes his life in his hand!'

'Dad, stop it! Can't you see you're freaking him out?'

'Ach, whisht lad, the man who can face a raging cougar with a knife will make mincemeat of a wee bit of rock like this. Come on, let's get the gear out before we get cold.'

I tried to think of a way out of what we were about to do. But their preparations were so swift I didn't have a chance, which was good, as the feeble excuses that came to mind were all lies. When the gear was laid out, Roger brought his tattered Bible from his bag and sat us down for what he called a quiet moment with the Mountain Maker.

He read the passage from the Old Testament in which King Saul's son, Jonathan, climbs a precipitous cliff with his armour bearer to face down an entire Philistine garrison after the rest of the army had run away. He checked that his armour bearer was willing to go and reasoned, as it read in his old translation, 'it may be that the Lord will work for us; for there is no restraint with the Lord to save by many or by few'. In true *Braveheart* fashion, Jonathan arrived on the ridge to the army's taunts only to wipe the smiles from twenty of their faces in the first thirty metres of his advance—at which point there was a mighty earthquake and the rest of the Philistines took to their heels. The Jews summarized Jonathan's exploit by saying, 'He hath wrought with God this day.'

'Aye, lads, and so shall we!' Roger said as he slapped me on the back. He prayed for us then, for protection and joy. 'Now Will,' he continued, 'if ye feel afraid that's okay. I would worry if ye did'nae feel it a bit in the pit of yer belly. But I will ask ye this lad: will ye face it now, today, and climb with us? If ye say nae, there's nae shame in it. But if ye come I promise you a rare experience that only one in a million lads yer age will ever have. So what d'ye say?'

They waited, looking at me. Like a rabbit caught in a car's headlights I stood there dumb. Then I heard myself say, 'Okay.'

'Good lad,' Roger said, 'let's do it.'

'Yeah, that's the spirit, Will,' Richard said. 'Dad's right, you won't be sorry.'

But I was sorry ten minutes later when, in my rock boots, harness and helmet, I watched Richard disappearing up the west face in front of me to the first pitch. Then it was my turn. Roger was beneath me to direct my movements if needed. Once I got more than ten feet up, though, I was paralyzed with fear.

'Will, listen to uz, lad, let yer body away from the rock. Aye, that's better. Now remember: three points of contact— use yer leg muscles more, nice graceful movements, aye that's it, that's it.'

I'd prayed while he was talking and now felt a new resolve enter my mind and limbs.

The ascent went on and on, from one pitch to another, me in the middle, Roger bringing up the rear and collecting the slings and chocks. Richard was a confident leader and appeared to feel as comfortable in this place as the ravens that flew round us. Roger gave me fewer and fewer directions, but his praise was extravagant with every new move I managed correctly. My heart was encouraged with every compliment.

When we arrived at the summit of the spire at last the feeling of achievement was intoxicating. It didn't matter that every nerve and sinew of my body was aching.

Richard was perched on his haunches grinning as I took my seat and unstrapped my helmet. 'Well, what do'ya reckon? Better than a beach holiday?'

I couldn't decide which was better: the glorious view or the knowledge that I'd conquered fear and risen to meet this challenge.

'Ye did better than anyone I've ever taken out for the first time. Why, I bet if ye got a few routes under yer belt this week ye could lead a climb before we get back to Lorton.'

'Oh, I don't know about that,' I said. 'My Mum would flip if she saw me here!'

'Yer in safe hands with oor Richard, he knows his ropes he does.'

While we ate lunch we decided that if the weather held we'd attempt some classic routes near Napes Needle on the far side of Great Gable on Saturday. We went down a gulley route called Central Jordan, which was a vertical crack in the spire, and made our way back to the camp along a forest track.

It was a triumphant return, and a dip in the icy pool and a bit of sunbathing on the bank of the Liza felt wonderful. When I got up, however, I was stiff in all sorts of places where I didn't know muscles existed.

'If you're hobbling like that in the morning, Will, you won't be tackling the Needle,' Richard said with a laugh.

'Well if that's the case then we'll all do something else and wait until Sunday. I din'nae want the lad to miss out, besides it would'nae be as much fun for us without him and there's plenty for lads to do around the camp for a day.'

Jan looked up from her book to smile at him. Hannah told me later that evening that for her dad to give up a day's climbing, when he was so close to his favourite routes, was a major sacrifice. I felt humbled by his kindness and was determined to climb again the next day.

But when I rolled out of my tent in the morning I felt even stiffer. And I didn't think I could blame any of it on my wounds.

Roger accepted it all in good grace. Roger, Richard and I decided to go fishing after breakfast. I was hoping Hannah would want to come, but she wanted to give Lewis more lessons.

'No, Lewis and I have another lesson this morning,' she said. 'He's doing so well.' She smiled at him and ruffled his hair and he beamed up at her.

I was jealous but too eager to get off fishing to let it bother me. Roger took the rifle and slung his axe through his belt. He gave me his Bowie knife to attach to mine. Richard had one as well, and we felt the part as we strode out of camp.

'They're good knives for general chopping and stuff but a bit big for whittling and such like. I did'nae know that when

I got it but I bought this one here from Finland which does uz better for fishing and carving.'

We only had one rod, but I remembered a few tricks that Stan had taught me. This was an ideal place to test them out and impress my companions.

Roger and Richard were keen to make me the fishing guru. I divulged the secrets that Stan had taught me but began to wonder whether I would disappoint them as I looked down into the dark pools, which appeared devoid of life. After about twenty minutes we found some nice dark overhung pools, which provided plenty of cover for any fish that might have made it this far upstream. We found some hazel fronds, out of which we whittled fishing rods. We borrowed fishing line from Roger's spool, used some corks from the camp as floats, and baited our hooks with fat worms.

Roger was insistent that he would try 'on-the-fly' this morning with his rod. I wasn't sure the water was moving enough where we were and suggested he try downstream where there was more current. Richard and I trailed our worms down through the deep pools right up to the banks which overhung the river. I was skeptical of our chances but was overjoyed when Richard had a bite. It was a small brown trout, and he jumped into the river to bring it to the other bank, where there was a nice shingle beach where I showed him how to gut it.

About half an hour later there was a rustling in the undergrowth behind us and Roger appeared, looking grumpy. 'I can'ne see anything downstream, how have you lads fared?'

When Richard showed him his fish Roger quickly exchanged his fly for a float and a nice juicy worm. We ended up spending the best part of two hours in that one spot, it was such good fishing.

I lost three fish in the space of twenty minutes, the last of which actually snapped the end off my makeshift rod. The others laughed as they watched the end of my rod and a float disappearing downstream and under the bank, but Roger used his stick to retrieve the line. He pulled in a nice brown trout and Richard caught another. As it was nearly lunchtime, we decided we'd perfect the technique of the Indian fiddle and cook the fish on the riverbank. It took us about an hour, but we produced fire. Roger was insistent that we try to cook the fish as he'd seen it done on a TV programme. We gathered large amounts of moss and laid it on the glowing embers, placed the fish on the moss and then piled more moss on top of the fish.

'Are you sure, Dad?' Richard asked.

'You wait, the two of ye and ye'll see! Nice steamed trout!'

He was right. We peeled back the skin with our knives and used our fingers to pick the hot flesh from the bones as we basked in the sunshine on the pebbly beach. It seemed incredible to me that we were eating fish we had caught and cooked in a fire we had made.

Richard and I lay back on the beach after lunch while Roger went upstream to catch more fish to share with the rest of the family. I drifted off, and when I awoke Richard was beside me reading his Bible.

'What are you reading?' I asked.

'The book of Acts,' he said. 'It's one of the best books of the Bible because it continues the story of how the disciples got on with the job after Jesus ascended to heaven.'

Richard went upstream to find his dad and, since I had nothing to do all afternoon, I opened the Bible to the book of Acts. Richard was right—it was a cool story full of adventure, narrow escapes, imprisonments, shipwrecks, beatings, stonings and chases. It would make a great film,

I thought. And when I'd finished I felt like I was beginning to understand conversion and baptism a little better. The church in those days seemed so organic and 'un-institutionalized'. The guys preaching back then didn't have just words but power as well. Here was a mission big enough for a man to give his life to.

As I gazed at the faces round the campfire that evening, full of the fish Roger had caught for dinner, I felt grateful to God for these friends who felt like an extended family, for bringing me here, for giving me this adventure. It was a glimpse of His goodness that I would need to carry me through the next day.

PART SEVEN

FAITH

22

DAMSELS IN DISTRESS

C louds moved in across the Irish Sea while we slept and shrouded Gable Crag and the other lesser giants that encircled our camp. From inside the tent I felt the cool gloom of the day.

Lewis had slept slumped against the edge of the tent and, having pressed the inner and outer tent together, woke to a wet sleeping bag.

'Oh, yuk! I'm soaking!' he howled.

'Well get up then,' I said. 'Get some wood for the fire and you'll be dry in no time.'

'But it's cold out there. I might catch me death.'

'You'll live,' I mumbled into my sleeve.

'I could get in with you, Will!' he said, nose peeping over the edge of his sleeping bag.

'Oh no you won't!'

The next thing I knew we were in the midst of a 'dead arm' fight. I only sacrificed one arm from my snug bag to meet the contest. Lewis shrieked and jumped round the tent while we belted each other until we heard Hannah's voice.

'What's going on in there, you two?'

Lewis was quick to gain the advantage. 'Oh, Hannah, tell him to stop! He's hitting me!'

The little wretch continued to pummel and kick me until Hannah threatened to come in and break up the fight.

'You ought to know better, Will. You're older and bigger than Lewis.'

'But I'm not—it's him. Lewis!'

'Ouch! Will, stop! Don't! That hurts!'

Finally Lewis unzipped the tent and went out to show her his bruises. I rolled over to the sound of her soothing words and tried to get some more sleep.

When I eventually emerged from the tent, Richard and Roger were already poring over their guidebooks, adjusting our plan based on the weather.

Hannah gave me disapproving looks over breakfast and Lewis sat close to her, looking up lovingly.

Although we had no idea whether the clouds would lift, Hannah and Jan decided to climb to the summit of Great Gable. Richard tried to convince Lewis to come with us to Needle Ridge. But the more Richard talked, the more convinced Lewis became that going with the girls would be safer.

But we could do the first part of the ascent all together, so we packed up and loaded the heaviest of our kit on to Alfie. 'Not really necessary,' Richard said. 'But all of our stuff is old and heavy and hey, Alfie's got nothing better to do!' We started up into the dark mists that overhung Great Gable and the surrounding fells. The path took us up what is called the Tongue, which led us right up to the point between Green and Great Gable. At Stone Cove, Jan, Hannah and Lewis ascended up into the clouds of Windy Gap while Roger, Richard and I skirted west underneath the great dark bulk of Gable Crag on a famous route called Moses' Trod.

This very path, Roger told us, was used by the legendary smuggler Moses Rigg as he brought his illegal whisky from his home in Dubbs Quarry a few miles away to places like Ravenglass. According to local folklore he was a gentle man and a fine wrestler. According to another legend, he kept one of his illicit whisky stills in a cave right at the top of Central Gulley on Gable Crag. Roger pointed high up into the mists and said that climbers had found a cave-like hut with a flagged floor.

I was intrigued by this famous Lakeland character and Roger told me he'd lend me a book called *George Ashbury* by O.S. MacDonnell.

'Some of the stories about Moses are pure legend, I'm sure,' he said. 'But it's not all folklore. There were those alive when MacDonnell wrote the book who could remember part of a whisky barrel being used for sheep dipping at Gatesgarth Farm in Buttermere.'

We continued on Moses Trod right the way round the ridge and then led Alfie down to Beckhead. We tethered him there in the shelter and removed his burden of climbing gear. From there we passed down and along the western edge of the Great Gable summits to arrive at another monumental landscape called Needle Ridge.

'This, Will, is "Lion Country"—a land of giants,' Roger announced proudly as we scrambled along the path. 'Great men made history here. I dare say ye would'nae have heard of the likes of Hasket-Smith, Solly and Slingsby, but these hills resound with their daring and courage.'

'Why? What did they do here?'

'Daring deeds, lad—not so they could be famous, ye ken. Nae, these men did what they did because they had adventure in their bones.'

'But what did they do?'

'Oh, I'll tell ye when we get there. Come on, keep going up this valley—we're nearly there.'

Roger looked back at me, struggling for breath, and smiled. 'Faith niver knows where it's being led, but it loves and knows the One who's leading. We'll be there soon— trust me!'

I felt that now-familiar fear when I stood gazing up at the huge knife-edged piece of rock. I had to steady myself on a rock behind to stop falling backwards. The mist swirled round it and droplets of moisture condensed on our jackets.

'Andrew's preaching his sermon round about now,' Roger said as he arranged the ropes. 'Ach, hope the lad's okay.'

'He'll be fine,' Richard said. 'What are you onto next week, Dad?'

'Next week's on faith ... should be good!' he said as he pulled on his boots.

'So,' I said, 'besides not knowing where it's being led, what is faith?'

Roger looked up at Napes Needle and smiled. 'Well now, faith is the art of holding on to things your reason has once accepted in spite of your changing moods.' He saw my blank expression and added, 'Will, I'll nae preach to you lad but if you ask me that in an hour or or so, ye'll get yer answer.'

As Richard started the first pitch of Napes Needle, I asked Roger to tell me more about the giants.

'You're standing at the birthing stool of modern climbing,' he told me. 'It all happened right here, and the bits that did'nae happen here happened over there on the Scafell Crags, the highest crags in England. On the ridge to the left there, Needle Ridge, British climbing moved on from men scrambling up gullies. Aye, some remarkable men declared the open season on ridges and faces that now make up the modern sport—Solly, a law clerk from

Birkenhead, and Slingsby, a great alpine climber, were here a little over a hundred years ago, clad in their clumsy hobnailed boots and tweeds. Do ye see that ledge up there? Aye, well it was there that W. Cecil Slingsby gave up his chance to be the first man ever up this ridge. Instead he allowed the much younger Solly to make the second pitch by standing on his mighty shoulders! It takes a big man to let someone else have the glory *and* to help them get it ahead of ye. It's nae wonder that Slingsby went on to fame in his pioneering climbs in Norway, with a giant heart like that.'

'That's cool,' I said to encourage him to keep talking while I kept my eye on Richard as he made his way up the first part of the Needle.

'Aye but that's nae all, Will,' Roger continued. 'This Needle here is also special because just eight years before Solly climbed that ridge, a twenty-seven-year-old lad called Walter Haskett Smith made the first solo ascent of the Needle. His accomplishment marked what is generally seen as the birth of rock climbing as a sport distinct from mountaineering. And Smith had nae ropes or friction boots, nae mobile phone or mountain rescue ... nae, those guys were derf! He had to leave his naipkin tucked into a crevice at the top to prove to anyone else who got up there that he'd made it first!'

Richard beckoned us to start the climb and, as before, I went in front and Roger directed my moves. It was a long ascent, and the last part was particularly difficult, but we made it to the top and spent a few moments huddled in the narrow space. I ventured a glance down through the grey mist to the enormous rocks below. Today there was no view, only danger; no real elation, only a desire to climb down as quickly as possible.

'Now, lad, did'nae ye have a question for uz?' Roger reminded me.

'Okay then, what is faith?' No sooner had the words left my mouth than I began to regret them. I couldn't explain why I was suddenly filled with foreboding.

Roger nodded to Richard, and they began to rig up a figure eight to my harness.

'What–' I began to panic.

'I said I would'nae give ye a sermon, William, and I won't. Tell me, d'ye trust that the rope can hold ye?'

I wasn't completely certain, but I guessed I wouldn't be up there if I didn't, so I nodded.

'Aye, and d'ye trust ma Richard with yer life?'

I hesitated, but I nodded again.

'Well, ye say it, but let's see whether ye really do. Faith is'nae saying it, it's doin' it.' With that, Roger tossed half of the rope over one side of the Needle and the other half down the other side. 'Aye, ye two, here are yer figure-of-eights. Ye know how to abseil—clip in, check each other, and off ye go!'

Richard grinned that wild grin with which he greeted danger.

I was a gibbering wreck. 'But there's no hand holds on that side, and you've not anchored the rope to anything ...'

'It's anchored to me,' Richard said. 'It's the only way from the Needle.' He got onto his belly and started to slither backwards to his precipice. 'I'll go one way and you go the other and my weight will stop you falling and vice versa.'

'Aye,' Roger said. 'Now crouch down and ease back slowly at the same time. Ye must go at the same speed or ye'll nae balance. Richard will reach the ground first as it's nearer on his side, but ye can trust him not to unclip. He's a good lad!'

Why can't he unclip? I wondered. And then it dawned on me. If he unclipped he'd send me hurtling to my death. I decided this illustration of faith had made its point. 'If it's all the same to you, Roger, I think it'll take enough faith for me to climb back down the way I came.'

Even in my panic I noticed the amused twinkle in Roger's eye. 'Noo, William, ye want to learn about faith, and I'm going to teach ye. Ye grow strong faith through strong trials. C'mon, clip in here and let's have some fun!'

'It's okay Will,' Richard said, 'trust us.'

With a sick feeling in the pit of my stomach I did as he said. The next thing I knew I was crouching down eye to eye with Richard. As I began to slither back all I could imagine was my body lying smashed on the rocks below. Roger coached us at the right speed as we lost sight of each other, and so the descent began.

'Aye Will, that's right, you can'nae see him, but yer trusting he's there!'

My life in the balance, the rope held and so did Richard's weight. Within the first six feet I managed to get my feet on the rock and leaned out under Roger's instruction.

'Now ye can pay out as much or as little as ye want and just walk or bounce yer way down the rock.'

'I think I'll just walk,' I said as I edged down a little further. The rock was wet but my boots still gripped and, the further I got, the more confidence I had. By the time I heard Richard saying that he was on the ground I was actually bouncing away from the rock and letting out more rope while in mid air. It was extremely cool!

Roger made it down and put his hand on my shoulder. 'Well done, Will. Ye'll hear many men tell ye all sorts of things about faith, but ye'll nae forget that sermon, will ye?'

I shook my head.

'It's not about words, it's about laying your life out on what God says is true,' Richard said.

And, for the first time, I could see that they were right.

We took a break and decided to have a crack at the Eagle's Nest, just above us on Needle Ridge. This mass of mountain ridge and deep cracks disappeared above the mist. Roger led the climb and we waited for him at what was called 'the dress circle'. It was getting colder and I was eager to start climbing again.

We made our way slowly to the two great parallel cracks about fifty feet above us. We reached a ledge near these cracks and then crossed them to the skyline on the left.

It was hard going and Richard often gave me the exact hand and foothold sequences over a specific section.

We were tiny as ants on this great rockface, exposed on all angles with nowhere to retreat. Roger met us at the ledge and we made our way up the second seventy-foot pitch to the Eagle's Nest. I breathed a sigh of relief in that clear fresh air when we finally made it. Richard made his way past us and up a further fifteen feet to the Crow's Nest, another famous perch, but I stayed put. We abseiled back to our gear and made our way back across the scree to Beck Head where Alfie solemnly waited for us.

Once again I felt an enormous sense of achievement, but I was also glad to be back on terra firma (and the firmer the better). As the adrenaline wore off and we approached our camp I felt the physical and emotional exhaustion take over. I dragged myself down the Tongue, eager to see Hannah and tell her about all I had done.

But there was an unusual stillness at the camp.

'They should have been back a long time ago,' Roger said. 'This is nae good.' He looked at his phone but knew there would be no reception. It was late afternoon and there was no sign of them coming down out of the clouds.

Richard looked anxious. 'Should we go now, Dad? With this mist it will get dark earlier and it'll take a while to reach the ridge again.'

'I know,' Roger said as he unloaded the donkey, 'but we'll wait a wee longer, get some food and rest and do a bit of planning first.'

Jan, Hannah and Lewis had set out for the summit of Great Gable from Windy Gap and their plan had been to come down the west face of Great Gable. But it was unlikely that they'd done this because they would have passed Beck Head on their way down and would thus have made it to camp first. We had to assume, therefore, that something had happened either between Windy Gap and the summit or halfway down the west side of the mountain. The plan was to form a pincer movement on the mountain and meet at the summit. Roger would go one way and leave Twiggy at Beck Head, where we had left Alfie a few hours before, and we would take Alfie up to Windy Gap and leave him sheltered on the leeward side. The animals had to be left because the remaining ascents could only be done on foot, but they were necessary in the case of an accident to carry the tackle needed to help anyone who was wounded back down.

Every muscle in my body protested, but the thought of Hannah, or Lewis or Jan, stuck high in the misty wilderness was a thought too terrible to bear. I'd heard Roger talk about the fate of those who had wandered too close to the precipice on the north face of Great Gable.

We packed provisions, warm clothes and two sleeping bags and divided the first aid kit. Then we knelt down to pray. I was impatient to get on with the rescue, and in my sinful ignorance I was angry with Roger for wasting precious time when the others might be in terrible danger. But, of course, his persistent dependence upon the Almighty God was the right course. And, as I was learning daily, none of what we did was possible without God.

As he finished, he prayed, 'Lord, I'm thinking of young David when his family were kidnapped and carried away by the enemy. And he called out tae ye for help and ye helped get them all back safely. Lord, we've done all we can to prepare but we know that the safety of oor loved ones rests in yer mighty hands, and we're trusting ye to help us. Amen.'

Richard had tears in his eyes as he gave his dad a hug.

'Now then, Richard, dun'nae give up lad, keep yer eyes and ears peeled, and I'll see ye both at the top.'

'We'll bring them back, don't worry,' I said.

'Good lad, Will,' Roger said, 'just watch yer feet up there in the mist on those rocks. There's a big boulder field near the summit and ye'll slip if ye rush. Just take it easy. Do what Richard tells ye, and I'm sure everything will be all right.'

It was a gruelling ascent up the Tongue again to Windy Gap, but we were there within an hour. Alfie, who seemed to sense that something was wrong, didn't tug or strain at the reins but made his way steadily. We left him cloistered by rocks and out of the way but in full view of the North East Ridge, so that we could easily see him on our descent. We'd arranged to call out to Roger as we made our way to the summit and would use our whistles only when we had found one or more of the party.

From Windy Gap, Richard and I went up the North East Ridge. Scrambling up the track and calling as we went, we ascended higher and higher into the mist and that strange mountain world. Richard and I separated across the

North East boulder field, as much as we dared. We called systematically and then listened for ten seconds, but there was nothing. Richard was a hundred yards off to my right. At one point I thought I heard something far away below to the left. I shouted again, this time directing my shout to where I'd heard the noise. There was no reply over the howling of the wind. The raven came circling out of the mist and Richard told me to move on up, which I dutifully did, allowing him to be the leader of the party as his father had commanded. But something like intuition stirred within me, and I continued to address my calls in that same direction as I moved up the boulder field, which got steeper and steeper as we neared the top of the great dome-like summit.

Suddenly there was the sound of a whistle from the summit and Richard shouted triumphantly and pointed, though there was nothing to see but the mist. Richard started running towards the top. I glanced back one more time and shouted in the direction of the sound. I heard the faintest of cries in reply.

It was certainly not the cry of a raven this time, but possibly the cry of a woman, though I couldn't be absolutely sure. Richard had disappeared into the mist to the sound of his father's whistle, and a strange choice lay before me. If I followed them I'd be obeying the instructions I'd been given, but I knew I wouldn't easily find the place where I'd heard the cry from the craggy rocks below.

After Roger's prayer I'd asked Richard on the ascent to Windy Gap about the story of David and his family kidnapped by the raiders. David had received a message from God, Richard said, telling him to pursue the enemy and assuring him that he would recover his family's property.

I felt a surge of excitement rising from deep within me. If God helped David, why couldn't he help me? And then I prayed out loud, 'Father, should I go down?' Although I can't say that God spoke to me audibly in response, a stream of thoughts raced through my mind with such speed that I didn't think it was possible I'd made it up myself. As I found out later they were, in fact, words straight from the story of David at Ziklag when God said to him, 'Go and you will recover all.' So I began my rocky descent, calling all the while to the person who I assumed was stranded somewhere below.

After about five minutes I could hear the voice more clearly and recognized it as Hannah's.

'Hannah, it's okay, I'm coming!' I shouted.

'Will? Is that you? I'm stuck on a ledge.'

'I'm coming.'

'Mum's fallen and hurt her leg ... is Dad with you?'

I made my way carefully round the ridge until I could finally see her. She was shivering and she'd been crying. 'Your dad and Richard are at the summit. Don't worry, I'll get you out.'

I looked around. She could climb most of the way off the ledge that she was on, but the last bit up to where I was standing was virtually impossible for anyone except the very tall because the last handhold was well out of reach. I didn't have any climbing gear with me, but I had an idea.

'Hannah, you can climb most of the way up this wall. I'll hang down and pull you up the last bit myself.'

She looked at me for a moment. 'Okay,' she said, 'I'm coming.' But as she neared the top of the rock face I could see she was very nervous. I made my way to the edge of the precipice and clambered down as far as I dared before securing my left hand on a good handhold and then extending my other arm down to Hannah. She reached up, but she wasn't near enough.

'It's no use, Will. You're too far away, I'd better go back. This is too dangerous.'

I paused. 'No, stay there while I get down just a little further.' I repositioned myself and my left hand found another crevice for a secure hold.

'Okay, Hannah, reach up one more time, but don't grab onto me just yet.'

She did, and I could see that if we did monkey grips, curling the ends of our fingers round, she would be able to take hold of my hand without jumping for it. She was starting to shake from holding on.

'Okay, can you reach up slowly and take my hand in a monkey grip so I can pull you up to the edge?'

'I don't know, I'm not sure. I'll be too heavy.'

I looked into her eyes. 'Hannah, it's going to be all right. Trust me. Stretch out your hand now. I won't let you go. Go on, now!'

I'll never forget the look in her eyes. With new determination and courage, she reached up and took hold of my hand. She was a lot heavier than I'd expected, but I tried not to let it show.

'Okay, that's good now. Slowly ... okay ... now let me take the strain,' I said. I began to pull gently and tensed my body even more. I pulled on my left arm, and slowly Hannah started to scramble up the rock face, leaving her position of security behind. I could feel the ligaments in my right arm tearing as I strained at her weight.

'Will!' she said as she saw the pained expression on my face.

I'm not sure I can do this, I thought. But I knew there was no way back now, and no chance that she'd be able to find the original hold if I lowered her again. I pulled and pulled, with every last ounce of strength left in me.

I was in so much pain that I had my eyes shut and my teeth clenched as I let out a pained growl. But then, just when I thought all hope was gone, I felt the pressure easing on my arms as Hannah found her first new handhold and positioned her feet to take the strain once more. I put my arm around her. We sat gasping at the top of the rock face, and she began to cry as she held onto me tightly and thanked me.

'It's okay,' I said. 'Everything's okay.' It was one of the finest moments of my life. For in that moment it didn't matter whether she would have me as a boyfriend or not—all I cared about was that she was safe.

Earlier in the afternoon, Hannah explained, Jan had slipped on the boulder field and badly sprained, or perhaps fractured, her ankle. So Hannah had left Lewis with Jan on the summit and started out into the thick mist to get help. She'd hoped to come down the southern nose of Great Gable and find us where we were climbing on the Needle. But in the mist she'd become disorientated, gone too far east and spent the afternoon scrambling among the rocks and boulders until at last she became marooned on a ledge far above the valley and far away from help.

As we neared the top I saw Roger tending to Jan. Richard had his arm around Lewis. They were all relieved to see us, and Hannah told them what had happened to her and how I'd rescued her. I tried to shrug it off, but Roger looked stern.

'Ye risked yer life doing that, Will. Ye both could have fallen, ye should have come for the rope. Ye ... ye ... ach, come here!' He grabbed me and pulled me close. He was tearful with relief as he said, 'Aye, but it's okay, thank ye, lad, ye did okay, thank ye for bringing ma wee lass back to uz.'

I winced a bit as he held me tight. Some of the ligaments in my arm were damaged and, though I knew they'd heal, the injury seemed to boost my heroism in the eyes of all standing around. Hannah brought me my coat and helped me put it on.

Alfie brought Jan safely the rest of the way to the camp and Richard, who went back by way of Moses Trod to pick up Twiggy, arrived back about the same time. Although no one spoke of it, all of us were thinking how close a call Hannah had had.

Although Jan was in good spirits, she needed medical attention. As we sat round the fire that night in a state of thankfulness mixed with exhaustion, there was a lot of talk about what should happen in the morning. Jan and Roger would have to go back, but Richard wanted to complete the circuit they'd planned—over into Wasdale and then back to Borrowdale. He argued that we were responsible and old enough to look after ourselves. Roger said he and Jan would talk it over and let us know in the morning.

Having had enough excitement to last an entire lifetime, I was quite prepared to go back. But I also liked the idea of continuing on into this mountain wilderness with Hannah, Richard and Lewis.

23

THE BRAVE MEN OF BUTTERMERE

The weather the next morning was uncertain, as was the mood of the group. Roger took Richard and Hannah for a walk and, when they came back, there was a hint of optimism in Richard's smile.

'The three of us can go on,' he said. 'But Lewis'll have to go back to his mum and dad because he's too young to be left.'

Roger was stern. 'I'll be taking the gun of course, and I suggest ye give uz the Bowie knife in case ye're stopped by the police. And mind that ye submit yerself to yer sister!'

Lewis was disappointed at first, but Jan soon had him anxious to get home and frighten his poor mother with all the adventures he'd had on the high hills.

After a few more farewells and cautions Roger, Jan and Lewis were on their way back down through the forests to civilization and we were left alone.

While the tents were drying we sat by the banks of Sail Beck to bask in this incredible freedom. Here we were, in these glorious mountains, with ponies and camping gear and enough food for the week.

Soon, however, Hannah was bossing us around to clean up the camp. Never having had a big sister, I wasn't used to being ordered about. Richard wasn't too keen about it either, but we put up with it as best we could as a deal was a deal and we'd promised we would do everything she said.

We rode off up the right-hand side of Sail Beck and over the Black Sale pass down to Wasdale. It was an old route used by pack ponies but many sections were extremely steep. While I was happy to dismount and lead rein along the narrow outcrops of rock, Richard and Hannah were eager to test their riding skills. Richard only dismounted twice, and Hannah finally lost her nerve on only one section. Although they were both excellent and experienced riders, I was sure one of them would meet with an accident and I was relieved when we made it to the base of the valley.

We rested at a waterfall called Ritson's Force, named after a man famous for his tall tales called William Ritson, who had once been proprietor of the Wasdale Inn. We continued into Wasdale, the remotest valley in the Lake District. When we rounded the corner of Kirk Fell into Wasdale, before us was the Scafell Massif, the highest lump of rock in England. To our right was the steep-sided valley of Wasdale, where the scree tumbles almost vertically two thousand feet into the dark, three-mile lake where we hoped to make our camp for the night.

Far away to the left I could still make out the mass of Great Gable and Needle Ridge where I'd rescued Hannah less than sixteen hours before. I was sure things had changed between us, but she was still keeping her distance, rarely looking me straight in the eyes for long. For the first time in my life, though, I didn't feel a need to rush in or make things happen or find out what she thought. I trusted that

God would work things out. This, I thought, was another kind of lesson in faith.

We drank ginger beer at the Wasdale Head Inn and reviewed the camping charges. After such solitude as we'd enjoyed in the Ennerdale Valley it seemed strange to be among other people. Richard suggested that, rather than pay to stay at the campsite there, we push on another four kilometres over Sty Head and onto Sprinkling Tarn. We bought a few postcards, mounted our ponies behind the pub like all good cowboys do, and headed off up another track which ran up Lingmell Beck to Sty Head.

Once at Sty Head we were really in mountain country, and we struck off to the east and the great slack and then dropped down to the dark emerald waters of Sprinkling Tarn where we set up camp. We only had one tent, but it had two compartments. Richard and I would share one, leaving Hannah the other for herself. The evening skies were clear and the fells deserted. We cooked beans and sausages on Roger's Primus stove, which took us awhile to get going and wasn't at all the same as cooking over an open fire.

After eating, we sat back to enjoy the tranquil evening. After about forty minutes, though, we were bored.

'How about an evening scramble up Scafell Pike?' Richard suggested with a grin.

'That's the highest mountain in the Lake District,' Hannah said. 'We're not doing that tonight.'

'C'mon,' Richard said. 'It'll be fun. Look, it's probably not even two kilometres away and we'll easily be back before dark. Even with you dawdling taking in the views,' he said as he poked her in the ribs.

She finally relented. 'All right, Richard Scott, but you have to promise not to do any spontaneous climbing. I don't want any cragging no matter how tempting the rocks are.'

He agreed and we took the ponies the first kilometre around Great End to the edge of the boulder field. The sun was still above the mountains when we tethered the ponies somewhere above Esk Hause and made our assent of the Scafell Ridge. As we reached the summit of England's highest mountain, the sun was setting in blazing orange and red way beyond the Isle of Man in the Irish Sea, and the mountain slopes were awash in colour.

After half an hour on the summit we descended in the blue stillness of the mountain air to the ponies waiting below. As the moon rose high over the Langdale Pikes, a glorious silver path extended before us across the tundra, leading back down to Sprinkling Tarn.

'Do you know,' Hannah told me the next morning as we were packing up our gear, 'riding bareback over the blue mountain tundra in the silky moonlight was like a dream come true.'

She seemed so at home up here with her little Indian pony. She was so beautiful, so full of pure life, so undefiled by the world. She wore her hair long, and it swept around her neck and shoulders like waves of deep auburn fire as she cantered across the high plateaus. As I watched her, there were moments when I lost confidence that God might bring us together. She was always friendly but gave me no reason to hope. All I had to cling to was the intuition I'd experienced at church and the memory of the way she'd held me above the precipice.

We saddled up and made our way up to Esk Hause and down Tongue Head to the picturesque cauldron-like hollow where Angle Tarn nestled under Esk Pike. The descent to Langdale Valley was extremely steep and no one attempted to ride their pony down the stone staircase that National Park volunteers had built to help stem the erosion. It was a slow descent, and Richard entertained us with the history of the very ground upon which we now walked.

'Well,' he said, and he lowered his voice, 'Hannah's heard it all before. It's a bit gruesome and I don't want her in one of her girly moods!'

'Gruesome? It's so beautiful here,' I said.

'Oh, don't you believe it Will, these quiet hills have stories enough to make your hair stand on end. Ask your Uncle George—he knows them all.'

'But he hasn't got much hair.'

'Like the smugglers old Lanty and Moses who survived the stalking attacks of the excise men and travelled all over these fells to ply their trade.'

'Your dad told me a bit about them the other day,' I said.

'Ah, but did he tell you about Boethar and his mighty men who defended these hills against the Norman conquest?'

'But your dad said it was King David in the Bible who had the mighty men.'

'Ah yes, one of my favourite bits of the Bible ... 2 Samuel 23:8.' And he began to bellow in his father's voice: 'These are the names of the mighty men whom David had ... Adino the Eznite, who lifted up his spear against eight hundred, whom he slew at one time. Eleazar the son of Dodo ... who defied the Philistines that were there gathered together for battle, and the men of Israel had run away. He arose on his own and fought the Philistines and even when his hand was weary he didn't let go of his sword. And the Lord wrought a great victory that day, and the people only came back to get the spoil.'

'Well, those guys sound like proper dudes, but I've not heard your dad talk about people like that round here.'

Richard looked pleased. 'No, I thought not. Well, that's what it was like here too at one time. It was the only unconquered part of England and, like David when he was on the run from King Saul, these guys lived rough and waged a guerilla war against a large enemy with only their knowledge of the high country and their awesome courage to keep them alive.'

'Sounds a bit like *Braveheart*,' I said.

'It was just like that—and worse. These brave men and women were the last people left standing after the invasion, and they lived like Robin Hood's merry men with their centre of operations in what they called the Secret Valley, which is what we call Buttermere today.'

'Oh, what, really? Buttermere?' I asked.

'Sure, it was the perfect place. The Normans had heard of a place called Little Norway but no one knew the mountains well enough to know where it was. Anyway, after the death of William the Conqueror his wicked son William Rufus decided he'd earn the respect of the nobles by squashing this pesky resistance. So he came up to Ambleside, just down there in the distance, at the head of Lake Windermere.' Richard pointed. 'He brought such a huge army with him that Boethar decided it was time to seek peace. So he sent his most noble and courageous lieutenant to meet King William and agree terms. And on this very track where we are now, Old Harry Knudson, or Ari, made his way over the mountains that last, fateful time with four other white-bearded elders from Buttermere.'

'Fateful? Why?' I asked, trying to imagine these men who sounded like Gandalf from *Lord of the Rings* making their descent to meet the dreaded king.

'Well,' Richard said, 'after a council in Langdale, they walked unarmed into the king's camp and were presented to him. Old Harry was a tall man, six feet, with a long white beard and ruddy face though he was over seventy years old.

He'd lived a life of adventure and the phrase that some use today, "to come out fighting like old Harry", says a lot about how he'd defended those he loved. When they made their request for terms of peace the king sat there and scowled and shouted, "These men are spies! Put out their eyes!'" At first the guards didn't believe he was serious and didn't move, but then the king shouted again, "These men are all spies, now put out their eyes!'"

'They didn't really, did they?' I asked, certain that Richard was embellishing it a bit for my sake.

'Will, don't forget what type of man we're dealing with here. William Rufus was so debauched and wicked that even the bishops of the day wouldn't give him a Christian burial. They only allowed his remains to be placed at Winchester. The guy was off his head ... and yes, he made his men do it right in front of everyone. When the guards moved away there were four men writhing around the floor in agony, but not Old Harry. He was standing.'

I could see what was coming. 'Oh, cool, did he grab a sword and lay into the guards?'

'No, he'd been sent to secure peace for the good of his loved ones and for their children yet unborn. He fought for that alone with words that took as much courage as the battles he'd fought with sword and bow. "Let me speak, let me speak!" he shouted above the cries of horror. "We are ambassadors come to seek terms of peace." But the king would not hear it. He sent them away so he could enjoy another night of booze and the women he'd kidnapped on his way through.'

'What happened to the men then?' I asked.

Richard walked more slowly so we'd be further behind Hannah. 'Well, this is the gruesome bit. For the next time anyone saw Harry and his ambassadors, they were crucified, naked and disembowelled on standards supported by horses and in front of a vast traveling army making their way up the valley to Grasmere.'

Now I was shocked. 'You're kidding, right?'

'Will, I told you this guy was evil. He put the remains of those brave men there to strike fear into the inhabitants of the valleys so they'd never meddle with the king again. But that's not the end, because–'

'Come on, boys, we're on the flats now. Let's get going and grab a cooked breakfast at the Stickle Barn!' Hannah raced down the valley and Richard on Twiggy and I, hanging on to Brigham for dear life, raced after her.

After breakfast we made our way in the hot sun along the road to Elterwater. There we found a bridge and a deep slate pool. Hannah gave Richard a run for his money, performing a series of spectacular dives and somersaults that put me to shame. We bought a pie and some Coke from the shop in town and ate lunch under the shady trees in the centre of the green.

'I know, let's go downstream to Skelwith Bridge and jump in at the waterfall!' Richard suggested.

But this time Hannah wasn't having it. 'No, Richard, there'll be nowhere for the horses and it's too far out of our way.'

'Oh come on, Hannah! We'll find somewhere.'

Richard seemed edgy, and Hannah nailed it. 'I knew I shouldn't have given you Coke,' she said. 'It always makes you funny and unmanageable.'

'That's rubbish, Hannah. Will, do I look unmanageable to you?'

I laughed. 'Oh no, Richard,' I said. 'Don't involve me— you know Hannah's always right!'

'Come on you two,' Hannah said. 'I have had a better idea. It's a secret, but if we get going over High Close Pass now we can be in Grasmere in time.'

Hannah wouldn't give us so much as a clue. It was hot work for the horses over more tarmac lanes, but we made the summit of the small pass. As we rounded the bend to begin our steep descent, we saw the panorama of this quaint dale. The exit was over another pass some miles in front of us.

'That's Dunmail Raise,' Richard said, pointing. 'And this is Grasmere, the place I was telling you about.'

'Oh yeah, you were about to get to a good bit ...'

'That's right. Where were we? Oh yes. So as the Normans came close to where that village is now legend has it that King William Rufus got his answer from heaven for his villainy. Out of nowhere came a sound that shook the earth and split the trees around him, sending knights crashing to the ground.'

'Oh come on, Richard!' I said.

'No, seriously. It's a local phenomenon called the Helm Wind. When two weather fronts meet near Cross Fell in the springtime they send such a sudden and violent wind down this valley that it's notorious even now.'

'Okay, so what happened next then?'

'Well, there was pandemonium in the ranks, and that wasn't helped by the wrathful arrows of Boethar's archers and vengeful warriors who descended upon them to pay them back for their slain leaders. The superstitious Normans fled, believing God was against them on account of William's torture of Old Harry, and as many as could ran back to Ambleside along with their repugnant king, who never set foot in Cumberland again. Old Harry was laid to rest over there just above the youth hostel.' He pointed to a small crag above the centre of the village. 'It's called Butterlyp Howe—we can go to check it out later if you want.'

'Yeah, I'd like to see that. Quite a man, Old Harry—bad way to go, though.'

But as we made our way to the village I wondered if that was such a bad way to go. Harry had lived to a good old age and had died valiantly trying to secure peace for his people. Maybe it was a heroic way to go after all.

We stopped at a little café next to a boating area on the lake. 'Right, here we are,' Hannah said. 'This is your surprise. Wait here and I'll talk to the manager and see what we can do.' She went inside.

We made quite a spectacle for the tourists, standing outside with the horses, but Hannah soon came out with the café owner and they appeared to be agreeing something. When he went back inside, she began to unpack her pony. 'Don't just stand there gawping,' she said. 'I've earned us a two-hour rowing boat, and we're heading off to that island to do some sketching and painting.'

'What?' Richard said. 'That's the surprise? Painting on an island? I hate art! And what did you trade for the boat?'

'I'm lending your Twiggy for him to lead kids around on. Don't look at me like that, Richard. Twiggy loves children, its why you got her. If you don't want to draw, you can swim or climb a tree or something. I've heard Will is good at art, and I thought he'd appreciate a bit of a quieter time after all this high adventure.' She looked at me for support.

'Well, yeah,' I said. 'Sounds great—I haven't got any gear, though.'

'I've got loads, and we can share the paints and water if we paint at the same place.'

'Cool,' I said. And it was.

Richard jumped out of the boat when we were clear of the shallows and said he'd swim to the island.

I offered to take the oars, but Hannah grabbed the one that Richard had been pulling on. 'It's okay, Will. I'm not a feminist or anything, but if we both pull together we'll get there quicker and have more peace before Richard gets there and starts whining about going back.'

So there we were, gliding together across the still lake in the afternoon sunlight. It was pure magic, although I didn't exactly know what I was doing with the oars. Hannah laughed and showed me how to roll my wrists properly. When we reached the island we had to fend off the geese with a branch and made our way up the little hill to an open grassy knoll among the Scots Pines where we sat down to select a view. We chose the view north toward Dunmail Raise and Helm Crag.

Richard soon arrived and began teasing Hannah for her spidery pencil work, but when he saw me working in earnest he left to explore the other end of the lake in the boat.

For the first time, I felt like Hannah got to see the real me. I inherited my artistic ability from my mum, and she and my school art teacher had helped me to be quite proficient with pencil and brush. While Hannah enjoyed art, she didn't have the same natural talent and became frustrated when she made mistakes.

'Oh, I just can't get the strokes right,' she said after a few attempts at the sky.

I glanced over. 'Well, it's better than my rowing.'

'Very generous. But seriously, what am I doing wrong? I mean, look at yours—you just do it so naturally.'

Although it was pretty obvious to me what was wrong, putting it sensitively wasn't so easy. 'Don't be such a perfectionist, Hannah. Your style is exact and controlled—it lacks feeling, flow, emotion ... that's all.'

She looked over at me, as if to see whether I meant more by it. Her cheeks went slightly red as she glanced down again. 'Well, I suppose. I don't find it easy like some people and perhaps I don't have your experience ... but thank you anyway for the tutorial.'

'Oh, Hannah, look, I didn't mean it in a critical way, really, it's just ...'

'Will, it's okay. I can handle criticism, it's only painting. Now get back to that masterpiece before I get more jealous.'

I didn't know how to take her behaviour. All I wanted was a sign or token that would give me hope. I'd thought that maybe wanting to spend this time alone together was such a sign, but I wasn't sure.

'Ahoy, you two lovebirds! I can see you cuddled up there!' It was Richard, standing in the boat waving. 'Are you coming back now, or shall I leave you there?'

Hannah flushed with anger. 'We are not cuddled up,' she called back to him. 'We're painting. Stop showing off or I'll get Dad to come and take you home.' She shook her head and turned to me. 'Too much caffeine makes him behave like an idiot.'

'Hey, it's okay. I don't mind.' I thought of reaching my hand across to hers as she began to wash her brushes. I let my brush touch hers, but she quickly moved it away and shook her brush dry. She must have realized what I'd tried to do. Or did she? My heart was pounding with the fear of being rejected.

'Well,' she finally said, 'I suppose we'd better get down to the beach before he starts bellyaching.'

'Yes,' I said. 'I'll get the things.' My heart sank. I decided not to mention anything again unless she did.

On the way down she wouldn't let me help her over the steep bit, which I thought was a bad sign, but we were soon in Richard's company and I was one of the boys again.

Back in Grasmere, Richard and I visited Butterlyp Howe while Hannah did some shopping. 'Howe means burial ground,' Richard said. 'There are loads of them all over the crags and fell tops around here.'

We stood silent for a moment at the place where this great man was buried. I thought of Harry and all he suffered. But I was also thinking of Hannah and wondered what she was thinking.

We met on the green and had an ice cream, but Hannah was very quiet.

She phoned her parents to let them know how we were doing, and I left a message on Mum's answering machine just to say I was fine. I'd already decided that if she picked up I wouldn't mention the rock climbing or the adults' early departure.

We headed out of Grasmere in the late afternoon and picked our way up Easdale and onto the fells once again. Richard was excited to camp at a place he'd camped with his dad when he was younger. He pointed toward a large waterfall at the head of the valley. 'That's Sour Milk Ghyll,' he said. 'Looks a bit steep from here but it's a bridle way and we'll be okay. Anyway, we came down worse this morning.'

He was right, and Brigham missed his footing only once. Soon we were high up above the valley in an isolated little corrie where Easedale Tarn sat in the shade. We were surrounded by the craggy summits of Tarn Crag and Slapestone Edge and Blea Crag.

We let the horses loose and they ambled down to the tarn to drink. Richard and I slept out under the stars that night, watching for shooting stars.

24

ANCIENT KINGS IN THE HILLS OF GOLD

'No really! Something's got me by the leg!' I shouted in panic. It was first thing in the morning and we were swimming out into the middle of the tarn.

Hannah laughed. 'It's just weeds, they won't hurt you.'

I wasn't sure I believed her but whatever it was didn't bite. The water was ice-cold but refreshing.

After packing up camp we led the ponies over the fell toward the head of the valley where the old packhorse route came up from Far Easdale to the mountain settlement of Watendlath.

As we rounded the crag Richard told me about King Dunmail, the last King of Strathclyde. Having heard all these stories from his dad, I think he quite enjoyed having someone to tell them to. And the history brought these places alive for me too.

'King Dunmail reigned over a thousand years ago,' Richard told me, 'and his little fortified city was just down there at a place called Wythburn.' He pointed down through the valleys to Thirlmere Lake. 'The valley's been made into a reservoir now but that was it, down there, and that's where he wrecked the lives of his people and his own family too.'

'Why? What did he do?'

Richard paused. 'I'll tell you what, Will. Now we're on more level ground let's open up the ponies and shoot over to that fell across there to get a better look at it.'

Hannah said she'd follow us. She was deep in her thoughts again and, though she seemed to love history as much as her brother, she wasn't in the mood that morning to hear of the folly of reckless kings.

It was an overcast morning so we arranged a rendezvous point before Richard and I raced over the kilometre to Steel Fell.

Far below the crags we could see the pass that bore the ant-like traffic from Grasmere to Thirlmere. Richard, still a bit breathless from the ride, pointed down to a pile of stones about thirty-feet square between the divided carriageways of the road. 'That's Dunmail Pass, and that pile of stones marks Dunmail's downfall.'

'What was his downfall?'

'Well, the man was a faithless idiot—a show off, I reckon. He was so confident in his great kingdom of Strathclyde, what's now Cumbria, and in his family connections with King Constantine of Scotland, and in his skill as a mighty hunter. He thought he had it all, but he didn't have one ounce of what Old Harry had, and when push came to shove he broke faith with his friends when he should have gone to Cheshire to fight at Brunanburgh. Not only was he disloyal to his friends, but he also led his people to near annihilation by his diplomatic incompetence and inaction.'

'How? Sounds like the guy never should have had any power.'

'Sure, you're right there. It's complicated, but he never made peace with the Saxon Dynasty who defeated his friends in Cheshire. Basically the guy was completely deluded by his own grandeur. But he got a nasty shock when King Edmund the Magnificent sent an army so huge that it could do a pincer movement on Wythburn from the north and south, finally defeating Dunmail just down there. The pile of stones marks the defeat.'

'Wow, and they're still there a thousand years later—that's cool. Is his body buried there?'

'He wasn't actually killed in the battle, but he was conquered and made to hand over all his regal regalia to Edmund. But Dunmail's sons wouldn't have it, so they ran off with their father's crown and sword and everything and chucked them into Grisedale Tarn, just out of view up there.' He pointed up a steep river valley above the battle site.

'I bet that Edmund bloke was cheesed off!'

'Oh, he was indeed. He put their eyes out for depriving him of the tokens of victory. Anyway, after that Dunmail made some arrangement with a prince in North Wales who needed a mercenary army to defend his borders. So he set off with his disgraced army and as many women as would follow him all the way down to the Vale of Clwyd, where loads died in wars when they could have stayed here and lived peacefully. After that,' Richard continued, 'not many people lived in these fells until the Norsemen moved in. It was their descendants, like Boethar and Old Harry, who defended the place from the Normans a hundred and fifty years later.'

I tried to imagine the swarms of bloodthirsty soldiers marching over the pass to war. What might have happened if Dunmail had been faithful to his allies? I felt sorry for him, making all those bad choices that people remembered him for over a thousand years later. The last thing I wanted to do was to leave a wake of disgrace behind me when I died. That pile of stones was a good reminder of how a corrupt man could so easily wreck the lives of others and change the course of history.

We met Hannah at Ulscarf and followed the fence over the crags and bog past Standing Crag to another bridleway that would take us to the tiny picturesque hamlet of Watendlath. We shared a pot of tea at the café and I took a great photograph of Hannah on her little pony at the historic packhorse bridge. We continued on the bridleway up Puddingstone Bank and over into Rosthwaite in Borrowdale and down to Grange for a picnic lunch.

The day was growing warmer, and after lunch another bridleway took us high onto the side of Cat Bells. From here we had an amazing view up Derwent Water to Keswick.

'Do you know much about Beatrix Potter?' Hannah asked as we went along.

'Well, I know she was from around here somewhere, and my mum read me her books when I was little, but I don't know much ...'

Hannah greeted this news with childish delight. 'Oh! You'll have to have a break from your history lessons, then! In the middle of the lake down there is St Herbert's Island. Do you see it? That's the island where Squirrel Nutkin rowed out to and had a run-in with Mr Owl. And Mrs Tiggy Winkle lives just on the other side of this fell.'

When we reached a small hamlet of white farm buildings, Hannah pointed. 'There Will, there you are— that's Little Town, where little Lucy lived in *The Tale of Mrs Tiggy Winkle!* Surely you remember that bit.'

'Oh Hannah, stop teasing Will,' Richard said. 'This is not a valley that should be remembered for baby kiddie stories. This valley was once the scene of a great massacre.'

'Oh Richard, not more gory stories,' Hannah said.

But I was all ears. 'Where was this massacre?' I asked.

'Just down there in the valley by the church. It happened a short while after Old Harry was laid to rest. After William Rufus had died, King Henry decided to answer the petitions of the local Norman baron, Ranulf de Meschine, and he got a back-up army. They had a spy who said he'd actually seen the valley and a spring campaign looked like a real goer. They battled their way to this very point at Little Town, but then they faced these four offshoot valleys you see in front of us now. That one on the right is the Newlands Pass into Buttermere, so they'd nearly found Boethar's secret hideout. Obviously the earl and his brother Aitken couldn't let that happen, so they made a midnight assault on the Norman army just down here on the other side of the river. They completely whipped the Normans and that church was built on the site.'

'Were they all killed?'

'No, a few got away. And Ranulf himself was still in Keswick ready to bring up the second half of the army the next day. But he didn't stick around to get his butt kicked. He went up north to Aspatria and joined his brother, who owned the southern half of what's now west Cumbria.'

We crossed the little bridge and went into the little Norman church. It was dark and cold and I shivered at the thought of the mass of corpses lying under the soil.

'All right, Will?' Richard asked when we walked back to the ponies.

'Yeah,' I said, but something about the story and the church reminded me of Uncle Sid. I was thinking hard about what had happened the week before in Cockermouth and how our family might be in danger. Since I knew there was nothing I could do before next week, I'd been trying, mostly successfully, not to worry about it.

On the south of the church Richard pointed. 'Do you see the summit of that hill? That's called Aitken Howe, and that's where Boethar's brother and chief general coordinated this battle. The foot soldiers could see half the stuff that was going on, but they trusted the man, who they called Well Beloved, who could see everything from his lookout. So they obeyed the orders of the horn blasts that told them when and where to advance.'

'Why did they call Aitken the Well Beloved?'

'I don't know—I always reckoned he was probably a really decent bloke who had time for people and who people went to with their troubles. Maybe the warriors bonded with him because of his generous leadership. But do you see my point?'

'What point?'

'Well, that we have someone who's also called Well Beloved who can see everything. All we have to do is tackle the part of the problem that's in front of us when he sounds the advance.'

'Oh, I get it now. God's like that, isn't he? That sounds a bit like something Aunty Dora told me. She said that our lives were like looking at the back of a tapestry, where it all looks a mess. So sometimes we don't like all the black thread God uses and because we're looking at the back we can't see how it adds to the pattern or makes any sense.'

Richard started to laugh. 'So it's only when you flip it over that you can see the pattern, the plan and all that ... nice.'

'Yeah, that's right. But she said it's only when you die that you can make out the whole picture and see the beauty.'

'But the Well Beloved always sees it all!' Richard dug his heels into Twiggy. 'Hah! Come on Will ... let's make some dust. I want to show you something.'

He sped off and I did my best to catch him up as we made our way up the left-hand finger of the Newlands Valley.

When we came through a small farm up against Scope End, Richard announced, 'Well, we're here.'

'Where's here?' I asked.

Hannah pulled up. 'Richard, I hope you haven't brought us up here away from our route just to show off more of your history knowledge.'

Richard smiled and whispered, 'No, not more battles, but gold!' He swept his arm across the landscape. 'Here, in these valleys all around, there's gold! Here, look at these names on the map ... Goldscope mine, there are holes round every crag right up to Dale Head where men found gold long ago!'

'Yeah, and cowboys too,' I said.

'No he's telling the truth, Will, I heard dad talking about it,' Hannah said.

'It's all documented in the books,' Richard added. 'Fancy that—right here, all around us.'

'But why isn't anyone mining for it then?' I asked.

But Richard didn't have a chance to answer. A shabbily dressed man had appeared from behind a farm building. ''Cause the rich folk have no backbone to invest in it,' he said, 'and the poor people have no grit to dig for it, that's why. Now what are you lot doing up here? Not been following me hav'ya?'

I was aghast. 'Mr Demas! What are you doing here?' There he was, looking as disheveled as ever and clutching a sack slung over his shoulder.

He caught me looking at the sack. 'Not 'ere to be questioned by bairns, it's my business and no one else's. But you lot are a long way from Loweswater.' He eyed me carefully, and his suspicion fed mine. What was he so keen to hide?

'We're on a trekking holiday,' Hannah said, 'and we're on our way back over the pass tomorrow when we break camp.'

'Oh aye, Miss Scott, and where are you camping tonight then?'

'We haven't decided yet,' Richard said, 'but we'll camp where we like if it's open fell.'

Jack Demas eyed him steadily and then turned back to me. 'Well I'll be keeping an eye on you from the fells. Make sure you don't stray where you shouldn't.' He turned back to Hannah. 'And I'll see you at the weekend in church, I suppose.'

A moment later he had trudged round the corner of the track and was gone.

Hannah shuddered. 'Oh, he gives me the creeps. I know I shouldn't say that, but he really does.'

'Well I've heard he's the richest man in the valley,' Richard said. 'I bet that's where he's been just now, getting gold ore from up there and now he's taking it back to melt down.'

'Richard Scott, you bet nothing,' Hannah scolded. 'We don't pass gossip in our family—honestly, you're as bad as the old women in church!'

'And you shouldn't speak disrespectfully of the senior members of the congregation. What would our mother say!'

They carried on their argument for a few minutes but I tuned out. Something Richard had said sparked an outlandish series of ideas. They were impossible, really, but so was the predicament my family might be in. What did I have to lose? I dug my heels in and shouted back to Richard and Hannah as I belted down the track. 'I need to speak to him! Won't be long.'

Brigham was soon trotting alongside Mr Demas, but he didn't turn to acknowledge me. It was as if he were expecting me. 'Well lad, let's have it. What do you want?'

I was taken aback by his directness, but I realized that he couldn't possibly know what I was about to say. 'I see your hands are healing. How's your back?'

He looked straight ahead and sniffed. 'Don't suppose you came all this way to make chit chat lad. Back's fine, stronger than most men half my age. Now what do you want?'

He wasn't making this easy for me. 'Well, you said something to me that day in the mine, when I got you out that you ... well ...'

He stopped and took hold of Brigham's reins. 'Aye, I know. I meant it, too—call it a Greek thing. You saved my life, now I'm in your debt ... though the Scot in me would wish otherwise. So tell me. What can a poor old miner like Old Jack do for the likes of you, lad?'

I paused for a moment, trying to remember how much I could tell him and what I had sworn to secrecy. 'Well, we might be in a lot of trouble and we need money and–'

'Wait a minute. Who's we? That lot back there?' He pointed back down the lane.

'No, not them. I mean my family—Granny, Aunty Dora, Uncle George ...'

He coughed and spat. His phlegm was black on the ground. 'I see. And do they know about this danger you say they're in?'

'No, and I swore to someone that I wouldn't tell them ... oh, it's so complicated, but if we're going to be safe we need money. Lots of money.'

'Safe from who?' When he looked up at me I was taken aback by the uncharacteristically soft look in his eyes. 'Safe from who, lad?'

I dismounted and walked round to stand in front of him. 'Mr Demas, I swear I would tell you if I could or if I thought it would do you any good. All I know is that serious trouble will come to us this week if ... look, please. All I ask is that you trust me.'

'Trust you, lad!' His voice rose. 'I haven't put my faith in another human being since they ruined me at the Loweswater mine. Now you turn up expecting the rumours of my wealth to be true and imagine that I'll give it to you but you can't, or won't, tell me where it's going and why. There's me telling people to mind their own business for forty years and now here's you expecting me to have a drop of my own medicine. Suppose you tell me how much. Can you do that?'

'About three million euro—so about two million quid.' I didn't dare look at him. This was a preposterous idea and I couldn't believe I was having this conversation. 'I mean, we'd pay it back!' I said quickly.

He laughed. 'Pay it back! I doubt it ... I doubt it.' Then he did a strange thing. He picked up his sack and walked away from me, glancing up now and then at the mine shaft entrances dotting Scope End Crag. He was muttering to himself. I wasn't sure what to do, but I decided to lead Brigham and follow him as he marched further up the small valley. 'Why should a man be in love with his fetters, though they be of gold?' he was saying over and over again.

'Mr Demas? Are you all right?'

He kept on walking. 'Aye, right enough, just thinking ... love his fetters, though of gold ... though of gold.'

'What do you mean?'

'Francis Bacon, lad—a clever man, but being clever ain't what counts in life.'

'What does then?'

He finally stopped and turned to face me. 'What counts is knowing when providence has found you and then ...' He paused and started up the track again.

'And then what?' I shouted after him.

'And then knowing what to do,' he answered as he kept on walking.

'But what about—what about what I asked you?'

'I'll see you on Sunday!' And he was over the rise and out of sight.

Richard and Hannah trotted up behind me then, full of questions. I told them I'd explain as soon as I was certain things were going to be okay. I toyed with the idea of confiding in Hannah so she'd think better of me, but I resisted the temptation. As we plodded back to the Newlands Pass I distracted Richard with more questions about the freedom-fighting heroes who had roamed the dales a thousand years ago. It was easy work, for he had plenty more to tell. Aitken and Boethar's tactical assaults, apparently, had earned them peace for a season.

'But,' Richard went on as he warmed to his subject, 'after this time of rest, another scheme was afoot. And it was a grand one. King Henry had weighed up Ranulf Meschin, trying to decide if it would be better for him to give the earldom of Carlisle to another more energetic nobleman and then make friends with these troublesome north men. But in the end he gave in to Ranulf's request for fresh troops from France for a new campaign in which they would fight the insurgents from the north, driving a large body of knights, archers and footmen down from Papcastle through what's now the Lorton Valley.'

'So there were battles being fought the whole way up the valley? And near Granny's house as well?'

'That's right,' Richard said. 'The dead were buried in places like Corn Howe and Branthwaite Howe, its what the name 'Howe' means, a burial site. So the Normans spent the second night of the campaign camping out on Lanthwaite Green above the lake before starting off on what they believed would be the last leg of their journey to discovering this infamous, secret valley.'

'They were only what, about two miles away?'

'Yes, about that. They were a far stronger and more numerous army than Boethar had, and they were ready for the final kill.'

'Cor, I wouldn't have wanted to be in Buttermere that morning—it's like the Battle of Helm's Deep in *Lord of the Rings*.'

'That's right, and the odds were not in their favour, but surrender wasn't an option after what had been done to Old Harry and the others. They knew that all they had left was to fight for their valley. They still had a few tricks up their sleeves, though. With a series of false fortifications and a mock withdrawal they convinced the Norman scouts that the secret valley was a valley up to the left, away from the lake. Had the enemy gone round Hause Point the game would have been over, as they could easily have spotted Buttermere from there. Fortunately for Boethar, the distraction worked and Ranulf flung his men headlong up Rannerdale into Boethar's trap. No sooner had the bloodthirsty Normans arrived at the steepest part of the valley than they heard a great sound behind them. It was Aitken and his chosen warriors, dashing over the rocks from above where they had been concealed, covered by the archer's fire. These valiant souls made their way into the thick of the fight to prevent a Norman retreat. Seeing his brother now in position, Boethar, who was commanding the battle from the Rannerdale Knotts above, sounded the horn to unleash the berserkers who leapt down into the mayhem to disembowel the knight's horses. Ranulf himself came down, but he was rescued by his men and, with another horse, he managed to escape back to Papcastle—never to venture into any of the valleys again. It was a total victory and Ranulf's brother William eventually made a treaty with Boethar, who retired to where he originally came from—Boet, or Boot as it's now called, near Ravenglass.'

'Wow, so it all ended happily ever after then.'

'Well, not exactly,' Richard said. 'Aitken the Well Beloved was killed leading his men to victory. His body lay in state in Boethar's house nearby and then was taken by horseback up the Newlands Pass to Aitken's Howe. He was buried there by the priest from Gatesgarth amidst a large company of mourners. They would never feel his love again, but they would now be able to benefit from it. As the Bible says, "Greater love has no one than this, that he lay down his life for his friends." That's exactly what he did and that,' Richard said, pointing up the ridge, 'is where he lies to this day.'

We decided to go up there, six hundred feet straight up to Knott Rigg, to camp for the night. From the summit of the pass we could see the only part of Britain that the Normans never set foot in, but I wanted to honour brave, loving Aitken. What would I do, I wondered, if I were asked to give up my life for another? I didn't honestly know. Being there at Aitken's grave, though, made me feel part of something vast and far greater than myself.

We talked long into the night. I kept catching Hannah looking at me in the glow of the Primus stove as she made us yet another cup of hot chocolate.

'Thanks, it's the best hot chocolate I've ever had,' I said.

Richard shot me a suspicious look. 'It's from Aldi,' he said, 'and if you want an extra spoon of powder just ask— you don't need to suck up.'

I smiled. I always knew where I was with Richard.

Before I drifted off to sleep I asked God for wisdom and strength to be like the brave men of the Secret Valley when it was my turn to face trial. I'd realized over the past week that, for all the honour and glory I'd received, killing the beast had been nothing more than a fight or flight thing. The real tests lay before me, down there in the valley. And they would require not reactions but considered responses, the actions of character.

Down there in the darkness were the ones I loved, in danger because of Uncle Sid's debts to men we'd never met. Down there was the river whose salmon stocks were threatened to near extinction by Chris Clegg and his mates. And down there was Chris's captivating sister Carrie, who I fancied rotten for all the wrong reasons. Going back would be bittersweet, and I hoped the holiday had prepared me for the battle.

PART EIGHT

HUMILITY

25

THE VALUE OF HARD WORK

A re you okay, Will? You look miles away.' Hannah came over to the edge of the ridge where I was gazing down on the valley.

'Um, no, I'm cool—just thinking about stuff. I guess I'm a bit sad this trip is over. I've had a really great time.'

'I know what you mean,' she said as she folded her arms and looked out across the mountains. 'It's been really special for me too.'

'Really?' I said.

'Yeah, really. We—well, that is to say, the weather and everything, and not dying on Great Gable, I suppose.'

'Come on, you lot!' Richard shouted. 'Sleeping bags won't stuff themselves.'

We packed the tents away and passed back along the ridge and then down the Newlands Pass into Buttermere. Richard pointed out the site of Boethar's mill and the place, far above, where Boethar had stood to coordinate the final battle. When we were about fifty feet above the lake I began to recognize familiar landmarks, including the spot where Harriet Armstrong's car had crashed through the wall and sunk in the dark waters.

As we neared the part of the wall that had been rebuilt, Brigham began to swing his head to veer away. I looked over to Hannah to see if she could explain this strange behaviour, but while she rode steadily on I noticed that Twiggy was also shying and trying to turn. Hannah brought him back into line with a tug of the reins, but I wondered if the ponies sensed this long-ago sadness. Something strange had happened here. Jack claimed to have witnessed it from a distance, but only Uncle Sid had actually been here. Had he really staged the murder of his unfaithful wife? I looked down into the dark watery depths and shivered.

Rannerdale came into view, and Richard pointed out the site of Aitken's last breath.

'Look, Will, next to the farm you can still find the foundations of the chapel the monks of Carlisle built on the spot where Aitken fell in the battle.'

As we passed there I wondered whether his brother had been watching as the Normans ended the life of this 'well beloved' man of the Secret Valley. How did Boethar feel, winning peace for his people at such a high cost?

We received a warm welcome at the vicarage and removed the saddles from the ponies for the last time. When the others had gone inside, I gave Hannah the picture that I'd painted on the island.

'Just to remind you of the holiday—and to thank you, you know, for having me along. It's been really good to do stuff with you and ... well, thank you.'

She gave me a kiss on the cheek as she accepted my gift. 'Thank you, Will,' she said. 'It's been a very special holiday for us all. And if you hadn't come along ...' she smiled. 'I might still be on that rock ledge waiting for help.'

I looked at her for a moment, still stunned by the kiss. 'It was nothing,' I mumbled.

She was looking down at my arm, where the bruising from the strained ligaments was now more obvious. 'I won't forget what you did, Will. You know that, don't you?'

'Yeah, I know,' I said.

As I led Alfie up the lane to Granny's I thought that if the sight of my bruised forearm would make her look at me like that again I wouldn't mind it never getting better.

Grandpa was home to greet me, as was Nelson, and Granny had been baking in honour of my return. Nelson, partly shaved and still bandaged, hobbled about in his excitement to see me.

'Sit down, lad, sit down,' Grandpa said. 'I want to hear all about your adventures and the peaks you climbed and your daring rescue of the fair damsel.'

'Let him rest, Reggie,' Granny scolded as she gave me a big hug. 'Can't you see how tired the poor lad is? My, Will, look how brown you are! But you need a rest. And a proper bath.'

'Nonsense, Elsie. The lad just needs to sit down here without your fussing,' Grandpa said.

In the end Granny won and I had a bath, but though I was tired I couldn't sleep. I was thinking about Hannah.

Andrew and Jane came round for dinner, and afterwards Grandpa took me and Andrew down to the river. When we arrived at Salmon's Leap, Grandpa produced three beers from his fishing bag.

'Elsie, won't let me have anything with the painkillers I'm on!' he said as he handed them out.

As we cast our lines, the talk turned to the Loweswater Show the following week.

'Lad, you must try your hand at Cumbrian wrestling while you're here,' Grandpa said.

'Aye, I'll tutor you, Will,' Andrew said. 'Your arm will be fine by then—and if not you can pull out.'

'I'm not sure,' I said. I couldn't bear the thought of being humiliated by the likes of Chris Clegg.

'It would be a shame not to try, Will lad,' Andrew said. 'With your agility and cunning, you'd be a natural.'

'Aye, a shame indeed, Andrew,' Grandpa said. 'I would have thought the beast slayer and the rescuer of damsels in distress would be up for a new challenge. But alas, he appears to be want to rest on his laurels now.'

'Aye,' Andrew said as he cast his line. ''Tis sad indeed when one so young and strong retires to rest on his laurels.'

'All right, all right,' I said. 'I'll give it a try.'

Grandpa smiled. 'Good lad,' he said.

As we headed home without any fish, Grandpa had to turn back to find Nelson, who had wandered off.

'You've been quiet, lad,' Andrew said as we continued up the knoll together.

I told him a bit about what had happened with Hannah over the last week.

'I just don't know whether she sees me as anything more than another kid brother,' I finished.

He nodded and stopped for a moment. 'I had to wait a long time, Will, to find someone like Jane. But I never lost hope that God had someone for me because of something your Uncle George said to me a few years back.'

'What was that?'

'It was a Bible verse actually,' he said. '"Seek first the kingdom of God, and everything else will be added unto you."'

'I've heard that one,' I said, 'but what does it have to do with me and Hannah?'

Andrew started walking again as he saw Grandpa coming up the field. 'Everything. If you go all out for God and his kingdom, you won't have to worry about any of the other stuff, including the person you're going to marry. George told me that the word "added" could be translated "overtake"—and that makes sense to me, because something can't overtake you if you're chasing it—or her, get it!' he added with a wink.

I smiled and nodded.

'I think,' Andrew said as Grandpa and Nelson came up behind us, 'it's more about becoming the right person than it is about finding the right person.'

I thought that sounded sensible when Andrew said it, although later I found myself wondering how I could make myself into the right person for Hannah—and I knew that wasn't the right way to look at it.

'What are you up to tomorrow then, Will?' Jane asked me as they were preparing to leave.

'Oh,' I said, 'I don't know, I think I'll just hang—'

'The lad's got a field full of thistles just waiting for him!' Grandpa said as he slapped me on the back.

Andrew raised his eyebrows and smiled at my long face. 'Hard work is becoming, Will,' he said.

I nodded, though I really couldn't see the connection with a field full of thistles.

The next morning Grandpa gave me a scythe for deadheading the thistles and a few safety tips. 'Your Granny'd never forgive me if you cut your legs off!' he said.

I nodded. I was stiff and sore, and after all that amazing freedom on the fells I still couldn't believe I had to spend my day doing this.

'It's as important to experience hard work as it is adventure, lad,' Grandpa said as he left me to go fishing, 'and I'd say you've had plenty of the latter recently.'

It was backbreaking work, and by lunchtime every muscle in my back and arms was aching. Granny brought a picnic for us all to have on the knoll, and when Grandpa joined us he said he was pleased with my progress.

I thought maybe his praise meant I could have the afternoon off, but I was wrong.

'You'd better get cracking at those thistles if you're going to get them done before bed, lad,' Grandpa said as soon as lunch was packed away.

I was horrified. The field was huge and I'd only done about a quarter.

'Reg?' Granny said.

'No, Elsie, Will wants to be a man, and to be a man is to know the value and dignity of work.'

'Yes, but Reg, the hay will keep to–' Granny began.

But Grandpa wasn't moved. 'Elsie, we're not raising hay here, we're raising a man. Right, Will?'

'Yes Grandpa,' I muttered.

Although my body protested with every swing of that scythe, there was something deeper in me that wanted to answer this call. I didn't understand it all, but I knew my grandfather did little without reason.

I soldiered on until teatime when Grandpa brought me some water and plasters for the blisters on my hands. He pointed out thistles near the edge that I'd missed and then left.

I wasn't completely alone. Carl Clegg passed by on his tractor a few times. He looked down at me with disdain, but I just waved and continued working. I'd also seen the Professor looking over the hedge at my progress a few times. When I neared his boundary he came over to the fence to greet me.

'Ah, William, I heard that you are finding the dignity of manual labour.'

'Something like that,' I sighed.

'Good, good,' he said.

I didn't see what was so good about it but I said nothing.

He watched me for a moment, stroking his beard. 'I had a friend like you once. She was despondent because she was always dreaming of doing great and heroic tasks. It took her many years to realize that her chief duty was actually to accomplish humble tasks as though they were great and noble.'

He paused and I wiped my forehead with the back of my arm. I bet this friend never had to deadhead an entire field of thistles in one day after a week's hard riding and climbing and rescuing damsels and slaying beasts, I thought. But again I said nothing.

'You see, William,' the Professor continued, 'the world is moved along not only by the mighty shoves of its heroes, but also by the aggregate of the tiny pushes of each honest worker.'

I nodded. 'I suppose,' I said. 'Just seems a lot of effort when it's only going to be winter hay for a donkey.'

The Professor looked at me for a moment and then a smile spread across his face. 'William, did not God say that the ground would yield thistles because of Adam's disobedience?'

I shrugged. I didn't mind the break, but I still had a lot of thistles to deadhead before I'd be allowed to get to bed.

'Yes, this is so,' he continued. 'And do you know what will happen to a society which scorns excellence in plumbing because it's a humble activity and tolerates shoddiness in philosophy because it's an exalted activity?'

'No, what?'

'Well, obviously, neither its pipes nor its theories will hold water.' He laughed.

I laughed, too. Perhaps, I thought, he wasn't totally bonkers after all.

As the sun began to dip behind Low Moor I paused to look out over the grassy field. I couldn't see a single thistle poking its spiky head through the grass. There had been literally thousands of them that morning, but I'd cleared them all by the sweat of my brow. Alfie wandered over and sniffed approvingly and I made my way to the house.

After supper Grandpa asked me to give Granny a break and do the dishes and get the hens in. I tried not to wince and said 'Yes, of course' as cheerily as I could.

As I passed the sitting room and said goodnight on my way up to bed I saw a satisfied smile on his face.

'Thank you, lad,' he said. 'You did a good day's work today. Would you mind giving me a hand in the vegetable garden in the morning?'

My resolve to become a man fought with my instinct to react sullenly. This wasn't fair. 'Okay,' I said. 'What time should we start?'

Although I ached all over, the morning's labour passed quickly as Grandpa and I talked. He told me that he'd always loved the idea of being self-sufficient and growing his own vegetables, but that it had become more difficult over the years. We dug the new beds that I'd started a few weeks before and did some much-needed stone picking and weeding. Before lunch we harvested some cabbages, gooseberries, red currants, carrots and beetroots. After I'd washed the muddy ones under the garden tap I went inside to find Andrew and Lewis waiting for me in the kitchen.

Andrew smiled. 'Well, aren't you coming, Will? We've got business to attend to,' he said.

Lewis had a mouthful of bread from the ploughman's lunch Granny had prepared for me. 'Yeah, Andrew's going to teach us and the Scotts how to wrestle, and we're all going to win at the show!'

I was tired and achy, but at least I'd get to see Hannah again. And, I thought, I'll be good at the sport so I don't have to worry about looking bad in front of her.

So after I ate what Lewis had left of my lunch we jumped in Andrew's car and headed to Loweswater.

As usual, Richard was excited about a new challenge. Roger was limbering up in his Ron Hill stretchy leggings and Jan was talking to him, though I could only hear his responses.

'Ach, dun'nae worry love, it's nae different than how the boys wrestle over the border ... Aye, I'm a bit older but I'll have more technique and sliggy than the younger lads ... Aye, I'll not do anything gyte, I promise.'

Hannah greeted us on her way to the paddock to groom her horse. She didn't care much about wrestling but she gave me a big smile as I waited to be put through my paces.

Andrew explained the rules and a few of the most common moves, like 'buttocking'—a term which sent Lewis into fits.

'Now remember,' Andrew said, 'in this type of wrestling there's no defence, only counter-attack.'

'Aye, it's like the wrestling we do in the spiritual realm,' Roger said. 'God does'nae provide any armour for our backs ... read it for yerself in Ephesians chapter 6, Will.'

I got the feeling that Roger, a bit like myself, was sure that he'd be a natural. But even though Andrew was very easy on him it quickly became clear that Roger, big as he was, would have to be content spending most of the afternoon lying on the grass looking up at the sky.

At first it appeared that I would be doing the same, as Richard was far superior to me and threw me at every turn. I felt angry and envious and blamed all the hard labour I'd had to do yesterday and today. Richard probably had all day yesterday to lie around doing nothing, I thought.

I felt better when Andrew praised Richard for his speed and agility. 'Aye, Richard, you've got a natural talent. You'll go far,' Andrew said.

From that point on I began to view my friend's skill not with green eyes but with a genuine pride. And I endeavoured all the harder to test his skill—not so much to win, but to make sure he had the best sparring partner possible.

I got a nasty shock, however, when Lewis sent me flying just as Hannah was coming back to the garden. The little shrimp made up for his lack of height by clinging to his victim and outmanoeuvring him at the last. It was the ultimate humiliation.

But she laughed and, after making no end of fuss over 'clever little Lewis', she came over to me. 'Oh Will, what a picture your face was. Don't look so glum, you can't be good at everything.'

I was able to laugh then. Seeing Lewis looking so pleased with himself, that he'd thrown 'the beast slayer', was ample payment for the humiliation.

I wondered, though, how I'd stand up to humiliation—if it came—in front of everyone in the valley at the Loweswater Show.

26

STAN'S SECRET

Get up! It's my first time in church and I don't wanna be late.' I thought it was a bad dream, Lewis appearing in my doorway and jumping on my bed. But he started a dead arm fight, and when we both landed on the floor I realized it was no dream. The thud brought Granny to the landing.

'What on earth is going on up here?'

'Oh, Mrs Wallace, Will's been rough with me again!'

'Oh Will, leave him alone and get down here or we'll be late.'

When I arrived at the breakfast table Lewis was being vague about whether he had in fact had any breakfast yet. It was the kind of response Granny liked, and she rose to the challenge of filling his bottomless pit with a generous serving of bacon and eggs.

Aunty Dora was already there, and when Grandpa appeared he was looking smarter than usual. 'Well come on, Elsie,' he said. 'Let's see this breakfast if we're going to have a hope of walking to church.'

He sat down in the stunned silence as if he hadn't said anything unusual. It had been over forty years since Grandpa had set foot in a church—not since little Elizabeth had died. What had happened? He ate his breakfast and glanced through the paper as usual, occasionally making remarks about the news as Granny and Aunty Dora tried to pretend they weren't over the moon with excitement.

It was a beautiful morning, and the five of us set out together. Lewis and I were soon ahead of the others and, as we neared the lane that led down to Mad Annie's cottage, we saw a smartly dressed figure making his way towards us. I didn't recognize him until he was nearly caught up with us. It was Stan.

'Don't mind if I join you all, it's such a lovely morning,' he said as casually as Grandpa had announced his intention to go to church.

I swallowed my surprise, but Lewis got straight to the point. 'Are you comin' to church too?' he asked.

'I am,' Stan said. He'd even shaved. He looked like a different man.

Lewis ran back to tell the others, and I quickly made a decision. 'Stan,' I said, 'I have to ask you something. I know it was you who texted Uncle Sid with my note the other day. Why did you do it? I mean, does he have something on you?'

He sniffed and smiled. 'No, he doesn't. Not really. I do the odd thing for him now and then to help out, but he doesn't own me or anything like that. The other day it wasn't Sid I was helping anyway.'

I was still angry. 'Well, I can't see how you helped me,' I said.

'No, it wasn't you either, lad.'

'Well, who then?'

He glanced back to see how far away the others were. 'I suppose you'll work it out sooner or later so I may as well tell you, but it's just for you, mind. I did it for our Annie.'

'Annie? Why Annie?'

'She's the only family I've got.'

Family? I tried to remember what Aunty Dora had told me. Ellen had had a two-year-old brother. 'You're her uncle? But you're the same age ...'

'Two years older, aye, but that's right. I was too young to remember much. I remember Ellen playing with me in the field at harvest time and down by the lake, but that's all. Mum and Dad took me and Annie back east that autumn and raised us together, like brother and sister.'

'But why all the secrecy?' I asked.

'After Dad died, Mum was in a tight spot. I was away a lot with the regiment, so she did the very thing Dad was too proud to do. She contacted Annie's father. It was a hard thing for her to do, but she did it. I'd grown up hating Sidney Armstrong, but deep down Mum knew it was the best thing and it turned out she were right. Her health was bad and she didn't have long. Sid came over and made arrangements for Annie to live here. Wanted to make amends, he said when I met him. Things were bad for me at the time. Mum was dying, the Mrs had just left and I was near retirement with nothing in mind. He said he could fix me up with a job over here—and that was it, basically.'

'I never knew,' I said. 'But I still don't get all the secrecy.'

'It's just the way Sid wanted it. He's very suspicious, you know. He didn't want people putting two and two together and gossiping about it. Anyway, it's worked out okay ... my job gives me plenty of opportunities to visit her and everyone's happy.'

We both glanced back. Lewis, who was walking backwards in front of the others, was waving his arms and jumping up and down. He appeared to be entertaining them with some long-winded tale.

'But how did you know I'd be following Sid that day?' I asked.

'Oh, easy,' Stan said. 'I knew from the moment you recognized him that day on the riverbank you wouldn't let it drop, so I just kept an eye out for you every Wednesday. I didn't want any trouble for her if you started blabbing.'

'I see,' I said. I glanced back again. Lewis was still holding forth. I took a deep breath. 'I won't tell anyone, Stan, but there's something else I need to tell you ... it's about the Cleggs. They're planning a big catch during the salmon migration in a few weeks.'

Stan nodded and smiled. 'Aye, I know about that, lad. But when and where is the thing, and then catching them in the act so's I can bring a decent case for the prosecution. I suppose they want you to go too?'

I nodded.

'Good. And would you be prepared to work for the fisheries, undercover as it were, so's we can catch them?'

'I suppose so,' I said. 'But listen, Stan, they know you might be there and Chris says he's got something planned to take care of you and any other bailiff who turns up uninvited.'

'Oh, have they?' Stan was quiet for a few minutes. 'Then we'll have to be careful, perhaps I'll have to bring my stick. When will he tell you about the date?'

'I don't know. He said he'd know more at the show next week.'

'Aye, that'd be right. He won't know when the river will be high enough for the fish to start their run up from the Derwent River. Well, you let me know what he says and we'll hatch a plan.'

'But you have to be careful, Stan. You don't know how dangerous–'

'Will, lad, you've no idea the places I've been and the things I've done. The only thing you need to worry about is that I don't forget where I am during the arrest and hurt someone. I know it looks like I'm pushing on a bit but some things are still the same, believe me, so don't you worry.'

The others caught us up at the junction and we made our way down the hill to the church as the bells rang out across the dale.

As I knew there would be, there was a bit of a buzz as we walked into church and people pretended not to look at us. I thought I detected a tear in Uncle George's eye as he shook Grandpa's hand and handed him a hymnbook.

The church was full. Jack Demas gave me a nod as we walked past his pew.

The branch in the dung had withered, as had the one in the rubbish. The grafted branch on the altar, however, had fully taken and was budding with young fruit. The stench was pretty powerful. Roger had said that people had been asking for a few weeks for the bucket to be removed, but he insisted it would be there to the end so no one would forget. One or two people had apparently left because of it, but many more had come to see what all the fuss was about.

Several prim and proper ladies from the Mother's Union kept turning around to stare at Grandpa, and every time they did Lewis waved at the spiteful old dears. 'Very friendly here,' he said.

'What's happening now?' Lewis asked about a hundred times before the service even began. 'Can I go sit with Hannah?'

'That sounds like a good idea, dear,' Granny said.

As Roger introduced the theme, humility, he invited George to do the reading again. 'This man is the meekest man I know,' he said with a smile.

I was surprised. I never would have described Uncle George as a doormat! He was a bit red in the cheek, but he walked up to the front with confidence. I watched him, trying to figure out what Roger could have meant. There was no posturing with George, no swagger, but he was a man's man in every way. And yet, though he was a strong, rugged shepherd, he was a servant of servants. If anything needed doing, fixing or cleaning, George could be found doing it.

'Aye, well, the first reading is a paraphrase from Paul's letter to the Philippians chapter two,' he began.

> 'Are you going to live selfishly for ever? Always trying to be a someone in front of others. Be humble instead, serve someone else before yourself. Quit only thinking of the 'Big Ego', look out not in for once. Have Jesus' attitude, for though he was God he didn't cling to that status but rather gave it up for us, choosing the position of a servant when he came as a man, even humbling himself to death on a cross. No wonder God exalted him to the highest position and with the greatest title that can be given to anyone in the universe. And no wonder at the name of Jesus every knee everywhere will one day bend and every tongue of every created being will acknowledge that Jesus Christ is Lord to the glory of God the Father.'

George cleared his throat and picked up another Bible. 'And the second reading is from Romans chapter twelve and verse three, and I'm reading this one in the King James version. "I say, through the grace given unto me, to every man that is among you, not to think of himself more highly than he ought to think; but to think soberly, according as God hath dealt to every man the measure of faith." And down to verse sixteen, "Mind not high things, but condescend to men of low estate. Be not wise in your own conceits."'

George went back to take his seat beside Jack Demas.

'Well,' Roger began, 'I suppose a sermon is the last thing needed to show humility. It's a virtue all preach, none practise, and yet everybody is content to hear.' As he continued, he picked up an apron from one of the chairs set out at the front and put it on. 'We live in a world that deifies the talented and famous, and dun'nae we all want oor share of pomp and recognition? But friends, talent is God-given. Be humble. Fame is man-given. Be grateful. Conceit is self-given. Be careful.' He paused. 'So I want to be careful today and do something that Jesus did for his friends. I know it'd be a better parallel to wash yer cars, but feet'll have to do.'

He invited a selection of people, none of whom seemed to know what was going on, to sit in the chairs at the front and take off their shoes. I saw some suspicious and frosty looks, but no smiles.

'Being a loyal subject in the kingdom of God is much the same as being a grave digger,' Roger said as they took their places. 'The only way up is down!'

With a basin of water beside him and a towel in his hand, he began to wash their feet. As he did, he apologized if anything he had said or done had offended them. He spoke to each person. He told some that he loved them. He asked forgiveness of others. Some he encouraged, and some he asked if there was any way he could better serve them.

There were a few tears, and I could see the hardness in many people beginning to melt. But not all. Mrs Pardshaw was at one end, and when she saw what was coming she rose and returned to her pew. Frieda seemed very touched by the gesture, although I noticed Hilda scowling from the pew.

Uncle Sid was up there, too, but he stayed and submitted to having his feet washed. It was hard to tell whether or not he was responding to Roger. He seemed to answer in just a few words.

When the service was over I made a point of catching Jack before he left. We made small talk about the weather and then he looked me in the eye and said, as if we were still talking about the weather, 'The answer to your question is yes, I will give you what you ask. Stuff's done me no good and may as well come to you.'

I couldn't quite believe what I was hearing, but I'd been thinking about how I'd respond ever since I rounded Hause End on Thursday. 'Could you meet me with it at Hause End at one o'clock on Wednesday? Wait out of sight around the first bend in that hollow.'

He frowned. 'What's going on? What are you up to?'

'Don't worry,' I said. 'Just stay hidden until I call to you.'

He shook his head. 'I don't like the sound of it,' he said. 'Who's driving you over there? It's not the police, is it?'

'No, trust me. I have sort of a ... gift for you too. It's hard to explain, but everything will be fine if you'll just be there but stay out of sight.'

Jack agreed and turned to walk away with a grunt. He'd seen someone approaching me from behind. I felt a bony hand on my shoulder.

'What are you doing talking with that man?' Uncle Sid asked.

'Nothing, really ... nothing,' I said.

He watched Jack with disdain. 'Good. I would avoid him, lad. He has nothing to offer but piteous stories about how the world conspired against him, "no good to man nor beast".' He glanced around and looked back at me. 'I got your note. Is there anything else I need to know? Anything you're not telling me?' His voice was shaky and I could tell that, for perhaps once in his life, he'd lost control of a situation.

'No, Uncle Sid, it's just like I said. I listened at the door and it sounds like they're sending some heavies up on Wednesday to pay you a visit.'

'That's just as I thought then,' he said. 'They'll be expecting to find assets that they can sell—paintings, antiques and probably the deeds to the house as well. But they're expecting way more than they'll find and I won't be able to pacify them easily.' He seemed to be talking to himself. 'I'd better go and talk to Stanley about it now so arrangements can be made.'

He was turning away when I stopped him. 'Uncle Sid, what would you do if I said I'd found the money to pay them back?'

'Are you playing with me, boy?'

'No, really. I know it sounds unreal, but I'm not making it up. You're the one who said we're in this together because they'll come after the family ...'

'Who have you been talking to? You gave me your word–'

'I haven't told anyone, honest.'

'And so where might this money be coming from, eh?'

'Well, I want to tell you but I can't—not until Wednesday afternoon. Can you take me to Hause End at lunchtime?'

His mouth dropped open at the mention of Hause End. 'What? There? Why—what is this?'

'Please, Uncle Sid? Trust me?'

He stared at me for what seemed like an eternity. 'All right, Wednesday. Meet me on the lane away from your grandmother's and I'll take you there.'

He went to speak to Stan and I rejoined the others. When Sid left to make his way to the graveyard I noticed Stan had a scowl on his face.

I walked over to him. 'All right, Stan?'

'Awey, Will lad, Sid's just filled me in. Seems like you've been busier than usual.'

'What do you mean?'

'Oh aye, he told me about Wednesday, and I don't like it. These are nasty people, and they're serious. I don't like it at all, lad. It's not a situation that I can control on me own and he won't hear of getting anyone else involved. He's too proud for that—and he's too afraid stuff will get out.'

'Why don't you let us help? Grandpa, the Scotts and me? We've got guns and we don't have to know everything. I've managed to get what they want, though that's a secret as well right now. With more people you gotta stand a better chance of avoiding trouble.'

'Will, this isn't a game or a movie. Some of these men might not think anything of cutting your fingers off one by one if they thought it would make Sidney find them another hundred grand! They'll be paid a percentage of the takings and they only have one way of asking. Sid thinks he'll be able to talk them round with the cash, but then he's deluded. These guys are subbies, probably pumped-up smackheads from Moss Side or something. When they see a wodge of ready cash, there'll be trouble. How easy would it be to pop off Sid and the French man and then make up a story? No witnesses.'

'Then let us help. Please. Who else can you trust? If Uncle Sid is over his head, who better than Grandpa and Roger? They're no strangers to that sort thing. Richard and I could be there to cover an entrance or something—you know, out of the way stuff. At least say you'll think about it,' I said. 'We only have one stab at this. And it's our family that's in danger here. Grandpa will want to know about it.'

'All right,' he said, 'I'll think about it.'

That was all I could do, though I doubted he'd risk falling foul of Sid by involving anyone else. I decided to talk to Grandpa if Stan didn't get in touch by Tuesday.

When I joined them again, Roger was talking to Granny and Grandpa about their fiftieth wedding anniversary. I'd forgotten it was only two weeks away. When George came over to talk with Granny and Grandpa, I smiled at Roger. 'Great sermon,' I said.

'Aye, well, it's like many things in the Bible. We can make them more complicated by talking about them. To be humble is to keep one eye on heaven and a right perspective of who ye are and what ye've been gifted to do—or nae been gifted to do.'

'Like you and me wrestling yesterday?' I asked.

He laughed. 'Aye, lad, well they say the hardest secret for a man to keep is his opinion of himself! And uz the great Scottish wrestler! And, by the way, it was good to see ye play the man yesterday with oor Richard.'

'What–'

'Aye, I saw ye—and the Lord did too. Reminded me of Jonathan after he saw David kill Goliath. The Bible says his "soul was knit to David's" and he "stripped himself of the robe that was upon him, and gave it to David, and his garments, even to his sword, and to his bow, and to his girdle." Aye, lad, d'ye see he would have happily let David have the throne that was meant for him by birth if it was the will of God? There's nothing more mighty in the whole of Scripture, except the cross of Christ.'

'Yeah, well, Richard's a mate, but you were washing the feet of people who don't like you much.'

Roger shrugged. 'To be humble to superiors is duty, to equals courtesy, to inferiors nobility.'

I thought about that kind of nobility all the way home. I hoped I'd have a chance to practise it.

27

MURDER MYSTERY AND THE MAFIA SHOWDOWN

*Enter not into the path of the wicked, and go not
in the way of evil men.*
—Proverbs 4:14—

'Think you could be a shepherd, lad?' George asked.

It was late Tuesday morning, and we'd just finished trimming the feet of what seemed like our thousandth sheep.

'Well, it's okay to be out and that. But is there any money in it?'

George laughed. 'No, lad, maybe them Texels are worth a bit, but there's no money in these fell sheep. Not any more.'

I'd been out on the fells with Uncle George all day Monday, bringing the sheep down. He'd let me drive the quad while he worked the dogs. It was awesome, but this foot rot session had been another matter.

I enjoyed spending the time with Uncle George, though, and the work had helped me focus on something besides what would happen on Wednesday. I'd been tempted several times to talk with Uncle George about it, but I was determined to give Stan until that afternoon before I told Grandpa what was going on.

Stan did call, though, to organize a planning meeting that evening down at Salmon's Leap.

Grandpa and I arrived first with our fishing rods and before long Andrew, Uncle George, Roger and Richard approached through the trees. Everyone looked serious and, as if by some unspoken agreement, we all kept our voices down. Grandpa cast his line while we waited and Richard helped me light a fire. When the sun dipped behind Low Moor, the woods were plunged into that familiar damp, blue stillness which I'd come to know so well. Suddenly there was a rustling behind us and Stan appeared on the outside of the circle of men round the fire.

'Oh!' George exclaimed. 'How on earth do you do that? You nearly gave me a heart attack!'

'Sorry I'm late,' Stan said. 'I had to check some things out at Cockermouth. Thank you all for coming. This is a very difficult and delicate situation, and I'm going to have to ask you all to be content with what information I can give you and ask for no more.'

Everyone nodded, silenced by his serious tone.

'Andrew and Roger,' Stan continued, 'what I'm about to say doesn't directly threaten you and the lad, and there's no pressure if you can'nae commit to what I ask. Major, George, I asked you here because there's trouble determined against you and your kin and I know you'll want to do what you can. All I can say at this time is that men, possibly four or five of them, from the criminal fraternity, are coming out to pay a visit to Sidney Armstrong at around fifteen hundred hours tomorrow. They're serious men, and they're coming looking for certain things from Sidney that he does not have.'

'So Sid's up to his neck in debt, is he?' Grandpa said. 'You say the men are serious. How serious?'

'Very,' Stan said. 'I've come from the Wordsworth Hotel just now. They're nasty-looking fellas. Two ex-military types and two handy lads with Manchester accents. And there's a Frenchman named Gerrand—he appears to be the mob's legal rep. They've come expecting a little trouble—I overheard them joking about it. They're looking forward to a bit of "country sport", as they called it, so they'll have side arms and the like.'

'Awey Stan lad, but what about the police, eh?' Uncle George asked.

'Aye, George, there is that. But first we need to get a package safely to Gerrand. And we need him to get away unmolested so he can bring the package to his employer. That package,' Stan paused to look at me, 'Will has secured by some secret means. It's a complete payment of Sidneys' debt.'

'It's complicated,' I mumbled as all eyes fell on me.

'The debt is very large and the package is therefore very precious. The fellas with Gerrand are subbies from Manchester,' Stan continued. 'They've come to remove antiques and such like. They have no idea the package is going to be handed over. And they mustn't know, either.'

'But why not? They work for the big man?' Andrew asked.

'Naev, that's the point, Andrew,' Roger said. 'They dun'nae work for Mr Big. They're hired muscle earning a few hundred quid, some kudos and a night in a hotel. I spent half ma life round these people, doing this sort of stuff. They'll be crackheads, screwed in their heads. If this package is half as valuable as Stan says it is, then they will nae think twice about taking it for themselves and shutting the mouths of any witness who'd mebbe bring word back to Mr Big.'

Stan nodded. 'Right, that's exactly it. The men who are threatening your family must get that package or we'll not hear the end of it. Gerrand must be allowed to inspect the goods, call his employer and then get away unmolested by the hired help.'

'Okay, Stan,' Grandpa said. 'I'm trying not to ask any questions that you cannot answer. But has Sid put you up to this?'

'No, Sid has no idea,' Stan said, 'and I'd like to keep it that way—although I don't think it'll be possible.'

'Okay, but do you have a plan?' Grandpa asked.

'Aye. It's not foolproof but it's the best we can do at such short notice. But first I need to know who's in.'

Grandpa nodded, and so did George. Roger nodded too.

'Are you sure, Vicar? You don't need some time to talk it over?' Stan asked.

Roger looked shocked, 'More time? They're ma parishioners, it's my duty. Whoever heard of a shepherd who did'nae take his rod to protect the flock from wolves!'

George smiled.

'Aye, Roger, but what about the lad? Will is already up to his neck in it, but Richard ... ?'

Roger looked at his son. It was obvious that Richard was game. 'Does yer plan allow for some lower risk positions for keen young lads?' he asked.

'Oh, Dad!'

'Aye, there are,' Stan said. 'Right, good, so that's settled. Andrew?'

Andrew smiled. 'Well, there ought to be a vet there to treat any of Roger's wounded sheep!'

Everyone else laughed, but Stan was still serious. 'Sure you don't want to talk it over with that pretty lass of yours?'

'No, definitely not. She'd never let me go!'

There was more laughter, and then Stan unfolded a map of the property to show us the plan of attack. Within twenty minutes the embers of the fire were glowing on their own in the woods as night fell and we all made our way up the field to the house.

Once we were alone in the yard Grandpa put his hand on my shoulder. 'Sure that money will be there?' he asked.

I hesitated just for a moment. 'Yes, I think so.'

'I don't suppose you're going to tell me where it's coming from?'

'Well, one day I hope.'

He shook his head. 'I just hope you won't land me in any more trouble with your parents.'

I opened the door. 'Well, Mum told me that trouble was your middle name!'

Grandpa laughed. 'Ha! One time maybe ... at one time.' He shook his head. 'You afraid, lad?'

'Yeah, I'll be glad when it's all over.'

Granny was already in bed, so we sat up by the Aga with some cocoa and he told me about the D-Day landing in France and fighting with the Chindits in Burma. The Chindits were special forces operating deep behind enemy lines in the jungles. He told me about how he and some men from a Gurkha regiment had stormed a Japanese gun placement under heavy fire and helped secure a great victory.

'Well,' he said finally, 'we need a good night's rest.' He put our mugs in the sink. 'You know, lad, something I've always found helpful was what Teddy Roosevelt said about conquering fear. At one time he was on the wild frontier and he said there were all kinds of things he was afraid of—from grizzly bears to mean horses and gun-fighters. But he said that by acting as if he *wasn't* afraid he gradually ceased to be afraid.'

'Thanks,' I said, 'I think I get it.'

When I came downstairs in the morning I found Grandpa cleaning his gun. Nelson stood by, eager for the fight even though Grandpa had told him that his injuries hadn't healed enough for him to join us. I realized as I watched him methodically cleaning his gun that morning that this was nothing new to him. It was the warfare of his youth.

I wasn't sure how much he'd told Granny, but as she made a fuss over him that morning it struck me that we were going to battle. Grandpa instructed me to call both my parents, which I did.

Mum said that everything was fine and they were looking forward to seeing me at the anniversary party next weekend. I left a message on Dad's answering machine and told him I loved him, which was a first.

Uncle Sid met me as planned at the end of the lane. He was quiet all the way to the lake, but as we drove over Langthwaite Green and approached Crummock he began to ply me with questions. I was purposefully vague in my replies.

Although I'd secured the money for him, what I hoped would happen first was of far more value to him and to Jack Demas than any amount of money. My palms were sweaty, but I held to my resolve. We were soon parked at the lay-by before the bend.

Without a word, Uncle Sid walked to the edge where his wife had plunged to her death. I walked behind him. I glanced towards the crevice where I'd asked Jack to conceal himself, but I couldn't see him. There was a brokenness about Uncle Sid. I could see it in the way he walked and I heard it in his voice.

He gazed into the dark waters fifty feet below. 'Why, why have you brought me here?'

My voice was a croaky whisper at first, and I had to repeat myself to get the words out. 'I want to know ... I want to know what happened here, to your wife. If you tell me what I want to know, then I will give you what you need.'

He spoke in a monotone, as if he'd rehearsed the answer many times. 'She was drunk, she drove out here alone and lost control of the car and ... and she died down there.'

I stepped forward. 'But you were there. You jumped from the car at the last minute–'

He spun round and grabbed me. 'Demas!' he shouted. 'You've been talking to him, haven't you? Siding with that washed-out tramp over your own family ... the man's a liar!' His hands bit into my upper arms as he shook me. 'And the money, I suppose that's a lie too, just a way to get me here?'

'No, no, that's not it at all. Honestly.'

He let me go. 'Well what is it, then?'

'I just—I just thought that after all that's happened, you might want to—'

'Might want to what? Want to what? And what makes you think I won't send you down there, eh?' He grabbed me again and held me near the edge.

'Because I know you're not a murderer!' I'd rehearsed that line in my head many times, but it sounded different to me now—now that my life was riding on what had only been a hunch.

He released me from his grip, but not his gaze. He was breathing hard and his face was ashen. Finally he turned slowly to face the precipice and gripped the wall with shaking hands. He was trying to hide them, but I saw the tears streaming down his cheeks.

'You want to know the truth, do you?'

'Yes. Please.'

'And you swear not to tell anyone?'

'Of course.'

'Then swear it!' he shouted to the lake.

'I swear it,' I said. 'I won't tell.'

'And I swear ... swear that vicar is getting to me with his preaching and his foot washing. Oh, to hell with it all, I'll not take all this to my grave. For God's sake, why should I?'

He looked up between the mountains and then down again into the black depths. 'You wanna know, boy? Well, you're wrong, I did kill her ... as good as, anyway. I drove her to it ... which is the same thing.' He took a long breath to steady himself. 'I ... I couldn't give her what she wanted. I was no good for her and her sort ... for all I tried. We did all right for money, but she hated me eventually for stealing her away from her sort, despised me. So she made the marriage a living punishment. She wasn't pure, do you understand, she wasn't faithful to me.'

He waited a few moments before continuing.

'That day started out like every other. She was drunk by mid-morning and said she was going to see her friend in Borrowdale—the dashing Colonel Palmers. I was the laughing stock and I told her I was coming too, to have it out with him. She taunted me, saying he was twice the man I was. Maybe he was, but I didn't care.' He looked up to the elephantine mass of Melbreak looming above the lake.

'You came down with her in the same car?' I prompted him.

Uncle Sid glanced back at the road coming down from Lorton. 'Aye, and we spent the journey opening old wounds ... everything ... every single thing. She'd drunk half a bottle of gin and she was hysterical, said I'd ruined her life, the only one she had. She said she'd end it today and take me with her to serve me right. She started screaming that she'd do it, that she'd bury us both in the lake. It got worse and worse until we came here to Hause End ... she put her foot down and I couldn't stop her ... I jumped from the car and she went through the wall here, screaming like a madwoman.' He hung his head over the wall as if he were about to be sick. When he turned back to me I knew he'd told me the whole truth. 'You're the first person I've told in twenty-two years—the length of my sentence. I've been punished for what I did ... in my mind, I mean. I sinned against both of them, Ellen and Harriet, and now I carry her in my conscience as much as any murderer.'

My voice came out as almost a whisper. 'But the vicar says that our sins were paid for at the cross–'

'So they say. Very convenient. Well, I've done my penance but I feel no different. It's probably worse now than it was then.'

'No, Uncle Sid, it's not about what you can do for God. Granny says it's what Jesus has already done. You've just got to believe him to be free.'

He'd composed himself a bit and I could see him returning to his usual self at the mention of Granny. 'Yes, well, if it works for my righteous sister then that's fine, but I've not come here to be preached to. Now what about this money?'

'Mr Demas has it,' I said as I pointed to the hollow in the crag.

'Demas? What? Demas is here? What is this, some kind of a trap? I knew I shouldn't have trusted you!' He grabbed me by the collar and dragged me to the hollow.

'No, that's not it! I just wanted to—'

Uncle Sid shoved me into the crevice. And there was old Jack, slumped on the ground gazing blankly out towards the lake.

He spoke as if in a trance. 'A suicide kills two people, that's what it's for.'

'Demas!' Uncle Sid shouted. 'What are you doing skulking round here?'

Jack spoke again, a bit louder. 'A suicide kills two people, that's what it's for.'

He got to his feet and looked Sid in the eye, but this time there was no anger or hatred—only the empty gaze of a man who has lived for so little. 'Arthur Miller wrote it. Had plenty of time to read plays, I have, stuck up there. Only he was wrong this time. Her suicide killed three, didn't it? I expect the silver is for you, Sid, but I'm giving it to the lad because he saved my life. He can do with it what he wants.'

Uncle Sid let go of me. 'So it's true. You did make the mines work.'

'Aye, we're not such failures as Harriet's folks had us down for. You and me both made things work in the end, didn't we? Anyway, it's all there. Take it. Take it all. Hope it does you some good.' He motioned to the wooden crates and started to walk, shell-shocked, towards Buttermere.

I was about to say 'thank you,' but I knew he wouldn't hear.

Uncle Sid lowered himself onto one of the crates and looked out to the fells. 'How did you know?' he asked. 'How did you know I hadn't killed her?'

'Well, I'd been thinking about it a lot, and the other night I was watching a Sherlock Holmes film with Grandpa. Holmes said, "When you've eliminated the impossible, whatever remains, however improbable, must be the truth." And then it all seemed to fit together. I mean, I knew you'd been here, old Jack told me that, but I also reckoned you couldn't have killed her, and that something like what you just said must have happened.'

'You risked a great deal on that hunch,' he said. 'You're a fool boy, thank God.'

I shrugged. 'Well, I never got the sense that Granny and Uncle George thought you had, and I think it was when I saw you with Annie that I was sure you weren't a murderer.'

We loaded the crates into the car and drove back in silence. To receive that level of help from a bitter enemy seemed to have humbled him beyond speech. He dropped me back at the lane at two o'clock and I ran home to find Grandpa loading up the Land Rover.

Nelson was primed and ready for the battle, but Grandpa was cool and solemn. 'Here's your gun,' he said. 'Did you check it this morning?'

I nodded.

'Well check it again, then jump in, there's a good lad.'

I did as he said and we started toward Lorton. 'Will, I want you to listen to me. You have a gun, but you must not point it at anyone. Do you hear? This is no wilderness adventure like the cougar. This is very serious. You're there because Stan trusts you to keep your head, and that gun is only to blow out their tyres if they look like they'll get away before the police come.'

We met Roger and Andrew in the village. Richard was already in position as a lookout on the Cockermouth road. Roger and Andrew both wore black, and Andrew was unshaven. Roger was also wearing a dog collar under his leather jacket. They looked the part.

'Wow, you guys look mean,' I said.

'Aye, lad,' Roger replied. 'Speak softly and carry a big stick and all that.'

Stan was with Uncle Sid at the big house across the fields in High Lorton where Grandpa and I were heading on foot. Our guise was that of a grandfather and grandson out rabbit shooting, which would enable us to get close to the enemy fully armed without raising suspicion.

It was ten minutes to three when we hastened over the stile. Grandpa had brought two dead rabbits that he gave me to sling over my shoulder and, in our hunting gear, we did look the part. Grandpa once again gave me his 'Fairbairn Sykes' commando knife to put in my boot. I hadn't seen it since the night I plunged it into the cougar.

'Here, I want you to have this, Will. I've taken it all over the world and it has seen me through some things. I have no sons to pass it on to, and I think you have earned it one way or another.'

I stammered my thanks, but there was no time to talk. We were at least ten minutes out of our agreed timing. If the enemy arrived early we'd all be in real trouble.

We were at the field boundary by Uncle Sid's lawn in eight minutes. I could see Stan at the front porch. We went through the small gate and concealed ourselves in a thicket of shrubs where we had a good view of the knoll where Richard was, nearly a mile away. We'd been listening intently for the last ten minutes and were sure he hadn't tried to reach us. I looked across the garden to the upper end of the long drive and saw Andrew and Roger jumping the wall and crawling through the dense rhododendrons.

Grandpa tried his walkie-talkie to contact Richard and let him know that we were in position. The signal hadn't been good in the village, but we were confident of a better reception in High Lorton since there was a clear line of sight. But we were wrong. There was crackling but no answer.

'Wretched, damn things, absolutely useless. This is not good, we'll have to improvise,' he muttered as he banged the instrument against his leg.

But we'd only been there a minute more when we saw some flashes of light from Richard's lookout position. It was Morse code. Grandpa was relieved. 'Good thing the sun's shining, but I've forgotten most things I ever learnt about Morse code. You don't know it, do you?'

It was a good day for the teenagers. 'Don't worry,' I said, 'Stan's been teaching me and I know a bit.' He repeated the message several times and I eventually got it transcribed onto a scrap of paper. 'Okay,' I said. 'It's CAR ... 2 ... VANS ... NOW ... NOW.'

Grandpa was decisive. 'Right. Let's get to our position. And remember: focus. Keep your eye on the target. Everything else is irrelevant.'

'Right, Grandpa.' I followed him across the lawn. Our advance was the signal for Stan to call for the armed response unit. I'd been rehearsing the plan in my head. We'd let the car through, but we wouldn't allow the vans to reach the house. We'd need to hold the vans so Gerrand could authenticate the loot, call his employer and get away through the stable exit before the police arrived.

My heart was beginning to pound, but I was trying not to act scared. We were walking along the drive with our rabbits when the car entered the gates. Grandpa motioned a welcome to Mr Gerrand, who looked like he was still suffering from hay fever. He waved back, a little nervously. I wondered if he recognized me. Grandpa handed me a cartridge and we slipped them into the chambers of our shotguns.

The white vans entered the gates just as we started to walk across the long drive. I let the rabbits slip out of my hand and they fell onto the drive in front of the oncoming van. As I stopped to pick them up, the van ground to a halt. The driver sounded the horn and made several rude gestures for me to get out of the way.

'He seems a bit upset,' Grandpa said with a wink. 'Think I'll go and see if he's all right.' The other van had also come to a stop and Grandpa stepped up to the driver's side window. 'I say, everything all right in there?' he asked in as cheery a voice as I've ever heard him use.

The huge man behind the wheel was swearing at us to get out of the way, but Grandpa was having fun. 'Sorry old chap,' he said. 'I'm a little deaf, could you speak up?'

This seemed to do the trick, for both men jumped out and started to mouth off. 'Suppose you're this bleedin' Mr Armstrong we're looking for? Well we've come to pick up a few things, and that gun looks like it's worth a few quid so we'll start with that, shall we?'

They were an ugly pair. The driver was about six feet four with muscular arms and a face like a bulldog. The other was smaller but wore such a mean expression that I'd rather have been caught by the bigger man if I'd had to choose. Both were dirty and greasy.

Grandpa didn't take his eyes off them but I stole a glance toward Gerrand. He was looking back at us but Stan was ushering him to the house. When Grandpa heard the heavy front door shut behind Gerrand he knew he had a little freedom to toy with the thugs. 'Oh, this gun is very valuable. It's a Holland Holland, given to me by General Ord Wingate's family after the Burma campaign and if you want it, you can have it ... one barrel at a time!' He shut the gun chambers and released the safety catch. 'Please,' he said, 'be my guest.'

It took the big man a moment to assess what the invitation meant, and when it eventually dawned on him he looked over at his shifty colleague, who was well aware of what had just transpired and was weighing up Grandpa's resolve to do what he'd said.

The smaller one spoke first. 'Come off it old man, you're not gonna use that thing on us. We're just the middlemen. See, I've got an order to reclaim valuables from your house against a debt you owe. Here, I'll show you the paperwork.' He began to reach into his pocket, where his hand had been itching to go since Grandpa had cocked his gun.

'Steady sonny!' Grandpa had his gun levelled at the man's face in an instant. 'Keep your hand where I can see it and the lad will relieve you of your *paperwork*.'

I handed my gun to Grandpa and gave the man a wide birth as Grandpa had shown me, approaching him from behind. I noticed Uncle George blocking the entrance to the drive with his sheep trailer, but the attention of the men was on the commotion we were creating so they didn't see him. I reached my hand slowly towards the man's pocket. I could smell his sweat and cigarette smoke. I steadied my hand. 'Don't act scared, don't act scared,' I told myself. I felt a hard metal object, a handgun, and pulled it out.

'You won't get away with this,' the man said. 'We're gonna come back and get you, both of you, and then you'll see ...'

I brought the gun round to Grandpa.

'Well, I'm glad I stopped you presenting your papers,' Grandpa said. 'It would have been very messy. Will, would you kindly frisk him and move on to his friend before the other two join us?'

Still shaking a bit, I recovered another gun, a knuckle duster and a flick knife.

'Right. You there, lie down on your belly, hands behind your head. And you—' he motioned to the bigger one, 'call the other two to join us as if nothing's wrong. Will, make sure this man gets down on the ground and cover him. Whatever he moves, blow it off. Except his head ... his mother will want something to recognize.'

I trained my gun and the man got down saying as he did so, 'Don't know who you're messing with here.'

My thoughts exactly I thought as I caught sight of Grandpa's steely gaze once more.

All of this had happened directly in front of the van and, though I wondered why the others didn't get out to see what was going on, they'd stayed in the van and seen nothing. They sounded their horn just as Grandpa forced the big ugly one to the side to call his colleagues.

Unfortunately the brute wasn't a very good actor, and whatever the men in the van behind saw in his face prompted them to spring out of the van fully armed with a baseball bat and a crow bar—and, no doubt, hidden firearms as well. These were the two ex-soldiers Stan had warned us about. They were big men but quick as lightning. Grandpa saw it coming but there was little time. Grandpa couldn't risk getting close to the man, as his gun was our only insurance. 'Idiot's let the cat out of the bag. Right, you, get down ... *now!*'

This all happened in a split second, but the big man was dithering about obeying the order. It seemed like he was suffering from brain freeze—he wanted to get down and save his neck but he was too scared to move. Either way it was dangerous for us. I didn't remove my gun from the sly man I was covering, but I backed up to the big man and tried a trick kids always did to me at school. The brute had his back to me, and I brought my heel down hard near the top of his calf where the blow would trigger that collapse reflex as I shouted, 'Down! Now!'

He must have outweighed me two to one, but he dropped nevertheless. Grandpa nodded approvingly and said, 'Right, drop back slightly. We'll need a bit of space to cover them all.'

As we took a few paces back, the other two arrived at the front of the van and saw their sorry colleagues face down. Just at that moment, Andrew and Roger appeared behind them from the rhododendron bushes. Roger swaggered over as if he were walking with his shoulders, forearms and slightly clenched fists held forward. He looked three times more intimidating than anyone else. Andrew followed suit and managed to look pretty hard himself.

Roger swiftly issued his ultimatum. 'Yooo, and yooo.' He sounded just like Billy Connelly. 'I'm givin' ye one chance to put doon those toys and join yer friends.'

The man with the baseball bat spat on the ground. 'This is a bleedin' joke is it? A vicar? What, you gonna get God to send down fire or what?'

They launched themselves at Roger and Andrew. One swung the baseball bat at Roger's head. He didn't move his body an inch but kept his focus on the thug's eyes. I drew in my breath. The blow would be hard enough to crack a skull. But at the last millisecond his left arm went up to receive the full weight of the attack. As the crunch came, Roger spat out, 'Yooo should nae take ...' His right fist landed like a sledgehammer on the man's unprotected face. 'The Lord's name in vain.' The man staggered back, stunned. He dropped the weapon as blood gushed from his nose.

Roger quickly closed the gap and grabbed his shoulder with his left arm. Then he winded him with a tremendous right punch that sent him to the ground, where he remained. Meanwhile, Andrew had been staving off the attack from the crow bar. The claw on the bar was five inches long and the man was swinging it so close to Andrew's head that I feared for his life. Andrew was agile but not used to this sort of wrestling. Ever keen to spot a weakness or mistake in an opponent, however, Andrew waited to see an opening while keeping a distance from the weapon. Another second and two swipes later, his chance came. The man teetered off balance for a split second as his foot caught the edge of the lawn, and Andrew moved in like lightning.

The man brought the bar up in a back swing as fast as he could, but he didn't have nearly enough speed to Andrew's block. With Andrew's huge hands now on the man's clothing, the weapon became useless. Andrew swung the man against the vehicle with such force that, when Roger finally secured the weapon, the man was found to be concussed from where his head had dented the side of the van.

Grandpa and I covered the remaining prisoners that Roger and Andrew hauled in while Andrew stripped the others of handguns and searched the vans to find a shotgun and two semi-automatic rifles. They were all laid out and made quite a stash of weapons for the police. Roger was jubilant, though his left forearm was badly hurt and possibly fractured. But, all in all, we'd had a lucky escape.

Suddenly there was a sound of bells. 'Sorry!' George shouted from the other end of drive. 'They insisted on seeing the robbers!'

Grandpa peered round the side of the van. 'Ah, the cavalry!' he said.

I couldn't look away from my prisoners, but I knew who it was as soon as I heard the voice. 'Churchill, come to heel!'

The Millstones parked their bikes against the side of the van and bustled over to see the men who had come to rob the big house.

'We were just doing the rounds to get signatures for the Cottage Hospital petition. George tells us there have been some unwelcome visitors,' Frieda said.

Grandpa was ready for some humour. 'Yes, I believe they've come up on a day trip from Manchester but I'm sure they won't mind signing the petition. They know how necessary hospitals are!'

Hilda came forward with the paperwork and looked down at the first man. 'Manchester! Such a dirty place!' She prodded the prostrate man with her umbrella. 'Do you think he can write?'

Roger didn't wait for an answer but grabbed the man by the scruff of his collar. 'Aye, he will,' he said. 'And if there's any more funny business ye'll not need a hospital, ye'll need a vicar!' He tugged the man up to standing and made him sign the petition. The other thugs were made to sign as well, as were we.

When we heard the sound of the armed response unit coming down the valley, Andrew and Roger melted back into the bushes. While we'd been signing the Millstone's petition I'd also noticed Stan loading Mr Gerrand's car with the silver and ushering him round the back of the house to the stable exit.

Grandpa told the Millstones to keep the event to themselves and they left soon after George had unblocked the entrance to allow the police through.

As the police arrived, Uncle Sid appeared at the doorway to see what the sirens were for. Stan followed him up the drive. Uncle Sid's jaw dropped when he saw the four prisoners and the arsenal of weapons.

Grandpa snorted. 'Hello, Sidney. We were out doing a bit of rabbiting when we caught these men snooping about.'

Sid looked puzzled and Stan winked at me. Two Vauxhall Carletons screeched through the gates and eight well-armed men in dark gear leaped out ready for action—only to be greeted by us. Grandpa was suitably vague and, after giving our addresses and brief statements, we were allowed to go. Grandpa and I walked down the drive, leaving the police to extract whatever information they could from Uncle Sid.

'Well done, Will. You kept your head where I've seen experienced soldiers lose their nerve ... I think a celebratory meal for the boys at the Kirkstile is in order!'

The others met us there at seven thirty. Stan was last to arrive, having only just said goodbye to the police.

There was a nasty bruise on Roger's arm. 'Ach, it's just a wee bruise—used to do that sort of thing all the time.'

Richard was a bit sore that he'd missed the action, but I could tell Roger was glad not to have had him in the thick of it. The pub was full of talk about the police arrests, though no one knew about our involvement as the papers wouldn't be out until Friday. We kept our voices down but spent several hours rehearsing the adventure.

'Right, my boy,' Grandpa finally said, 'it's time to be heading home. This old man is getting tired.'

Once we were home I called my dad to tell him about our adventure. He was amazed by the tale but was glad I was all right.

'I think it's a good thing you're coming home soon,' he said. 'Try not to get into any more life or death situations before we come to pick you up, all right?'

I promised, but I felt a heaviness at the thought of leaving and going back to Liverpool. I didn't ask him for an update about how things were going with Mum.

Granny didn't say anything to me about our 'rabbiting trip', but I heard Grandpa getting a right roasting in their bedroom as I lay awake that night.

PART NINE

SELF-CONTROL

28

THE LOWESWATER SHOW

'Cor, look at it—it's not let up for hours.'

It had rained solidly all day Thursday and into the night. Grandpa motioned me back to the fireside. 'Yes, it's a fair amount of rain is that, enough to get the salmon running. I think I'll get you to find me some worms tomorrow.'

'Is worming for salmon difficult?'

Grandpa leaned forward. 'No, it's simple enough. You just need a couple of juicy worms wriggling at one end, then some weights a few feet away to hold the worms down in the current.'

I nodded as he used his hands to demonstrate.

'Now the trick, of course, is to trot the bait down the riverbed in front of the fish's nose,' he said. 'The salmon, who by nature don't spend time feeding until they finish their epic journey to the spawning grounds upstream, will only bite by a hunting instinct—and that only when the prey is dangled in front of its nose! We'll get out tomorrow afternoon and have a go if it clears a bit.'

By Friday the Cocker had risen over a foot and we were all keen to see whether any salmon had made their way up this far from the broad stretches of the Derwent at Cockermouth, of which the Cocker was a tributary.

The torrents of rain did abate, and so we went down to the river after lunch on Friday. Grandpa was a master at it. He took his old split cane rod up the river where, after only twenty minutes, he'd caught a fish. When I heard the splashing I raced over to see the first catch of the season, and it looked to be an absolute monster—well over twenty-five pounds.

'Ooh, he's a big fella, what a beauty.' The silver giant thrashed and jumped around for a few minutes but then broke the rod and line. We could see the rod end with the remainder of the lines sculling over to the far bank.

'Quick, lad, if the line pulls through the eyelets we'll lose the fish for sure,' Grandpa said. 'Get your kit off and grab it!'

In the heat of the chase I was keen to obey and, despite the strong current, I'd stripped to my boxer shorts in minutes and leapt from the bank. A few strokes had me on top of the rod.

'Grab the line first!' Grandpa shouted. 'The line!' He was laughing and Nelson, who hated to miss any of the fun, wanted to jump in too. Grandpa kept him to heel while I grabbed the line, and then the rod, and swam back. I could feel the fish pulling against the line but I made it back to the bank. I held it out to Grandpa, but he shook his head. 'No, I lost it, Will. It's your turn to try now.'

And so I began my wrestling match with what became known as the 'Leviathan of Salmon's Leap'. This monster had travelled two thousand miles, and I was determined he'd be my first salmon. It took about an hour to land and I was nearly half a kilometre downstream by the time I was able to tire him out. Most of that time I was actually in the water, sometimes actually being pulled out into the deep. I had no shoes on and struggled to get a good footing. At one point he came powering toward me and darted between my legs. The line got badly tangled, and the fishing line cut into my hands, but I didn't let go. Spurred on by cheers and barking from the bank, I finally won my prize and carried it to the shore.

It was a twenty-nine pound cock fish with a large hooked upper lip. I'd never seen Grandpa so excited, 'Now this is a proper fish, lad! Well done, well done ... oh, this is something you'll not forget, ooh, just look at it!'

As we started to gather my clothes, Stan appeared. 'Good job, lad,' he said as he admired the fish. 'Now don't forget that I'm taking you to see my friend at the field sports shop in Cockermouth before you leave to get you a proper knife.'

But he had other reasons to be cheerful. 'It's unusual for the rivers to be so high this early in the summer. I'm guessing this'll bring out the poaching gang. And we're ready for 'em,' he said.

I felt a dread in the pit of my stomach.

'It's the show tomorrow,' Stan continued, 'and you say that's when you're gonna see Chris Clegg again?'

I nodded.

'Well you know everythin' your Grandpa and me's been saying about the fish stocks and how important it is that we stop this gang? If the likes of them carry on one more season, you can forget wild salmon up here like that one. The sport will be dead. The rivers will be dead.'

Grandpa nodded. 'Stan and I were discussing this last night. He's been talking to the police, Will. They've agreed to let you be Stan's insider into the Clegg gang. They'll wire you up so we can gather evidence when they strike.'

'Have your spoken to his parents yet?' Stan asked Grandpa.

Grandpa shook his head. 'No, I wanted Will to agree to it before I spoke to his father.'

Stan looked sterner than ever. 'Listen, Will. This will be more dangerous for you than anyone. You'll have no gun, and whoever the Cleggs are bringing in as muscle will be unpredictable characters. If they suss what you're up to then you could get hurt—badly hurt.'

'I'll do it,' I said. 'If my Dad says yes.'

Grandpa nodded. 'Good lad, I'll call him tonight.'

As we walked up the hill we kept to the woods, as it would be dangerous for me to be seen with Stan. He told me how the police would fit me a tracking device and live-linked microphone system that would enable me to record the other's voices, thereby gathering evidence for the trial if an arrest could be made.

Granny was suitably impressed by my catch and insisted on taking photographs. Grandpa and I spent the rest of the afternoon examining maps of the river and likely netting points.

After our supper of fresh salmon that night Grandpa called Dad. They had a long conversation and then Grandpa passed the phone.

'Sounds like one adventure after another,' Dad said. 'What was I saying just the other day, Will?'

'I know, Dad. It's just—well, this is important, and ...'

'Tell me,' he said. 'Is this something you really believe in or are you just getting caught up in all the enthusiasm?'

I told him about the salmon I'd caught and what incredible creatures they were and how everything that I'd learned about the river that summer had made it so precious to me. 'Dad, I won't go if you say not to, but I've got a chance to make a real difference here.'

There was a moment of silence. 'I still can't quite believe I'm talking to the same boy we packed off from the city seven weeks ago,' Dad said. 'I'm not sure what they put in the water up there, but ... yes, yes you can go, but promise me that you'll do everything your grandfather says.'

I agreed and passed the phone back to Grandpa.

I left the room and they talked for a while longer. It was a very long conversation for two people who hadn't really talked for ten years. I was trying not to listen, but I couldn't help overhearing snippets. They talked about me and about Mum and about Dad's business problems as well. Grandpa seemed to be making him some sort of offer, too. 'You'll think about it then?' I heard him say. 'She might as well have some benefit from the estate now ... Yes, I would say Will has already settled well here ... No, no, I won't mention anything to him now. If you and Suzie agree then you can tell him yourself when you're up next weekend for the party ... No, don't mention it ... Yes, well, you can thank me later.'

Although I wondered what they were talking about, with the Loweswater Show the next day it wasn't long before my mind was racing with thoughts of Cumbrian wrestling, horse jumping and Hannah, and the Cleggs. I was very excited but also more than a little nervous.

The next morning Granny was up and away early to set out stalls for the Mother's Union. It had rained heavily again during the night and the morning was overcast with the promise of later sun. Grandpa took me and Lewis down after breakfast.

'Is the show a big event, Grandpa?'

'Never used to be before the Millstones retired here,' he said as he struggled to get the Land Rover into fourth gear.

'The Millstones? They don't organize it, do they?'

403

He laughed. 'No, but they did take over the car park stewarding when they heard that there were some people who parked illegally in the lay-bys and snuck in.'

'Oh, right. What was their solution?'

'Oh, it's worth seeing. In fact some miss the show jumping so they can watch. Basically, they redirect all traffic into the parking field.'

'All the traffic? But what about people who want to pass through?'

Grandpa snorted. 'Well, unless they have a very good reason for passing through they don't stand a chance!' The showground was in a beautiful spot, flanked by mountains with the small lake of Loweswater glistening in the morning light. Lewis and I left Grandpa at the judge's tent and found Andrew, who roped us into helping put up the Cumbrian and Westmorland Wrestling Association's tent.

It was almost up when we got there, and our job was just to re-tension all the guy ropes while Andrew hammered some of the pins in further. Lewis and I were working around to another side when we heard a large clatter and Andrew crying out. We raced around to the other side to find Andrew struggling out from under twenty or so wooden pallets that had been stacked high near the tent.

'Somebody knocked them onto me,' he said as we helped him to his feet. 'Aah, my leg. They fell on my calves ... Let's have a look.' He sat down again and pulled up his trouser legs. The swelling and bruising was already visible.

'Andrew, that looks really bad,' I said. 'Who would do such a stupid thing? They could have killed you.'

He rubbed his wounds. 'Ooh, there's a few people who would rather an outsider wasn't winning the cup again this year. Do us a favour and go see if Archie is anywhere near.'

I did a quick circuit of the vicinity, but he was nowhere to be seen. We helped Andrew into the tent, where he found some ice and bandages.

More and more people arrived in a steady stream. There were trail hounds, horseboxes, cattle, sheep and ice cream vans. The show started officially at midday with a fell race in which Uncle George had, for many successive years, been the victor. I saw Uncle Sid at the judge's tent. He looked happier than usual and beat Grandpa by nearly a metre in the long distance fly-casting competition. He acknowledged me with a nod. I could tell from Grandpa's hand gestures that he was telling Sid about my epic salmon. I visited Granny and Aunty Dora, who were too preoccupied with the cakes and flower arrangements to talk. As I passed by the main gate I saw Hilda and Frieda flagging down cars.

'Yes, hello, it will be five pounds for the car, just follow the signs ... What's that? Yes, yes, I'm sure you are my good man, but I've heard it all before. Don't want to make a fuss now, do we? Best to come quietly especially with a queue forming. Five pounds, thank you. Now just follow the signs ... and don't forget to look in on the W.I. tent!' The bewildered man drove his Mondeo into the field, following the signs.

'Another skiver?' Frieda shouted from the booth.

Hilda adjusted her cardigan. 'Yes, that one said he was going fell walking!'

'The cheek of some people!'

I ran into Hannah just as the horse riding competition was beginning. She looked great. She was wearing cream jodhpurs and a navy jacket with brass buttons. The effect with her dark auburn hair was stunning.

'Hi, Will, just the person–'

'Wow, Hannah, you look ... great.'

She blushed. 'We got the outfit second-hand, you wouldn't believe the prices of these things but, you know everyone has to have them for jumping so ...'

'It really suits you. I hope you do well today.'

'Well Tonto's on form. I think the holiday really got him into shape and ...' She broke off and looked around at the milling crowds. 'Look, Will, stuff's been up in the air for me a bit recently and, well ... I don't feel I've been very fair to you and and I just wanted to ... oh, look, it's in this letter, if you read it later somewhere quiet ... it's all in there, okay?'

I nodded. 'Okay,' I said. I folded the envelope and put it into my pocket. I'd never really seen her flustered before but I knew she was nervous about the competition. Lewis appeared then, just as 'Hannah Scott' was called over the tannoy. She jumped really well and only clipped two rails.

Roger, Richard and I all greeted her outside the gate with high praise. She'd taken the lead, and many who had ridden before her were seasoned professionals from outside the county.

When the referee announced Carrie Clegg as the next rider I went back to the ring to take a look. She wore a bright red hunting jacket and her blonde hair was in a net. She looked pretty awesome in the saddle too, but I pushed those thoughts to the back of my mind. She wasn't what I wanted although the physical attraction was still, almost overwhelmingly, there. She rode well and, though she lacked Hannah's style and grace, her pony's hooves didn't clip a single rail and she won by two points.

Though I wanted to go back to commiserate with Hannah, the Cumbrian wrestling was next and I still hadn't found Chris Clegg. So I made a beeline to the beer tent, where I was quite certain I'd find him.

I was right. They were all there, including Archie Pritchard, who was leaning up against the bar looking intimidatingly at every man who came in. Chris seemed pleased to see me, though, and he introduced me to Archie, who didn't seem overly impressed, and some other people as well. Chris bought me a pint of lager and, as he rattled on about the height of the river and where certain people had seen salmon running, I saw Carrie come into the tent. She was flushed with excitement after her win. Her face lit up when she saw me. 'Well, Will, did you see me whip everyone? Should have seen the Scott girl ... nearly in tears, sorry bitch.'

I tried not to flinch.

'Bet she thought she had it in the bag. Come on, Chris, get us a drink.'

While Chris got her a pint, she asked me about how my grandfather and I had rumbled the four Mafia thugs. She said it was all over the papers. 'That's so cool,' she said as she gulped her beer.

I felt a flush of pride. I told them as much as I could without giving too much away. I brought the conversation back round by telling Chris about the salmon I'd caught the day before just above Salmon's Leap.

His eyes lit up. 'Told you, Starky,' he said to one of the grim young men propping up the bar with Archie. 'Them fish are right up and there was more rain last night. I say we wait a few more days till the rest of the fish make it as far as the Great Bend and then we work our way up from't waterfalls. What d'you say? Tuesday night? Archie, what do you say? Reckon those mates of yours from Workington will be okay with that?'

Archie drained his pint. 'Well, me marras are doormen, so they won't get away from't pubs 'till gone midnight, but yeah, if you can miss a bit more beauty sleep, I think that'll be all right with 'em.'

I made a mental note of the locations they mentioned and the names of the men I'd been introduced to.

Jane came in then, and I edged behind Chris.

Archie leered at her. 'You're Andy's bit of fluff aren't you? Not a bad looking lass, suppose you've come t'tent 'cos you fancy a real man, eh? I'll sort you out all right if you come over here, lass.'

She glanced at him as she ordered her lager and lime and more ice for Andrew's leg. 'I'm glad my fiancé didn't hear you insult me like that. And, for the record, you're the last person a woman would ever possibly want to be with—as you've no doubt realized from your other failures with the opposite sex.'

Jane picked up her drink to leave.

'Hope you like him as much when I push his face in the dirt today,' Archie snarled. 'I hear he's had a little accident with the pallets, poor wee lad. Maybe you should take him back yam to the south with the rest of 'em namby-pamby Bible bashers.' Jane ignored the comments and walked out with her head held high.

Carrie thought it was funny, and it was painful to have to try to act the part as the undercover agent. The beer had gone slightly to my head and I was wondering how I might fare in the ring in my state when Carrie told me she wanted to tell me something.

'Not here, you wally, out back. Come on.' I followed her round the back between the marquee and row of portaloos. When she turned round to face me I saw that she'd taken off her cravat and unbuttoned her blouse a few buttons.

'Bet you wanted to do this for a while,' she said as she pushed against me.

'Uhh, well, I ...' The combination of beer and sheer physical attraction fuddled my head. I smiled like an idiot and struggled for something vaguely sensible to say. Turn around and leave now, a faint voice in the back of my head insisted.

But it was too late. As she put her arms round my neck, any thoughts of self-control all but disappeared. I found my arms going round her as our mouths met. Nothing had really prepared me for the power of this passion and, even though I detested the taste of cigarette smoke in her mouth, at that point I didn't want it to stop.

That voice deep within me was still screaming, though, faint as it was. I felt like I was looking down at myself, disgusted, but unable to control my physical body.

I ignored that voice as best I could, though, until I heard another, familiar, voice behind me. 'Will? Is that you ... oh, God, it is!'

I pulled my face away from Carrie's in time to see Hannah standing there, her eyes welling up and her mouth open in shock.

I wanted to run after her but stood still. I felt caught. What could I say? And, I reasoned, I was a 'double agent'.

Carrie laughed. She still had me in her arms and pulled me close again. 'Looks like goody two shoes is still sore after losing the riding—and maybe something else as well!'

I gave a half-hearted laugh. 'Yeah, anyway, look, I'm going to have to get going or I'll miss the wrestling.' I pried myself away from her grasp.

'Oh yeah, Carl will be getting ready too. He's expected to clean up this year for his weight. Come on, let's go.'

As I followed her onto the path I noticed the Professor standing near the tent. I was sure he'd witnessed the crime of passion.

'Oh, hi Professor, I was just ...'

He came over and pointed his stick at me disapprovingly. 'The happiness of a man in this life does not consist in the *absence* but in the *mastery* of his passions. So says Tennyson and you, young sir, have made Hannah very unhappy ... bad form.' He pointed to my mouth. I wiped it with the back of my hand and saw it was smeared with lipstick. I wiped it again in disgust. The Professor meandered away, tutting.

Things could not have been worse. And, as the tannoy announced the first round of the wrestling, I remembered the letter from Hannah in my pocket.

29

IN THE RING

*You know how, at the games, there is only one
prize for the winner?
So run to win! Athletes don't indulge in an
unhealthy lifestyle
and they just do it for a laurel wreath, which
withers a week later!
You and I, on the other hand, fight for an
eternal crown.
So, spiritually speaking, don't run half-
heartedly, make sure every punch connects.
I make sure my physical appetites don't control
me and lead me off track,
in case having been a trainer to others, I myself
am rejected at the finish line.*
—1 Corinthians 9:24–27, paraphrase—

It seemed like most of the valley had gathered on the grass
bank overlooking a grassy arena about twenty feet square.
The lower weight classes went first, and a robust, ruddy mix
of young farmers gathered near the tent for the contest.
Lewis had entered as well, and he had the crowds in fits of
laughter on his second bout by clinging feverishly to the
reigning belt holder, a very angry Mr Carl Clegg of Kern

Howe Farm. Though Carl tried everything in his power to wrench, swing and shake him off, Lewis held on.

Lewis was delighted with the whole idea of wrestling and was quite at home with the audience. The best part of all was that he could irritate Carl Clegg beyond reason and he knew Carl wouldn't hit him because of the referee. After several minutes Lewis began to get a fit of the giggles and eventually had to let go. He fell onto the grass clutching his ribs and laughing out loud.

'Oh, let's do it again!' he said as Carl stomped back to the tent scowling. The referee gently explained to the young contender that his turn was over until next year and so Lewis joined me and Richard.

I glanced around for Hannah, but she was nowhere to be seen. I didn't dare read the letter with Lewis and Richard there. I'd have to wait to find somewhere quiet after my turn. Richard had a number of fights and won them all. He showed the same grace and agility that he did on the rock faces, and throughout the afternoon he rose up the ranks of contenders.

My heart was pounding as I was called to the ring. It felt like the gate going up in the film *Gladiator*. I walked out and grappled my lanky opponent as we waited for the referee to start us off. My opponent was a young shepherd from Alston. He wore the traditional gear—a white vest and leggings with a pair of embroidered black velvet trunks over the top. I wasn't expecting to do well, but as we tugged and wheeled each other about I managed to yank him and buttock him onto the ground.

Lewis was delighted, of course, and he whooped and cheered. 'Mighty Beast Slayer!' he shouted. This started people pointing and talking about me, and in my vanity I lost concentration during the second bout and found myself expertly flung onto my right shoulder and over into the grass. On the third bout I was more focused and, when my opponent tried to right buttock me, I counter-attacked by pulling him away as hard as I could and twisting him to the ground. I was jubilant. It was an unexpected bonus, and I grinned as I shook his hand. As the winner of that round I was paired next with Carl Clegg.

'Now then Will, lad, I'll show you how to wrestle properly,' he said as we walked out together. 'Don't worry, I'll take it easy on you.' We shook hands. He was much bigger than me and I was still feeling a bit limp from my bout a few minutes before. As we began I noticed how hard his arms were against my neck and with what ease he buttocked me half into the crowd. All the best moves I tried were useless against Carl, who outweighed and outpowered me.

Carrie called out from somewhere above me. 'Come on, Will! Get it together.'

As I stood, apologizing to the spectators I'd nearly knocked over, I felt a hand on my shoulder. It was the Professor again. 'William, do not play your "king" as if you're afraid he will play an "ace".'

I walked back to the centre wondering what that meant and assumed the position. When Carl's hands were linked behind my neck he gave me a few sharp pulls. 'Back for some more are you, Will lad? Well it's all for free ...'

As the referee had told us to start I didn't wait for him to finish his patronizing speech. With all my strength I did what I'd seen Andrew do to the crow bar thug on Wednesday. I tightened my grip and wrenched all of Carl's bulk from the ground, yanking him backwards on top of me. The backward movement had me reeling to the ground but, with my last ounce of strength, I was able to twist Carl so that he landed squarely on his back with me on top of him. The crowd gave a hearty cheer for the cunning I'd used, but Carl was badly winded. When he did eventually get up he was seething about being cheated out of a straight victory.

I was sure I'd re-torn some muscle in my forearm that had been mending nicely since the climbing rescue. As I massaged it, I thought again of Hannah and how I'd betrayed her. I looked round, but she was still nowhere to be seen. I noticed Roger had joined the men in the tent and was nodding with approval, as were numerous other wrestling veterans who sat on a bench with pipes and flat caps.

Carl saw me nursing the injury and was quick to exploit it in the next bout. He pulled at every point against the torn ligament and, after thirty seconds of excruciating pain, I couldn't resist the jerks any more and found myself flattened onto a hard patch of earth. Carl was above me and his saliva was dribbling onto my face. 'There, that's you seen to,' he panted, 'and now we'll see what Bible boy's got in him.'

We shook hands and Carl was given a rest until it was time for him to face Richard.

When the match was called I was standing with Richard.

'Now remember,' Andrew told him, 'there's no defence, only counter-attack. Clegg's a bully, he fights with human anger. You saw how Will outwitted him—if you can find some chinks then the belt could be yours. I'm serious, Richard. I believe you can do this.'

Richard was nervous but Roger steadied him as he entered the ring. 'Play him fair lad, that's all uz ask.'

Carl easily took the first round—it was over in a matter of seconds. Richard was shell shocked, but he got back to it straight away and with a monumental heave he had Carl off the ground and twisted flat on his back in no time. It was a serious piece of skill, and I saw the same old men smiling as the enraged Carl jumped up, wiping the grass from his tracksuit.

As they went down for the third and final bout I could hear Carl's bitter words from where I was standing. 'The Bible boy thinks he can throw? Well I'll show you how we do throwing up here and you won't be getting up after I've landed on you with my elbow.'

I looked to the referee, sure that he'd heard it and would disqualify Carl. But he did nothing. There was a lot of chatter behind him, which might have accounted for his apparent deafness.

As he called for them to begin, Carl went straight to work fulfilling his threat. Before Richard had time to counter-attack, he was lifted off his feet. I think Carl could have successfully thrown Richard there and then, but he was keen to do it right in front of Roger, Andrew and me. He stumbled over to glare directly at me as his victim wriggled unsuccessfully. In that last split second Carl bent his knees slightly in order to get a better hold before felling Richard. It was a mistake from which he would never recover—though no one, least of all Carl himself, could have anticipated what Richard would do next.

As Carl's chunky legs bent they presented a foothold for Richard. He sprang up them through Carl's grip, completely over balancing him. It looked to most of the audience like he'd shot straight over Carl's shoulder, but this was just a trick of perspective. The two of them ended up in what looked like a fireman's lift, and a moment later Carl went crashing to the ground to the sound of enthusiastic applause. The old men gave him a standing ovation.

'Eeh, I's not seen a fella move like that since Jim Harrington leapt over Ian Potts at the Allendale show int' seventy nine,' one of the men called to the referee.

Richard was greeted with hearty congratulations and Carrie walked away as Carl stood in the ring swearing that it wasn't a proper move and Richard should be disqualified. But no one was listening to him.

When I left to try to find Hannah, Jane was still fussing about whether Andrew should wrestle with his leg injury.

I went back with Richard to the Scott's car, where we found Jan. She told me that Hannah had just left to take her pony back to the paddock and pointed to the lone rider disappearing down the lane. As Richard talked on and on about the wrestling, I turned away and pulled Hannah's letter out of my pocket.

Dear Will,

I've chosen to write this down because it's difficult for me to say things like this in the right order. I think this is the hardest thing I've ever had to do, and I hope you can be patient.

You may have felt my behaviour toward you a bit strange over the last week, particularly after you risked your life for me on Great Gable—for which I am very grateful, as you know. I've had to do a lot of thinking and talking with my mum about things that are going on in my life. But now I think it's a bit clearer and I wanted you to know where I am.

All my life I've prayed for God's choice for someone for me to spend my life with. In my mind I'd always pictured an older person—not really old, but more mature than me and probably a pastor or missionary or something. But something happened in church a few weeks ago when I saw you, and I knew the Lord was saying that you were the one. At first I fought the idea—not because you're not nice, because you are, but you were so different from what I expected.

Please understand I haven't meant to hurt you by being distant—it's just that I've been confused. You're so much younger than I am and from such a different background. But over the last few weeks, since I've seen you with my family and the way Dad, Richard and Mum love you and speak about you, it's made more sense to me. Being on holiday really helped to make things clearer too, since I needed time to think and pray about it.

I don't really know what you will make of this letter or if you have started to feel the same way I do, but I would like to talk with you when you've had a chance to read this and pray about it.

Yours affectionately,

Hannah Scott

PS Please don't show this to Richard.

'Will ... Will, are you all right?' Jan was looking at the letter in my hand.

'Where's Richard gone?' I asked.

'He went to watch his dad wrestle. Are you all right? You seemed a hundred miles away.'

'Oh, I ... um, I was just reading something.'

She smiled. 'Hannah's letter?'

I nodded.

She offered me some juice. 'Here, have some of this and sit down for a minute. You look exhausted.'

I sat down in a deck chair and took a sip as the guilt really started to sink in. 'I don't know what you must think of me.'

'Yes, Hannah told me about the letter and what happened at the beer tent. Have you only just read it?'

I nodded again.

'I thought so,' she said. 'Tell me, do you feel the same way Hannah does?'

I looked up at her. 'Yes, I do. That day at church the same thing happened to me, and then ... the holiday and ... stuff.' Then I tried to explain my role as a double agent in the poaching ring, but the more I tried to make it sound like a James Bond 'deed-for-king-and-country-thing' the sicker I felt.

'It's all just such a mess,' I said finally. 'I wouldn't blame Hannah if she never spoke to me again.'

'Oh Will, you're so young and serious. Everyone makes mistakes. Right now Hannah thinks she's just made a bigger mistake than you did by giving you that letter, but I don't think so.'

I looked up again. 'You don't think so?'

'No, I think she took a big risk, but I don't think it was a mistake to tell you how she felt.'

I drank some more juice and thought for a moment. 'Do you think I'll marry her?'

Jan laughed. 'Will, you're fifteen years old! God may have a very good reason to put you two together, but he'll do things in his own time. You have a long way to go before you're ready to commit to Hannah in the way she'll need.'

I felt as if two great worlds had collided. 'A long way to go? But all my friends have girlfriends.'

She leaned forward and touched my hand reassuringly. 'Before a man can be a lover, he has to learn to be a warrior. I mean, he has to learn how to fight for and protect the one he loves. And I know you're thinking that means doing something heroic like rescuing her on the mountain, but that's not what I mean.'

'What do you mean then?'

'God will lead you, perhaps by giving you something for which you must wrestle—you know, to learn endurance.'

'Oh right, I think I see, but this summer's been like–'

'A good start,' she said. 'But you're still learning to stretch your wings and finding out your limits. It's a wonderful time for you, and for Hannah and Richard.'

'Yeah, but I mean everyone ...'

'Oh I know what most everyone else your age is doing. They think passion is love, and when it fizzles out a few months later they move onto someone else, expecting the next person to be the answer. You don't need that heartache, Will, and neither does Hannah. You need to get to know each other carefully, mentally and emotionally.'

'She probably hates me now anyway.'

Jan sighed. 'Will, I've prayed with her since she was a little girl for a dashing prince to sweep her off her feet, and you have all the right ingredients.' She paused and smiled. 'You just need a little more baking time, that's all. I'll talk to her again for you. She's not the first girl to be shocked by God's choice for her, you know.'

'What do you mean?'

'I mean me, Will! I was just like Hannah, with high ideals for the strong Christian husband who I'd been praying for year after year. And then one day I met Roger and I knew it was him and I just couldn't believe what God was showing me.'

'Why?'

'Because he was in prison and was just about the roughest man I'd ever set eyes on!'

'In prison? This I have got to hear!'

She looked out toward the lake. 'Yes, in prison. I'd joined our local church's prison ministry team. I'd never been inside before and it was quite a shock to the system—all those locked doors and angry men. Roger was serving time for an armed robbery and he was sitting at a nearby table talking to a woman I assumed was a prostitute who turned out to be his sister. We were waiting for our prisoner and I couldn't take my eyes off this enormous, scary man. And as I looked into his eyes the Lord showed me all the hurt and pain that was in him and it was almost too much for me. I began to cry, and that's when I heard the Lord tell me, "Jan, you go and love him." I was completely shocked—I mean, what could I do?'

'Wow,' I said. I still couldn't quite picture it. 'But does God always set people up like that?'

'Well, perhaps not exactly as he did for me, but I think it's something that he's very interested in. Maybe he only gives audible prompts to very stubborn people!'

We both laughed.

'So what happened at the prison?' I asked.

'Well, when Genie left I went over to his table as he finished his coffee and asked him his name.' Jan smiled. 'I must have sounded so stupid ... anyway, he was a bit suspicious at first. He thought I was working for the police and had come to get info out of him about the gang he worked for. But I kept visiting him and, eventually, his heart softened and he gave his life to Christ. When he was released in 1981 we were married, although my parents hit the roof. And then he started to train for the ministry. So there you go. I thought I might have been left on the shelf, but God is full of surprises!' She reached over and touched my hand. 'So Will, don't worry about being too much of a sinner in our family—you don't even get on the scales! Come on, let's go and see how those men are doing. I heard Andrew was hurt before the match.'

I helped Jan with her crutches and we arrived at the ring just as the finals were called. It was Andrew and Archie, and it was clear that Andrew was in a lot of pain and worn out from the five other men he'd felled to make it there. Archie looked a lot fresher as they entered the ring, squared up and shook hands. As the match began both men circled and Archie pulled down hard onto Andrew's swollen calf muscles as they padded back and forth. Archie tried a few moves but Andrew's counter-attack was strong and swift and within minutes Andrew had used his favourite outside stroke to bring Archie down.

Archie cursed and tried to kneel on Andrew's calf as he got up. The referee cautioned him over the language but didn't see his deliberate foul. Andrew didn't lose his cool but got up and limped to centre. The flat-cap men called out encouraging comments and the referee asked him if he wanted to call it a day and go out undefeated.

'No,' Andrew said, 'I'll see it through.'

Archie licked his lips as he looked at the big silver cup on the table in the judge's tent. Being the champion heavy-weight wrestler carried huge kudos with it round these parts. The two men locked again, and this time Archie pushed and pushed Andrew back onto his bad leg as they circled the ring until there were great beads of sweat running down Andrew's face. He winced in agony under the strain.

It was too much for the old men. One of the fiercer looking of them said, 'Awey Pritchard, can'st thou not fight like a gentlemen seeing his leg is badly?'

A few others in the crowd also booed at this cowardly spectacle, but it didn't affect Archie in the slightest. It looked like Andrew was about to give way as his leg began to buckle, and with one last heave Archie tried to drive him over onto it. But Andrew knew full well Archie's lust for success, and he faked the buckling of his knees and then exploited his opponent's last thrust by cross-buttocking him with such force that he ended up in the crowd with Lewis's ice cream all over his face.

The crowd erupted and everyone stamped and cheered—everyone except Archie and Lewis.

'I hope you're going to get me another ice cream. It were a 99 flake!' Lewis cried.

Andrew stood to full height with his hands on his hips and laughed like the Jolly Green Giant before he went over to help Archie up and offer him a handshake.

'Get way from me you devious, cheating loser!' Archie shouted and pushed his way through the crowds. This behaviour won him a one-year ban from the Wrestling Association.

At the awards ceremony immediately following, Richard, Andrew and the other winners of the various weight classes collected their cups amidst enthusiastic cheers.

I was really proud of Andrew for not shouting out about the foul play, and I was also chuffed to be Richard's mate as he stood there clutching the smaller cup. Just this morning he'd been an outsider and complete unknown. Next year he'd be better weighted to suit his class and maybe go on to win bigger titles.

The victories were tinged with the sadness of my spectacular failure with Hannah, but at least Jan had given me cause to hope.

30

ONE RIOT, ONE RANGER

Break thou the arm of the wicked and
the evil man.
—Psalm 10:15—

I tried to look my best for church the next morning, but I felt like someone had gouged my stomach out with a shovel. My stupidity was still taunting me, despite Jan's gentle words. As we sat down in our pew the rains pounded on the roof of the church. It had rained all night and the river was still rising.

Hannah and Richard were leading the music as usual, but Hannah didn't make eye contact. She concentrated on looking after Lewis, who had brought his whole family along. To compound my misery, Roger was preaching the final sermon in his 'fruit of the Spirit' series. And self-control was the last thing I wanted to hear about. As he railed from the pulpit on a society that puts football players, movie stars, rock musicians and politicians with little or no self-control on pedestals, I sank deeper into my seat. Andrew hobbled to the lecturn to read excerpts from Paul's second letter to Timothy.

'But know this for sure, that in the last days perilous times will come: For men will be lovers of themselves and lovers of money, big mouths and big heads, disrespectful to God and disobedient to parents, unthankful, unholy, unloving, unforgiving, always slagging people off, having *no self-control* ...

But you've heard what I teach and seen how I've lived a faithful Christian life in love *and how the world kicks me around for it, as they do to all of Jesus' true followers.* So as the world gets worse, you get better, by applying two things to your life: first, my solid example and second, what you've learned from the God-breathed scriptures. Then you will become a mature, steadfast man of God, armed and dangerous for all the good work He has for you.'

When Andrew sat down again Roger's tone was softer. 'So ye can see that the Lord has allowed each of us the potential to be mighty, powerful, and a force to be reckoned with in this world. A twelve-bore shotgun is packed with power, but that same weapon needs to be handled and aimed using self-control if it's not going to blow yerself up. Now I know that some of ye here hate yerselfs because you can't control yer temper, yer diet, or yer tongue, but I want ye to be encouraged that the same one who tamed the waves can tame ye when ye let him have dominion over yer life. He would'nae be a very powerful King if he could'nae subdue his kingdom, would he?'

'Aye,' he continued, 'so confess yer sin and allow the Conqueror to work in yer life and dun'nae struggle alone without him. Dear old Peter, who lost his way a few times, was able to write before his death about what had changed him. He said in his second letter that "His divine power has given unto us *all things that pertain unto life and godliness,* through the knowledge of him who called us to glory and virtue." Did ye hear that? His own mighty power gives us everything we need to live a life of glory and virtue as we come to know him. Have ye ever heard such an extraordinary thing as this? No wonder it's called the Good News!' He fumbled back through his tatty Bible and continued. 'Whereby are given unto us exceeding great and precious promises: that by these you might be *partakers of the divine nature,* having escaped the corruption that is in the world through lust.'

He looked up and grinned in my general direction. 'Aye, that's right—the divine nature! He puts it in all of us who are in him! That's what I've been banging on about these last nine weeks, 'cos it takes a lot of persuasion to get a man to give up the keys to his own life. But trust uz, ye can equally be assured of this as well: if a man trusts, like Peter did, only in the saving and life-transforming power of Jesus Christ, then he will have an abundance of fruit in his life. For Jesus alone is the root that produces love, joy, peace, patience, gentleness, generosity, faith, humility and self-control. Amen.'

I went to shake his hand as soon as the service was over. 'Thank you,' I said.

'Aye, lad, I heard about yesterday from Jan. Sounds like ye weren't so clever. Do ye like this other girl?'

'What, Carrie? No, not like that—she's nice and everything, but not like Hannah.'

He looked at me with his lion-like stare and spoke in a low voice. 'Will, you have a call from Almighty God on yer life, and you're packed with potential, but if ye go around thinking with yer groin ye're gonna screw up yer life and mess up ma wee lass, too. And if ye do that then I'm not gaun ta be happy and I'll be talking to ye. D'ye understand?'

I swallowed hard and nodded.

'I'm forgiven for my past,' he said, 'but I can'nae undo the effects of half the trouble I made because the message only reached me later in life. Ye have a chance to get things right the first time, so don't screw up by trying to be like every other daftie ye see on the telly. Life is not a dummy run, laddie. It's for real.'

I nodded again. 'I really wish there was something I could do.'

'Ach, lad, just leave Hannah alone for a day or two while she sorts herself out and then see how she is.'

Grandpa, Stan and Andrew joined us to talk about the team they'd been forming to patrol the river on Tuesday night. We were to meet the big wigs from the Environment Agency and a special operations guy from the police in Cockermouth on Monday.

I thought a lot that afternoon about what Roger had said to me. When I talked with Mum later in the evening I told her about the police operation on Tuesday.

'Your dad mentioned it to me, Will. It sounds dangerous and you sound a bit down. Are you sure you should go ahead with it?'

'Yeah, I'm in it now.' I didn't dare get my hopes up about her conversation with Dad and I didn't ask. I explained what I could about Hannah. She sounded very interested and said she was looking forward to meeting her again at the party next weekend. I wasn't feeling so hopeful.

On Monday morning Granny and Aunty Dora were busy planning flower arrangements for the weekend and I was roped into helping them wash old bits of crockery. As I dried a vase and put it back on the dresser I glanced up at the photo of the Wallace boys. There was Grandpa with his arm round Uncle William, and beside them were Cyril and

Paul. 'Aunty Dora,' I said, 'did you ever try to get in contact with Uncle Cyril after the war?'

Aunty Dora looked up at the photograph. 'Yes, I did, but your grandfather wasn't keen. Cyril sailed away to Canada in 1940, after that argument, and I couldn't get any of the veteran or government agencies over there to trace him.'

'But why didn't Grandpa want to see him?'

She took a long deep breath. 'Oh, Reggie thought we should have stuck together after Mum and Dad were killed. I think he found it hard to forgive Cyril, but things just happened and we can't go back now. I've not seen him since I was ten and I doubt I ever will. Anyway, let's get these dishes sorted out.'

After lunch Grandpa and I made our excuses and got into the Land Rover with Nelson, as usual, taking the centre seat.

It had been raining on and off all day and I was glad not to be outside for once. Nelson was considerably improved in health and determined not to miss another adventure. Grandpa snorted as Nelson reached his paws onto the dashboard and farted. We opened the windows and drove through Lorton and up over the rise into Cockermouth. The meeting wasn't held at the police station as I'd assumed it would be but in a disused warehouse on the far side of an industrial estate.

'No police station, lad,' Grandpa said as he turned off the engine. 'Walls have ears, and we've got to be careful this doesn't get leaked.'

There were also two unmarked transit vans parked outside. Just inside the garage-style door Stan was chalking out a map of the river with terrain features and markings for the likely salmon-holding dubbs. Standing around him was our little team, including Richard. There was a suited man from the Environment Agency and a stocky policeman dressed in jeans and a t-shirt.

'Wow,' I whispered to Grandpa. 'They've got a lot of gear.'

Grandpa smiled. 'There's nothing as likely to produce peace as being prepared to meet the enemy!'

Stan was still working on his map when the man in the suit introduced himself and started talking. 'Thanks for coming, everyone. My name's John McLeod. I'm Stan's boss, and I just want to highlight a few things before Stan and Eddie get into the logistics of tomorrow night. You may or may not know what a state we're in here, but I have to tell you that only two percent of the salmon rivers in the North West are stable as we speak. Pollution is a problem, but poaching, and particularly poaching by large, organized groups like the one we're dealing with here, is a massive threat. I know old boys who tell me how the banks of the Cocker were lined with fish only a few decades ago, but the stock has fallen so sharply that we run a very real risk of losing the fish altogether in the next ten years if the poaching goes unchecked. I know I'm preaching to the converted, but your help is critical because we're understaffed for these types of operations. We've brought Eddie in because he has a special operations team that the agency has used in Lancashire and we've had some good nights out, so I'll hand you over to him.'

Eddie was smiling. 'Thanks, John. Yeah, well I don't know a lot about fish but I do know a thing or two about catching the bad guys. In fact, catching them is easy enough—it's catching them red-handed with solid incriminating evidence that can secure convictions that's the difficult thing. Which of you two lads is the insider?' I nodded, and he took me over to a table piled with bags and boxes. 'Tell me, Will, do you like James Bond?'

I grinned. Who didn't?

'Well, you can call me "Q", and this is our underground warehouse of tricks. But we only get one stab at this and we can't afford to screw up. We'll never be able to do an op like this again. They'll see us coming a mile away if we screw up this season, and they won't come back next year for a second helping!'

'Aye,' Grandpa said, 'Musn't fight too often with one enemy, or you will teach him all your art of war—Napolean I think.'

'Yes, that's precisely it,' Eddie said. 'See here, this is the latest recording equipment used by all the top agencies. It's a one gigabyte, waterproof recording pod—and this baby here is a transmitter so I can hear it live and back it all up in the mobile control centre parked outside. The microphone will be attached to the outside of your clothing, and it's essential that you record as much as you safely can without being caught. In case any of them get away in the dark, we need their names—we need for you to be able to ID them. Otherwise we haven't got a case. Chris Clegg's mobile phone SIM card would be a handy trophy as well. I'm also going to fit you with a tracking device, which is basically as much protection as you're going to have.'

I was about to ask why that was when Stan turned from his map. 'Will,' he said, 'this ain't gonna be like the other day at all. It's gonna be dark, and things might be unpredictable. If we know where you are then we'll have a better chance of getting to you if things get out of control.'

With this sobering thought I was presented with the tracking device. It looked rather like a rubber pill. 'It has a five-hour battery life,' Eddie said, 'and can either be taken with food tomorrow or as a suppository.'

I was about to ask what a suppository was, but I guessed as the men chuckled.

'Aye, Will, it'll have to go in one way or the other!' Stan said.

I agreed to swallowing the device and Stan began to talk us through the different scenarios. There was a lot of information to absorb.

They wanted to be upon the gang just as they were dragging their first stretch and thereby catch them, net in hand, before the fish were taken. Grandpa, Richard and the others would be watchers, positioned at outposts around the target zone. They would radio in if they saw some of the gang escape the trap. It wasn't likely they'd have trouble, but Eddie cautioned them to radio in rather than attempt an arrest themselves.

Stan had pictures of the members of the gang he knew about on a flip chart, along with their likely roles in the catch. There were a few question mark cards to make up for the bouncers from Workington. Stan didn't seem at all bothered about them. 'What? A few weightlifting posers pumped up on steroids? Believe me, on a dark night there's a world of difference between a kid like that and a soldier who knows what he's about!' 'Aye,' Roger said, 'One riot, one ranger!'

I looked round at him. 'What does that mean?' I asked.

He looked at Eddie. 'Time for just one story?'

'Okay,' Eddie said, 'if it's good!'

'Oh, it's good all right. "One riot, one ranger" were the words of Texas Ranger Bill MacDonald when he got out of the train in Dallas to face a town in a state of riot. The mayor wanted to know why the Texas Rangers had only sent one man to handle a whole town gone wild. And that was his classic reply: "One riot, one ranger." True story! And it was'nae long before law and order was restored, just like Stan'll do tomorrow night. Right, Stan?' Stan nodded.

After the meeting, Eddie took me to one side. 'Will, Stan says he's going to give you some combat training tomorrow. I want you to listen carefully to what he says. I'll see you tomorrow night and get you rigged up. Get plenty of sleep tonight and tomorrow afternoon, and don't wear clothing that makes too much noise as it'll affect the recording quality. This head torch has a blue-ish light ... take that too, as it might prevent Stan from clobbering you in the fray!'

Contrary to Eddie's orders I hardly slept that night. I met Stan at the old quarry in the Wild Wood after breakfast. Being up there again was eerie.

'I've brought you here because we mustn't be seen talking—and I also wanted you to remember the last time you were here.' I looked around. I could still see the blood on the rocks and felt on edge at the memory of the beast coming at me.

'Aye, that's right,' Stan said, as if he'd read my thoughts. 'You feel alert, don't you? Most people spend their whole lives inside a comfort bubble and don't know that feeling, the rush of adrenaline that makes you fight to stay alive. Well tomorrow night you might need more than just adrenaline, and your Grandpa's said I can teach you a thing or two so you can stay alive if things turn nasty.'

He moved into the base of the quarry and took his jacket off. Underneath he was wearing a vest that revealed what good shape he was still in for a man of his age. He made me promise never to use the things he showed me that morning unless my life was severely threatened. Were it not for the danger of the situation facing me that night, someone my age should not have known those things at all. Suffice it to say that I did feel very dangerous walking back through the woods to Granny's after two hours sparring with Stan. Stan hadn't taught me a tenth of what he knew, but it was all we had time for. I had a new respect for the SAS and understood why he had such confidence in the face of whatever Chris Clegg and Archie Pritchard could devise against him.

Stan was concerned about knives and gave me a few more tips on the walk home. 'Forget what you see in the films, Will. If someone comes at you with a knife, you have a 90% chance of serious injury in the first three seconds. And I'm talking about myself here, too. Martial arts training will only buy you another two seconds if the weapon is in the hands of a reasonably agile opponent.'

'Then what do you do?'

'Depends. If you have a weapon, move back to give yourself space to deploy it.'

'Yeah, but I'm not going to have a weapon,' I said.

'Even so, distance is still your biggest friend. Just get away from that knife if you can.'

'And if I'm hemmed in?'

'Then you do everything you can to close the gap between you and the weapon. Sacrifice your hand if you must, use the back of your arms. Don't expose your main veins but jump on him, get him down, just don't allow him ... or her ... any space to move.'

'But then what if I can't get the knife away and I'm injured?'

Stan looked at me and pointed two fingers at my eyes.

'Eye gouge?' I said in alarm.

He carried on walking. 'Aye, if you want to stay alive. Or throat ... Listen, Will, this is no game. I don't know how many of these guys there are going to be, and I may not be able to get to you. If you want to survive you'll have to use force and techniques suitable to the threat.'

'Okay,' I said, 'I'll do my best.'

'Good, good,' he said. 'Who dares wins, lad!' He left me on the edge of the woods and I went home for lunch and a troubled afternoon sleep. Grandpa woke me at seven for dinner and afterwards we met Eddie, who was parked in the yard in his van. Grandpa was cheerful as usual but Eddie was more serious as the operation got underway.

He looked at Nelson, who was riffling his way through the baggage. 'You bringing this little fella as well, Major?'

Grandpa grinned. 'It's not the size of the dog in the fight but the size of the fight in the dog! This here is a plucky little fighter and he's looking forward to a good night out.'

Nelson pricked up his ears at the word 'fight' and began wagging his stubby tail.

Eddie fixed me up and I swallowed my transponder. 'When it comes out you can keep it as a souvenir.' He said with a smile.

Grandpa made me take his Commando knife again with very firm instructions. 'It's hard not to kill someone once you start playing with these things, so only get it out if you think your number's up.'

I called Chris Clegg at nine and he said it was all set. A few were meeting for a drink at the Wheatsheaf in Lorton for last orders and the others were going to meet in the field near the Big Bend. I agreed to join them for a drink, and an hour later I was walking through the drizzle to the pub. Chris, Carrie, Carl and the cousins from Buttermere who I'd seen at the beginning of the summer were all there. Carl wasn't happy to see me but Chris offered to get me a pint. Having learned something from my lack of restraint the other day I ordered a Coke, even though it earned me a few glances.

Archie and the two that had been with him at the Kirkstile a few weeks back came in a short while later, and we all sat round with our drinks until chucking out time at eleven thirty. I kept my jacket on so as not to give the game away and managed to record some interesting conversations. I rode on the back of Archie's Toyota Hilux with Carrie. She tried again to make moves on me, but I wasn't having any of it this time. She was still gorgeous, but I knew now that I could never be satisfied with just that. Fortunately it took all my nerve just to hold on for dear life as we bounced down the track, so I didn't need to do much to put my resolve to the test.

We were soon at the field and left Archie waiting by the gate for his 'marras' to arrive. It wasn't long before a Mitsubishi Shogun made its way down to the river with Archie hanging on the side. All lights were now off and I stuck as close to Chris as I could so I could record all the instructions. I felt isolated and exposed there among them. I still liked Chris, and I did feel like a traitor, but like Stan said, sometimes you've got to decide whether you're on the cross or banging in the nails. Tonight it felt like a bit of both.

What I didn't know was that his new friendship with Archie, combined with his ego and great love of gangster films, had got him in way over his head. As four big men approached the rest of us down by the nets, it was clear that they weren't there to take orders from Chris.

'Okay lads, thanks for getting here, let's get these nets to the river.'

One stepped forward. 'Steady up, lad. Archie says there's a scrap to be had. We're here to break heads, marra, not ponce aboot wid nets. Now where's this Stan the man?'

Chris told them to keep their voices down, but they took no notice as they swung their bats and strutted about.

'Amphetamines,' Carrie whispered. 'These idiots are pumped up and going to get us caught. I told Chris not to let Archie talk him into this.'

Chris kept running his hands through his hair and telling them to keep the noise down. But he almost got himself punched by one of them called Brian who was going round asking the other men, 'D'you have a problem?'

The cousins and Carl had changed into wetsuits and were dragging their nets to the river. Brian thought he'd seen Carl 'looking funny' at him and was following him down to the river to 'give him a talking to'.

Carl was panicking, trying to look busy by the river as Brian approached. Archie went after Brian to try and divert an unnecessary bloody nose for Carl.

Meanwhile, I was looking around for the team to get here before there was serious trouble. Where were they? Things were getting out of control.

At that point one of the other bouncers pointed to a lone figure walking across the field toward us with a stick. As if by instinct Chris started toward the river while the three bouncers and Archie's two friends formed a protective barrier of muscle around the operation. I knew it was Stan, who was drawing the gang's attention away from Roger and Andrew who were, by now hopefully, sneaking along the edge of the field under the cover of the hedgerows. Stan hadn't wanted to expose Roger and Andrew to the danger of concealed weapons until he'd 'taken a wee look' himself. As Roger had said, 'One riot, one ranger'!

As Stan came within striking distance, one of the bouncers challenged him with his baseball bat. 'La'al bit late for you to be up, old fella?'

I knew what was coming next so I shielded my eyes as Stan switched on his powerful torch and shone it directly at the men who were now ten feet away. He'd have his own eyes shut too of course. This was a ploy to deprive them of their night vision.

'I'm the water bailiff for Her Majesty's Government, and you're all under arrest for illegally poaching salmon. Lay down your nets and weapons and I'll go easy on you,' Stan said.

The big men started laughing. 'Awey, old man, and what if we don't? What you gonna do about it? Tickle us with that la'al walkin' stick?'

'It's Stan,' Chris whispered to me and Carrie. 'Come on, let's get these fish while the lads give him what he's been asking for.'

As we started to cross the river I could still hear Stan's voice clearly above the laughter. 'Which stick? This one?'

Stan's torch went off then and I looked back over my shoulder to see the five men dropping in quick succession with shouts and groans accompanied by the hideous sound of wood on bone. Before they had time to get up, Andrew and Roger broke cover and were confiscating the weapons. I didn't see much more as we slipped out of sight, but I heard Roger's harshest Glaswegian accent bellowing for the men to stay down. The two vans were racing across the field and Stan had moved on to Brian, Carl and the cousins. Archie, seeing the cavalry, scarpered across the river and began heading up the opposite bank.

'Quick, up there,' Chris said. 'Follow Archie, it's our only way out.'

I had no choice but to follow. I knew I could be traced with the tracking device and it was the way to make sure Archie didn't go free. We crossed the river at the shallowest point and stumbled up the bank into the trees. Carrie slipped on the bank, but Chris didn't wait for her. When I stopped to give her my hand she pulled hard and then pushed past me. Just like on the first poaching trip, I realized she would happily have trodden on me to save her own neck. I staggered back but regained my grip and leapt up the bank. I couldn't let them get away. I looked back across the moonlit river and had a clear but fleeting view of Stan dispatching Brian and the others. Brian's screams of pain had the cousins and Carl surrendering, their hands in the air.

Beyond the woods at the top, we caught up with Archie. He'd hit his head on a branch and was seething with anger, as was Chris. Archie was spitting nails as we ran along the field. 'Someone has shopped us all right, and when I find out who it is I'm gonna do more than break their legs.'

Chris was swearing with every step too. I was terrified and more determined than ever not to blow my cover. How long before their suspicions settled on me?

As we got clear of the Big Bend area and headed toward the upper stretches of the river, Archie told Chris to shut up. 'Wisht, there's someone up there in't trees. Becky's little helper, I bet ... come on, let's have crack with him,' he said as he pulled a knife from his belt.

I knew it would be one of the watchers, but who? What if it was Grandpa or Richard? Meeting Archie and Chris in the state they were in would be very dangerous. We moved up onto the knoll. The lone figure reeled back in fright as we came upon him in the clearing, above the river.

'Who are you and what you doin 'ere?' Archie shouted with a raised arm as he caught hold of the watcher.

'Nothing! Let go of me!'

I almost fell over in shock. It was Hannah.

'What? A girl?' Archie said with contempt. He let go of Hannah, who shrank back against a tree.

Carrie stepped forward. 'It's that vicar's daughter!'

Just then the walkie-talkie in Hannah's hand crackled. 'Station Two, targets approaching your position, stay concealed, over ...'

Chris lunged forward and grabbed the receiver. 'She's with them! The bitch is with the Beckies!'

My mind was reeling. Where was Richard? Surely Richard would be with her, but where? Knowing him he'd be off to the edge to get a better look. I had to intervene and buy us some time, but to give away my involvement would be fatal because all their wrath would fall on me. I was in a very tight spot, but not nearly so tight as the one Hannah was in when Archie grabbed her again.

'Who shopped us, eh? How'd they know where we'd be, eh?' He waved his knife in her face. 'I'll carve your pretty face right here if you don't tell me now.' She looked away from him.

There was no decision to make. I stepped forward and gently took hold of his hand and moved him away. 'Come on, Archie. That's not going to help. I have what you need,' I said. Amazingly, he listened and stepped back for a moment while the penny dropped. I moved over to Hannah and she reached across to hold my sleeve.

'It's you, isn't it? You told 'em ... I'll rip your skinny head from your shoulders!' Archie screamed at me.

But as he lunged forward, Chris grabbed him. 'Wait, Archie, he said he had summ'it for us.'

Archie was temporarily stayed as Chris looked at me. 'Well,' Chris said, 'what is it?'

I undid the microphone gear and showed it to him. 'It's the recording with all the evidence and names and stuff and all that we were going to do.' He reached out to grab it but I closed it in my fist. 'You can have it if you leave Hannah out of this.'

I knew the information was backed up on Eddie's computer, but I was desperate to buy some time.

Chris was furious. 'Why'd you do it, Will?'

'Because you wouldn't listen to me. I told you that the river stocks were too low but you wouldn't listen ... and because you were going to have my friend hurt ... and I couldn't let you.'

'What? That washed up drunk?' Chris spat.

'And what are y'doing defending that goody-two-shoes bitch?' Carrie screeched.

'Haven't you guessed yet?' I asked as I edged still closer to Hannah.

Carrie cackled defensively. 'Her? You've got to be kidding!'

I took no notice. 'Now d'you want this stuff or not? You'll still have a chance to get away.'

Chris looked for a second and then snatched the gear. 'Double-crossing git, yes, we'll take it. But you can have a taste of your own medicine, see how you like it now with Archie.'

Archie stepped forward again. 'I'll have to be quick with you, boy, or they'll be on us up here. So what's it to be? A broken arm or a broken leg, eh?'

This was the sort of wrestling he liked—no rules and an opponent half his weight.

I didn't hesitate as he came nearer. In a flash, the Commando knife was out of my boot and in his face. 'You have what you want if you get past this.'

He swayed back in shock and then crouched lower, like a tiger waiting to pounce. 'Come on, Will, you'll not be quick enough for me lad.'

I wasn't about to be patronized by him. 'I was quicker than a cougar. You shouldn't be too much trouble.' The words were barely out of my mouth when two very strange things happened.

First, a gentle stream of words ran through my mind. 'Okay, Will, that's enough.' They weren't cross words, but they were comforting words, as a father would use with his son as he took his tools out of the son's hands to show him what he could do. This voice seemed to come from outside myself and took me by surprise. I halted for a second, wondering what course of action I should take to obey it.

The second strange thing, that happened almost simultaneously, gave me more clarity—though more dilemmas. Hannah turned her head to my ear. 'Will,' she said, 'I think the Lord's just shown me that he wants you to put the knife down.'

'Put it down?' I said. 'It's all we've got!'

She leaned over again. 'No, Will, we have him ... and each other, I think this is a test.' She squeezed my arm again but she didn't seem afraid.

So there I was, with one last chance to defend the girl who I loved above my own life, and God was asking me to drop my defence and trust him instead. Since it came to us both I had no doubt that the voice was God's, and I felt a great excitement rise in my heart alongside the fear as I threw the knife into a nearby tree.

Archie looked at me, baffled. 'Eh? What'd you do that for?'

As I spoke, I sensed a power and authority in my voice. 'I won't fight you. God will do it.'

I felt Hannah feel down my arm and place her hand in mine as the menacing giant stood tall against the silhouetted trees and started to move closer.

'Well, lad, I don't see God anywhere. Where is he?' Archie asked.

Chris and Carrie were laughing too, but I didn't take any notice. Being right with God and being next to Hannah was enough for that moment.

'All right, lassie, you'd better run along,' Archie warned. 'You don't want to share what Will's about to get.'

Hannah squeezed my arm tighter. 'I'm staying here with him,' she declared.

My trust was shaken for a moment as he closed in on us. At the last second, we both inhaled sharply but neither of us raised our hands as he raised the knife.

The first thing I noticed in the dreadful moment that followed was a shadow that moved behind Archie. I knew it was Stan, and I also knew what would happen next. There was no sound until Stan's left boot came down hard on Archie's upper calf and his left arm went around his neck. Gasping in terror, Archie was yanked back off balance as Stan took hold of the forearm that held the knife. Archie's face held a look of utter disbelief. Stan dropped him to the ground and brought his now straightened arm down hard over his knee. The snapping noise and Archie's scream made Hannah wince and recoil.

Stan was unmoved. 'Good evening, Mr Pritchard. You're under arrest for illegally poaching salmon, as are your friends the Cleggs.'

'My arm! My arm! You've broken it!' he yelled with a high-pitched, almost womanish wail.

'Yes,' Stan said, 'aren't you lucky it's nothing worse.'

Chris had already started making his way back into the woods but was set upon by Richard, who had him to the ground without injury until Stan could bring the tie wraps to cuff him as he'd done to the others. Carrie had run off to save her own skin and promptly ran headlong into a branch. She broke her nose and was knocked unconscious as she hit the ground. Hannah left my side to administer first aid to her.

Within half an hour they were all heading toward Workington Police Station in secure vans and we were all wandering home in triumph.

I was allowed to escort Hannah home across the fields, and we had plenty of time to talk as we made our way over the meadows and stiles hand in hand. We were still quite shaken by our near miss but also exhilarated by the last-second deliverance.

She was still a bit shy of me but accepted my apology for what had happened at the show. 'Well, we don't have to talk of it again, it's done ... it's past now, let's talk about something else.'

We reached the paddock where Tonto was still grazing in the half-light. As we mounted the stile above the vicarage we could see the reflections of moonlight on Crummock Water twisting up the length of the valley.

Tonto came to Hannah and they nuzzled each other. As the moonlight shone silver on her face I would have risked a kiss but I knew, like Jan had said, that it wasn't my time. And it was perfect right then just being with her. The last thing I wanted to do was destroy something so beautiful by pushing it.

'I've had the best summer of my life up here,' I said.

She didn't look at me but she whispered, 'So have I.' She paused. 'Do you think you'll come up again soon?'

I hesitated as it dawned on me that we'd soon be parted. 'Hannah, I er ...'

She flung her arms around me. 'Will, you won't forget me when you're back there, will you? I mean, you won't forget what God has shown us, will you?'

I was taken aback by her sudden show of emotion and I realized for the first time just how strongly she felt. 'Hannah, I could never forget you,' I said. And then it came out. 'I, er ... I love you.'

She held me tighter and I held her, too, for a moment. Her head was buried in my neck, and by the gentle shuddering I could tell she was crying.

I didn't know whether I'd upset her and wasn't sure what to do, so I just held on and waited. After a moment Hannah pulled away and dried her eyes. She patted Tonto reassuringly and then looked at me. 'I will wait for you, however long it takes, I will wait.' She bent forward and kissed me on the cheek, and I could feel her tears on my face as she moved away. 'I can make my own way,' she said. 'No, you get some sleep, you must be shattered.'

I heard Roger and Richard walking down the lane to the house as we parted. Hannah was halfway down the field when I called to her. 'Have you got internet access?'

She turned. 'Internet? Yes, why?'

'I need to find a missing sailor. Can I come over tomorrow?'

'What? Of course you can, but what ...'

'Don't worry! I'll tell you tomorrow!'

31

THE REUNION

Thursday morning I was up before anyone else. I let Nelson out and took care of the chickens for Granny. It was a beautiful fresh day. The rains had passed and washed everything clean. I went through the yard across the road to check on Alfie. He was behind one of the two barns and was happy to see me—and the carrots I had for him. I was back inside and putting the kettle on as the clock struck eight. I'd only had about six hours of sleep, but I couldn't wait to get to the Scotts. My mind was racing.

'I'll be back at lunchtime,' I told Granny.

'All right, dear. Just make sure you're back for lunch as I told George you'd help the men with the marquee this afternoon.'

Hannah spotted me from her bedroom window as I came down the lane on Granny's bike. She opened the window to greet me. 'Is that my brave, handsome rescuer?'

I dumped the bike in the vicarage garden and climbed the drainpipe to her window. 'Is that my fair Juliet?'

'Will, you mustn't. That rusty old pipe might not hold!'

'I'll go down if you give me a kiss!' I looked up with a mischievous grin and she gave me a peck on the cheek.

'Now get down, or I'll get my dad.'

I climbed down and was confronted by Jan as I turned to the door. 'Ah, Romeo. Good morning. I trust you slept well after your adventures?'

'Oh, yes, fine thanks ... Jan, I wondered if I could ask for your help. Richard says you were a librarian once, and I need to find someone ...' I went on to explain about Grandpa's brothers—how Uncle Will had been killed at Dunkirk, how Uncle Paul had been shot down in his Spitfire, and how Uncle Cyril had fallen out and gone away.

'Well there are no guarantees, Will,' Jan said, 'but there have been a lot of ex-servicemen sites set up in the last few years and they've really made information so much more accessible.'

She took me inside where Hannah was waiting with blushed cheeks and a smile.

She helped me and Hannah start with a Google search through every veteran association associated with the British merchant fleet of that era. After two and a half hours we were just about ready to give up when we found a site called 'Veterans' Affairs Canada'. We clicked on it and found loads of information about the Canadian merchant fleet. We followed the link to their veteran's page and found Archibald Wallace, complete with an address at Gravenhurst in Ontario. I couldn't believe it.

'He probably joined their navy when he moved there,' Jan said as she peered over our shoulders. We emailed the veteran's association and told them we urgently needed to contact my great uncle. A letter would take too long, we said, if he wanted to make it to his long-lost brother's fiftieth wedding anniversary. All we could do was wait.

After lunch back at Granny's I spent a gruelling afternoon helping to put up the marquee for the weekend celebrations. Stan popped by to fill us in on progress with the poachers. It appeared that all was going well and that after Eddie had taken witness statements from us it would all be very damning.

'I'll take you into Cockermouth on Friday to give your statement, lad, and also to buy you that knife I've been promising you.'

We were just breaking for tea when there was a clattering of hooves up the lane. Hannah jumped off Tonto and led me into the field away from where anyone would hear as the marquee men whooped and whistled.

'Don't mind them,' she said. 'You're not going to believe what's happened.'

'Did the veteran people email you back?' I asked.

She shook her head. 'No, much better. He called Mum just now.'

'Who? The veteran people?'

'No, silly, Uncle Cyril himself! The veteran's association had phoned him and passed on the details we gave them. He was a bit defensive at first, as you can imagine, but you know what Mum's like. She talked him round and ...' She had her hands clenched and she was doing little excited jumps.

'Come on, Hannah, what is it?'

'Will, he's coming! He's actually coming! Dad said he'd pick him up from the airport, and that swung it—he's actually coming, Will! We did it!'

I was totally overwhelmed and, for the umpteenth time that summer, I found it hard to believe what was happening.

Hannah helped Granny serve the cold elderflower cordial to the workers as I tried to take in what we'd just accomplished. As the marquee went up and I hammered the steel pins into the ground I began to see my family being put back together. I remembered to thank God for it. Hannah spent the evening with us at the farm and got on really well with everyone. She proved to be more than a match for Grandpa's wit, which he loved. He kept looking over and winking at me during dinner, but other than that he didn't do anything to embarrass Granny or me. Andrew and Jane came over after dinner and we played Scrabble and spent a long time dissecting the events of the previous night. Hannah cleaned up in Scrabble and grew more and more in Grandpa's estimation.

I called my mum after dinner and told her all about the night before. She'd been worried, I knew, but she said again that she was looking forward to seeing Hannah. I talked to Dad, too, and he was more interested in the action and all of Stan's heroics. I gathered enough courage to ask him how things were going with mum and he said, enigmatically, that everything was about to change and that I should be prepared for a shock on Saturday. He wouldn't give me any more details. Were they going to get a divorce? Who would I live with? And where? Would I still be able to get to see Hannah and all my new friends in the valley?

In the vacuum of uncertainty many of the old doubts and fears crept into my mind as I went to bed that night. I felt like I did that first night I came to the valley, lonely and insecure. I read a few Psalms and then, as I'd done many nights that summer, I cried out to God for my parents.

In the morning I did a bit of preemptive packing. I could hardly believe that I had only one more night in the little room that had been my home for the last three months. So much had happened.

That morning Stan and I went with Grandpa to give our witness statements, and after an hour at the station Stan took me to the tackle shop and chose me an expensive-looking knife from behind the glass cabinet doors. It wasn't long, but I'd learned that, apart from hacking, a short-blade was far more manageable for most jobs. It had a fine, chestnut leather sheaf and an extra pocket that held a fire steel for making sparks for fire. It was perfect.

'Reindeer bone handle ... Original Finnish Puukko Knife ... Aye, that's what you want,' Stan said with a smile.

'But Stan,' I said, 'it's so expensive—you can't.'

He handed it to me. 'Will, I want you to have this so's you can remember all that we did together this summer. It'll last you long after I've gone if you look after it ... it's a good knife. Them Sámi people in Finland haven't got much to do in the long winters so they make the best knives you can get. And don't worry about the money.' He smiled again. 'I'm getting a bonus this month from Sid!'

I could see he wasn't going to get any more sentimental than that, so I took the knife from him as reverently as if it had been presented to me by a king.

I wandered up Station Road while Stan went to see if Grandpa had finished at the police station. I came to Mitchell's auction rooms. I'd never been in before, so I followed some farmers inside to see what it was like. It was a big warehouse, full of antique furniture, doors, sofas, fireplaces and the like. I walked around and eventually came to a central area where the auctioneer's stand was, as well as a series of rising bench seats where people gathered and chatted.

I was wondering how it all worked when I was knocked from behind.

'Sorry, lad.' A large, hairy man dumped a box of bric-a-brac by my feet. 'Can't see a thing, carrying these big boxes.' He wiped the sweat from his brow.

'Is it all your stuff?' I asked him.

'Nay, marra.' The big man laughed. 'It's all me father-in-law's from Whitehaven. He's just died and the wife has got us clearing all the stuff out. "Take it to auction," she says ... and there's plenty of it an'all.'

As he went off for another load I looked down at the contents of his father-in-law's life. What a strange thing, I thought, to leave it all behind. As I reached down to pick up an old toy tank something else caught my eye. It was a small piece of torn, purple material and, as I pulled at it, the man came back with another box. I stood up with the tank in one hand and the torn piece of purple ribbon in the other.

'Oh, you caught me being nosy, sorry.' But I looked down again and realized it wasn't just a piece of ribbon I had in my hand, for hanging on the other end was a dark metal cross.

I stared at it for a moment. I knew somewhere deep down that I was holding something precious, but I wasn't sure why.

'You all right, marra?' the man asked as he straightened up.

'Yes, I'm fine ... tell me, what do you know about this cross?'

'Oh don't ask me, marra. Take it if you want it, the old fella was always collecting that sort of junk.'

He went off again and I wandered back to the entrance, gazing at the cross. I was still looking at it outside when Stan caught up with me. 'There you are ... come on, your grandad's finished and wants to get home. What's that you have there? Hey, it's a Victoria Cross! Where did you get that?'

For a moment I didn't answer. It couldn't be. This wasn't possible. 'I got it in the auction ... but I ... well ... hey, listen. Do you mind not mentioning this to Grandpa just yet? I have to see someone.'

Stan smiled. 'Aye lad, all right, but I think I know what that is and I think you'd better be careful.'

I asked Grandpa to drop me in Lorton and made my way across the field to Uncle Sid's house. He came to the door and showed me into his study. It was the first time we'd talked properly since the drama of the week before, and I could see the dust was still settling for him.

'Well, nephew, it's been quite a week. Yes, quite a week. Stan told me about Tuesday night, and I've heard from my colleagues in France who tell me the items we sent them have arrived safely and cover the debt with interest. It appears that I'm doubly in your debt. Would you like a drink?'

I nodded. 'Uh, just something soft, you know.'

He poured me a Canada Dry in a tumbler and then poured himself a whiskey, which he raised. 'Here's to you, my boy! I wasn't wrong to trust you.'

I blushed and took a sip.

He wanted me to fill in as much detail as I could about trapping the poachers, and I was glad to oblige. He listened with interest and asked questions.

I saw the invitation to the golden wedding anniversary on his mantelpiece. 'Are you planning to go?' I asked.

He looked down at the floor. 'I think it'd be more enjoyable for my sister if I weren't there.'

There was an awkward pause, and I stepped over to his desk and placed the cross in front of him.

For a moment he just stared at it, then at me. Then he turned his head away as tears began rolling down his cheeks. 'What? How? It's not possible ...' He shook his head.

I went round to his side of the desk and put my hand on his shoulder. 'I found it in a box at Mitchell's just now. I think God wanted you to have it.'

Uncle Sid's shoulders shook. 'I was such a fool ... a reckless, selfish fool.' He took a key from his pocket and opened a drawer in his desk. He took out a dark metal safety pin with a piece of the same ribbon attached. He carefully placed them together, and they were a perfect fit. There was no doubt that this was Uncle William's Victoria Cross medal that Sid had borrowed and lost in a bar fight in Whitehaven over fifty years before.

When it was time for me to leave I summoned up a bit more courage. 'Uncle Sid,' I said, 'for what it's worth, I think you should be there on Saturday.'

'I'll think about it,' he said. 'Now get along.' I was nearly out the door he called me back. 'You're a good lad ... thank you.'

Friday afternoon was all work and preparation. Everything had to be perfect, and even Lewis promised to wash. Hannah, Richard, Lewis and I were in charge of getting the garden in order, and Granny was a relentless taskmaster. In the evening I heard a car pull into the yard and peered out my window. It was Uncle Sid's BMW and Grandpa, who was passing through the yard on his way down to the river, greeted Sid warily. It was in this yard that Grandpa had beaten up Sid's friends all those years back, and now here they were again. I prayed that Grandpa would be able to forgive him. Grandpa stood and talked in cordial tones, but his arms remained folded.

Granny joined them, and it was obvious from his body language that Uncle Sid was apologizing. When Sid put something into Grandpa's hand I saw Grandpa stagger. Granny steadied him, but she was also holding Sid's arm. I decided to leave the window. All three were crying, and it didn't seem right for me to watch. I sat on the bed for a few minutes, but when I heard another car door open I went back to the window.

I watched Sid shut the back door of the car and introduce Granny to her niece, Annie. She was dressed immaculately and stood awkwardly on the drive. Granny stood for a moment and then, all at once, she recognized her dear friend's face in the daughter that stood before her. I went back to my packing then. I was getting a bit tearful myself.

Sid went fishing with Grandpa and stayed for supper. It was tense at times, as everybody was learning to adjust after such a long enmity, but it was a start—and that was more than I could have hoped for.

Late Saturday afternoon Lewis and I took up our post, helping the guests to park in the field as they arrived.

'We should charge 'em all five pounds, like at the show,' Lewis said with a mischievous grin.

Grandpa and Granny stood by the marquee, which was erected in the field with views across to the mountains. Uncle George had a new suit and looked almost respectable, although he always said that no matter how you dressed a farmer you couldn't hide the fact that he was one. He was talking to Jack Demas, who had also scrubbed up for the occasion.

Uncle Sid occupied a quiet table in the corner where he was attentive to Mrs Pardshaw. She was wearing a smart navy suit and eyed the other guests with suspicion and disdain as they passed near her table. The Professor was feverishly escorting the Millstone sisters to some seats in the shade. He seemed all in a flutter. Would this be the night he'd finally win Frieda? Mum and Dad came together and Louise, wearing a new Laura Ashley frock, ran to me and gave me a hug. We hadn't seen each other for nine whole weeks and had only talked briefly once on the phone when I was in hospital.

She put a Game Boy in my hand, 'Sorry, couldn't resist.'

'It's okay, keep it.' I said.

'You've changed, you have,' she said as she stepped back. 'I know! You're bigger and uglier!'

She ran off, and I chased her. Dad stopped me from doing a proper tickling job as she wasn't to get grass stains on her dress.

Mum started fussing over me as soon as she got out of the car. She licked her thumb and tried to wipe a mark off my face.

'Mum don't,' I said. 'It's not dirt, it's a cut!'

I introduced her properly to Hannah, who was wearing a silky, full-length, navy blue dress. She looked like someone out of a film, so serene and elegant. Was this really the girl God had kept for me? All seemed too good to be true. Mum dragged her off, and soon they were in deep conversation as Dad and I looked on.

'Come on then, Dad. What's this big surprise?'

Dad smiled and put his arm round me as we walked up to the marquee. 'Will, that's for me to know and you to find out after I've had another chat with your Grandpa.'

I left him with Uncle George and went back to my post, where Lewis was doing his best to marshal the never-ending stream of vehicles.

As the Professor passed by on his way to the gents he said, 'I have been hearing about your exploits. Almost the perfect ending to your summer, I dare say?'

'Well, nearly, there's still ...'

'Ah, no more doubts about the future, young Hamlet. "There is a divinity that shapes our ends, rough hew them how we will." Why do you keep these anxieties—have you learnt nothing here?'

He didn't wait for an answer, and a few moments later Hannah came running over. 'I saw my Dad's car on the lane—he's back from the airport!'

We left Lewis to carry on his good work and headed over to the yard where Roger was helping a tall elderly man from the car. You would have thought them old friends from the banter and the old man, who was definitely a Wallace by the look of him, was making nervous jokes as he looked round the yard.

I wanted to go and meet him, but Hannah stopped me with a nudge as she saw Dora entering the yard with an empty tray. She looked once at her oldest brother and smiled as she passed. But then, as she neared the alley by the back door, she stopped. The tray fell from her hands and clattered on the tarmac as she cupped her mouth with both hands. She turned slowly and faced Uncle Cyril as the tears began to run down her cheeks.

For a moment he hung his head and then he looked at her with tear-filled eyes. 'Is that you, little Dora?'

She nodded.

'Can you ever forgive me for running away?'

She ran to him and held him tight. 'Cyril ... oh Cyril ... it's really you ... how did you know?'

As the old man began to explain what had happened only days before, Grandpa came out with some guests. He stopped in his tracks and gasped. It was the only time I'd seen him speechless. He took hold of Uncle Cyril's shoulders and just stared. His mouth moved, but if there were words I couldn't hear them. Aunty Dora clutched both of them and tears began to run down Grandpa's cheeks, too. Hannah wouldn't let me stick around to watch any longer.

The top table was lengthened for the new guests, and what followed was a magical evening of laughter, tearful speeches and dancing. Granny and Grandpa couldn't have wished for a more perfect night to celebrate their fifty years together, and I couldn't have wished for a better finale to the summer that changed my life.

In Grandpa's speech he called everyone's attention to his 'plucky little grandson' and, after extolling my development over the summer and all I'd done, he called me to the front. He held up Uncle William's Victoria Cross. I noticed that Uncle Sid had meticulously stitched the two bits of ribbon together, making it one again.

'This was given to your namesake, William, for his heroism at Dunkirk. I'm giving it to you tonight in front of all these people to show the world what I think of you, and what I know you'll become one day. As the ribbon has been mended, so you have helped stitch up what was broken in our family since you came to us nine weeks ago. Keep this safe and remember to live as our Billy did, in the service of God and his fellow men.'

The whole marquee erupted with applause and I saw that my Dad was the first on his feet, his eyes moist.

As the evening drew to a close, I noticed Hannah looking over the table at me. Her eyes told a story I knew only too well. Whoever said parting was such sweet sorrow hadn't been sitting on my side of the table that night. Amid the euphoria of the night there had been this dreadful parting looming at the back of my mind and, as the evening came to a close, it felt almost cruel.

We walked together outside in the cool of the evening. The sunset had Grasmoor on fire and Hannah held my arm as we looked over to the Buttermere fells and saw the crown of Great Gable shrouded by pink clouds.

'I meant what I said Will, you know ... about waiting for you.'

I knew it, too, for she never exaggerated or said things for effect. It was just one of the things I loved about her.

Just then I saw my dad coming out of the marquee, and I knew he'd be looking for me. The anxiety rose in my stomach, for I knew he'd want to get away early as we had a long journey ahead. I wanted to have a last proper goodbye with Hannah, but even that was taken from me as Dad came over.

'Hello, Hannah,' he said. 'Forgive me, but I must speak to Will for a moment ... but you can come too if you like.'

He led us round into the courtyard between the two barns, across the road from the farmhouse. It was where I'd stood with Stan that night two months ago after I'd been caught poaching. Dad stood in the centre of the yard. 'Well,' he said, 'you've probably forgotten, but I was going to tell you something tonight before we left—after I'd had a chance to talk with your grandparents.'

'What is it, Dad?'

'Well, as you know, we've had a bit of difficulty shifting those flats I did in Birkenhead and things weren't so hot with the bank. That night when I spoke with your grandfather on the phone he put an idea in my head and I've done the figures and it's our only way out ... in fact, it's a very shrewd financial move for all of us.'

'What is?'

'These!' he said, with his arms outstretched.

'What?'

'These barns. Your grandfather is going to give them to us to convert into houses, and we're going to sell up in Liverpool and move here. What do you say to that?'

I hugged Dad with relief and joy. 'Yeah, that would be fantastic ... Hannah, did you hear that? We're moving up here!'

But there was one last thing, and it was the biggest thing. 'And Mum?' I asked.

Dad laughed. 'Hasn't she told you?'

'No, told me what?'

'Well, we've got a long way to be where we need to be I guess, but she says that she'll give it another go if I agree to get some counselling. Well, I'm not going to say no, am I? So we spoke with your parents on the phone last week, Hannah, and they've agreed to go through some marriage guidance stuff with us twice a month at your place. You know, with homework as well, and we'll take it from there.'

I didn't know what to say. Maybe the Professor wasn't mad after all. It was the perfect ending to the perfect night ... the perfect ending to the perfect summer.

Of course, I was young then and did not know that it was really only the beginning.

AUTHOR'S NOTE

WE OUGHT TO BE GIANTS

"This world doesn't need more grown-ups. It needs more Giants."

....

Will Houston, aged 16 years

In a play by the Russian writer Anton Chekhov one of the characters says, *'The Lord God has given us vast forests, immense fields, wide horizons; surely we ought to be giants, living in such a country as this.'* What did he mean, Giants. Surely he wasn't just talking about physical giants, like the ones in fairy tales. He was talking about those people, maybe even some people in our own families, whose love, courage, sacrifice and wisdom have made such a huge difference in our lives. I bet you've dreamed about being like some of those amazing people, too—even if you haven't thought of them as Giants. But why are there so few Giants in our world? The sad truth is that there's a dark power hard at work in all of us, trying to keep us as dwarfs. It's an earthly pull towards greed, envy, bitterness,

459

resentment and choosing the easy way out that, in the end, will leave us empty shells of the people we were created to be. Even scarier still, there's a default setting deep in us that seems to naturally embrace darkness and dwarfdom. But that dark power, frightening as it is, is nothing compared to the power that can make us into Giants. The Giant-making power is eternal and stronger than anything or anyone—as Will Houston discovers in this story.

Such thoughts first sparked the idea of writing a book, but who was I to think such things—a dyslexic whose English teacher wanted him taken out of her class! Besides, I didn't have time to write a book. Not until I was diagnosed with cancer. Having cancer helped me to realize how short life can be. That disease showed me what's most important, what I wanted to be most of all and what's worth living—and dying—for. So I began writing the story in a hospital bed in Whitehaven just before my surgery, and I continued writing the first seven chapters during my months of recovery. The rest was written and reworked over several more years.

Will Houston did not become a man in one summer, not really, and he did not become a Giant either, but he did see Giants, and when he saw them he knew what he wanted to become. I hope the lessons he learned, the mistakes he made, and the adventures he had will inspire you also to live a bigger, fuller life.

I extend special thanks to my wife Ruth, who spent countless hours with me creating the characters and proofreading my dyslexic, typo-ridden garble. In many ways, she was the inspiration for Hannah and parts of the love story.

My thanks also go to those at our local church who set themselves to pray every day that this project would bring glory to God. I'm humbled by their support and faithfulness.

And to the dedicated team at Piquant, particularly Pieter and Elria who believed in this project from the start and have been more encouraging than they will ever know. Also my superhuman editor Tara, who made the manuscript into a book—they must have good coffee in the US.

And, lastly, to my children Abigail, Thomas, William and Jonathan: thank you for your patience, dear ones. I hope when you are older you will see that this book was the best thing I could have accomplished for you too, and for those that will come after.

In the film version of *Lord of the Rings*, Galadriel says to Aragorn (the yet unrevealed and uncertain man with a king's responsibilities lying before him): 'You have your own choice to make, Aragorn ... to rise above the height of all your fathers since the days of Elendil, or to fall into darkness ... with all that is left of your kin. *Namárië.* (Farewell.) *Nadath nâ i moe cerich.* (There is much you have yet to do.)'

Yes, there is.

Henry Brooks
www.giant-shoulders.com

For other titles in the Will Houston series, visit
www.picfic.com

To meet the author, visit
www.giant-shoulders.com